Joseph Henry Shorthouse

Sir Percival

A story of the past and of the present

Joseph Henry Shorthouse

Sir Percival
A story of the past and of the present

ISBN/EAN: 9783744749145

Printed in Europe, USA, Canada, Australia, Japan

Cover: Foto ©Raphael Reischuk / pixelio.de

More available books at **www.hansebooks.com**

SIR PERCIVAL

SIR PERCÍVAL

A STORY OF

THE PAST AND OF THE PRESENT

BY

J. H. SHORTHOUSE

AUTHOR OF
'JOHN INGLESANT,' 'THE LITTLE SCHOOLMASTER MARK,' ETC.

'I sawe a damoysel as me thoughte, alle in whyte with a vessel in both her handes,
and forth with al I was hole.'—*Le Morte D'Arthur, Book XI.*

London

MACMILLAN AND CO.

AND NEW YORK

1887

Printed by R. & R. CLARK, *September 1886.*
Reprinted October (2), *1886, 1887.*

TO

THE REV. FRANCIS MORSE, M.A.

CANON OF SOUTHWELL

VICAR OF ST. MARY'S, NOTTINGHAM

AND RURAL DEAN

This Volume is Dedicated

WITH

THE GRATEFUL AND AFFECTIONATE REGARDS

OF A LIFETIME

PREFACE

TO THE NEW EDITION

Since the publication of this book I have been informed that the use of their family name, coupled with the mention of Dr. de Lys of Edgbaston in the Preface, has been the cause of misunderstanding and of annoyance to the De Lys family and their friends. There is no connection whatever between the incidents related in this book and the family history of Dr. de Lys. No member of that family was ever a Protestant or Jansenist. I have therefore substituted a different name in the present Edition.

J. H. S.

CONTENTS

CHAPTER I

CHAPTER VII

CHAPTER VIII

CHAPTER IX

CHAPTER X

CHAPTER XI

CHAPTER I

I suppose that no one ever denied that Kingswood was a beautiful house, though some may have objected to it on the ground of inconvenience. It stood in the centre of an agricultural and wooded country, remote, with one slight exception, from any mining or manufacturing population. It was immediately surrounded by acres, or, I should rather say, miles of chase and forest, untouched since the Saxon time, when it had been the favourite hunting-ground of king and etheling. Through miles of tangled fern and forest glade the narrow, unkempt drive led to the house, a series of low, almost detached buildings surrounding a quadrangle. The entrance hall was said to date from the Saxon time; but if this cannot be accepted, the house itself as a whole was certainly one of the most ancient inhabited houses in England. The deer came up unchecked, amid the beds of fern, to the long low front, which was more regular than the other sides of the quadrangle, with small windows at regular intervals at some height from the ground, which lighted in fact only the upper rooms, and pierced in the centre by a gateway in a low cupolaed tower. This front was said to have been added in the reign of Henry the Seventh, when the house was restored after the wars. Inside the quadrangle, in the centre of the gravel, stood the tall pillar of a sun-dial, erected on a base of four steps, and having four gnomons, one on each of its four sides. Opposite to the entrance gate, up a flight of curved steps, was the door of the great hall. The stone door frame, supported by pillars in half relief, and carved with a profusion of armorial quarterings, was carried up to the roof, and, at the time of which I speak, was in perfect preservation, having some years before been most carefully restored. It gave a richness and perfection to this aspect of the house which it would otherwise have lacked. The rest of the quadrangle was most irregular in character, having square projections and windows both square and circular in mullioned stone frames, roofs of distinct buildings and of different heights, and chimneys of every form and size. In certain sheltered parts ivy and other creeping plants had grown up the walls, but in general the mellowed stone-work was perceptible, interspersed in one or two places with the small red brick-work of the Jacobean time. Not a stone was allowed to decay without being replaced, and this exquisite nicety and perfection of detail, contrasted with the rustic woodland surroundings, was the distinct charm of the place.

Inside, the hall reached to the roof, and

was lighted by two high square windows, with diamond panes of glass, on either side of the door. It was entirely panelled, as indeed was the whole house, with oak. On the right hand, as you entered, was an immense stone fireplace which reached to the rafters of the open roof, and was carved with an elaborate sculpture, representing Actæon being devoured by his hounds. The other furniture consisted of a comparatively modern oak table of massive size, two or three high-back chairs, some skins of deer thrown upon the hearth, and a curious collection of armour arranged along the upper part of the walls. This armour was considered to be one of the curiosities of the place. The tradition was that it consisted of pieces of armour which were too old and obsolete to be used when a troop was equipped for the king's service at Edgehill, and that, as very few of the more modern weapons, offensive and defensive, survived Marston Moor and Naseby to return to the ancestral home, these relics of a still remoter past were re-arranged and burnished up to make the best show they could on the denuded walls. They certainly, except perhaps to the eye of the expert, presented in no way an imposing appearance; but for this reason, perhaps, they were the more valuable. I think I have heard of gorgeous suits of restored steel armour, at which some have been inclined to scoff.

To the right of the hall, by the side of the fireplace, was a door opening into an apartment which contained a staircase. These staircases were a feature of Kingswood. They were innumerable; indeed the several parts of the house were so disjointed and the storeys so irregular that there was little communication between them, and almost every part required a separate staircase. These were generally composed of a number of short flights consisting of three or four steps each, and went wandering and twisting about in all sorts of surprising directions. They were all panelled

with oak, most of it bleached almost white
with age and sunshine, and twisted and worn
out of its original shape, as were also the irregular steps. They were ornamented, sparsely,
with pictures, mostly of the Dutch school;
and I do not know that I delighted in anything more during the long years of childhood
—and how long those years of childhood were!
—in this wonderful house, in which I found
so much delight, than I did in brooding over
some exquisite bit of landscape or winter
skating piece, some meadow scene of Cuyp
or some wayside group of Berghem, standing
out, a brilliant gem, from the waste of pale
oak panel, which contrasted and yet harmonised so perfectly with its repose and with
its truth.

The presence of these pictures in such profusion at Kingswood is easily explained. After
the Restoration, while the great estates and
palaces belonging to the family, or which were
obtained by them, were being recovered, and

nursed, Kingswood was the residence with which crippled fortunes obliged them to be content; and the exile, who returned from Holland with his king, had contracted a taste for the Dutch school of painters, and yearly imported works of the best masters. There was then no landscape school of art existing in England, and this taste, though creditable, was not, I think, surprising.

A doorway, by the side of the staircase I have mentioned as being close to the hall, led into the drawing-room, which was situated at the back of the hall and faced the south. This room had a more modern appearance than most of the other apartments. It had been decorated in the last century during a temporary residence of the heir of the dukedom. The oak panelling had been painted white, and wreaths of fruit and flowers carved in wood, after the manner of Gibbons, had been introduced. The alternate spaces were filled with silver sconces, and between them some of the best pictures and portraits in the house had been hung. Close by the entrance door was a portrait by Gainsborough. It represented a boy dressed in what the last century chose to called a Vandyke costume—a costume familiar to all from the celebrated pictures of the Blue Boy. It was, I have always thought, the most speaking and life-like portrait I have ever seen. I thought so as a child; I have had good cause to remember it since.

Were I writing only to please myself I should never tire of dwelling on the charms of this wonderful house, but I fear at the outset to weary my readers with too much description of that which cannot have the same charm for them which it has for me, and it may be wiser, therefore, for me to introduce at once my first personal experience—the experience of a little girl of three—of my home.

One night, I know that it was night by the candlelight everywhere, and by the great fires burning all over the house in the lobbies and halls, it seemed that my ordinary life ceased, and that I entered into fairyland. About the usual time of my going to bed Mrs. Poins, whom I then regarded as my special property, but who I have had, since, reason to suppose. combined for my especial benefit the functions of housekeeper and voluntary head nurse, came to me and told me that I was to be dressed and go downstairs to dine with his Grace. I was immediately attired in white, with a gold sash. I know that especial care was taken with my hair, a proceeding which I particularly disliked. I was taken by Mrs. Poins, who struck me as being also elaborately dressed, down the great staircase—not the one I have already described, but another which occupied a sort of tower in the south front of the house, next to the drawing-room. This staircase, that night perhaps for the first time, but certainly often afterwards, impressed my childish fancy, as resembling, or perhaps, indeed, as being, Jacob's Ladder, so high it was, so full of steps, so crowded with stately forms of ladies and gentle-men in jewelled costumes and gold frames, ascending and descending, as it seemed to me.

From the bottom of the staircase, through .one of the innumerable little lobbies, with a brilliant fire, and two or three Dutch land-scapes dreaming their sweetness away in quiet corners, we entered, by a small private door, the dining-room, which looked on to the court-yard towards the north. It was not a large room, but its aspect in some respects was strik-ing. I thought so as a child, and, remember-ing it as I write, I think so still. It was lined, of course, with oak; but whereas the rooms that faced the south and the sunshine had their panelling blanched and paled, the rooms that faced the courtyard and the north were dark and sombre with age and gloom. A lofty chimney-piece of carved wood, on the shelf of which stood a row of old Rhenish wine-glasses, occu-pied the end of the room by which we had entered, while at the opposite end, which communicated with the great hall, there was a black buffet or sideboard, with tall flagons of antique plate. There were no pictures on the walls, but the black oak was covered in places by squares of old tapestry, the colours of which were yet bright. Between each of these pieces of tapestry were silver sconces of great size, holding candles.

In this, as it seemed to me, awful and mystic apartment, I was placed at a table— a little child three years old, Mrs. Poins standing behind my chair—in solitary company with a kindly and very beautiful old gentleman, as he seemed to me, whom I had previously seen but seldom, but whom I knew to be the Duke. He was dressed in ordinary evening clothes, but wore a broad blue ribbon across his chest. Behind his chair stood a personage in black, and before the great buffet was another magnate, also in black. Now in ordinary life, and by daylight, I knew these two great personages intimately, and did not scruple, if my fancy led me so to do, to pull them by their whiskers and beard. Even at that solemn moment I knew that they were Mr. Priest, his Grace's body-servant, and Mr. Giles, the head butler, but seen under these awful circumstances, and impressed by the extreme gravity of their demeanour, they seemed to me transfigured, so to speak, and I should not have dreamed of claiming acquaintance with them. Other beings, in gorgeous raiment, but whom I seemed also to have a dim consciousness of having known under widely different aspects, flitted about the room.

Every detail of that stately meal is distinct in my memory even now. Of course I must have had very little given me to eat, and I do not remember the taste of anything. What I do remember is the amused, kindly, and concentrated attention of which I was the centre—the reserved and stately, and yet real and even humorous enjoyment in which

every one entered into the spirit of the hour.
Finally, a tiny drop of some sparkling
wonderful drink was given me, and Mrs.
Poins, leaning over me, whispered : 'Bow to
his Grace, darling, and drink.'

And I see now, in my old age, the gracious
kindly face of the old noble bowing to the
little child over his lifted glass.

I never heard any explanation of this
night. I can only suppose that, my aunt
being indisposed, it occurred to some one that
the sight of the little girl at table might
amuse the Duke, and that this earliest recollection of my girlhood was the result of this
humorous fancy.

My aunt, I called her so, but she was
really my great-aunt, was the second wife of
the Duke of Cressy and de la Pole, of one of
the proudest families that the world has ever
seen, in whose veins ran the blood of Valois,
of Plantagenet, and of Anjou. She was herself the daughter of a Dean, and of a distin-

guished family, in no way unsuited to her lofty alliance, but she was, what was still more, the gentlest and kindest woman that ever lived.

In those early days when I had been sent, a little child, from India, my girl-mother lying dead, the Duke and Duchess only came down to Kingswood at intervals. But the place had a singular fascination for his Grace as advancing years told upon him—the visits to this retired spot became longer. Gradually all ties to the gay or political world became weakened, and at length, when I had reached the age of twelve or fourteen, the Duke and Duchess, resigning their magnificent palaces and country seats—all the grandeur of society and all the leadership in Government—to the Marquis of Clare and his wife, settled down with most perfect satisfaction to a life of absolute repose.

Some three or four years after the death of his wife my father was killed in some nameless skirmish with a frontier tribe, in one of those little wars which occupy a paragraph or two in a morning paper. I am only a woman, and my opinion is of little worth, but I have often thought with surprise that what seems to me to be a unique characteristic of the English race is not more thought of than it is.

I say the English race, because I have a distinct idea in my mind, though it is somewhat difficult of expression—the great victories of the world, the victories that have triumphed over death and hell, have been won, for the most part, by the English race; the noble and the peasant standing side by side, and 'jeopardising their lives unto the death in the high places of the field.'

I would cut out my tongue rather than it should speak a word that would imply disparagement of that 'thin red line' that has won for the world priceless victories which never would have been won but for that superb characteristic of the English race, manifested as much in the peasant as in the noble. But after all there is something in the gift —the supreme gift—of leadership, and there is a class in England, history teaches us so on every page, without whom the world's victories would never have been won.

> 'Their graves are severed far and wide
> By mount and stream and sea.'

Civilisation pursues its beneficent march, forwarded, for the most part, by this glorious English race—forwarded too, for the most part, by these little nameless wars. Three lines only in the gazette, but some bright young life is laid down without a murmur— not a vulgar life, but a life the offspring of a family, the flower and type of the human race —some home is made desolate, with no thought save 'we have done that which it was our duty to do.' I have been told by clever men that in the days when Rome was the mistress of the world something like this was also known. Whether it were so or not I cannot say.

By the time I had attained the age of seventeen or eighteen years the life at Kingswood had become so settled and regular that I fancy even a conventual household could scarcely surpass it for regularity and repose.

We breakfasted in a room in the south-west angle of the house beyond the drawing-room. This room was chosen in preference to one in the east front, which might have seemed more suitable for a morning-room, because it communicated with the library, which was situated in the west front. The Duke received few letters or papers, all business letters being disposed of by the Marquis or his agents. The Duke opened a paper two days' old, and gave us an account of such news as he thought would interest us. Immediately after breakfast he retired into the library. Exactly at eleven his horses were brought to the door, unless the weather was very unfavourable. He had two rides, which he never varied, one for each alternate day. The one lay towards the west, through the chase and wooded lanes, with here and there a breezy common, and led you at last to a country town. Here the accustomed horse stopped of his own accord at the agent's gate, where the Duke sat for a few moments in his saddle in consultation, then on to the rectory, where, if the rector and his wife were at home, his Grace would alight and take a glass of sherry. Were it market day, he would pass through the market-place and speak many a gracious word.

The other ride lay due north, entirely through the chase, through tangled thickets of twisted thorn and holly, with distant glades of oak and beech ; at last, on a rising ground, a ruined tower and a flash of far-off sea. After lunch, should the weather be propitious, the carriage came to the door exactly at three. For the Duke and Duchess there was only one drive, and this lay towards the east. Why

they never visited the market town which was
the scene of the Duke's morning ramble I
never knew; but they never did. The road
lay through the chase for about a mile till it
reached a quaint little church—a spot so dear
to me that I shall presently describe it more
fully—and, after a further stretch of chase and
open common, passed a group of cottages, also
connected with the story I have to tell, and
then, by a long reach of country road, well
kept, came, at the end of some two miles or
a little more, to what might be called a considerable town. Its position on a river, navig-
able, for the few miles which lay between it
and the sea, for ships of what in those days
was considered a respectable size, had made it
in former days a port of some importance; and
some small deposits of coal and ironstone had
encouraged enterprising persons to erect more
than one quaint little factory, which in no
degree detracted from the picturesque aspect
of the place. There were old - fashioned

wharves and offices, sleeping in the sunshine, with bales of goods and strange-looking cranes and landing-stages; very seldom, if ever, did we penetrate so far as these.

This was particularly the Duchess' drive, and had only two objects in view. The first in position was the parish school, which was situated at the entrance to the town. Here on alternate days the carriage stopped. Her Grace alighted and entered the school. The Duke never accompanied her; for half an hour, or sometimes more, he would remain quite silent in the carriage, open or closed according to the time of year. As the carriage always stopped precisely at the same place the aspect of the scene was invariably the same, yet it never seemed to weary the Duke. I know from frequent experience the sight that met his eyes. Opposite the school was a stone garden wall, above which in the season apple and pear trees were in blossom. Beyond this was a little cottage of two stories occupied by a cobbler, whose work was exhibited in an old-fashioned bulkhead window. Day after day this confined view seemed to satisfy the Duke. Whether he saw it at all, what thoughts, what recollections of a long life passed in the gay capitals of Europe, filled his mind, during these quiet afternoon hours, who can tell?

He was satisfied with the narrow prospect from the windows of a brougham, but in summer from an open carriage there was a wider view. Past the old garden wall, with the ruddy apples perhaps overtopping it,—past the cobbler's hutch,—the eye wandered down a picturesque bit of street winding between irregular red and white houses, with here and there a projecting sign. Overhead was the wide expanse of the English heaven—that gentle heaven of pale blue sky and passing cloud. Over the tiled roofs that formed the line of the street rose against the sky the red cupolaed tower of a Queen Anne church. The narrow winding footpaths were paved with irregular and broken flags and the gutters with pebble stones, amid which grass and dock leaves forced their way. Every now and then as the Duke sat, patient and silent, in the warm sunny street, a solitary figure would approach along the pathway, giving a momentary life and even excitement to the scene. A perceptible quiver of interest passed through the perfectly trained servants ; none ever passed, were it even a stranger tramp, without raising his hat—without receiving a touch of the hat from the Duke.

Inside the school the Duchess took a class, now of girls, now of boys, now of infants. Some survival of the early training of her life, in her father's parish, made it impossible for her to pass her life without some such effort for the good of others. I have ample knowledge, from certain experience, that these efforts of the Duchess were productive of exceeding good.

The object of the drive on the alternate

days took the carriage a little farther on into the centre of the little market-place, where was a stone market hall supported by pillars. The visit was so arranged as never to fall upon a market day. Here the carriage always stopped at a small shop kept by two old ladies who were sisters—a book, stationery, and Berlin wool shop. The visit to these old ladies was the one dissipation of her Grace's life. It was her Regent Street and Piccadilly. Any new book which the unerring judgment of the Misses Smith assured them would meet the approval of their patroness was always procured. The Duchess was devoted to the writings of Miss Yonge, but, as it was obvious that it was impossible for that lady to keep her Grace supplied with a new work on each occasion of her visit, she was obliged to depend upon the taste and instinct of her friends, and I have reason to know that the trust was never misplaced. The Duke invariably accompanied his wife into this shop; seated on a chair by the counter he appeared to take the greatest interest in its entire contents, not at all excluding the wool and crewel work. His taste in novels was limited. He thought it proper to admire Scott, considering his principles correct and even excellent, but it is my conviction that he was often bored by Scott's novels. The writer of fiction whom he really unaffectedly admired was the late G. P. R. James. The tone of his novels, he said, was invariably high, his English style unaffected and pure, and his stories interesting. But what really delighted him was Mr. James' knowledge and grasp of French history and life. The Duke had been, in his youth, an attaché to the embassy in Paris during the Bourbon Restoration, and his judgment on this point was worthy of attention. He has often pointed out to me the minute knowledge of old France possessed by Mr. James, extending to the points of junction of bye and cross-roads in the times of the old provinces. This

visit to the Misses Smith and the talk with
which it was accompanied—much of which
was regularly repeated—was always a source
of pleasure on both sides. The Duchess sometimes purchased articles at the other shops in
the quiet square, but rarely alighted.

In the winter we dined in the room looking
on to the court, which I have already described
as the scene of that never-to-be-forgotten evening; but in the summer we dined in the same
room we had breakfasted in, in the south-west
corner of the house. This room had two
windows looking towards the south and one
towards the west. This western window, the
three windows of the library, and the rest of
the windows in the west front, looked on to
what was called the Wilderness, but what was
really an apple and pear orchard of immemorial antiquity. A long straight path ran
up the middle of this piece of ground, and
terminated, at some considerable distance, at
a neglected terrace, with stone balustrades

and urns, overlooking 'the chase,' with a distant woodland of massive thorn-trees and oaks, and groups of Scotch firs against the western sky. As the Duke sat at dinner, at the end of the table opposite to this west window, a glory of sunset light suffused the Scotch firs and the apple blossom, set in the dark blue of the evening sky.

The other two windows of this morning and dining room looked out on to the garden, the only flower garden of the house. This was a square plot of ground, extending along the entire south front, and, being exactly square, occupying, of course, a considerable extent of ground. It was laid out in formal beds, and terminated at its farthest extent with an immensely broad gravel terrace, commanding a magnificent view of chase and woodland towards the south. I always regretted that we lived so much towards the south and west; but I had one consolation. My own sleeping room faced the east, and reminded me always of that chamber of the House Beautiful, where Christian slept, that was called Peace, and faced towards the sun rising. The morning glories over wood and meadow fill my heart at this moment, so many years after, with gratitude and joy.

When we were alone we spent the evening in the library, which, as I have said, adjoined the room in which we had dined. I think I enjoyed this hour more than any other of the day. The Duke, as was natural from his extraction and early residence in Paris, was greatly read in French literature, and had collected a large number of French memoirs of the last two centuries. He delighted in Montaigne, and would read to us passages of the old humorist's courtly French with a grace and ease that made it impossible to miss the meaning. There was a rumour that in the last days of the true Bourbon Monarchy this brilliant young English noble, himself of royal French blood, whom the king deigned to call 'Mon Cousin,' had formed an attachment to one of the princesses. The Duchess would sometimes, by way of courtesy, introduce her name, saying, 'I believe you knew the Princess —— very intimately;' and the Duke would never fail to observe that she was 'une vraie fille de France'—a true princess of the Blood-Royal.

As I recall these stories and such as these, there mingles with the regret that so much was passed unnoticed, and is forgotten, the pathetic sorrow that, the loved and familiar voices of our youth being for ever silent, we shall never hear the like any more.

CHAPTER II

PORT-ROYAL DES CHAMPS

I HAVE spoken of a quaint little church
standing in the chase some mile or so on
the road to Rivershead, as the little town,
which was the object of the Duchess' afternoon drive, was called. I never approached
this little church but I was reminded of
those mysterious chapels in the forest-wilds
of the 'Morte d'Arthur,'—'an olde chapel
in a wast land,' as one is called; 'an olde
febel chappell,'—and I could have fancied
almost, when the hush of summer noon stilled
the sense of the present, and lulled it into
dreamland, that this was the very chapel
whose door Lancelot had found 'wasted and

broken, and within he saw a fair altar, richly arrayed with cloth of silk, and a candlestick of silver that bear six great candles; and when he saw this sight he had a great will to enter into the chapel, but he could find no place where he might enter,' for though the door was not broken, yet it was as old, perhaps, as the 'Morte d'Arthur,' and it stood open all day long; and although the passage was open, yet the place felt so holy and pure, in the fresh forest air, that I might well understand that a man, 'sinful and unconfessed,' might, indeed, find no place where he might enter.

The church was very small, and had an appearance of extreme antiquity, rumour even asserting it to have been built in the Saxon times. It was built of timber, interspersed with rubble stone and plaster, and roofed with tiles. It consisted of a nave and chancel and a north aisle, separated from the rustic nave by low pillars, with round arches, carved with rude fretwork. It had an oaken porch, open at the sides, and covered with devices and figures of saintly life, worn and defaced with age. It was surrounded by immemorial yew-trees of great size, pollarded and contorted into every variety of strange form, and producing a mystic depth of light and shadow on moss-grown roof and stained wall and fretted oak, which seemed at once to perfect the harmony with the strange romantic past, and to fall in unison with what the village folk conceived of truth, and heard from Sunday to Sunday within its walls—the struggle of light with darkness, the triumph of the light, the mystic Love that pierced the shades of death, and won, by force of sacrifice, its secrets from the grave.

Beyond the nave, the half of the north aisle, towards the east, was enclosed with an oaken screen, elaborately carved, and said to be of fourteenth century work, and beneath the tiny window towards the east were traces of a separate altar. Within this sacred enclosure were the seats appropriated to Kingswood, and here, on Sunday mornings, when the Duke and Duchess attended service, we used to sit. At other times I sat in the nave facing the chancel and altar, in one of the plain oaken seats or forms, which had remained unaltered from the pre-Restoration times, before the first pew had entered the churches of the land.

The chancel was very small, with no seats or stalls of any kind, but with one or two quaint seventeenth century tablets on the walls. The small east window contained some scattered antique glass displaying armorial bearings. These always reminded me of George Herbert's lines :

'Onely a herauld, who that way doth passe,
　Findes his crackt name at length in the church glass.'

One of these small panes was pointed out to visitors as being different from the rest. It was beautifully painted, and represented a knight, bareheaded, kneeling in a forest, through which was shining a bright light, as of the sun. In the distance, exquisitely delineated in the most delicate miniature, was a city with spires. Above, on a scroll, was the word 'Parcyvale.' This fragment was evidently of foreign manufacture, but all trace of its history or meaning was lost. It was supposed to have been one of a series, of which it was the sole survivor.

The only other objects of interest in the church were the oak screen work and a recumbent effigy, much defaced, outside the screen in the north aisle. This was supposed to have been brought from a neighbouring monastery at its destruction. All trace of the person whose memory it was intended to perpetuate was lost, but round its base was carved a series of small figures representing the different occupations of the thirteenth or fourteenth centuries—a fowler, a huntsman, a carpenter, a smith ; these gave an unexpected interest and value to the tomb now that its original purpose was quite missed and forgotten.

Some distance beyond the church, about half way between it and the group of cottages I have spoken of, was the parsonage. It had been a woodman's lodge, and stood within the gates of the chase. It had been altered and enlarged some years before I first knew it, when the Rev. Charles de Foi came into the parish.

As I write this name for the first time in this story which I have undertaken, very boldly as it seems to me, to tell, I cannot refrain from tears, so touching and precious are the memories which the name recalls, to an orphan girl, of him who was as dear to me as any parent could have been.

He was of French extraction, as his name implies. His grandfather, who was of noble birth, had been brought up among the Jansenists or Port-Royalists. Travelling in England in the last century, he had become acquainted with some of the leaders of the evangelical revival in the English Church, notably with Samuel Walker of Truro. He recognised this religious movement as so similar in its ideas to that in which he had been brought up, and was so impressed with the beauty of the English service and ritual, that he decided to adopt this country as his own. He transferred his property to England, and established his only son, who had been trained to the medical profession, as a physician in London, where he obtained considerable reputation among the nobility, especially those who were well disposed towards religion. This son married an Englishwoman, and brought up his son Charles to the English Church.

The fortune of his father, the old French *émigré*, had been considerable. It had been increased by the thrifty French habits and by the emoluments of his own profession; and about the time that his son Charles went to Cambridge he retired from London and settled himself in one of the market towns on the Thames with his two daughters, both of them younger than Charles.

The young Charles inherited the character of his grandfather. The doctor was a man of imposing manners and of blameless life, but was not a man of strong religious instinct, whereas his son combined in a remarkable degree the characters of a gentleman and of a saint. His grandfather had lived to a very advanced age, dying in his ninety-fifth year; and his grandson, who was then in his fifteenth year, had enjoyed the priceless advantage of several years' intelligent intercourse with such a man.

He had listened with absorbing interest to the old gentleman's narratives of his youth and of his ancestors—to his descriptions of 'la belle France,' of beautiful and gay Paris, and of the holy people, nobles and ladies of rank, who, in the midst of a gay world, had confessed Christ and endured suffering and persecution at the hands of the Jesuits and of a misguided king. He had listened while his grandfather had told him how gentlemen of property had given up their parks and houses to be appropriated to school-houses and play - grounds, and how these little academies were organised and governed by men of the highest learning and piety. How some of the finest verses in Racine's tragedies were meditated whilst he was a boy at school amid the woods of Port-Royal; and how at Chênet, at des Troux, and at Paris—at these retreats sacred to religion and to learning— the fact was fully proved that it is only where religion sanctifies and purifies the heart and life that anything worthy of the name of education—that dare presume to call itself the highest achievement of learning — can exist. In these sacred retreats the vaunted results of Jesuit teaching were outdone, for those were based only on the necessities of policy, and were practised only for the benefit of a party and a sect; these were based upon the inviolable laws of righteousness and the will and purpose of God. New associates were continually quitting the world and bringing their children to these homes of culture and of peace. The spacious gardens blossomed as the rose, and the walls resounded with hymns of prayer and songs of praise. In these Christian academies was inculcated that pure idealism which is the foundation of all true faith; which, taught by the Greek Plato, is the foundation upon which true Christianity rests — an ideal purity and morality, not the lax expediency of casuists. Here Arnauld published his work on frequent communion, deploring the levity with which many in those days approached the sacred mystery, urging the necessity of genuine fruits of repentance before the blessings of

faith can be won, and insisting that no repentance can be termed evangelical which
arises from a fear of punishment and is
ignorant of, and uninspired by, the love of
God acting and reacting in the soul. The
most prized possession of the old man, the
ornament most admired by the boy, and
which he wore as a man, was a seal, the device
of which was a crown of thorns from which
emanated rays of light. Underneath was the
motto 'Scio cui credidi,'—'I know in whom I
have believed.' This relic, which had descended to the old man from his grandfather,
was one of those engraved in memory of the
miracle of la Sainte Epine, by which the niece
of Pascal had been cured of her loathsome
and distressing malady; which grace, the old
gentleman told the boy, had so sensibly
touched that great and intellectual man, as
being bestowed upon one who was not only
related to him in the flesh, but was also his
spiritual daughter in baptism,—'sa fille spirit-

uelle dans la baptême,'—that his spirit being quite occupied by the thought of it, God inspired him with an infinity of admirable thoughts upon miracles which may be read in his books, and which, by giving him new lights upon religion, redoubled the love and the respect which he had always felt for it.

One particular anecdote which the old man was never weary of repeating, and which the boy never forgot, seemed to me admirably to describe the peculiar combination of the gentleman and the priest which existed in Mr. de Foi.

When Monsieur l'Abbé de St. Cyran was in prison at Vincennes, where he suffered much privation,—his books, papers, and pens being for a time withheld from him, and the avarice of the jailer depriving him of sufficient food, his dungeon being damp and exposed to the weather,—it was the custom that all the prisoners should attend Mass once a day. The abbé noticed that several of these, among whom

were two or three persons of distinction, im-
prisoned for political offences, were very thinly
clad.   Monsieur de St. Cyran immediately
packed up some of his books, which had at
last been allowed him, and sent them with a
letter to a lady of his acquaintance in Paris,
requesting her to sell the books, and with the
money to buy a supply of clothing for the
prisoners ; 'and I will also thank you, madam,'
he wrote, 'to buy some clothes for the Baron
and Baroness de Beausoleil.   Pray let the
cloth be fine and good, such as suits their
rank.   I do not know what is proper, but I
think I have somewhere heard that gentlemen
and ladies of their condition cannot appear
without gold lace for the men and black lace
for the women.   If so, pray get the best ; let
all be done modestly, but yet sufficiently
handsomely, that, in looking at each other,
they may, for a few minutes at least, forget
that they are captives.' The lady remonstrated
with him, suggesting that the money might

be better employed; but he answered, 'I do not believe that He who commands me to render unto Cæsar the things that are Cæsar's will account me a bad steward for giving modestly to each according to that rank in which *He* placed them.' The clothes were purchased and sent to the prisoners' apartments, who never suspected whence they came. They only observed that Monsieur de St. Cyran himself was destitute of those comforts, and concluded that his having been alone forgotten was a judgment upon him for his heresy.

Amid these influences was the education of Charles de Foi, as an English churchman, laid. He combined, as was far more common at the end of the last century and at the beginning of the present than it is now, the beliefs and instincts of an evangelical and a high churchman. He was deeply impressed with the individual life and power of Christianity which pervaded and actuated the evangelical leaders of the past and present century, while his inherited instincts as a Catholic attached him with enthusiasm to those Catholic aspects which are so prominent in the English Church. That it should be supposed, he has often said to me, that any discord should exist between these two instincts of Christianity is one of the most striking instances how an uneducated prejudice and superstition may mislead men. I only knew him in advanced age, but I can well imagine what he must have been as a youth—tall and slender, of a gravity beyond his years, of a religious sweetness of demeanour which at once propitiated and restrained.

His father was a man of learning, not only in his own professional studies, but in the higher literature; and he had set his heart on his son's distinguishing himself at the university. There was everything in his son's disposition and breeding to facilitate this design. His ancestral instincts, derived from that Port-Royal community which might well

be called a sacred college, which equalled the
Jesuits themselves in their zeal for learning
and in their skill in imparting it, paved the
way, in his case, for a brilliant collegiate
success.

About the time that Dr. de Foi came to
reside in the little town on the banks of the
Thames, one of the most beautiful estates in
the neighbourhood had been purchased by a
Mr. Mainwaring, a man of very large property,
the result of several generations of successful
commerce, and of considerable political influence. He was a member of parliament,
and was supposed to possess very considerable
influence, both in his relations with the Premier
and with the Chancellor of the Exchequer. He
was, moreover, a man of refinement and culture,
having been educated at Eton and Oxford,
and, enjoying the reputation of wealth that
doubled itself every few years, his acquaintance
was sought for by all. He had more than one
son, and one daughter who already gave

promise of exceptional beauty, and of whom
he was extremely proud. Mrs. Mainwaring
was an invalid, and Dr. de Foi, as a friend,
became interested in her case, and was able to
give her considerable relief. The families soon
became acquainted, and the young people were
often together.

In the gardens at Wotton, as her father's
residence was called, and in the meadows on
the banks of the Thames, Charles de Foi saw
a great deal of this beautiful girl. He always
maintained a guarded reserve in speaking of
this companionship; but I can well believe,
judging from what we know of her after life,
that Julia Mainwaring's somewhat *borné* life
was struck through with a sudden light—that
her nature, essentially a noble one, was startled
from amidst the commonplace surroundings of
a gay and fashionable life into the perception
of an ideal existence of which she had never
dreamed. I say a *borné* life, because, though
the position her father occupied, and the *entrée*

into society of every kind which was open to her, might seem to render such a phrase inappropriate, yet, inheriting no ancestral culture, and deriving little from the members of her family, for her father's occupations kept him entirely engaged, and her brothers were ordinary young men of not the highest fashion, her acquaintance with Charles de Foi was a liberal education of the loftiest kind. To Charles de Foi himself she became the central figure in the woven tissue of a many-shaded, many-coloured existence. Around her his fancy wrought the threads of his intellectual life—his dual intellectual training, the humanism of the classics, the severer, but still strangely mysterious rule of the mathematics, the ecstatic striving after the spiritual life, springing from the intense religious instinct which he had possessed from a child. In this paradise of the soul Julia Mainwaring, moving in her perfect beauty through the flower gardens and by the shining river of her home, was exalted to an ideal loveliness and grace by the golden halo of pure thought and holy aspiration in which he lived.

At the time that Charles de Foi went to Cambridge, and indeed for many years afterwards, it was necessary that candidates for honours in classics should have obtained honours in mathematics also. Mr. de Foi always considered this to be an admirable rule, and regretted its abolition. He considered that it had been of exceeding value to himself. For the first part of his residence at the university it enforced an almost entire attention to his studies. In those days undergraduate life at Cambridge was a very different thing from what it has since become. Athletic sports were only just beginning to be talked about. The occupations of the idle undergraduate were driving, horse-racing, gambling, and drinking. The relaxation of the reading men riding and card-playing. Religious life and activity were represented solely by the evangelical revival, and principally in the person of the Rev. Charles Simeon of King's, whose weekly teas were the resort of all religiously - minded candidates for orders. To these meetings, which were open to all gownsmen, Charles de Foi soon found his way. There were many inducements for him to do so. Mr. Simeon had been at Eton, and he had been extremely fond of riding, which was Charles de Foi's favourite relaxation. Mr. Simeon was besides a remarkable instance of the combination of religion with high breeding. His family in the past had been connected with John Hampden, and in the present generation branches of it had merged in the families of the Welds of Lulworth and of Vaux of Harrowden. Charles de Foi became extremely attached to this remarkable and holy man. He has often described him to me. 'His courteous and refined manners, and his humorous quaintness, won upon all hearts. At the entry of each gownsman he would advance towards the opening door, with all that suavity and politeness which he possessed in a remarkable degree, and would cordially tender his hand, smiling and bowing with the accomplished manners of a courtier; and I assure you we deemed it no small honour to have had a hearty shake of the hand, and a kind expression of the looks, from that good old man.

'He was seated in a high chair by the side of the fireplace. Before him were the benches, arranged for the occasion and occupied by his visitors; even the window recesses were furnished with seats and were filled, for Mr. Simeon had taken the greatest care to make the windows air-tight, and even put them to the test of a lighted candle. "I shall be very willing," he would say, "to catch from you any cold which you catch from the draft of my windows." In the meantime, two servants would be handing tea to the company—a part of the entertainment which most of us could have well dispensed with, as it somewhat interfered with the evening's proceedings; but it was provided in kind consideration for our comfort and ease.

'If any stranger was introduced to him at these meetings he would forthwith produce his little pocket memorandum-book, and enter with due ceremony the name of his new acquaintance, taking care to inquire his college, and such other matters as he deemed worthy of being registered. Sometimes, too, he would comment, in his own way, upon the name he was writing, or make some passing quaint remark, which would put us all into a good humour.'

I am sure that there were points upon which Mr. de Foi did not sympathise with Mr. Simeon. It does not seem to me to be of any importance to inquire what these points were. Where a sympathy of nature exists differences of detail are of little importance. The personal admiration and attachment which

Mr. de Foi felt for his teacher were unbounded.
'One of the most striking things that was ever said to me,' he would say, 'was said to me one day by Mr. Simeon on the grass plot before Clare Hall.

'You may suppose that I am opposed to those who earnestly advocate extremes, and that I am in favour of a golden mean. You are mistaken. I go far beyond them; I am for all extremes. The truth does not lie in the middle, or in one extreme, but in both extremes. I am for all extremes—for Paul and for John, for Calvin and for Arminius. "Well, well, Paul," should I say, "I see that thou art beside thyself, go to Aristotle and learn the golden mean." I formerly read Aristotle, and liked him much. I have since read Paul, and caught somewhat of his strange notions, oscillating (not vacillating) from pole to pole. Sometimes I am a high Calvinist, sometimes a low Arminian, so that if extremes will please you I am your man; only remember it is not *one* extreme that we are to go to, but *both* extremes. We shall both be ready, in the estimation of the world, to go to Bedlam together.'

When Charles de Foi returned to his home he found his relationship to Julia Mainwaring to be in the most favourable condition. Mr. Mainwaring was extremely attached to him, and indeed the fascination of his character and manner was such that none could resist it. He appeared to desire nothing more than that Charles should marry his daughter, but he was very averse to his taking orders. His desire was that Charles, after distinguishing himself at the university, should go into Parliament. There would be no difficulty in finding him a seat—it was before the passing of the first Reform Bill. With the wealth and influence which he would command, with the fascination of his own manners, the fluency of his speech, and the charms of his wife, there seemed to Mr. Mainwaring's fancy no limit to his probable success. Mr. Mainwaring was honestly and profoundly attached to his only daughter. He was intensely proud of her, and he had quite sufficient culture to appreciate the highest kind of man, and to desire that she should gain such a man for a husband. If Charles de Foi took orders all this prospect would be changed. It was not only that the highest possible success attainable in the Church would be very different from the success upon which he had set his heart, but he had sufficient insight into character to perceive that his daughter was not suited to be a clergyman's wife.

Mr. Mainwaring did not say much at first to his intended son-in-law, but in his second and third year he spoke to him several times very seriously on the subject, setting before him how bright his future might become, and how ruinous both to his own interests and to those of his wife persistence in taking orders would prove. Charles's father also spoke to

him more than once, and it was plain that his
wishes were entirely in accordance with those
of Mr. Mainwaring.

Charles de Foi went in for the mathematical examination at the end of the year,
and came out a wrangler some places higher
than was expected. During the vacation he
had another very serious conversation upon
the old subject, and returned to Cambridge
for the classical examination in the Easter
term. He was exceedingly disturbed and
troubled in mind. Apart from the pressure
that was put upon him to induce him to
give up his intention of taking orders, in
resisting which he knew that he should have
no support from his father, he felt a growing
conviction that Julia was not suited for the
life of even a dignified clergyman's wife.
He could perceive that her father's judgment on this point was a correct one, that
the qualities and aspirations which would
make her the excellent and even exemplary

wife of a nobleman or statesman, were not such as would make her happy in the narrower walk he proposed to lead her in. His perception of this fact increased every day.

The all-important examination was fast approaching—the examination upon which so much depended, and towards which so many years of patient labour and of enthralling study and imagination had tended, and it may be thought that his mind must have been distracted and completely paralysed by such discord of emotion; but Charles de Foi possessed a spell which allays the trouble of the mind, which clears the intellect and enables it, freed from distracting perplexity, to concentrate itself upon the duty of the hour, in the certain confidence that the future will be guided by an unerring Intelligence. Religion is a spell for all necessities of life, but in no necessity is it more beneficent or powerful than in that of mental effort and concentration. Once again, in this supreme moment of his life, the old training of Port-Royal did him yeoman's service.

At no period of his life, not even in this crisis, was religion dissociated from education. He frequented Mr. Simeon's Friday evenings with the greatest regularity, and sought every opportunity of conversing with him, and seeking his advice.

One sunny afternoon, just before Hall, walking upon the grass plot in front of King's, he found the opportunity of opening his heart and his circumstances to his aged friend. Mr. Simeon had the warm and eager manners of a foreigner, which qualified him so perfectly to comfort and to guide.

'My young friend,' he said, 'this is no strange thing that has happened to you. I remember the time when I was quite surprised when a Fellow of my own college ventured to walk with me for a quarter of au hour on this grass plot, so much was I a man wondered at.

'Many years ago, when I was an object of much contempt and derision in this university, I strolled forth one day, buffeted and afflicted, with my little Testament in my hand. I prayed earnestly to my God that He would comfort me with some cordial from His Word, and that, on opening the Book, I might find some text which should sustain me. It was not for direction that I was looking, for I am no friend to such superstitions as the "Sortes Virgilianæ," but only for support. I thought I would turn to the Epistles, where I should most easily find some precious promise; but my book was upside down: so, without intending it, I opened on the Gospels. The first text that caught my eye was this: "They found a man of Cyrene, Simon by name: him they compelled to bear His cross." You know that Simon is the same name as Simeon.

What a word of instruction was here—what a blessed hint for my encouragement! To have the cross laid upon me, that I might bear it after Jesus. What a privilege! It was enough. Now I could leap and sing for joy as one whom Jesus was honouring with a participation in His sufferings. Things are strangely altered since those days. At the beginning of this term 120 freshmen were introduced to me.

'Let us think how it lies with you. The first alternative is to give up your sacred call and adopt a life such as they follow who have never had such a call. I do not think that we need speak much of this: but the other choice is, perhaps, more difficult to decide. Say that you marry this girl whom you love, and, against the wishes of her father and of her family, perhaps her own, take orders, are you prepared for what will follow? I know my own needs. I entreat you and all my friends, when they feel themselves especially near to God, to remember one who has so much need of help. If I know anything of the human heart you will require all the help from her who will be always at your elbow, whose wishes you will be bound to consult, if your own spiritual welfare and the interests of your Master's kingdom are to be promoted. I advise you to think most seriously of these things.'

The examination took place, and the lists came out. Charles de Foi's name was second in the first class. Then he came home. His heart was torn by contending emotions. His mind was full of love to God, of love for Julia Mainwaring, of enthusiasm for the studies and ideas that had been present with him day and night for years past. As he travelled home in the mail - coach this exciting conjunction of ideas kept possession of his thoughts.

On the afternoon of his arrival he found that what would now be called a garden party, but was then called a 'fête champêtre,' was to be held at Wotton, at which the most distinguished personages were expected from London. It was one of the first *fêtes* of the season, and was to be particularly brilliant. Charles had heard of it before from his sisters, and had timed his arrival at home, as he thought, so as to avoid it; but his sisters urged upon him the propriety of being present, though it were only for an hour; and having rested a little from the fatigues of his journey, he dressed and repaired to the grounds, whither his father and sisters had already preceded him.

The roads outside the gates were crowded with brilliant equipages, and thronged with servants; and the exquisitely-kept lawns, sloping to the river, were brilliant with a gay and fashionable assembly, attired in a profusion of bright colour, and an exaggeration of form that would now appear grotesque. Through these crowds, composed for the most part of entire strangers to him—through this strange maze of form and colour, De Foi threaded his way. The day was brilliantly fine; music floated on the air, and gaily-dressed servants moved about attending to the wants of the guests. At last De Foi reached a comparatively open space in front of the mansion, which, being unshaded by trees, was too hot to be attractive. Here, just beneath the terrace upon which the house was built, stood a group of the most distinguished guests, and Charles, standing in the shade, recognised Julia Mainwaring, and by her side a man, several years his senior, of exceptionally fine and lofty appearance. He was dressed in more sober colours than most present, but still in the highest fashion of the day, and wore close-fitting hose, or tights, as they were called, which showed his figure to great advantage, frilled ruffles at the shirt front and wrists, and a broad blue ribbon across his chest.

Julia was looking especially lovely. The somewhat fantastic fan-shaped hat or bonnet which she wore, and the full sleeves of her dress, which made some women look ridiculous, were toned down by her perfect figure and by her height, and appeared merely fit and becoming. The two appeared to Charles to be on terms of friendly intimacy.

'Can you tell me, sir,' said De Foi to a gentleman who stood near him; 'can you tell me who is that gentleman with the Ribbon of the Garter, who is speaking to Miss Mainwaring?'

'That, sir,' said the other, 'is the Duke of Cressy and de la Pole. People are saying it will be a match.'

As he spoke, with a sudden flash of light across De Foi's spirit, the divine leading shone bright and clear.

He made his way across the intervening grass, and approached the group. Julia came forward to greet him with manifest delight.

'Will your Grace allow me to introduce to you Mr. Charles de Foi, a near neighbour and a dear friend, who has just taken the highest honours at Cambridge?'

The Duke bowed with great politeness.

'I am very fortunate,' he said, 'in making so distinguished an acquaintance. Are you proposing to enter Parliament, Mr. de Foi?'

'No, your Grace,' said Charles quietly but very distinctly; 'I am looking forward to taking orders in the Church.'

Julia looked up suddenly into his face, and her cheeks flushed.

'It is the loftiest profession on earth,' said the Duke, with greater courtesy even than before, 'and the country is deeply grateful to men of distinguished attainments who devote themselves to so beneficent a calling.'

Charles de Foi spent the rest of the day in retirement and prayer, and the next morning he went up to Wotton again and had a long walk with Julia Mainwaring in the meadows by the river.

I have heard very much of what passed between these two, but it does not seem to me that it would be becoming to relate it here: it jars upon the sense to write down words that reveal the most sacred feelings of the heart. It must be sufficient to say that they mutually agreed to part, with tears on her part, with ill-suppressed emotion on his. It sounds little to say. A harrowing chapter in a novel, a scene of rant upon the stage, would doubtless display the genius of the writer with greater effect; but for me these few words must suffice.

Charles de Foi returned to Cambridge and was present at the sermons upon the Holy Spirit which Mr. Simeon preached that autumn before the university in St. Mary's. None who attended these sermons could forget the impression made upon the mind—the appearance of the church, crowded in every part,

the Heads of Houses, the doctors, the masters
of arts, the bachelors, the undergraduates, the
congregation from the town, vying with each
other to hear this aged and venerable man.
His figure remained in Charles de Foi's memory
to the latest hour of his life.   His fixed coun-
tenance, his bold and yet conciliatory manner
of address, his admirable delivery of a well-
prepared discourse, his pointed appeal to the
different classes of his auditory, the mute attention with which they hung upon his lips,
all composed the most solemn scene he had
ever witnessed.

He had heard that Julia was engaged to
the Duke of Cressy, and when he came home
at Christmas he was told that the marriage
was to take place in London at the beginning
of the year.   The Mainwarings, he was told,
were in town and would not spend Christmas
at Wotton.   It seemed, therefore, as though he
might stay safely at his home without fear of any
painful meeting, but a meeting there was to be.

A few days after Christmas, on a market day, he was passing through the little town. It was a bright winter's noon. The clean houses and the small fresh-looking shops were gay with Christmas goods. As Charles de Foi came out of a bye-road into the High Street, he was aware of a magnificent carriage, apparently quite new, with a pair of horses whose cost it would be rash to estimate, which was standing at the door of one of the principal shops. The market crowds that thronged the pathways enabled Charles to stand for a moment unnoticed before he passed on. The street was full of country carts, of noises of children and of hawkers' cries, of country men and women, of farmers, and of young gentlemen followed by their dogs; but the occupant of the carriage seemed absolutely indifferent and unconscious to all. She lay back in her seat motionless, in an attitude of impassive rest. The exquisite delicacy of her complexion was untinged by the faintest glow, and the expression of her features, chiselled as by a Grecian sculptor, was almost insolent in its superb repose—too indifferent to be haughty, too serenely unconscious to condescend to pride. After a moment's pause Charles de Foi passed on, slightly raising his hat, expecting as slight a bend of the haughty head.

No!—a flush, like the loveliest glimmer of the early dawn, passed over the marble face, the set and chiselled lips parted with a radiant smile, and the cold imperious eyes melted into tenderness that was pathetic to see. She leaned forward eagerly in the carriage and held out her hand.

'Good-bye!' she said.

The shock of the surprise was too great for the young man. He took her hand, but could not speak. The next moment the servant came out of the shop with a message; Charles stood back and raised his hat—a moment's pause, face to face, as she sank back into her seat—and, with a sudden start and scramble of the priceless horses, the carriage swept off down the crowded street, making the market people on every side start back.

He never saw her again. Once or twice he knew himself to have been in the same room with her in London, but he never consciously saw her again. After twenty years of a brilliant and useful life she died of a fever caught in Rome. Some short time after her death, almost indeed as soon as he had seen it in the papers in the London parish in which he worked, Charles de Foi received a letter from the Duke begging him to visit him.

'Mr. de Foi,' said the Duke, in the library of his town mansion, into which Charles had been shown, 'I owe to you my wife. I owe to you twenty years of greater happiness than falls to the lot of most men. Not only because you resigned her to me, but because the great and noble qualities

she possessed—how great and noble none
can know but myself—were developed—she
herself said, called into existence—by her
early intercourse with you. I have often
suggested that we should ourselves endeavour to renew the intercourse, but she
always declined. On her death-bed she said
to me, "I should die happy did I know
that you would see much of Charles de Foi.
None can know him without being the better
for it."'

Mr. de Foi came down with the Duke,
shortly after, to Kingswood. He made the
acquaintance of the clergyman at Rivershead,
and found in him a congenial friend. He
was in need of rest; indeed his health had
so much broken down that he had been
compelled to refuse more than one important
living in London which had been offered to
him. He requested from the Duke the
appointment to the church in the park, an
extra - parochial donative with no visible

source of income, and found work in conjunction with his friend at Rivershead. By
this long chain of circumstances it was that
I made his acquaintance when I was brought
to Kingswood, to my aunt, as a little child.
He was then a man of between fifty and
sixty years of age. He had a great reputation
among the servants of the Kingswood household, and many of them would walk down to
Rivershead on a fine Sunday evening to hear
him preach, either in the parish church or in
a mission chapel which, it was reported, he
had won from dissent. On Sunday mornings
he read prayers and preached in the little
church in the chase, and, if the weather was
propitious, the Duke and Duchess attended
the service. It was the opinion of the
servants, however, that Mr. de Foi was
'quite another man' in the pulpit here from
what he was at Rivershead. 'He preaches
before his Grace on Sunday mornings, Miss,'
Mr. Priest has said to me more than once,

implying that under these circumstances it could not be expected that the sermon would be suited to the understanding of the household.

The old-fashioned High Church notions of Mr. de Foi led him to the observance of many practices, since supposed to be modern innovations, a generation at least before Ritualists, so-called, were heard of. He observed the eastward position at the Holy Communion, he invariably bowed to the altar, and he read morning prayers on Wednesdays, Fridays, and Saints' days in the little church in the chase. The bell was rung to call to these services, but no one was ever known to attend, until one morning, when I was about eight years of age, happening by chance to be in the neighbourhood with my nurse, I insisted upon going in, and, conceiving an intense liking to the ceremony, we never, or rarely, failed to form the entire congregation. After service Mr.

de Foi generally accompanied us towards the house, and in this way the friendship between the man and the child—the kindly interest on the one hand, and the intense devotion on the other—grew up. It was in these walks, through the beds of fern and bracken, that I began to love him, and even as a child to apprehend the lofty teaching of his Christian Idealism.

CHAPTER III

'My dear,' said the Duchess to me one morning after breakfast, when the Duke had gone away into the library, and we had retired into the east front, where the Duchess' rooms were, 'my dear, the Duke is so kind as to invite a young relation of mine to come and stay with us for a time.'

I was at that time somewhere about twenty-two years of age, and the prospect of another inmate among the quiet surroundings of Kingswood was not without its interest.

'I hope,' continued my aunt, 'you will not ask me what relation he is to me, for I

have never been able to make it out. My
mother's sister married the old Lord Guion,
Earl of Castle - Guion, in the peerage of
Ireland, and Viscount Guion in the peerage
of England. He had three daughters—Lady
Elizabeth, Lady Sarah, and Lady Grace.
Lady Grace married Sir Phelim Massareen,
of a real old Irish family. They had one son,
who died in France, I think at Boulogne, some
years ago, leaving an only child, a boy, whom
Lady Elizabeth has brought up at Eton, and
of whom she is exceedingly fond. You remember Lady Elizabeth, I dare say, when she
was here some years ago. She is a wicked
old woman, and I do not wish to see her here
again. Lady Sarah, on the contrary, is extremely pious—far too pious to belong to the
Church of England. She lives at Bourne-
mouth, and sees nobody except her doctor
and the minister of her chapel. She is a
Christadelphian, or a Swedenborgian, or a
Malthusian, or something of that sort. The

old Lord Guion was a very singular man. He was possessed of immense estates both in England and Ireland. He was exceedingly disgusted and alarmed at the passing of the Reform Bill—the old Reform Bill, my dear, I mean. He believed that all property was insecure. He took advantage of the Irish Encumbered Estates Act, though his estates were not encumbered—far from it. He sold all his English estates—he had no son or male heir. He was a very shrewd old man, and it was a period of great prosperity. He sold all these estates to great advantage, and invested the money in the funds. It is said to amount to several millions,—I am sure I don't know,—and is well known in London as the "Guion money." It belongs entirely to Lady Elizabeth and Lady Sarah, and Lady Sarah won't touch it,—the Malthusians won't touch money, I believe,—and it will all come to Sir Percival, so it is said.'

The Duchess stopped to take breath. I

knew most of what she told me before. Indeed, she had told me most of it herself several times, but I listened with interest under these altered circumstances.

'And Sir Percival is coming here, aunt?' I said.

'Yes, my dear. Lady Elizabeth has written to ask it. The Duke likes Lady Elizabeth. He says she is of the old Irish-French school. The fact is,' continued the Duchess, sinking her voice a little, 'I do not mind telling you, my dear, because you are a very sensible girl —the fact is, Lady Elizabeth says there is a designing young woman—young person, she calls her—who has made a great set at Sir Percival, not so much, Lady Elizabeth is certain, for his own sake, or for the sake of the Guion money, but solely to spite Lady Elizabeth herself. She is kind enough to say that she has such a lively recollection of the intense stupidity and quietness of Kingswood, that she thinks that no place could be so suitable to send her nephew to for a time. I expect him to-night.

'The Massareens,' continued the Duchess after a pause, 'were always impecunious; indeed no Massareen was ever known to have a penny. They lived in a great tumble-down house with a great kitchen, which was open to all the country round. If anybody sold them a horse, or anything else, they used to come and live with them and eat the value out; but this sort of thing, you know, my dear, could not go on for ever, at least not with Encumbered Estates Acts, and all that. That was why Sir Percival's father died in France, at Boulogne.'

My maid told me that evening, when she came to my room before dinner, that Sir Percival had arrived. 'He had brought a servant with him,' she said, 'and Mr. Priest had told her that he was a very handsome young gentleman. He was then dressing for dinner.' I went down into the drawing-room, I must confess, a little sooner than usual, that I might be with the Duchess when the guest was announced.

I have already said that the drawing-room was the most modern-looking room in the house, but I should like to be a little more particular in describing it. It was a large room, decorated in the last century. Into the original wainscotting carved panelling of fruit and flowers had been introduced, forming wreaths and festoons in strong relief. The walls had been painted white and relieved with gold. Between the wreaths and panelling were placed portraits in oil, mostly full lengths, and beneath these were smaller paintings and groups of miniatures, and one or two cabinets of French marquetry. At one end of the room were two doors, one communicating with a small lobby opening to the hall, the other to one of the numberless staircases I have described as existing all over the house. Between these doors was a portrait by Gainsborough of a boy in a fancy dress of blue silk standing in front of a green landscape, with what always seemed to me an inexpressible look of vividness and of youthful grace and life.

The Duchess was sitting by the hearth knitting. She knitted an immense number of worsted stockings and comforters, which she gave to the children in her schools. She was excessively fond of knitting, and indeed I have arrived at the conviction that, to persons of a not very originative habit of mind, there is no occupation so attractive as this, for it combines, as none other does, the ease of mechanical operation with the delight and satisfaction of skilled result. I was standing by her side, as I remember, in a white dress, in the shade of one of the silver candelabras which lined the room, when the door leading to the staircase was opened and a servant announced—

'Sir Percival Massareen.'

I looked up, and, by the side of the Gainsborough boy, I saw, in the open doorway, another boy. He was tall and fair, quite a boy, but, as far as I could see, very handsome, with a strong clear-cut face. He was, of course, in modern evening dress; but his fair throat, and the white of his large falling collar and of his linen, gave him, in the shadow of the doorway, no such dissimilar look from that of the pictured figure by his side. He stood for a moment motionless, as though shy and afraid to advance. Then, probably seeing nothing alarming in a most benevolent-looking old lady knitting stockings, and a pale girl in white, standing under the branched shade of the candelabra, he came forward into the room.

The Duchess rose and met him with outstretched hand.

'I am so glad, Percival,' she said; 'I have never seen you since you were quite a little boy. I should not have known you again.'

He took her hand, and bowed with a winning grace. He was certainly, in the clear light, very handsome — a winsome, kindly lad.

'This is Constance Lisle,' the Duchess went on; 'you are some sort of cousins, I suppose. I may call myself aunt to both of you; but Constance always seems near to me, because she has my own name. My name was Lisle, you know.'

I don't think that Sir Percival knew anything about it, but he looked very pleased and friendly at us both.

'The Duke will be here directly,' said my aunt. 'Have you ever met, Percival?'

'I remember his Grace once at Eton,' said the boy, 'on a 4th of June.'

He spoke with perfect ease, as though familiar with titles and the phrases of London speech—with, perhaps, a touch of the modern careless freedom and absence of form, but in his case so toned down by his sweetness and deference of manner as to lose all its harshness.

The Duke came in soon after this, and we went in to dinner. We were all delighted with our guest. He chatted of his past life, and the time he had lived abroad, of Eton, of Lady Elizabeth, of his examination for the army. He showed a sense of fun, of a perception of the humorous side of character; but he never, in word or tone, displayed aught save a pure and modest spirit within. If he had met or seen anything in his boyish life that was contrary to such a spirit as this it seemed to have slipped off him without leaving a trace. As I sat opposite to him at the table, listening to his guileless talk, I was racking my brain to remember why his name was familiar to me, when suddenly there rushed into my mind the recollection of the great treasure of the library—the black-letter folio of the 'Morte d'Arthur' by the old printer Caxton himself, which the

Duke had caused to be brought from Hartfield, the great house of the dukedom, that
he might delight himself with it in his retirement. I could recall nothing of the story of
Percival save one sentence—that, as I remembered, he had 'kneled doune and made
his prayer devoutely unto almighty Jhesu,
for he was one of the best knyghtes of the
world that at that tyme was, in whome the
verry feythe stode mooste in.' I do not
know how it was, but I suppose that on
some occasion, while the Duke was turning
over the precious leaves, to entertain me
with the marvellous book, this sentence had
struck my girlish fancy, for I seemed to
see the quaint spelling of the lines impressed on the white cloth before me; and
I do not know that I should feel ashamed
to acknowledge that there, at the table, I
prayed to the Almighty Jesu—I had learned
from Mr. de Foi the habit of instinctive
prayer—that this lively, pleasant boy might,

in his calling and walk in life, achieve a
fame not dissimilar to that of his namesake
of the knightly romance of old.

After breakfast the next morning my aunt
said to me :

'Constance, my dear, you had better take
Percival through the gardens. There is no
shooting at this time of year, I believe,' she
said; 'and, perhaps, even if there were, he
would like to see something of the place
first.'

The Duchess in her secret heart detested
shooting; I believe that she even considered
it a brutal and disgusting occupation: but it
was part of the institutions of the country
—like the judges of assize, and hanging,
and grand juries, and many other things
which it was proper for men to do.

Sir Percival did not seem at all unwilling
to go, and we went out, through a porch
under an exquisite oriel window, and covered
with roses and clematis, in the south front,

into the flower gardens. It was a fine morning in late spring.

We went out at once on to the soft, mossy lawn, and turned round so that Percival might see the long, low front of the house. It lay broken into endless variety of bay and mullioned window, and ivied buttress, and low projecting tower, in brilliant sunshine and deep shadow, and enspiritualised, it seemed to me, by the fleeting clouds that swept over the sky.

'Is it not a beautiful house, Sir Percival?' I said.

He looked at it for a moment as though rather puzzled, then he said:

'I suppose it is.'

This is the time to ask him about the 'Morte d'Arthur,' I thought.

'Do you like Tennyson, Sir Percival?' I said.

He looked perplexed for a moment, then he said:

'Oh, yes. I have read his poems. I like them very much.'

'Do you like the " Idylls of the King ?"'

'Yes,' he said, rather doubtfully; 'I don't think I have read them all.'

'You know,' I said, 'they are taken from the old romance of the 'Morte d'Arthur.' The Duke has a wonderful black-letter copy of it, printed by Caxton. I must ask him to show it to us. You know there is a Sir Percival in it. That is why I should like you to see it.'

'No,' he said, 'I did not know that. What sort of fellow was he?'

'He was one of the best knights of the world, that at that time was,' I said, repeating the phrase that was engraven in my memory as in brass, 'in whom the very faith stood most in.'

'That sounds well,' he said. 'I am glad he was so good a fellow as that. It is well to have a fellow like that of your name to follow.'

'He was one of the very few,' I said, 'who saw the Holy Grail.'

As I said the words the sunshine seemed brighter, the old house seemed to stretch before us in a more entrancing beauty, the great elms upon the lawn towards the west cast a calmer shade.

'Oh, I know,' said Sir Percival; 'that was the cup of the Sacrament, or something of that sort, was it not?'

I suppose he thought, from something in my face, that I was shocked, for he immediately went on—

'I beg your pardon; I did not mean to be irreverent. Tell me what it was.'

He uttered these last words with such a winning sweetness that I liked him more than ever.

'It was the Holy Vessel of the Sacrament,' I said, 'that was used by our blessed Lord Himself, and could only be seen by the perfectly pure in heart and life.'

He turned to me again in that half-puzzled, wondering way in which he had looked upon the house, but he did not say anything more.

We went on in the morning sunshine through the parterres, all sweet with perfume and glistening with morning dew; passed some gardeners who were mowing the lawn; and went through a low oaken door in the high wall into the kitchen garden, which lay towards the west, beyond the south front of the house.

Sir Percival did not seem inclined to talk much, and I did not feel quite certain what to say. We walked, therefore, mostly in silence beneath the high wall that stretched before us, as it seemed, without limit, covered with fruit-trees in blossom. Every now and then I pointed out some exceptional plant,— a tobacco plant, or something of that sort,— but my companion seemed *distrait* and silent beyond his wont. It occurred to me, sadly, that we were not getting on very well.

The great garden sloped very slightly towards the south-west, and in the corner in this direction was another low doorway, which opened at once upon the chase. This had always been a favourite spot with me from my childhood's days. On either side of the door, within the garden, were tool-houses, within which were kept mysterious implements, and which oppressed my senses as I entered them with a strange earthy smell. When you had taken down the great bar that fastened this door you came out upon a cart road formed along a sort of natural terrace, along which stretched a row of ash-trees of great size and age. Beyond this the chase sloped away towards the west, with a rapid decline, into a dingle or valley in which the oaks and ashes, sheltered from the wind, had grown to an enormous size; and beyond the dingle, and through the vistas of its woods, the valley opened out with an expanse of woodland as far as eye could reach. I had not been able to choose my hour for bringing my companion to this spot, or I should probably have preferred a fine evening; but when the door in the wall was opened, and we stepped out upon the chase, I was content.

The radiant summer sun, alone in the cloudless sky, flooded with light a world of young green foliage, unruffled by touch of storm or age. A flickering haze, drawn up from the marshy park-land by the heat, quivered over the delicate green of the grass, and of the young oak leaves, and of the larger foliage of the ashes, and protected it from the killing sunlight that annihilated all other colour in its blaze. From the green forest-world below the haze ascended against the worn, pale blue of the heaven, also killed by the blazing light, and softened it also into a tender mezzotint, blending, with the green of earth and the golden light, into an opal veil, as it seemed, of crystal amber, in which the vast expanse of woodland, a world of invisible

life and possible activity, lay brooding in a
sleep of silence and of rest.   Beneath the
spreading branches of the trees flitted stealthily
the forms of deer, and other creatures,
more swift and active, stirred the fluttering
leaves.

I stood for a moment dazzled by this
glorious sight.   Then I turned to my companion and looked eagerly into his face.   He
did not notice me, but stood looking before
him with something of the same expression I
had noticed before, but, as I thought, with a
look of greater insight, as though some perception of a hitherto unknown fact was forcing
itself upon his mind.   I would not speak;
some instinctive power within me kept me
silent; but with all the force of an intense
desire which sprang up suddenly within my
soul I begged him to see!   'O Percival!
Percival!' though not a sound was uttered,
yet the words seemed to form themselves
within the murmuring breeze, and throughout

the rustling grass, and along the spreading branches of the ashes. 'See! only see!'

He looked steadily before him for some seconds, then he turned to me with the old, puzzled, winsome look.

'It is very odd,' he said; 'ever since I have been out with you I seem to have felt some new, strange way of looking at things, as though things I never thought of were coming into my mind—as though I should be able sometime to see and do things which I have never seen, never thought that I should do. I must have seen many such a place as this, but they never looked like this to me before.'

'You cannot think,' I said, 'how I love this place. I want you to see it as I see it. I have never lived anywhere else; I have hardly ever seen anything else.'

'But it is not only places,' he said, 'other things seem different to me since I knew you.'

We went back to the house along the cart road, beneath the spreading ashes, and after this sudden experience and confession we felt little more of shyness or embarrassment, but could walk silently side by side without awkwardness or any sense of the necessity of speech. We went round to the northern front, through the wilderness, or orchard, and into the silent sunny quadrangle, through the low cupolaed arch.

After lunch, as I was helping the Duchess to dress for her drive, she said :

'I hope you like Percival, my dear; how did you get on with him?'

'I like him so very much,' I said. 'I love him dearly; I am sure he is good. He will grow up to be a great and a good man.'

'You must be prepared to find him deeply in love with you in a day or two,' said my aunt, smiling.

'I think not, aunt,' I said.

'He told me before lunch, after you came

in,' said my aunt, 'that he had never had such a walk. He said that walking with you was like walking with an angel, and that you had the loveliest face that he had ever seen. You *have* a very sweet face, you know, Constance, my love,' continued my aunt in a rather injured tone; she always looked upon me as peculiarly of her own family, almost her child, as well she might, and was jealous in respect of me.

'I am afraid boys do not fall in love with angels, aunt,' I said.

Though I spoke sadly, I confess that I was pleased to hear what she said, so pleased that I was almost frightened. 'If I do not take care,' I thought, 'it is I who will be hopelessly in love in a day or two.'

'Poor boy,' said my aunt, 'I wonder that he is so good, brought up as he was, and with that wicked old woman to influence him.'

That night after dinner the Duke, at our

request, had the priceless Caxton brought
into the drawing-room, and read to us all
that he could find, or chose to select, concerning Sir Parcyval. The Duke was a
beautiful reader, and was very familiar with
the old English of Chaucer and his fellows,
and understood their system of rhythm, of
final syllables, and much besides, which he
had often explained to me. Percival listened,
I could see, with much interest, and looked
at the great black-letter folio with awe, as
well he might.

'But this knyght,' the Duke read, 'that
foughte with Syre Percyval was a proved
knyght and a wyse fyghtinge knyghte, and
syre Percyvale was yonge and stronge not
knowyng in fyghtyng as the other was.
Thenne syre Percyvale spak fyrste and sayd
syre knyght hold thy hand a whyle stille,
for we have fouzten for a symple mater and
quarel over longe, and therefor I requyre
thee tell me thy name, for I was never or

this tyme matched. Soo god me help sayd that knyghte, and never or this tyme was there never knyght that wounded me soo sore as thow hast done, and yet have I foughten in many batails and now shalt thou wete that I am a knyghte of the table round, and my name is Syre Ector de marys broder unto the good knyghte syr launcelot du lake. Allas said syr Percyval and my name is syr Percyval de galys that hath made my quest to seke syr launcelot, and now I am seker that I shall never fynysshe my quest, for ye have slayne me with your handes. It is not soo said Syre Ector, for I am slayne by yoore handes, therefore I requyre you ryde ye here by to a pryory, and brynge me a preest that I may receyve my saveour, for I may not lyve. Alas said syre Percyval that never wille be, for I am so faynte for bledyne that I maye unnethe stande, how shold I thenne take my hors.

'Thenne they made bothe grete dole out

of mesure, this wille not avayle said sire
Percyval. And thenne he kneled doune and
made his prayer devoutely unto al myghty
Jhesu, for he was one of the best knyghtes
of the world that at that tyme was, in whome
the veray feythe stode moost in. Ryght soo
there came by, the holy vessel of the Sanc-
greal with alle maner of swetnes and savour,
but they coude not redyly see who that bare
that vessel, but syre Percival had a glemer-
ynge of the vessel and of the mayden that
bare it, for he was a parfyte clene mayden,
and forth with al they bothe were as hole of
hyde and lymme as ever they were in their
lyf dayes. Thenne they gef thankynges to
god with grete myldenesse. O Jhesu said syre
Percival, what maye this meane. I wote ful
wel said syre Ector what it is. It is an holy
vessel that is borne by a mayden, and therein
is parte of the holy blood of oure lord Jhesu
crist blessid mote he be, but it may not be
sene said syr Ector, but yf it be by a parfyte

man. Soo god help me said syr Percyval I sawe a damoysel as me thoughte alle in whyte with a vessel in both her handes, and forth with al I was hole.'

When he had finished the reading, the Duke told us in his simple way, with a manner which he always had, as though his chief object was to imply that he knew no more than we did, that Sir Percival was hardly treated in the 'Morte d'Arthur.' In the French books he had a romance all to himself, and occupied the same position that Sir Galahad does in the English romance, but that when Sir Thomas Mallory undertook to translate these French romances into one book, he would not omit any one of them, and was therefore obliged to cut out all the deeds of poor Sir Percival, which were identical with those of Sir Galahad, and leave him in a very secondary position.

The reading was over, and the Duchess had retired for the night; the whole house was wonderfully still, the staircases and lobbies, antique and roughly panelled as they were, were alight with fires and candles in silver sconces, and full of strange gleams and mystic depths of shadow. Percival and I wandered out of the drawing-room, and found our way to the great hall. Before the stone fireplace, carved with Actæon and his dogs, lay two or three stags' skins with the antlers still attached, a dangerous practice, but peculiar to the house. The fire had been fed with a huge log of wood, which had burned very low. There was little other light in the hall. The flicker of the expiring flames that leaped up suddenly and fell again lighted the oak panelling, the massive door-ways, and the armour that had been discarded as useless, centuries ago, the faded brightness of which still shone upon the walls.

Avoiding carefully, trained as I was by long custom, the branched antlers, I stood at one side of the stone fireplace by the expiring blaze. Sir Percival stood opposite to the hearth looking fixedly into the fire. His youthful, handsome face and boyish figure in modern evening dress contrasted strangely with the old-world surroundings, toned and mellowed by the disappointments, the sorrows, the losses of ages of men. It seemed to me that spiritual beings, fairies and ghosts, the true owners of the scene, were only waiting the removal of our intrusive presence to resume their rightful possession.

'I like that fellow, Constance,' Percival said,—he had mustered courage to call me Constance within the last few hours, and my aunt had encouraged him to do so,—'I like that fellow Sir Percival, and I am glad that I was called after him. He was young and not knowing in fighting as the other was; and in the book he was dispossessed of his birthright, and took the second place. I like him.'

The expiring log sent up a sudden and final flame that lighted all the hall. Percival looked up suddenly into my face and went on as though remembering the rest.

'And he saw a damoisel all in white with a vessel in both her hands, and withal he was whole.'

The transient gleam faded from the lofty hall and left no other light save the dim glimmer of the candles, and we shook hands and said good-night.

The next day we went a ride together in the afternoon, while the Duke and Duchess drove into Rivershead. Percival had ridden with the Duke in the morning, and proposed tennis to me in the afternoon, as there was a court laid out for visitors on the farther part of the lawn. I was soon, however, able to convince him that I was a wretched player. It was quite an agreeable surprise to me when I hit the ball at all, much more when I sent it in the right direction. Percival therefore, who was a superb player, soon got tired of this, and was quite willing to ride with me, or to do anything else to escape such an infliction. Here I was at an advantage, for I was a quite fearless rider. I had a perfectly trained lady's horse, and would gallop with him to any extent, whereas the Duke's sober riding in the morning had not been at all to Percival's taste. We rode out through the chase, towards the north, to the ruined tower.

It was a sober afternoon following the glories of the previous day. A vast pall of thunder - cloud stretched over the entire heaven, but towards the west and north a broad belt of clear sky let in the light. The sun was not low enough to allow its rays to be seen, but its light above the thunder-pall produced an effect of crystal clearness and brilliancy, both on the horizon and across the broad landscape beneath the cloud,—an intense distinctness in the outline of every object, far more intense than could have been possible in the light of the sun.

We soon got into a gallop over the rough grass of the chase. It was dangerous no doubt; but all riding is dangerous, and our horses knew the country, and for this afternoon, at any rate, we escaped without accident. Thus galloping, with an occasional walk, we reached the dark tower, and stood beyond it on the grassy knoll looking over the channel and the distant coast-line. Here and there in the far distance, below the dark rain-clouds, the sun's rays were shining through the crystal air. It was a lovely scene—the broad channel in shadow, but in clear light, dotted with white sails—the distant hills lighted with the misty, slanting rays which gilded the under edges of the clouds, and softened their rugged, storm-laden forms. Then we turned our horses' heads, and pacing round the grassy knoll, reached the southern side of the tower and drew rein, facing the chase over which we had come.

There were no distant rays of sunlight here. The dark pall of cloud stretched nearly to the horizon, with only a narrow line, in the far distance, of solemn light. Beneath the dark canopy lay the vast extent of woodland, unbroken by spire or tower or house. Every tree, almost every leaf, stood out with awful distinctness in this strange light, which could not be called the light of day. A wild wind swept over the wood, bending and driving its waving branches into fantastic forms. The scene was terrible in its distinct, colourless gloom.

It seems to be generally accepted as a fact that childhood and youth are thoughtless and gay. I can only say that not only in childhood, but in youth, I had fits of nameless, inexplicable terror, nay, of horror, which I never experienced in later life. Whether children, being nearer to the unseen, have consciousness and instincts which older people have lost in a grosser tabernacle of flesh, I cannot say; all I know is that as I sat upon my beautiful horse by Percival's side that afternoon, an intense dread and horror settled upon my mind.

The cold clearness of the forest glades, the strange forms that rose against the mystic sky-line in the distant south, sent flashing into my mind something I had heard the Duke read about what would happen to the world when the sun had expended its heat. Here, it seemed to me, was the awful cold and gloom of the final day—a world without a sun—a world without a God.

In my helplessness and terror I turned to Percival for help. He was sitting well back in his saddle, his hands straight down upon the pommel; his pose, and that of his splendid horse, perfect as that of the figures upon a Græcian frieze. The outline of his clear-cut face, and the tossing crest of his horse, chafing against the rein, stood out in the clear, sombre air. I drew my breath again freely in the sense of his strength and repose.

'Constance,' he said, 'this is grand : this forest, this wild, tossing woodland, this dark sky, is what the knights often saw in their quest.'

CHAPTER IV

A CHANTREY OF PRIESTS

I HAVE said that the Duke had for years resigned all public life and functions to his eldest son, the Marquis of Clare. He had one other son, who was a diplomatist, and resided constantly abroad with his family. Every now and then, when any particular business required attention, the Marquis would come down to Kingswood to consult with his father, with whom he was on the best possible terms.

I never exactly knew why, but I did not like Lord Clare. He was a very handsome man of about forty-three years of age. He had inherited the beauty of both his parents, and his mother's winning ways, and this last circumstance had made him very popular, especially in his youth, at school and college, and assisted, more than anything else, in making him, what I always fancied him to be, a thoroughly spoiled child of fortune. His father idolised him ; the words 'my son' conveyed to the old noble the sense of all that was honourable and to be prized in human nature.

'My son,' he would say to me, when we were riding together; 'my son is a far greater noble than I could ever be'—(I need not say that I did not in the least agree with him)—'his mother was one of nature's peeresses, and he inherits her manner.' The Duke addressed his son as 'George' from duty, but he would have greatly preferred, had he followed his own taste, giving him his title, or, better still, addressing him as 'my son.' He has confessed this to me.

'In France,' he would say, 'the greatest

noble never speaks of his father otherwise than as "Monsieur mon père." It is considered that there can be no higher title. I wish it were the custom in England.'

On one occasion, when I was a little girl, we spent a few days at Hartfield, the ducal house. I was particularly impressed by the great Vandyke room, hung entirely with portraits by Vandyke. What impressed me most was the similarity of expression in all the portraits. They all wore their eyes, so to speak, exactly like the king—or rather, they all tried to do so, some succeeding much better than others. Whether this was a Court fashion of the time, or whether it was a mannerism of the painter, I never knew; but the fact impressed my childish fancy very much; in fact, fascinated it. I spent all the time I could spare before those marvellous gentlemen and courtiers of that melancholy past.

The expression in the king's eyes seemed to me, always, as though he saw something many thousand miles away, and never, by any possibility, could see anything between himself and it. All his servants seemed to me to imitate this expresssion with more or less success. The most successful seemed to me to be the beautiful and gallant Lord Caernarvon, whose eyes seemed to me more beautiful and *distrait* even than the king's.

Now, when I grew older I never saw the Marquis of Clare without being reminded of this old childish fancy. Not that the expression was exactly the same. It was not that the Marquis seemed to see something a very long way off, but that he never seemed able to make up his mind whether it was worth his while to see anybody, or anything, or to say anything at all. Lord Clare was very polite, and was especially courteous and considerate to my aunt, his stepmother. This ought to have conciliated me, but I always fancied that he acted thus, not from any regard to my aunt, but simply from the supreme instinct

and conviction that whatever a Duke of Cressy
and de la Pole did must necessarily be absolutely right, and that had his father chosen to
marry a kitchen-maid his conduct would have
been exactly the same. I may perhaps have
wronged and mistaken the Marquis, and the
reader may think, before this story ends, that
I did.

When Lord Clare was expected at Kingswood the entire household was excited; any
conceivable fault, I believe, would have .been
forgiven to any member of it except want of
attention to the Marquis. The most careless
and casual expression of preference on his part
was treasured up and remembered. The Duke
was constantly on the look-out for these chance
expressions, for the Marquis was anything but
an 'exigeant' person, and rarely in fact seemed
to think it worth while to have a preference.
Anything, however, that he was supposed to
prefer—any choice wine, any particular horse,
which he may have praised or honoured with

an approving glance, was henceforth devoted to his service. A particular room was always appropriated to him, but I never could learn that he had expressed any particular liking for it. He was supposed to be partial to snipe shooting, but I never knew upon what grounds, and I suspect that his fondness for this form of sport was very languid.

Two or three days after our ride to the dark tower Lord Clare was expected at Kingswood, and arrived some time in the afternoon. We, Percival and I, did not see him before dinner. Percival had met him in London, and they seemed to be on familiar terms. The evening impressed itself on my recollection, and I may be excused for remembering it.

The only conversation I recall at dinner was something between the Marquis and my aunt on the subject of politics. The Duchess had innocently asked what was going on in the political world.

'I really don't know,' said the Marquis; 'I have long since ceased to take the slightest interest in politics. My father,' and he glanced up the table at the Duke, who was listening, as he always did, with intense interest to his son's talk,—'my father would have liked me to take a leading part, but I always told him, What can you do? It is impossible for a noble to lead a democracy. The moment you begin to reason and argue with people you may as well be a socialist at once! I was terribly near getting into office once: had the Buck-hounds offered me!'

'But there is Lord St. Julian.'

'Oh yes, there is Lord St. Julian,' said the Marquis; 'but Lord St. Julian is not a noble, really, though he comes of the great Julia Gens. He is a Professor. The St. Julians have always been too clever, and himself particularly so. He wants that touch of stupidity which is absolutely necessary to a true noble. You will not find the true nobles B——t, or

R——d, or B——m and C——s, messing in party politics with a democratic House of Commons.'

After dinner the Duke, as was now his wont, went into the library for a little rest; but Lord Clare and Percival came into the drawing-room to us, and Mr. Giles brought us tea.

'I hear'—said the Marquis, as he seated himself courteously by my aunt, 'the Duke tells me that you are going to have Virginia Clare down here. I wish you joy of her.'

'Why?' said the Duchess anxiously; 'is she not nice?'

'Oh, I don't quite see her running with Constance, that's all,' said the Marquis. 'She is an agnostic, you know. "I am an agnostic, Lord Clare," that is what all the little girls say now. I always want to say, "That is exactly what I should have expected, Miss Smith;" and the boys, too, go about volunteering the quite unnecessary information that they know nothing.'

'How sad!' said my aunt.

'The coolest thing I ever heard, I think,' said Lord Clare, 'was said to me by a young fellow the other day. He told me it was immoral in *me* to believe anything which *he* didn't understand. "Then, my dear fellow," I said, "I shall believe in nothing." It wasn't original. Dr. Johnson said it. Perhaps that was why it didn't impress him much.'

'But she is very handsome—Virginia, I mean,' said my aunt; 'she gave great promise of beauty when I saw her last.'

'Oh yes, she is handsome enough,' said the Marquis, 'much more than can be said for most of your clever girls. We are a handsome family, no doubt,' he added, with a curious expression which was not a sneer and yet was like one—'we are a handsome family, no doubt, whatever else may be said of us. I think my father gets more beautiful every time I come down. She plays tennis superbly. You know her, Massareen?' he continued, turning to Percival, 'you are a kind of cousin, surely.'

'No,' said Percival, 'I never heard of her before.'

'Oh, I beg your pardon,' said Lord Clare, 'I forgot, you are on the Duchess' side,' and he bowed to my aunt, as who would say, 'No greater honour a man could have.' He did it so perfectly that for a moment or two I quite liked him.

The Duke came in soon after, and his son joined him.

Percival and I amused ourselves at the piano. Percival was fond of singing, and wanted to improve himself. My aunt pursued her knitting. So an hour passed. Then my aunt made a move to leave the room, and began to put up her knitting. The Duke was putting up some papers. Percival and I came up to the hearth, and stood before the fire. Lord Clare left his father for a moment, and came and leant on one end of the great carved mantelpiece, looking, as I thought, with some interest at Percival.

Percival was standing on the hearth, looking, as was his wont, straight into the fire.

'How happy we are here!' he said. 'Why should we ever change? I am so sorry this Virginia Clare is coming. I am sure I shall not like her.'

'I would not be so cock-sure of that if 1 were you, Massareen,' said the Marquis. 'I would not mind taking fairly long odds that she bowls you over in five minutes. She is simply one of the loveliest girls I ever saw.'

'What? an agnostic!' said Percival.

'Yes, agnosticism and all,' said Lord Clare.

I looked up at him as he spoke, and saw with astonishment that the cold, indifferent look was gone out of his eyes, and that he was regarding Percival with a glance of interest and even pity; then I was still further surprised and astonished to find his eyes turned upon me.

I dropped mine in a moment, and the Marquis said :

'You won't take it, Massareen, but I am going to give you some advice. You say that you are happy now—don't change. I remember a sentence in the Eton grammar—it's Cicero, I think—"Incredibili *Constantia* sunt cursus stellarum." My advice is, imitate the stars in their incredibility—but the Duchess is tired,' and he moved forward to open the door for my aunt.

I did not understand all this at the time, but the next morning after breakfast Percival said to me :

'That was a very pretty compliment the Marquis paid to you last night, Constance.'

'Compliment ?' I said.

'Yes; "*Constantia* cursus stellarum," you know. It isn't in the Eton grammar. I believe he made it up himself. But he began again a few minutes after when we were smoking. "Did you ever read Jane Austen's

Persuasion, Massareen?" he said. "No? Well, read it. There is a woman in it, Anne Elliot, the most perfect thing ever done. I never knew more than two women in real life that I have thought of so much. A man may be proud to have walked up the streets of Bath on the same pavement which Anne Elliot's feet pressed; and I declare to you, Massareen," he said, flinging his cigar into the fire and taking another—"I declare to you that no girl ever reminded me of Anne Elliot so much as Constance Lisle."

'You may imagine,' continued Percival, with boyish candour, 'how astonished I was' —but I could not be angry with him, I was so astonished myself.

'If he were not married,' he went on, 'you might be Duchess of Cressy and de la Pole before long.'

'That I should never be,' I said.

The Marquis and Percival went out fishing that day. They were out to lunch, and we did not see them till the evening. I fancy there must have been guests to dinner, for I cannot recall any incident that took place.

The next morning the Marquis left. After breakfast Percival said to me:

'What do we do this morning, Constance? What are you going to do?'

'I am going to church,' I said. 'It is St. Peter's Day, and Mr. de Foi reads prayers in the little church in the chase. Will you come with me? it will materially increase the congregation. Otherwise there will be only Mr. de Foi and myself.'

'Oh, I will go gladly,' he said; 'I would go anywhere with you.'

He was very friendly with me now in a boyish way.

'If you will come out with me on to the lawn,' I said, 'I will read to you the Keble for St. Peter's Day. You said you liked the Keble I read to you the other day, Percival.'

'Yes, I did,' he said heartily; 'I liked it

very much.   I should like to hear you read now.'

We went out into the parterre, before the south front.

The wall that enclosed it on the left hand and separated it from the chase was of considerable height, and afforded a very convenient shade from the morning sun.   Beneath this wall garden chairs had been placed, and to these we betook ourselves.   The wall was a remarkable one.   It was built of old blocks of stone, not very large, and was covered with clematis and straggling creepers, but every now and then there were built into the wall remains of carved work and tracery and architraves.   It was supposed—the house was so old and no particular records existing of it, so that much of its history was lost, and the walls and courts and the very ground itself were so full of unexpected remnants and relics of the past that the wisest antiquarians were at fault—but it was supposed that at some very early time a chantry, or religious foundation for priests, had been joined to the kingly manor, and that the remains of such ecclesiastical architecture had been built up into the garden wall. However this may have been, the wall, at some distance from the house, was pierced by a very beautiful archway of small dimensions, enclosing a door of antique oak, also elaborately carved. Over this archway had been introduced into the wall a curiously-carved cornice or architrave coming down to a point. When I was a little child and was allowed by my nurse to play on the sunny side of the lofty wall, this mysterious door greatly impressed my fancy and excited my wonder. I knew nothing of what was beyond, but it seemed to my childish imagination a vast and gloomy world, full, doubtless, of strange terrors and dangers, and from whence, over the protecting wall, black clouds and storms came drifting from the north and east. I did not know in those childish days that through this door, at which I looked then with so much wonder, I should pass at the most solemn moment of my life.

When we had reached the wall we found that the sun had already advanced so far towards the south as to take away all shade, and we therefore walked once or twice up and down the broad path beneath the wall before seeking a cooler seat elsewhere. I showed Percival the curious carvings, and told him what was guessed at of their origin,— the chantrey of priests within the king's house, —and I pictured as well as I could, second-hand from Mr. de Foi, that delightful long-past time when the secular and the religious life walked in amity hand-in-hand—when the king or noble collected within the walled para-dise of his home all that the world recollected of learning, or had taught itself of handicraft; and in the midst of the wilderness of waving forest and of wilder men, kept alive the culture and the religion that was to bless an aftertime.

We found our way after this to a tulip tree
on the lawn, which cast an alluring shade,
and I read to Percival the Keble for St. Peter's
Day : of the Apostle, who, sleeping the night
before his expected execution, dreams of the
Master whom he had denied, yet loved, of

>   Th' inverted tree,
> Which firm embraced, with heart and arm,
> Might cast o'er hope and memory,
> O'er life and death, its awful charm.
>
>   .　　　　.　　　　.　　　　.
>
> Touch'd, he upstarts, his chains unbind,
> Through darksome vault, up massy stair,
> His dizzy, doubting footsteps wind
> To freedom and cool moonlight air.
>
> Then all himself, all joy and calm,
> Though for a while his hand forego,
> Just as it touch'd the martyr's palm,
> He turns him to his task below :
>
> The pastoral staff, the keys of heaven,
> To wield awhile in gray-hair'd might ;
> Then from his cross to spring forgiven,
> And follow Jesus out of sight.

When I had done, I sat silent, turning over
the leaves.　　Percival did not speak.

'Oh, Percival!' I said at last; 'listen to this. This is what I read on Ascension Day, not so long ago. That was before you came.'

And I read—

Soft cloud, that while the breeze of May,
   Chants her glad matins in the leafy arch,
Draw'st thy bright veil across the heavenly way,
   Meet pavement for an angel's glorious march.

My soul is envious of mine eye,
   That it should soar and glide with thee so fast,
The while my grovelling thoughts half-buried lie,
   Or lawless roam around this earthly waste.

Chains of my heart, avaunt! I say:
   I will arise, and in the strength of love
Pursue the bright track ere it fade away—
   My Saviour's pathway to His home above.

    ·   ·   ·   ·   ·

The sun and every vassal star,
   All space, beyond the soar of angel wings,
Wait on His word: and yet He stays His ear
   For every sigh a contrite suppliant brings.

He listens to the silent tear,
   For all the anthems of the boundless sky—
And shall our dreams of music bar our ear
   To His soul-piercing voice for ever nigh?

    ·   ·   ·   ·   ·

Percival sat still when I had finished, looking straight before him, with the old puzzled look in his hazel eyes. His eyes were a combination of gray and brown, and seemed the inheritance of different races. Did they foreshadow and predict, in spite of the coldness of a northern race, the possibility of an instinct of fancy and of faith?

I sat looking at him for a moment, hoping that he would speak.

'It is so strange to me, Constance,' he said, of a sudden; 'all so strange. Of course, I've been to church and heard sermons, and I know we ought to pray, and all that; but I never knew any one who seemed to see all this as you do. It seems to be so real to you. Do you really mean that you hear this

"Soul-piercing voice;"

that you see Him; that you see Christ, as you see me, as you see the Duke?'

'Yes,' I said; 'I do.' It escaped me before

I was aware. It hardly seemed as though it were myself that spoke the words, so suddenly, so confidently, had they leapt forth. The boldness of the assertion struck me with a kind of awe, and I buried my face in my hands.

'You have something,' said Percival, beneath his breath, 'which I have not.'

The time was approaching when we were to go to church, and we went out through the mystic doorway into the chase. For the first hundred yards there was a narrow footpath through the grass that led to the carriage drive. It was a fitful summer morning, with soft sunshine breaking out from passing rain-clouds, and sudden showers that scarcely moistened the ground.

As I had warned Percival, he and I formed the entire congregation.

'That man reads well,' Percival said, as we came out. 'I like to hear the prayers read sometimes without music. One seems to understand them.'

'Let us wait and speak to him,' I said; 'I should like you to like him. Perhaps he will come to lunch.'

Mr. de Foi came out of the vestry, and came up to us at once.

I thought Percival must be struck with his venerable appearance and mild, beneficent air.

'Sir Percival Massareen,' I said, as I shook his hand. 'Will you come to lunch, Mr. de Foi? there is no one at the house but ourselves.'

He did not accept or decline, but walked by my side.

'You have had the Marquis down,' he said; 'was he well?

'Yes; he seemed quite well: didn't he, Sir Percival? But we are going to have another guest, a Miss Clare, a most beautiful girl, Lord Clare says.'

'It is a pleasant day, Sir Percival,' Mr. de Foi said.

'Yes,' said Percival, as I thought, somewhat bluntly; 'it is. I think one ought to be thankful for every fine day. My father used to say the only thing we had to do in this life was to seize on the brightness of the present. Every pleasant moment, every day passed with some success, was so much snatched from inexorable fate.'

Looking back afterwards on this most eventful day, I think I see that Percival was beginning to feel the reaction from an unaccustomed strain, and that from the religious effort of the morning his thoughts had reverted, with relief, to the unrestrained life his father had led; but I did not see this at the time, and perhaps I did not act wisely in what I did.

'Mr. de Foi,' I said, 'I wish you would tell Sir Percival that beautiful story of your grandfather, the Vicomte de Foi. It will not take long, and it has something to do with what we were talking about in the garden before church. The story about Mademoiselle Desessart, I mean.'

'Yes, it is a pretty story,' said Mr. de Foi; 'and there is a certain appropriateness in telling it to Sir Percival, because it is related of one who, though he was my grandfather, in youth, in rank, and in grace resembled himself.'

Percival bowed at this speech, but, I thought, with some shyness. I began to fear that the old - fashioned, half - foreign manner of Mr. de Foi would estrange him.

'My grandfather,' said Mr. de Foi, 'was the second son of a French noble, and was called the Vicomte de Foi. His grandfather had been an intimate friend of the celebrated Abbé de St. Cyran, of Port-Royal. The family had always, therefore, been "bien reglée," and the Vicomte's father, the Marquis de Foi, held an appointment in the family of Monseigneur le Dauphin, father of the unfortunate Louis XVI., whose household was very religious. The Vicomte's elder sister, Madame la Comtesse de Civrac, a very beautiful woman, who had married a relation of the Duke of that name, was truly religious, having been brought up by her parents in all the traditions of the Port-Royalists. She was devotedly attached to her younger brother, whom she kept constantly with her, and endeavoured to preserve from the contagion of the Court and the world. In this, to a great extent, she succeeded. The Vicomte, when he had attained his twentieth year, was a man of what was called in those days "une conduite parfaitement régulière." He was extremely handsome, tall, and of a perfect figure. He was sincerely religious; he took the sacrament every fifteenth day, and his sister's heart overflowed with gratitude to God that her prayers had been answered. But though the Vicomte preserved so fair an appearance before the world, he was not altogether satisfied in his mind. He was a favourite among his companions. He mixed freely, as did all his family, with the Court and the world, and he was oppressed with the apprehension that the paths of the religious life were rough and stony, and that to follow them would entail a sacrifice of so much that was dear to his habits and to his taste that he would be miserable for life. This feeling and this dread, which had been growing upon him for some time, were accelerated by some trifling incidents which happened when he was a little more than twenty years of age, and became extremely oppressive. He was ashamed to confess his trouble to his sister, or to any human being, but he had been trained to the habit of prayer.

'The chateau of the Comte de Civrac, where he almost constantly resided, was situated on the bank of the Seine, some distance from Paris. One night in the spring of the year he had retired to rest, after a visit of some days to the city, in a troubled frame of mind. The difficulties of maintaining the religious life appeared to him to be more insurmountable than ever, and the gloomy future that lay before him seemed more oppressive and dark. In this mood he fell into an uneasy slumber, from which he awoke a little before sunrising. The chamber which was appropriated to him was situated in a wing of the chateau which faced the east, and looked out upon the Seine. In front of his windows were groves of thorn - trees — " les belles aubepines " my grandfather always called them—at that time of the year in full blossom. On the other side of the river was a forest of oaks. The night had been very warm and the windows had been left open, and when the Vicomte awoke the room was full of the delicious odour of the hawthorn and of the sweet morning air. The rising sun, not yet visible, sent in advance of his rising, a roseate light and glow, soft yet brilliant. An inexpressible sense of peace and joy suffused the Vicomte's spirits as he awoke. There was not, as he described it, any sense of personal presence, but the whole universe seemed instinct with peace and light. The words were impressed upon his mind with an overpowering force, "My yoke is easy and my burden is light." "Only follow Me," an all-persuading voice seemed to say, "and the troubles and fears that haunt you shall vanish away. There will be no un-happiness, no regret. The pleasures you fancy that you will have to renounce are not pleasures, are not even such as you yourself really covet. The pleasures which you are formed to enjoy are of good report, they are all compatible with the Divine will; there is no voice that will call you to renounce these."

'The Vicomte rose from his bed in a rapture of gratitude and joy. The load that lay upon him was not only taken away, but a world of joy and pleasure seemed to open before him wide as life itself.

' He had been engaged to return to Paris that night to attend a ball at the Hotêl du Valois-Desessart, given in honour of the eldest daughter of the duke of that name, who was that night to be introduced into society. The Vicomte's first idea was to send an excuse and remain at the Chateau de Civrac. It seemed to him, in his excited state of mind, that a gay and brilliant ball, at which all the rank and fashion of a luxurious city would be present, would be the last place in which he could expect to find pleasure and satisfaction—that among the thorn bushes of the park and on the banks of the placid Seine, with some holy book for his companion, he should pass the hours far more in accordance with that beautiful and holy life to which he felt that now at last he had devoted himself for good and all. But, to his surprise, he was not allowed to act thus. He heard a voice, clear and distinct as the one which had brought him such comfort in the early morning, saying to him, " Go to this ball." Its insistence upon his spirit was too great to leave a moment's doubt as to his conduct. He returned to Paris in the morning to his father's *hôtel*, and at the proper time he dressed for the ball. He remembered to his dying day the dress which he wore—a peach-coloured suit embroidered with silk.

'When the ball began the Vicomte, being a graceful dancer, and, from his father's connection with Monsieur le Dauphin, of distinguished rank, was chosen to dance in the first set, which was led by the Duke and Duchess and by Mademoiselle du Valois-Desessart and her partner, a prince of the Blood-Royal. In the same set there was dancing an exceedingly pretty girl, a cousin of the young lady of the house, and of the same age, a Mademoiselle Desessart, who was being brought out at the same time as her more distinguished relation. It fell to the Vicomte's lot to dance chiefly, in the elaborate yet slow dances of those days, with this lovely girl. She was wild with delight and hope, with the prospect of years—endless years—of gay pleasure and of reckless life and joy. The Vicomte listened to her delight with sympathy and friendliness.

'Suddenly, in a pause of the music, the voice which had before guided him again penetrated his senses with its all-commanding power.

'"Speak to this girl of the love of God, of her Saviour, of the unimaginable joys of the spiritual life."

'The suggestion seemed so preposterous to the Vicomte that he hesitated to obey. He even went through a figure of the dance without response. But the insistent voice repeated with still more irresistible authority, clear through the dance-music of the violins, "Speak to this girl of the love of God, of her

Saviour, of the unimaginable joys of the spiritual life."

' The Vicomte obeyed. He began by asking his partner if she knew his sister, Madame la Comtesse de Civrac; he then told her how beautiful and pious she was, then of her care of him, then of his troubles and doubts, then of his experience at sun-break that very day. The girl probably at first thought that he was mad. She listened at first with amazement, then with wonder and with awe. She had never heard such words before. She had a father, to use my grandfather's own words, "très dérangé dans ses mœurs." Her mother was a perfect woman of the world, devoted to play. The director of the family was an abbé equally "livrè au libertinage et au jeu." No such thoughts as these had ever before entered her mind.

' More than once or twice during this memorable evening, as the choice of partners in the several dances, or as the chance intervals of dancing permitted, did the Vicomte obey to the letter the Divine voice.

'They parted at last on the great staircase of the *hôtel*, and her eyes were moist with tears.

' " I thank you, Monsieur le Vicomte," said this lovely child, for she was little more, "for what you have said to me to-night. I shall never forget it. I have never in my life heard a single syllable of such words as you have spoken to me. I have read in some fairy tale of angels who came down from heaven to a marriage festival and brought untold blessings. Are you *quite* sure," she added, smiling through her tears, "are you quite sure, Monsieur le Vicomte, that you are not an angel? Shall you really go away in a common coach?"

'Four days after the ball the Vicomte, who was again in Paris, received an urgent request that he would go to the Hôtel Desessart, not the Grand Hôtel of the Duke, but a smaller one, where the father and mother of his lovely partner resided. He immediately complied, and in the afternoon was ushered into a salon, where in a few moments the Marquise Desessart, his young friend's mother, joined him. She was evidently distracted with grief, but was able to control her feelings so far as to speak calmly.

'" Monsieur le Vicomte," she said, " I have ventured to send for you at the earnest entreaty of my daughter, with whom you danced several times at the Hôtel du Valois-Desessart the other night. My daughter is dying of virulent smallpox. The physicians assure me that she cannot possibly live through the night. You will understand, Monsieur le Vicomte, what an overwhelming affliction this is to us all. You will perhaps be able to understand what a terrible stroke this must be to a poor child just entering life, with prospects that were entirely fortunate and gay."

' " But for you, Monsieur le Vicomte," the Marquise went on, commanding herself with great difficulty, " but for you, my daughter says, and says truly, she would at this moment be tossing on her death-bed mad with despair and rage. She is perfectly happy—she has no fear of death—she has no regret for the joys she has only just tasted—for the bright world and life, a glimpse of which only she has seen. Monsieur le Vicomte, my daughter never in her life heard any whisper of the matters of which you spoke to her. Neither Monsieur le Marquis nor myself have ever been 'dévot.' Monsieur l'Abbé, though a delightful man, is not 'dévot' either. It is wonderful to be in my daughter's room. I do not know anything of these things," said the poor Marquise, " but I should think it must be like heaven. My daughter says that her heart is full of nothing but ' the love of God, of her Saviour, of the unimaginable joys of the spiritual life.'　These are her very words.　She says that she will not see you, though she would like to kiss your hand. She says you saw her only once when she was beautiful and happy; she would like you to remember her as she appeared to you that evening.　When she meets you in the courts of heaven perhaps she will be beautiful again."

'The Marquise paused for a moment, but the Vicomte could not speak.

'"I am charged by my daughter to give you one other message," she continued, "and I must do so, though it scarcely seems polite.　You will pardon a mother, Monsieur le Vicomte, in such a case as this.　My daughter says," she went on, "that she charges you on her dying bed, solemnly before God, that you go on as you have begun.　She has no other distress but in the thought that in the long years to come you may fall away."

'The Vicomte made no further effort to conceal his emotion. He went down on his knees on the parquetry floor of the salon, and as well as his choking voice permitted him, solemnly, in the presence of the Marquise, dedicated his life to God; and,' concluded Mr. de Foi, 'as confidently as I can assert anything in this life, I am certain that never in word or deed was he false to his vow.'

We walked for some moments in silence, then Mr. de Foi said:

'The Constable of France, Anne de Montmorency, when he was dying of his wounds, refused a confessor, saying that it were a brutish thing, after having lived fourscore years, not to know how to die a quarter of an hour. It may have been true in his case, I cannot tell; but had she been left to herself how could a child like this, so young, so lovely, so ignorant, have known how to die? To my mind it shows the infinite mercy of our Father in Heaven, that He is pitiful not only to the aged, and the poor, and the afflicted, but to the young, and the brilliant, and the rich.'

We reached the house as Mr. de Foi said these words, just in time for lunch. A few moments afterwards, as we went into the dining-room, I said to Percival:

'That was a very beautiful story, did not you think?'

'Yes,' he said, 'oh yes. Very pretty— very French.'

CHAPTER V

IT was my afternoon to accompany the
Duchess to the schools, where I also took a class.
We took Mr. de Foi with us in the carriage,
and the Duke, instead of waiting outside the
schools as usual, drove with him farther on
into the town, and we found him patiently
awaiting us when we came out. I took my
class as usual, but I confess that all the
time I was thinking of that beautiful and
pious Vicomte de Foi, who was just the
age of Sir Percival Massareen.

We drove home in a soft glow and shimmer of summer light. The murmur of the
breeze across the woodland, the steady

rhythmical patter of the horses' feet, soothed the senses into repose. A great calm and peace seemed to settle down upon the world, with all its troubles and cares. Sitting with my back to the horses, as we reached the higher ground I could see the vast stretches of forest and chase, bounded in the distance by the flashing waters of the channel and by the pale, transparent azure of the northern sky. The Duke and Duchess seldom spoke when driving, and I had nothing to interrupt the course of my own thoughts. Something in the placid landscape seemed to foreshadow and to harmonise with an indistinct glimmering of what I began to fancy would be my future fate—the only prevision vouchsafed me of what that future would be.

I do not know how Percival had occupied himself that afternoon. Unless he is constantly fishing or playing tennis, I do not know how a gentleman passes his time in the country in summer. Miss Clare was expected to arrive before dinner. Guests always arrived at Kingswood late in the afternoon, and, as the drive from the nearest railway station was a long one, they were always conducted to their rooms on arrival, and no one expected to see them before dinner.

I dressed as usual, and went down by a distant staircase, through the hall and small lobby into the drawing-room. As I passed through the hall the full summer light was shining on the old breastplates and helmets, and on the wide open fireplace, before which a great hydrangia stood in flower. I remembered the night not long past when Percival had stood upon that same hearth, then glowing with a dying fire. In the lobby the silent landscapes upon the walls greeted me with the long fellowship which the entire house and all that it contained seemed to have contracted—a fellowship in which no jarring note, no inharmonious shade or sound seemed possible, so hallowed and so gracious by long companionship had every familiar object become.

I opened the door into the great drawing-room and went in. The lobby, lighted by day only by an arch, opening upon the adjoining staircase, was in soft shadow; but the drawing-room, with its white and gold panelling, was full of summer evening light. The moment I opened the door the future of my life was revealed to me.

Standing in the farthest of the three windows looking into the garden, which occupied the left-hand side of the room, was the most striking-looking girl I had ever seen, talking to Sir Percival. I say a striking-looking girl advisedly, for the word describes her more perfectly than any other that I can think of. She was surpassingly beautiful, but it was not her beauty that struck you—even in her beauty it was not the faultlessness of her features or complexion, but a kind of effulgence of beauty that filled the room—as, if you could conceive of a goddess of beauty, you would have said, 'It must have been something like this'—so, in the same way, it was not anything in particular that she did or said that was attractive, it was a sense of attraction that overpowered you. The moment that I saw them together I knew that Percival was hers.

I believe that I did not hesitate for a second, but came up the room to her at once with outstretched hand.

'I hope you have had an easy journey,' I said—I would not say that I was glad to see her. 'I am Constance Lisle.'

'I have heard of you,' she said. 'I wonder that we have not met before.'

'You have been abroad,' I said, 'and we live so quietly here. I have hardly ever been in London.'

'Yes,' she said; 'what a strange old-world place it is! I suppose you are quite fond of it.'

'Kingswood?' I said.   'Yes, I love it very much.'

She did not reply; she was looking at me with a searching gaze that made me almost shrink, then she turned away as though she had completely satisfied her curiosity.

'I have been telling Sir Percival,' she said, —they seemed quite old friends,—'I have been telling Sir Percival that I am the sworn enemy of everything that is old.   That I detest the social system which is the curse of civilisation. That I wish to subvert and destroy it all.'

'But how are we to live?' I said, not knowing what to say.

'Every one will share alike,' she said. 'Every one will have two hundred and fifty pounds a year.'

'But,' said Percival hesitatingly, 'if no one has more than that, no one will be able to pay for pictures, or to keep horses, or anything.'

'Oh, yes, they will,' she said.   'Everybody

being provided` for, they will paint pictures and do things for love — love of the race. Everything will be for the race, nothing for self.'

'H'm, er!' said Percival doubtfully, 'and if they breed horses for love, who will ride them?'

'Oh, everybody will ride them,' she said. 'Everybody in turn.'

Percival did not seem to see it. He shook his head with a puzzled air.

'You are very rich, are not you?' she said, looking at him steadily with her intense gaze.

'I?' he said, laughing. 'No; I haven't got a penny. Never had one.'

'Oh, but you are going to be rich, or something. I know all about it — all about the Guion money. You must give it all to us. It must all go to the socialist propaganda. It will be a great help. It is several millions, is it not?'

The Duchess entered at this moment and greeted Virginia with great kindness. Very soon afterwards the Duke appeared, and we went in to dinner.

Virginia sat at my aunt's right hand, Percival next her; I sat opposite. She sat down at once, and did not rise as the Duke said grace.

Virginia looked round the room with curiosity, as well she might.

'What a very curious room, uncle,' she said. She was the granddaughter of the Duke's only brother, dead long ago.

'And this tapestry,' she went on, 'I suppose it is very old?'

'It is supposed to be as old as the thirteenth or fourteenth century, my dear,' said the Duke. 'Some people consider it to be as curious as the Bayeux.'

'It is very ugly, uncle,' she said.

'Well, my dear,' said the Duke, looking up at it as though for the first time, 'it is not beautiful, according to the modern canons of taste.'

'It is very valuable,' I said, 'and would sell for a great deal, which might be given to the socialist propaganda fund.'

She shot a glance of her eyes across the table at me, like the glitter of a rapier flash. 'Oh,' it said, as plainly as words could speak, 'we are going to fight, are we?'

'No, it would not,' she replied, quick as thought. 'Under the socialist propaganda no one would buy such—things.'

'Are you a socialist, my dear?' said the Duke with bland inquiry.

'Oh, I am worse, uncle—much worse. I am a *Petroleuse.* I would destroy everything—everything there is.'

'Everything!' said the Duke vaguely, as though the conception was too large for him to grasp at once, 'everything, dear me! that seems a great deal.'

'My dear,' said the Duchess, by way of

changing the conversation, 'do you know how your uncle the Dean is ?'

My aunt was always uncomfortable and nervous at conversation which she thought improper before the servants.

'No, aunt,' said Virginia; 'I never see anything of them. I never go to the Deanery. I have long since given up public worship of any kind.'

'But don't you like the Cathedral music ?' I said, more for the sake of saying something than for anything else.

'Oh, the music is so bad !' she said.

'I think,' she went on, after a moment's pause, 'if I could join any form of faith, I would join the Quakers. They seem to me to be the most open to all influences of light. But I have long ago renounced all forms of faith.'

I did not dare to look at my aunt.

'The evolution of theology, you know, aunt,' she went on, calmly, 'is quite as clear

as the evolution of the human race.' (It
must be clear indeed, then, I thought.) 'It
began with nature worship, the cult of the
cosmic deities; then through scio-theism,
the deification of ancestral ghosts or ancestor
worship; then through fetishism and totem-
ism to the present state of intellectual shadow
worship.'

I did not know then, but she told me a
day or two afterwards, that she had been
reading in the train as she came down an
article by one of the leading scientists of the
day. She lent me the magazine, and, as far
as I could understand the article, I fancy
that she had got, as Lord Clare would have
said, 'a little mixed.'

No one seemed able to grapple with the
ancestral ghosts, so she had the conversation
all to herself.

'I suppose,' she said, 'that mankind will
always find some incentive to moral action
in symbols. So long as the Christian faith

is admitted to consist of mere symbols, I do not know—I really do not know—that I should object to it so much. Some of its shadow worship is beautiful—quite beautiful. But when these shadows are imposed upon us as realities, then it becomes the highest duty of us all to show that these dogmatic idols have no greater value than the productions of men's hands — the stocks and stones which they have replaced.'

I am ashamed to say that I looked at my aunt with apprehension; I do not know with what foolish apprehension. I was quite wrong. She was looking fixedly at the silver sconces on the table before her. Evidently no power on earth would be able to force from her a single word. Percival looked very much perplexed. He did not like, poor boy, to be told of any duty, incumbent upon all, which he felt he could not understand or sympathise with. He looked across the table at me. I felt quite unequal to the emergency, and turned, as a last resource, to the Duke.

I was instantly relieved. A look of trouble and anxiety was upon the Duke's face, but it did not seem to me that it had anything to do with 'scio-theism,' or the worship of ancestral ghosts. There was a general appearance of uneasiness among the domestics at the Duke's end of the table. Something was wrong with the chablis.

Mr. Priest withdrew a few paces, and stood apart, like some superior intelligence whose advice was not required at this particular juncture. Mr. Giles advanced to the table, and with an air of quiet and unobtrusive rectitude, which it would have been impossible to surpass, presented his Grace with a cork. The Duke took it—looked at one end for some moments very attentively; then he turned it round and looked for the same length of time, and with equal care, at the other end. Then he returned it to Giles with a gesture of superb resignation, as though he had said:

'I accuse no one; I blame no one. It is inexplicable; but let it pass—let it pass. We will return to the ordinary and trivial avocations of life.'

He turned to us, and, evidently perceiving that Virginia was dominating the conversation, addressed himself to her.

'I beg your pardon, Virginia; you were saying—— ?'

The effect was irresistible. I caught Percival's eye. He threw himself back in his chair, and a horrible dread seized me that he would burst into a boyish roar. The warning look of my eyes struck him, and he restrained himself.

Virginia was evidently very much vexed. She flushed all over, and bit her lip—a peculiarity we soon became well accustomed to. My aunt came to the rescue with great success.

'I was thinking,' she said to the Duke,

'that, if to-morrow were fine, it would be very nice to drive, after luncheon, to Merrivale. I owe Mrs. Merrivale a call, and the young people would like to see the abbey. I am sure, my dear,' she said to Virginia; 'I am sure you would like to see the ruins. Constance is never tired of wandering among them.'

So we escaped any more shadow worship for that night.

Virginia, indeed, seemed mostly put out with Percival and me, not at all with the Duke, to whom she devoted herself during the rest of the evening, and evidently entertained him very much.

'A very nice, well - mannered young woman,' he said to his wife at night; 'and her socialistic notions sit with a very pretty quaintness upon her.'

The Duchess told me this long afterwards, for she did not at all agree with her husband at the time.

I woke early the next morning, with a

perception of loss, with a devouring sense of disappointment and sickness of heart. The moment my eyes were open, before I had time to realise even that I was awake, this cruel torturer seized upon me. In a moment or two I knew what it meant. It meant that Percival could never be mine. It meant that I knew this with a certainty that made all effort, all struggle useless—nay, unbecoming and unimaginable.

I lay for some time silent in the summer morning light. I thought of the Vicomte de Foi, and of that wonderful morning in the chateau by the Seine. 'He had been trained in the habit of prayer.' At least I may say this much of myself too. I came down with the aching restlessness assuaged, the heart-pain allayed and stilled.

After breakfast the Duchess said:

'Constance, my dear, you had better take Virginia round the gardens. We do not go to Merrivale until after luncheon.'

I knew what was passing in the minds of every person at the table, for the Duke had left.

'Percival will do that, aunt,' I said; 'he knows the gardens by this time as well as I do.'

I looked up as I spoke, and met Virginia's eyes. There was a flash of true friendly admiration in them that spoke more clearly than words:

'You are cleverer even than I thought.'

Some time afterwards, when I looked out of a high staircase window towards the south, I saw that they had soon exhausted the gardens, and had taken to tennis on the lawn. Then I remembered what Lord Clare had said about Virginia's perfect playing. I had intended to go down to the Duchess, but when I saw them I changed my mind. I went back to my room. I put on a hat, and went out upon the lawn.

It was beautiful to see them play; so

perfectly matched were they that it seemed as though the game was almost robbed of its individuality, and had become automatic.

I went up to Virginia.

'Lord Clare told us what a beautiful player you were,' I said. 'Sir Percival will be so glad. I cannot play at all; I cannot even hit the ball.'

'No; riding is Constance's strong point,' shouted Percival gallantly across the lawn. 'She is the most perfect horsewoman I ever saw.'

'You must let me see you ride,' said Virginia, serving her ball. 'It is the rarest thing in the world to see a girl ride well; and I think'—and she returned the ball—'I think there is no more beautiful sight.'

'You ride?' I said.

'Oh yes, I ride; but if I ride myself, I cannot see you.'

'I do not see that,' I said.

'No; it does not seem very reasonable

when one comes to think of it,' said Virginia, returning with perfect ease and success a volley from Percival of more than ordinary swiftness.

As we went into lunch some time afterwards Percival said to me :

'What do you think of her? Is she not splendid ?'

'Yes,' I said, 'Percival, but her principles are very sad !'

'She thinks a great deal of you,' he said in rather an injured tone ; 'she says you are the cleverest girl she ever met.'

Immediately after lunch, the carriage coming to the door, we set out for Merrivale. My aunt and Virginia occupied the principal seat, Percival and I sitting with our backs to the horses. I sat opposite to the Duchess.

We drove for three miles through the chase towards the south on a descending road, all the beauty of the massy summer foliage and the wealth of grass and flowers and birds and butterflies on every side—a sense of beauty and of peace seemed to fill the vast horizon as far as eye could reach.

After passing through several gates with lodges we finally left the park by great lodges with double gates, and entered on a country road which led us through one or two pretty villages and country places, with commons and green spaces and old roadside taverns and farms.

As we were passing along the level road and were rather silent, Percival said to me:

'I have been thinking of that story of Mr. de Foi's, Constance, and I don't think I like it even so much as I did at first. It does not sound true, somehow. I don't mean that it didn't happen, but it does not seem true in itself.'

'What story was that, Constance?' said my aunt.

'The story of Mademoiselle Desessart, aunt,' I said.

'I should like to hear it,' said Virginia;
'do tell it, Sir Percival.'

'Oh, I can't tell it,' he said; 'Constance
will do it justice.'

I told it as shortly as I could, and not
nearly so effectively as Mr. de Foi had done.
My aunt had often heard it before, but she
never heard it without tears.

'Well,' said Percival, when the story
was finished, 'what do you think of it, Miss
Clare?'

'I am thinking about it,' she said.

She evidently did not choose to speak
before the Duchess.

We had by this time left the level road and
come to a wooded valley that rose suddenly
in front of us, and up which we drove with
slackened pace. Down the valley, as we
ascended it, we met a considerable stream or
even river, the source, indeed, of the stream
that gave its name to Rivershead. As we
slowly ascended the steep road the vast banks

of foliage spread themselves away on either side. The rushing river flowed round rocky islands, crested with beech and oak saplings, and spread itself into broad pools, in which the trout were leaping ; hares and pheasants flitted across the road.

Virginia was evidently touched by the beauty of the scene.

'How beautiful this is!' she said. 'I do not think that any country in the world is so beautiful as England in summer.'

'England is beautiful all the year round, my dear,' said my aunt severely.

After we had ascended the valley for about a couple of miles we crossed the river by an ancient bridge and came to some lodge gates. Inside the gates, in a sweep and amphitheatre of wooded hills, stood the ivy-covered ruins of an abbey, and beyond, over a wide expanse of park studded with spreading oaks, a large and stately house. Here the Duchess turned us out to go to the ruins, while she drove up to the house. 'We might come up afterwards,' she said, 'and have some tea.'

We followed a path to the left across the grass until we reached the ruins, which lay in a little hollow immediately over the stream. They were not extensive, but the parts that remained were very perfect. The long and narrow nave, the tracery of the western window, and the southern transept were quite perfect; but the northern side of the choir and the northern transept over the river were gone. The eastern window was a blank open space.

I conducted my companions over the ruins, which were entirely overgrown with ivy and fringed along the tops of the walls with saplings, mostly ash. Flights of jackdaws kept up a ceaseless chatter over our heads. Lying in the grass of the chancel, which was kept closely mown, were three or four stone effigies of knights in armour which had been removed from ruined tombs. They were in remarkable preservation, but stained and moss-grown from damp and age.

The walls were so high and narrow and the ivy and foliage so thick that the ruins felt damp and chill after the blazing afternoon sunshine, although the blue sky was stretched cloudlessly over our heads. When I had exhausted all my antiquarian knowledge I pointed out to my companions a staircase in the corner of the southern transept, and advised them to ascend it.

'It is rather steep,' I said, 'but I believe quite safe, and there is a beautiful view. I have been up so often I think I will not come. I will wait for you in one of the seats in the choir.'

They went up gladly, and I returned to a rustic seat in the chancel. This part of the ruins was warmer and more cheerful than the nave. The sun shone brightly on the grass, and cast the shadow of the chancel arch, which was quite perfect, on the ground at my feet.

At my back was the rushing river, and at my feet the mailed figure of a crusader half-buried in the soft, mossy turf. From where I sat I could look down the narrow green nave to the perfect tracery of the western window and to the sunny wooded heights beyond.

The gloomy, ivy-covered ruins oppressed me with a sense of sadness and melancholy which I had never felt in them before, though I had often visited them on far more cheerless days. The flowing river hurried past with a weird and dreary sound; even the chatter of the jackdaws seemed subdued to a mournful note; and a low, sad murmur swept through the ivy and the grass. If I had been really alone, I should have wept.

From where I sat I could not see the others when they had reached the top of the wall. They stayed some time, charmed, no doubt, with the lovely view.

Suddenly I was aware that they had descended, and were entering the choir by the chancel arch. In the lovely setting that surrounded them I thought it would have been difficult in all England to have found so beautiful a pair.

'I hope you have enjoyed the view,' I said.

'It is lovely,' said Virginia kindly; 'thank you so much for sending us up. I wish you had come.'

She looked radiant with happiness and beauty.

'I have seen it so often,' I said, 'and the steps are very slippery and steep.'

The words sounded strange as I said them, as though spoken by some one else. These are not the only steps in this life, I thought, that are slippery and steep.

We went farther up the choir and stood beneath the east window, where the sun shone warmest upon the grass.

'The view of the nave, and the rose tracery in the west window,' I said, 'is considered, I believe, very beautiful from here.'

We stood for a moment silent, then Percival said :

'Well, we have never heard your opinion of Mr. de Foi's tale, Virginia'—he called her Virginia now.

'Oh, I hate it!' she said, almost fiercely. 'It is false and sickly in sentiment, it is obsolete and *passé* as these crumbling ruins of an effete superstition, which make one's flesh creep even in the sunshine.'

Percival seemed surprised at her warmth.

'I did not know it was so bad as that,' he said.

'I never see ruins like these,' she went on, 'but I think of some lines of a poet, I don't in the least know who, I heard some one quote :

> "The crumbling ruins of fallen pride
> And chambers of transgression, now forlorn."'

'They are Wordsworth's,' I said,—Mr. de Foi had long ago taught me to love the 'Excursion,'—'but I do not think that he is speaking of abbeys like this, but of ruined castles where wicked and cruel deeds were done.'

'It is the same thing,' she said; 'indeed the abbeys were worse. The nobles would never have gained the power they had to oppress and crush the people but for the terror of the priest and his superstitious faith. And to think of the nobles in your story living in selfish luxury amid a starving and wretched people, and, not content with earthly luxury, inventing for themselves spiritual luxuries as well! All religion has been invented for the selfish satisfaction of the rich.'

'But if they are so happy and satisfied,' I said, 'it is strange they should have invented a religion. I should have thought that religion was for the miserable and the sad.'

'Yes, that is just like one of your sayings,' she said laughing; 'you certainly are the cleverest girl I ever met. But it won't do. There are sorrows in all ranks. Nature is cruel, wicked. That is a fact that must be faced. The death of that poor girl in your story was wicked and cruel. But religion is cowardly as well as selfish. It is the duty of a reasonable being to face the shadows and spectres of existence like a man, not to run sobbing, like a child, into its father's arms.'

She was standing, in her beauty and in her fierce scorn, on the spot where the high altar of the faith she so despised had once stood. The sun was shining full upon her, till she seemed almost dazzling in contrast with the green background against which she stood.

I looked at her in silence.

'The shadow of existence has crossed my path through you,' I thought. 'It is you who are cruel. You have robbed me of my friend; would you rob me also of my Heavenly Father's love?'

Perhaps she read in my eyes something of what was passing in my mind, and guessed the rest, for she turned to Percival and moved away.

'Constance does not like such talk as this,' she said; 'let us go out of these chill ivied walls into the free sunlight again.'

We went across the sunny lawns, and by the stone terraces and statues, to the front of the house. The old servant who let us in was a friend of mine.

'Her Grace is in the drawing-room with Mrs. Merrivale, miss,' he said.

Mrs. Merrivale was rather a fashionable gay woman, but she was sincerely attached to my aunt, and was kind to me. She was pleased to see us all; and after we had had some tea, she took Virginia and Percival, with whom she was evidently struck, to see some curiosities in the great gallery, which were considered to be some of the sights of the county.

'I dare say you will like to stay with the Duchess,' she said to me, 'you have seen the wretched old things so often.'

It was very hot, and we had had a long drive, and my aunt, in spite of her tea, was plainly on the point of taking a nap.

'Do not stay with me, my dear,' she said dreamily, but she was asleep before she heard my reply.

I went softly to one of the tables, upon which books were lying, and took up one of them by chance. It seemed to open of its own accord at these perfect lines, which seemed written for that hour and place, and for myself alone.

> We are like children rear'd in shade
> Beneath some old-world abbey wall,
> Forgotten in a forest glade
> And secret from the eyes of all,
> Deep, deep the greenwood round them waves,
> Their abbey, and its close of graves.
>
> But where the road runs near the stream,
> Oft through the trees they catch a glance

Of passing troops in the sun's beam—
Pennon, and plume, and flashing lance,
Forth to the world those soldiers fare,
To life, to cities, and to war.

And through the woods, another way,
Faint bugle-notes from far are borne,
Where hunters gather, staghounds bay,
Round some old forest lodge at morn,
Gay dames are there in sylvan green,
Laughter and cries—those notes between.

 .   .   .   .   .

Long since we pace this shadow'd nave ;
We watch those yellow tapers shine,
Emblems of hope over the grave,
In the high altar's depth divine.
The organ carries to our ear
Its accents of another sphere.

Fenced early in this cloistral round
Of reverie, of shade, of prayer,
How should we grow in other ground,
How should we flower in foreign air ?
Pass, banners, pass, and bugles cease,
And leave our desert to its peace !

We did not see much modern literature
at Kingswood, and I had never read Mr.
Matthew Arnold's poems. I read these lines

over several times in the quiet room. There was no sound but the happy murmur of the great gardens without. I felt inexpressibly soothed and calmed. Presently my aunt awoke.

'What have you got there, my dear?' she said. 'Have you anything pretty to read to me?'

I sat down by her and read the whole of the poem 'Stanzas from the Grande Chartreuse.' Some of the lines I did not like so much.

I had just finished when the others came back. The carriage was at the door, and we drove home, mostly in silence. Virginia and Percival were rapidly reaching that stage of mutual understanding when silence ceases to be embarrassing.

CHAPTER VI

THE day on which we had driven to Merrivale was a Friday. The next morning the
Duchess was not very well. She seemed to
have been over-tired. I spent most of the
day in her room, reading to her when she
wished it, and sitting by her when she wished
to be quiet.

The next morning, Sunday, she was much
better, but did not feel strong enough to go
to church. The Duke came up to her room
after breakfast.

'We must not keep Constance here all
day,' he said; 'I can sit with you as long as
you wish it.'

We were not at all surprised at this, for the Duke never went to church unless my aunt went.

I dressed in time for church, and went down into the garden where Virginia and Percival were sitting. Virginia had arranged for herself two or three of our old-fashioned uncomfortable basket-chairs into a kind of lounge, and, lying on these, she was reading Shelley. I think she must have brought the book down with her, for I do not know that there was a Shelley in the Kingswood library, at least I never saw one.

It was again a lovely morning, and its beauty seemed at once to exhilarate and soothe. I do not know what influence had been working upon my spirit during the quiet hours of the previous day, or during the night, but I seemed to feel a dawning hope springing up in my heart that all was perhaps not over, and that Percival would even yet come back to me. When I say 'come back,' I see now that I thought foolishly, for he had never belonged to me; but I did not know that so clearly then. As I came across the lawn in my white and pink summer dress I fancied the walk to church through the flowery meadows of the chase, the morning service, the hallowed and the gracious influences of the time. What would happen who could tell ?

I came up to the two, who were seated under the tulip-tree, where we had read Keble together, some few paces from the garden door, with its mysterious tracery, half hidden by the climbing tendrils of the clematis and the rose. They both looked up with a friendly air, and Percival rose.

'It is time we started for church,' I said. 'My uncle and aunt are not coming, so we must walk. Are you coming with me, Percival ? '

It would have been better perhaps if I

had not asked the question, but I was only a girl.

Percival looked uncertain. I saw that he glanced at Virginia, who seemed to take no notice, and turned over the leaves of her book. But although she seemed so indifferent, I saw that she raised her eyebrows in a way peculiar to her, to which we had become accustomed. I remember Lord Clare saying once that she was particularly 'fetching' when she raised her eyebrows. She had such a superb look of lofty pity, and of friendly, arch contempt.

'I think not to-day, Constance,' said Percival. 'I think I shall stay with Virginia, if she will let me.'

I believed then, and I believe now, that if she had not raised her eyebrows at that moment he would have come with me. I think now that it would not have made much difference in the future if he had, but I did not think so then. I fancied that he did not look very comfortable as he said the words, and I thought that Virginia saw it, and felt it necessary to come to his aid.

'You had better stay with us for once, Constance,' she said. 'You religious people ought to mortify yourselves now and then, and stay away from church, you value yourselves upon it so inordinately.'

'That is hardly fair,' I said, as gently as I could. 'How can we help valuing what is so delightful and precious to us?'

'There is something in that,' she said, turning over a leaf. 'Percival, you had better go. You see what a bad boy you will be if you do not. I will not be responsible.'

I looked up at Percival and smiled.

'There!' she said, turning another leaf, 'a heart of stone could not resist that pleading look, that witching smile. Percival, go!'

I should have looked at her reproachfully, but she kept her eyes fixed on the book, though she seemed to see everything.

Percival did not stir. A sense of pity for his evident embarrassment rose in my heart, and I turned away. Before me, in the full sunshine, lay the long wall, with its strange, worn tracery, the mystery of my childhood's days, half hidden by the leafy tendrils that crept over it. The sight is impressed on my memory clear and distinct, as though I saw it now. For a moment it was brilliantly plain, then it became misty and dim.

I reached the doorway in a second or two. It might be fancy, but I thought I heard her say, 'And you do not even open the door for her,' but still, happily for me, Percival did not stir. The door was fastened with a great antique iron latch, which had often before given me trouble. It seemed to-day to open of its own accord. I closed the door softly behind me, and went out on to the pathway in the chase.

As I closed the door it seemed as though

I closed behind me youth and life and love.
The massive oaken door, studded with heavy
stanchions and nails, swung to relentlessly,
as though it shut me out from the lovely
sunny garden, and from all my girlhood and
my youth. It seemed as though I left my
youth behind me with that brilliant pair,
and chose at once a sombre and a serious
life beyond, far beyond, my years. 'They
were together all yesterday,' I thought,
'surely he might have come with me this
once again.'

I turned with a sinking heart towards the
flowery stretches of the chase, then in a
moment all was changed. The gentle breeze,
which had risen with the sun and followed
it from the east, stole across the meadow
flowers and the grass, laden with the scent
of the summer morning, and murmurous with
distant sound. An inexpressibly sweet and
delicate melody penetrated my sense. I was
about to say that the air was full of the sound

of church bells, but in saying this I should have been altogether wrong. There was no perceptible sense of hearing, but a perception of melody in the mind which was independent of the ear, or rather which received the impression of music through the ear, after the sound had become so attenuated that all effect upon the ear itself was lost. I have experienced this feeling since, but never with such enthralling effect as upon this, the first occasion. I am convinced that I heard— heard, that is, with the spirit—the church bells ringing for miles around, though the nearest churches were probably almost, if not quite, beyond the reach of ear.

The effect was inexpressibly spiritual and delicate, far beyond the most exquisite music of sense. It seemed to solace the troubled mind with a distant echo of the music of heaven, to suggest to the distracted thought all the 'comfortable words' that promise companionship and presence and succour in time of disappointment and of desertion, and of a lost hope. 'I am with thee always,' a sweet, clear voice seemed to say. A sense of fellowship, gracious beyond the tenderness of women, accompanied my steps. In that walk across the chase to church no one shall ever persuade me that I was alone.

.　　.　　.　　.　　.

We dined very simply on Sundays, more like a kind of supper, most of the servants being at liberty. After dinner that night in the drawing-room the Duchess asked for music, and Virginia sat down to play. She played superbly, but refused to sing, solely, I believe, because her voice was not equal to her skill.

She played some brilliant pieces—I do not now remember what they were. Indeed, I think that soon she did not know herself. She seemed to me to be improvising, or, if she did not do that, she threw so much of her personality into the piece that the conception of the composer was well-nigh lost. I am far from saying that she played without soul, but I should say that she played without rest. She seemed to play as though music were not a teacher, but an inarticulate cry—as though she refused the healing message of harmony, and cast it back, in its own notes, against the sky. She played a piece at last with intense feeling, but with a restless, passionate violence, as of despair; then she dropped into a sudden adagio, and, concluding with some chords of exquisitely-modulated rhythm and cadence, she sprang up from the piano, and, clasping my arm,

'Constance,' she said, 'sing! I want to hear the human voice.'

The clear, simple notes—solemn, yet, ah! how sweet!—filled the room with a sense of rest and stillness after the storm of passionate sound—'He shall feed his flock like a shepherd, and he shall gather the lambs with his arm—with his arm.'

I had a mezzo-soprano voice of small compass, but clear and firm, and I sang the air through in F.

'He shall feed his flock like a shepherd, and he shall gather the lambs with his arm, and carry them in his bosom, and gently lead those that are with young, and gently lead—and gently lead those that are with young. Come unto him all ye that labour. Come unto him all ye that are heavy laden, and he will give you rest—will give you rest. Take his yoke upon you and learn of him, for he is meek and lowly of heart, and ye shall find rest—and ye shall find rest unto your souls.'

Then again the sweet, clear chords, clear as the proclamation of an angel, sweet and pure as the dying thanksgiving of a saint, filled the room with the trustful silence of the soul.

Virginia came up to me as I rose, and put her arm round me.

'I could wish to sing like you, Constance,' she said. 'You have something which I have not.'

They were the same words that Percival had used.

The next week or two passed much in the usual way. It was fortunate for me, in one sense at least, that Percival had been with us so short a time before Virginia came, for there had not been time for the desire that I knew existed in my aunt's mind, that I should marry him, to grow into a suspicion or expectation that such might be the event. I avoided riding with Virginia and Percival in the afternoons as much as I could.

'Why are you not riding, my dear?' said my aunt, looking at me inquiringly, as I got into the carriage to drive with her and the Duke to Rivershead. 'It is not your day at the schools.'

'They like riding together, aunt,' I said.

'It would not be a bad match,' said the Duke. 'He will be very rich. She would make him a noble wife.'

The Duchess said nothing, but she looked wistfully at me.

'She will make him a noble wife,' I thought,

as we drove through the chase. 'Does she love him? She cannot love him so well as I!'

Indeed I often wondered whether she loved him at all.

That Sir Percival loved her no one could doubt. His whole nature seemed brightened and intensified.

'It is just what he wanted,' I thought; 'but it is sad to think that she cannot lead him to the highest things—the highest life.'

I often spoke to Mr. de Foi about them. He entered kindly into the matter. He said nothing that would lead me to suspect that he had penetrated my secret, but he had always treated me with such a fatherly tenderness that it did not seem strange to me that he did so now.

For some few weeks the quiet hours passed after this fashion. I never spoke to Percival of Virginia nor to Virginia of Percival, and neither of them ever spoke of the other to me. Percival would, I fancy, have been glad to do so ; but, in the first place, he was so much with Virginia that he had not much opportunity, and, in the second place, when he did attempt it I did not encourage him. Some strong, but I hardly know what, impulse forbade me to say anything in disparagement of her to him, even though it might have seemed that the highest motives impelled me to do so. I did not know till months afterwards that they understood each other.

One morning, at breakfast, Percival opened a letter with an expression of disgust. We had only one post every day at Kingswood, which a boy fetched from the nearest post town every morning. This letter was a summons to Woolwich for his final examination, and a residence of some months was required. The light died out of his bright boyish eyes.

For the next day or two I saw little of either of them except at table. It seemed to me as though we were leading the old uneventful life we led before they came.

After Percival had left Virginia became very companionable. She was always charming to the Duke and to my aunt, but now she seemed to seek my society, and we spent much time together on the lawn and in the garden walks.

The morning after Percival left the Duke said:

'Now that you have lost your escort I must find a pony-carriage for you young ladies. The distinction is fine, I allow,' continued his Grace musingly, 'but I think it is a true one, between two young ladies on horseback, followed at some distance by a groom, and the same young ladies driving themselves in a chaise, with a boy behind them. I for one, at any rate, prefer the latter.'

'Constance is very kind,' the Duke went on, after a pause, 'in adapting her pace and her talk to the needs and the capacities of a very old man; but I could not inflict the penance upon two young ladies.'

This referred to the occasions on which I had ridden with the Duke, and had never spoken unless I was spoken to; but we both of us perfectly understood that his Grace did not want either of us as a companion in his morning rides: to have maintained a conversation with the lively Virginia on these placid occasions would have been equivalent to a popular *émeute* in his Grace's experience.

A day or two after this conversation the pony chaise arrived from London. It was a most dainty affair: two delicious little cream-coloured ponies, and a most delicate chaise, with a boy-groom to match. It was used, alas, for so few times!

I believe that Percival wrote at first every day, and I am equally certain that Virginia was bored and annoyed by the frequency of these tokens of affection. She used to glance over them rapidly, and put them away at once.

One morning, soon after breakfast, I went

out on to the lawn, and found her sitting on her wicker chairs near the tulip-tree by the wall. One of Percival's effusions was in her hand, which hung listlessly towards the grass.

She looked up with a smile of welcome, and I sat down.

'What are you looking at me for?' she said, after a minute or two had passed.

'I am wondering whether you love him at all,' I said. I know not why, but my tongue seemed suddenly loosed.

'Who? Oh, Percival,' she said, taking up the letter into her lap. 'Oh yes, I love him. He is such a dear boy—such a boy,' she added, after a moment's pause.

Then suddenly she looked up, and an altogether different expression animated her strong and beautiful face.

'Constance,' she said, 'tell me; was there never anything between him and you?'

'No,' I said; 'never! He never loved me; never would have loved me.'

By a sudden inspiration I seemed to see this last truth now for the first time.

She gave a kind of sigh, as it were, of relief.

'Yes,' she said; 'I love him. He will grow.'

'He is another man,' I said, 'since he loved you. It was just what was wanted to draw him upwards, to raise him above himself. Oh, Virginia, lead him to the highest life!'

She sprang up so suddenly that I rose also, not knowing what was to come.

She seized me by both my hands, and held them down at arms' length.

'Constance,' she said, 'you are a glorious girl! I love *you* better than anything in the world besides!'

CHAPTER VII

SOME days, or it may have been weeks, for the hours passed so evenly that we lost count of time, and I think I recall one, if not two, visits from the Marquis during this time; but, however, some time after Percival had left us, Mr. de Foi was lunching at Kingswood. He told us, in the course of luncheon, of an epidemic fever that had broken out among the wharves and old lanes and warehouses at Rivershead, and was puzzling the doctors a good deal. It was not an alarming fever in its first appearances, its characteristics being troubled sleep, or slight forgetfulness; but it was extraordinarily fatal in its results. On the second or third day the patient frequently died; if he lived over that time he recovered. Some physicians supposed that it was a species of Oriental fever brought to Rivershead by the foreign sailors that sometimes came up to its wharves.

However this might be, Mr. de Foi said that it was spreading among the townspeople in a manner that was almost alarming, and had even crept up into some of the neighbouring villages. He advised us to be careful in our rides.

Two or three days after this Virginia came in to luncheon with an excited manner. The Duke was that day lunching at the Rectory at the market town. He did this sometimes when he had more business than usual to talk over with the agent. We were, therefore, alone at lunch.

Virginia's maid, an excitable girl, had been telling her a gruesome story of the spread of the epidemic, and of the panic that it was causing

among the people. In particular, she had heard
that the contagion had reached the little village
beyond the church in the chase, and she had
harrowed Virginia's feelings by telling her of
a poor woman who had been attacked by the
disease, and was lying absolutely untended—
deserted by the panic-stricken people. Virginia poured all this sad story into our ears.

Suddenly, towards the end of lunch, as Mr.
Priest was devoting himself with extreme
attention to the Duchess—he always made
a point of this when the Duke was absent—
Virginia said:

'Aunt, I shall go this afternoon and see
this poor woman.'

'My dear!' said the Duchess, quite
aghast.

'Yes, I shall; it is horrible to think of her
being so deserted.'

'But, my dear, it is very infectious. You
know that Mr. de Foi particularly warned
you not to ride in the neighbourhood of

Rivershead. Will you not wait, at least, until the Duke returns?'

'No, aunt; I shall go at once. It is horrible to think of this poor woman deserted and dying, and no one to aid her. How could we stay here and think of it? If you are afraid of my coming back, I will not come back; if you are afraid of the carriage coming back, I will walk.'

'If you go,' I said, 'I shall go with you.'

'Nonsense,' said Virginia, almost angrily; 'what good would that do?'

'My dear,' said my aunt, with that touch of pride which she so seldom exhibited, but which became her so well, and to which there was no reply; 'if it is right for you to go, it is Constance' duty too.'

'Mr. Priest,' said Virginia, 'will you have the goodness to order the pony carriage for three o'clock?'

'Certainly, Miss Clare.'

I have sometimes wondered to what command Mr. Priest would not have replied in the same terms.

The dainty pony chaise came round into the quadrangle at the hour appointed, and we got into it: Virginia, of course, driving, as she always did. We drove out through the cupolaed archway into the chase.

It was intensely hot. The cloudless sky was one blaze of dazzling light; not a breath of air stirred the drooping foliage. The deer were herded together under the largest spreading trees; every creature of the woods, every bird and insect, was still. A flickering air, like a shimmer of fairy fire, played above the ground and through the vistas of the faded forest; and in the distance, over the shores of the channel, a thin mist rose over the fetid mudbanks and the dried-up courses of the streams.

As we drove on in silence a feeling of intolerable dread and apprehension seized upon me, a horror of a great darkness—an absolute physical darkness in the midst of the intense blaze of the afternoon heat. I tried to pray, but the power of thought and of sustained intention deserted me. I could only realise the sense of approaching evil. I felt as though, in my desperation, I could snatch the reins out of Virginia's hands.

The impulse became too strong to be resisted, and, regardless of the presence of the boy behind us, I said:

'Virginia, stop! I beg of you to stop! For Percival's sake, for my sake—you say you love me—I beg of you to stop! I have a sense given me that the errand on which you are determined is needless—worse than needless. Were it otherwise I would not stop you, but I am confident that it is not the will of God that we should go on. The air is full of evil omens: let us turn back.'

'Turn back!' she said; 'do you suppose for a moment that I shall turn back? I did not wish you to come, but having come, you must go on.　You speak of evil omens.　Do you think that this would not be a day of evil omen to me were I to turn back?　I know nothing of your spiritual visions and insight and warning voices.　I understand only a commonplace morality which teaches me to visit the helpless and the sick.'

I think, as she spoke against visions and of the duty towards the sick, a vague idea was forming itself in my mind that He who originated the visitation of the sick was revealed to some by a ' vision of angels which said that He was alive ;' but she went on before I could frame such thoughts into a reply.

' Besides,' she said, ' we are nobles, and it is our duty everywhere to face death.'

I cannot describe the proud look with which she said these words.　She seemed to have forgotten for a moment her socialistic creeds.

' Did you never hear,' she said, ' of the girl at Gorhambury, or one of the historic houses —I forget which ; it is not so long ago—who was dressing for dinner, and her muslin caught fire, and in a moment the toilet-table and the curtains were in a blaze. She ran down the great staircase screaming for help, and when they met her she said, "Never mind me; save the house!" What have we girls done that we should be less brave than she was?'

'Did she die?' I said.

'I forget,' and her proud eyes filled with tears. 'I only know I thought it the noblest story I had ever heard.'

She brought her whip down softly over the lovely ponies, and we flew rapidly over the scorched spaces of the chase.

We passed the little church that lay silent and peaceful in the sunshine, and passed out through the lodge gates, bowling down the country road into the little village street.

Always silent and deserted, it seemed to my feverish fancy more deserted and more silent than usual. Not even a dog started out to greet us. A perfect silence—a silence which it seemed impossible to break, so still and fixed was it—brooded over the wide village green and the rows of cottages.

Fringing the narrow paths that led up through the gardens were rows of white lilies, all in full bloom. Their rich, oppressive odour filled the air, and struck the sense, already prostrated by the heat and by the fatal shadow that hung over the sunny land, with a feeling of sickness as of the heart.

'It is the valley of the shadow of death,' I said involuntarily but aloud.

We had received careful instructions as to the house we were in search of, and Virginia pulled up the ponies at a cottage some half-way down the street. The blinds of the windows were all down, every window closed.

A momentary feeling of relief, which I repressed as selfish, passed through my mind. The poor woman must be gone.

As we paused for a moment in uncertainty, the groom standing at the ponies' heads, a woman, the first living creature we had seen, came out of the cottage exactly opposite, and crossed over the green to us.

Virginia spoke to her.

'We came to see after Mrs. Wilde,' she said; 'we heard that she was ill, and had no one to see after her.   She is not dead?'

'No, my lady,' said the woman, who was evidently much impressed by Virginia's appearance—'leastways, I believe not.   I was in with her this morning.   I don't like to go in more than I can help, because of my master and the children; but I thought she seemed comfortable like when I left her.   Her husband, my lady, works at the docks, and is a deal over at Brisport.   He's there now.   Mr. de Foi has written to him, I believe.'

'I shall go in, then, and see her,' said Virginia.

'I reckon you'd better not, my lady,' said the woman; 'it's terribly catching this fever, the doctors all say.'

We left this good woman talking to the groom, who no doubt gave her his opinion of our folly, and went up the narrow pathway between the rows of stately lilies, the over-powering odour increasing at every step. The door was on the latch, and we went in. The interior was close and stifling beyond endur-ance. We opened the windows at once.

'I shall go upstairs,' said Virginia; 'you had better stay here. If I want you I will call. Too many people in a sick-room are no good.'

This was quite true; besides, I had no right to assume equality with her on this errand of mercy. But for her I should not have been there at all.

She went up the narrow, twisted, wooden stair, and I remained below. I sat down and looked round the room. It was an ordinary cottage room, well furnished for its class. A Bible, Baxter's *Saints' Rest*, and two or three other books, lay on the window-sill.

I looked out down the village street. The chaise had left the door, and was standing at a little tavern at the lower end of the village, surrounded by a small group of admirers. The groom volunteered the statement to me afterwards that he had gone there to give the ponies oatmeal and water as it was so hot.

I returned to my seat; all was quiet upstairs. I had not sat many minutes when some one knocked at the door.

In answer to my invitation to enter the door opened, and a nice-looking, respectable girl entered.

She appeared to have heard something about our visit in the village, and to be rather surprised and embarrassed.

'I came to see after my aunt, Mrs. Wilde,' she said.

She was very quietly and suitably dressed, but was covered with dust, and seemed ready to drop with fatigue.

'You seem very tired,' I said. 'Will you

sit down and let me get you some water? I think there is some in the inner room.'

She really was not able to do anything else. I fetched her some water which I had seen through the open door, and she drank eagerly.

'I am Miss Lisle,' I said. 'I live at Kingswood. Miss Clare, the Duke's niece, heard this morning that your aunt was ill, and that there was no one to nurse her. She insisted on coming down to see after her. She is upstairs with her now.'

The young woman seemed very much astonished.

'The Duke's niece!' she said. 'I have seen you, Miss Lisle, at church when I have been here with my aunt.'

'How did you hear that your aunt was ill?' I said.

'My uncle comes over to Brisport on his work,' she said. 'He stays with us. This morning he had a letter telling him. I was out of service.   The people I was with have failed, and I was out of place.   I set out at once and walked over.   It is fifteen miles, and it was very hot.'

'Will you have any more water?' I said; 'I do not know that I can get you anything else.'

At this moment we heard a noise on the stairs, and Virginia came down.   She certainly was a strange sight in such a place.

'I think Mrs. Wilde seems very comfortable,' she said.   'She is asleep; and it is sleep, not lethargy.   I took lessons at the hospital at Charing Cross, and I know.'

'This is her kind niece,' I said, 'who has walked fifteen miles in the heat to help her aunt.'

Virginia went up to the girl, took her two hands in hers, and shook them.

'How good of you!' she said.

She took the girl upstairs, and left her with her aunt, after giving her, I fancy, some

P

instructions. Then she came down again, looking, as I thought, rather *distraite* and tired, and we drove back. The heat seemed more oppressive than before: it was no wonder that we were still.

We went to our rooms as soon as we got home, but we found little coolness there. Even as the sun set the sultry heat appeared to increase. The dusk of evening, the gathering gloom, seemed to make it more painfully felt. Virginia was unusually quiet at dinner, and no one else spoke at all.

The great drawing-room was lighted dimly with shaded lamps. Every window was open, but no breath of air, no breeze of freshness or of life, stirred the tremulous light.

'Sing us some of your *Messiah* airs, Constance,' said Virginia. 'I am tired, and it is too hot to talk.'

I went to the piano and sang, hardly knowing what I sang.

'Every valley shall be exalted—shall be exalted, and every mountain and hill made low—the crooked straight—the crooked straight—and the rough places plain.'

The bright light shone on the music page before me, but beyond the great room lay in solemn gloom, dim in the shaded light. I could see nothing of Virginia but a mass of white in one of the deep embrasures of the windows, open upon the sweetly - scented but motionless night. Beyond her, dimly in the background, I could just perceive the Gainsborough boy. My aunt, I knew, was asleep. The Duke was still and motionless, as was his wont. I sang on.

'Who shall abide the day of his coming, and who shall stand when he appeareth ? for he is like a refiner's fire.'

The solemn, plaintive notes, wafted on the perfect stillness, wandered out into the darkness of the distant night, but from the distance came no response.

'He was despised and rejected of men—a man of sorrows—he was despised—rejected—rejected of men.'

I sang till I could bear the strain of gloom no more. I turned the music desperately again.

'Speak ye comfortably to Jerusalem, and cry unto her, that her warfare—her warfare is accomplishëd.'

The sudden change and clearness of the notes aroused my aunt.

'Thank you, my dear, thank you!' she said. 'That is very nice. It is quite late.'

The Duke shook my hand with more than usual kindness as I left the room.

'Good-night, my dear. I heard all that you sang,' he said. 'Thank you very much. I would sooner hear you sing those airs than —than go to church.'

He meant it so kindly that I could not say :

'That is very sad, your Grace.'

But, as I lay awake in the awful darkness,

which the stifling heat seemed to bring more near and to make more real, the reiterated phrase came back to me, repeated over and over again in the mystical rhythm of its tone, far into the sultry stillness of the summer night—

'Her warfare is accomplishëd.'

CHAPTER VIII

LADY ELIZABETH

'IF you please, miss,' my maid said to me the next morning when she came into my room, 'Miss Clare's maid says that her lady is not well and will breakfast in bed.'

I got up at once and went to her room. She seemed sleepy, or in a kind of stupor. Then I went to my aunt's room.

'Aunt,' I said, 'Virginia has the fever. I knew it last night. We must send for Doctor James and telegraph for Percival.'

'You are frightened, my dear,' said my aunt, 'and fancy the worst. How could you know it last night? Send for Dr. James by

all means, but to bring Percival down would
be very foolish.'

'He must be sent for, aunt,' I said, in the
greatest distress; 'I should never forgive
myself else.'

I wrote a note for Dr. James and a
telegram to Percival, and sent them off by
a boy. In the course of the morning the
doctor arrived. He was a very old friend,
and we felt great confidence in him.

Virginia continued in the same condition,
only the stupor increased. She seemed to
be lying in an uneasy sleep, troubled by
disturbing dreams. The doctor shook his
head. The symptoms were all those, he said,
of this strange epidemic.

'I should like, your Grace,' he said to my
aunt, 'I should like to telegraph to London
for Sir Felix Weston.'

He was the great fever doctor of the day.

Late at night Percival arrived. He seemed
dazed and astonished rather than distressed.

In the fulness of his youth and activity he could not grasp the idea of danger or of death. I let him come into the room for a moment, and he stood silent and awestruck by the bed where Virginia lay murmuring incoherently in her restless distress. It was evident that she was perfectly unconscious of what passed around her. I sat up with her all night.

The night was rather cooler than the previous one. There was a slight breeze, which the doctor welcomed as the beginning of a change. Nevertheless I sat by the open window by a shaded lamp. I had brought up a volume of Mrs. Hemans' poems—poems which Mr. de Foi had taught me to admire, and of which I was very fond. Over and over again, during that long sad night, I read a poem which I had often read before, but which never seemed to me so beautiful as now. I shall copy it here. It may speak to some others as it spoke to me.

MUSIC AT A DEATH-BED.

Bring music! stir the brooding air
　　With an ethereal breath!
Bring sounds, my struggling soul to bear
　　Up from the couch of death!

A voice, a flute, a dreamy lay,
　　Such as the southern breeze
Might waft, at golden fall of day,
　　O'er blue transparent seas!

Oh, no! not such!　That lingering spell
　　Would lure me back to life,
When my weaned heart hath said farewell,
　　And passed the gates of strife.

Let not a sigh of human love
　　Blend with the song its tone!
Let no disturbing echo move
　　One that must die alone!

But pour a solemn-breathing strain
　　Filled with the soul of prayer!
Let a life's conflict, fear, and pain,
　　And trembling hope be there.

Deeper, yet deeper!　In my thought
　　Lies more prevailing sound,
A harmony intensely fraught
　　With pleading more profound.

A passion unto music given,
   A sweet, yet piercing cry ;
A breaking heart's appeal to heaven,
   A bright faith's victory !

Deeper !   Oh ! may no richer power
   Be in those notes enshrined ?
Can all that crowds on earth's last hour
   No fuller language find ?

Away ! and hush the feeble song,
   And let the chord be stilled !
For in another land ere long
   My dream shall be fulfilled.

The next morning Sir Felix arrived, having travelled by the night express. As he came into the room, where I was sitting by the bed, a wonderful sense of power and of help seemed to enter with him. It seemed to me as though it were impossible for disease to exist in the presence of that composed manner and step.

Sir Felix held a consultation with Dr. James, who had returned to Kingswood early in the morning. We understood that the great doctor was very much interested in the peculiar characteristics of the singular epidemic which was despoiling the neighbourhood.

Virginia lay in the same state all day. Her face was slightly flushed, otherwise there was little change in her appearance. Mr. de Foi came about lunch-time and stayed most of the afternoon, in hopes that some return of consciousness might occur, but it never came. I lay down for a time, that I might be ready for the night. Sir Felix saw his patient more than once. He held a parting consultation with Dr. James, and left in the evening to catch the night mail to town.

All through the long night of gloom and sorrow I sat waiting for one connected sentence, one glance of recognition, one word of recollection and of love, but it never came. I could do nothing but moisten the parched lips, sprinkle the troubled brow.

Dr. James saw her in the morning. 'In

another hour or two,' he said, ' there would be a change. We should then know the best or the worst.'

About eleven o'clock Percival came to the door, and I let him in. Mr. de Foi, he said, was downstairs. We stood together by the bedside.

Virginia moved slightly, as though conscious of a fresh presence. A deeper flush spread over her face, but the troubled, restless look went out of it, and the faintest of all possible smiles seemed to settle upon her lips.

' Fetch Mr. de Foi,' I whispered; 'she is going to awake.'

But before he could stir I caught him by the arm and held him fast. She opened her eyes full upon us—her magnificent and speaking eyes. A still deeper flush, a smile of life and joy, a look of greeting and of return, as it were, to the world of hope and light and love, shone from her face with a beauty that was not of earth. She raised her head slightly with an effort.

'Percival!' she said—then she was gone.

.   .   .   .   .

Then followed a sad and terrible time. We buried Virginia in the little churchyard in the chase. The weather suddenly changed, and rain fell continuously for a week. Her father and two brothers came down to the funeral. They were not sympathetic or congenial people, and the hours dragged desolately by. What I should have done without Mr. de Foi I do not know. I followed her to the grave. I think nothing could have kept me away.

Percival returned to town the next morning with the others, and we were left alone: how grateful the solitude and silence were I cannot say! The Duke had been extremely shocked by what had happened; he aged perceptibly in a few hours, but he seemed to wish me to ride with him, and I did so every morning, attended by two grooms, for I did not

know what might happen at any moment.
Mr. de Foi lunched with us every day, and
was our greatest support.   After some weeks
we went to Hartfield for a few days, but the
Duke was uneasy away from Kingswood, and
we came back.

The autumn drew to an end.   About the
end of September Percival came back, having
passed his examination.   I did not think that
he was at all improved.   I loved him as much
as ever, but I did not like him nearly as much.
He was less of a boy, more manly in every
way, but he seemed to me to have lost more
of the freshness and purity of soul in those
few weeks than all the previous years of his
chequered youth had stolen from him.   I
fancied that his love for Virginia had called
up an ideal within him, and that the shock of
her loss had thrown him back upon his sen-
suous nature with disastrous force; as a man
who has had a glimpse of heaven, and lost it,
may be in a worse state than if he had never

gained an insight into its sacred depths. He seemed to have seen a good deal of London society in the intervals of his studies; and I even fancied that I could discern the influence of the 'designing young person' that Lady Elizabeth talked about. But I said little to him about his London life; he was honestly interested in his professional studies, and in a day or two I was thankful to find that he fell back into his old self again, and became once more the simple, boyish Percival of the past. He seemed to feel the influence of the place, and I thought, 'he feels the presence of a lost loveliness, of a lost companionship, the recollection of which sweetness makes the stately walks and the long terraces of the garden dearer to him than other places are.'

I used to watch him with a wondering tenderness, but I very seldom said anything to him beyond ordinary commonplace talk. I think that I was awe-struck. I think that I had a feeling that he no longer belonged to me, in any sense—that it no longer pertained to me even to endeavour to influence him for his good. That dying girl's face seemed ever to stand between me and him. The tone of her voice, the single word 'Percival,' uttered with her last breath, seemed to have stamped and claimed him for her own for all time— nay, beyond all time. I felt a half weird sense that, so long at least as he was at Kingswood, she was training him, that she was leading him even then.

'I had a letter this morning from Lord Pangbourne, your Grace,' he said to the Duke one day at luncheon—he always addressed the Duke with a pretty deference in this way. 'I think that I shall get the appointment to Suakim. His lordship says that I have passed my last exam. very well, but I know what that means. I have to thank your influence, sir.'

'There is great competition, I suppose,' said the Duke, 'for these things.'

'Oh yes.   I shall be hated awfully for my luck.'

So in a day or two he left us and went to Egypt, where, I believe, he had something to do with engineering, or the Canadian boatmen, or something of that sort.

But, one morning at breakfast, there was his name, Lieutenant Sir Percival Massareen, in a paper two or three days old, in a telegram from Suakim in connection with some sortie in which our troops were engaged under a very galling fire, when he had ridden round the enemy's flank, or done something in bringing off a wounded comrade, that made people talk of him for a day or two; and men went about London saying that they knew him very well; and he was recommended for the Victoria Cross, and got it; and when two or three months afterwards, after General Gordon's death, the troops came back, he brought it down with him from Windsor, where the Queen had pinned it on his breast herself, and

Q

I saw it many times. I am sorry that I cannot give a better account of this affair, but Percival always said that it was nothing, that he had done no more than any one else did or would have done, and that it was all his luck.

Percival did not stay with us at this time more than a day or two. He went back to London and stayed there, as was natural perhaps at his time of life; but we heard presently, even at Kingswood, some things which did not make us very happy about him, and once, when Lord Clare was down, he said at dinner:

'I would get Massareen down here for a time if I were you. I don't fancy that he is getting into very good hands in London. That Guion money hangs in the air, like a curse, over him.'

Some little time after this my aunt received a letter from Lady Elizabeth Guion, inviting herself to Kingswood, 'on very particular family business,' she said.   My aunt reluctantly gave way.

'She is a wicked old woman, my dear,' she said, 'and I never wish to see her again.'

In due time this 'wicked old woman' arrived. She was certainly wonderful to look at. She wore a drawn-silk bonnet of enormous size, lined with white satin, which framed a fine old delicate face, surmounted with iron-gray curls and traced by deep lines. She had piercing gray eyes, which animated, you could not say lightened, her face. She usually wore a long cloak of navy blue, and carried in her white, shrivelled hands, which were covered with rings of untold value, an ivory-headed and gold-mounted cane. She was for all the world like an aristocratically-fashionable witch.

She had the reputation of being extremely witty and of saying the most cruelly offensive things, but I was conscious that we did not see her to advantage in these respects, for she

was evidently exceedingly anxious to propi-
tiate us, and especially to remove any unfavourable impression which the Duchess might
have formed of her. She began at once to say
pretty things to my aunt, or rather she was
constantly talking at her through others, and
especially through the Duke.

'How delightfully *reclus* and peaceful
you are here, Duke,' she said, at dinner, on
the second evening of her arrival. 'I could
fancy myself once more in Paris, in the old
days, among *les grandes dames* of the Faux-
bourg. There was a pretty phrase, I remember, often in their mouths, "*L'impiété perd
les jeunes esprits.*" Ah! in those days it was
the best fashion, for women at any rate, to
be *dévotes!*'

Even the Duke was unable to repress a
slight smile, but there was a glance of kindly,
and even tender, recollection in his eyes that
deprived the smile of all offence.

Lady Elizabeth lost no time in informing

us what her mission was—to promote a marriage between Percival and myself. She
spoke to me about the matter with the most
wonderful freedom and candour.

'I should have liked him to have married
that other girl very well, my dear,' she said
to me as we were sitting, fortunately for me,
alone; 'the girl that died, you know. She
was a fine, outspoken girl, of good form, and
with a will of her own, and she would have
made him a good wife. But she is dead——
And, by-the-bye, my dear, those stupid doctors let her die. As soon as Percival told me
about it, I said, "She didn't die of fever at
all, she died of sunstroke." But you were
all in such a state of panic about the fever
that you misled the doctors, and they never
know anything but what you tell 'em. I
always tell my doctor that. But, however,
I was saying I should have liked Percival
to marry her, but she is dead; and I don't
know, now I see you again, but what I

prefer you. You have a look somehow—
what shall I call it?—*Je ne sais quoi*—
lignée?—*famille?*—no; not even *spirituelle*.
Something beyond that. Something like your
own name, my dear; but even beyond that.
I cannot describe it, but it is worth all the
white and pink in creation. If you could
but get that look into *his* children, my dear,
you would have the loveliest children in
England.'

I did not wonder that some people were
staggered at Lady Elizabeth's manner of talk.

'I have told Lady Elizabeth,' said my
aunt, 'that I should like to see a union
between you and Percival more than anything besides. May I say anything to her
from you, my dear?'

'Had we not better wait until he makes
the proposal, aunt?' I said.

'Perhaps we had, my dear.'

'God bless you, Constance!' Lady Elizabeth said to me as we were all gathered in

the hall to wish her good-bye. 'I have been a wicked woman, my dear; but I don't want him to be wicked, somehow. That sort of thing has been overdone.'

She said this out aloud so that every one could hear; then she got into the brougham, with her maid, and her crutch, and her blue cloak, and her foreign courier on the box, and I saw her no more.

CHAPTER IX

SHORTLY after this extraordinary visit Percival
came down to Kingswood.   He had evidently
been sent down by Lady Elizabeth, and on
the first evening he was not at all in the best
of humours.   In a few hours, however, he
settled down, as he always did, into the old
Percival again, only I thought that he was
more like the old Percival than ever, more like
him than he had been on the occasion of his
last visit.   He was not in the least altered by
his campaign, and even his London life seemed
to fall off from him after a few hours spent
in the placid atmosphere of Kingswood.   It
seemed to me sometimes, as I looked at him,

as though the intervening past might have been a troubled dream, and that we might be sitting together, as in those spring days when I had seen him first—seemed, I say, but only seemed. I knew very well that those days could never be again. He did not appear to think so constantly of Virginia as before ; but I fancied that she was not so much forgotten as some might have supposed —as my aunt, I believe, did suppose. He used to come to church with me now, and I read Keble to him on Sunday mornings as of old.

'Percival,' I said to him one morning, after one of these readings, as we walked to church across the chase, 'I should so like to hear Mr. de Foi preach at the chapel in Rivershead this evening. I have not heard him there for a long time. Will you drive me down ?'

'I should like nothing better,' he said, with animation ; 'Sundays are so awfully dull.'

I had better confess at once that, in proposing this little scheme, which suddenly occurred to me, suggested, perhaps, by the fineness of the morning, I was actuated by purely selfish motives; I was not thinking of Percival at all. It will be difficult for those who live an active or gay life to understand — to realise the habitual quiet and seclusion in which I lived, to appreciate the enjoyment that such a variation as this promised. It was quite as delightful to Percival as to me.

'The chaise will be at the door at a quarter to six, miss,' said Mr. Priest to me, as I came out from luncheon. He had evidently put himself in my way on purpose. 'We are so pleased that you should go down with Sir Percival to hear Mr. de Foi at Rivershead.' The household evidently considered it as a tribute to the correctness of their religious taste.

We spent the afternoon as usual on Sun-

days, sitting about in the broad shadows on
the lawns.   Punctually to the hour, after
we had had some tea, the chaise was at the
door.

We had sent away the delicate pony
chaise, to which such distressing memories
clung, at the earliest possible moment.   No
one could think of driving it again.   The
chaise at the door was one belonging to the
house, with a large seat and sweep of dash-
board in front, and a smaller seat behind for
the groom.   It was drawn by a very beautiful
and favourite mare, named ' Music.'

Percival cast a scrutinising glance over the
equipage, as he drew on his gloves. It was
faultless in every point.

' Awfully clever thought this of yours,
Constance,' he said, as we drove out of the
quadrangle, lying flecked with shadow and
light in the afternoon sun.

We drove across the sunny chase, past the
silent church, and through the lodge gates

down the village street, bright and quiet as on that terrible day. Two years had passed since then, yet even now I dared not look at the fatal house, though I knew that for three seasons the white lilies had withered and been cut down.

As we passed down the long straggling street into Rivershead, passed the schools, and drove into the little town, the unusual aspect of the place struck me with a feeling of inexpressible delight. The cloudless blue sky, untainted by a wreath of smoke, the clear sharp outline of every gable and roof and quaint front, the peaceful quiet aspect of every familiar corner, so different from its usual work-a-day look, filled my heart with an inexpressible thanksgiving. I saw the numbers of people in the streets, far more than on ordinary days, all clean and neat and happy, the bright pavements, the girls in their best dresses walking with their lovers, with a sense of gratitude and peace. I thought that this was going on all over England, in its degree, in all places, at other times so desolate and forsaken in misery and grime. I saw all this with gratitude and peace, in which feeling, doubtless, the unexpected holiday I was myself enjoying had something to do. We drove through the narrow winding streets, by the river and its wharves, all wearing an aspect strange and idealised, and pulled up before the chapel door, leaving the chaise to the groom.

As we entered the chapel Percival suddenly said to me:

'Constance, do you remember that afternoon in the ruined abbey, when we asked Virginia what she thought of Mr. de Foi's story, and she said that girl's death was cruel? Do you think that she was right?'

'I cannot tell,' I said, for there was no time. 'We cannot ask her now.'

It was a curious place. An old chapel panelled with oak and with high square pews.　At the upper end were three plain windows, high up in the wall, and underneath an altar richly vested and decked with vases of flowers.　This was almost the only thing that marked the place as belonging to the Church of England.　A pulpit and desk stood on either side, and over the former was one of those terrible sounding-boards, supported by a chain, which always suggest a horrible catastrophe should the chain break.　Round the rim of the sounding-board, over the preacher's head, were engraven the words, 'I have determined to know nothing among you save Jesus Christ, and Him crucified.'　There were galleries round the room, and the summer afternoon sun filled the place, which was crowded with people, a very large proportion of whom, I was surprised to see, were men. All these things I noticed as we entered the chapel, where some one seemed to be on the watch for us, and we were shown into a pew not far from the pulpit.　The evening service

was sung by a choir in the gallery, and Mr.
de Foi ascended the pulpit to preach.

'Is it well with thee? is it well with thy
husband? is it well with the child?'

I cannot judge of the sermon, it is too
much wrought into the issues of my life, but
I copied it from Mr. de Foi's MS., and I put
it down here in full.

THE SERMON

'"Is it well with thee? is it well with thy husband?
is it well with the child?   And she said, It is well."

'Surely a great thing to say.   What more
can be said of any of us?   It is well.   But
what was the case of this woman who said
that it was well with all the dearest ties of
her life,—herself, her husband, her child?
She had longed for a child—a child had been
given her of the Lord,—that child was dead.
"Is it well with thee? is it well with the *child?*
And she said, It is well!"   What can this
mean? and moreover, if you will read the

story, you will see that the prophet has no after-thought, no intention of improving the occasion, of drawing a lesson from it. He does not know that the child was dead. He only asks the question in kindliness, because she had entertained him when he passed that way. He says himself expressly that he did not know that the child was dead—"The Lord hath hid this thing from me," he says—and yet this woman, when this yearned-for child—this child who was of an age to draw the heart-strings closer, who in his death-struggle had "sat upon her knees till noon," —was dead, says, yet she says, in answer, not to a sermon, but to an ordinary inquiry, "It is well." What does this mean?

'But before we answer this question let us think for a moment what the question is, "Is it well with thee? is it well with thy husband or thy wife? is it well with the child?"

'Is it well? Will you answer this question,

not to me, but to yourselves and to God? Is it well?

'We live in an age of boasted freedom, in an age of free thought, of free inquiry; no man hindereth us. We stand at the junction of two ways, we are free to choose. We may refuse Christ, or we may accept Him. We may believe in God, or we may deny His existence. Say that we have rejected Him,— Is it well with thee? is it well with thy husband or thy wife? *is it well with the child?* Have you escaped the common lot of humanity, have you escaped the disappointment of frustrated hope, have you escaped bereavement, death; death in all its forms; death, I grant you, at times beneficent, peaceful, the fitting end of happy finished life; but death also of another kind, unlooked for, cruel, needless—nay, to the finite sense, blighting, unreasonable, brutal even? Have you escaped the troubles of this life, penury and hunger and despair? have you escaped the tedium of

existence, the weariness of life, the desire—
the wild desire to be anywhere except here?
Is it well with thee?

'As I stand here in this place, having
taken upon myself this awful task—a task
none the less awful because repeated so often
—of speaking to you of God, as I look upon
your faces raised to mine, there are few that
are not familiar to me. Nay, as I look
around me, and the summer evening light
shines upon them, I do not know that there
is *one* of whom I know nothing, and the most
of what I know has something to do—much
to do—with sorrow and with bereavement
and with death.

'They will tell you—if you go to the
learned men they will tell you—that this
faith which we preach is "shadow worship;"
that it has no foundation in fact; that it
cannot stand for a moment in competition
with an alkali or a gas. Shadow worship!
I am speaking now, not to scientists or men

of learning, I am speaking to women weeping over the lost, I am speaking to fathers, to husbands, to men who, apart from their own feelings, have the added chivalrous instinct of sympathy with the pain and suffering of the long-loved wife, and I ask them, Is it well with the dead child?'

The preacher paused, and looked for a moment as though he would have said more, but there was something in the restless tremulous movement before him that warned him, and he went on in a calmer voice:

' "And she said, It is well." What can this mean? The answer is not far to seek. The child was the gift of God. If the Lord hath given in mercy, surely it must be in mercy that He takes away. "The Lord gave, and the Lord hath taken away, blessed be the name of the Lord." "It is well." I do not say that it is an easy confession for any of us to make; but I say that it is an impossible one save to the man or woman who acknowledges that the gift was the gift of God.

'Then what is the will of God? It seems an important question. Every morning and evening we pray, "Thy will be done;" and it would seem to be futile to pray for that the meaning of which we have no conception. Is it the will of God that sorrow and sin and suffering should prevail? He gives, and we are satisfied and glad, and ask no questions; but why does He take away?

'Ah! if I could answer this question you would no longer need to sit here, even for a moment, to listen to me.

'But I can tell you, without a second's hesitation, what *is* the will of God.

'The will of God is righteous dealing, and love, and forbearance, and hope—forward-looking—and joy. You know what these words mean. These are not shadows. You know that, in proportion as you follow after these things, the sky is brighter above you,

and in your dwellings is fulness of joy. You
know that the common daylight is transfigured, that the daily task is hallowed, that
the familiar faces of those with whom you live
shine with a lustre of beauty and of peace;
and why? Because you have entered into the
will of God. Try it; try it only for a week.

'For, as you try it, you will realise this fact,
above all others, that not only is every single
act of self-sacrifice, of love, of kindliness,
blessed in itself, in its immediate result, not
only on yourself, but on others—not only on
others, but on yourself—but that every single
act, however trivial and small, is not isolated
and alone, but is part of a higher life, of a
more perfect existence, of a loftier intellect, and
a diviner Love. Every single act of sacrifice is
part of the great sacrifice that

"Hallowed earth and fills the skies."

Every act of love and kindliness is only possible because it is part of the divine love;

nothing can exist save as the result of the existence of its perfect ideal, and the ideal of perfect existence is God.

'So perfect is this dilemma that abroad, where men think with greater boldness than in England, and follow their conclusions to the logical sequence, thinkers have boldly adopted the conclusion that there is no such thing as love or hatred, no such thing as virtue, no such thing as vice; that every emotion of the mind towards what, they say, is ignorantly called good or evil, is only the result of the healthy or unhealthy action of the gastric juice. That a mother's love is nothing but healthy digestion; that a mother's prayers and despair over a wild son spring from nothing but an unhealthy action of the liver. A creed, you say, ghastly and dreary. It may be so, but a creed logical at all events; for, believe me, if you once admit the absolute reality of certain principles of existence—nay, of one of them only, say of love—you have no alternative but to believe in the existence of a divine principle, which is God.

' Many of you are in the habit of reading the magazines of the day, and you know these things as well as I do. You know that there is a party at home who, as these people abroad would destroy Christianity by denying the intellect, would hope to destroy it by crushing emotion and imagination. They know that so long as these remain in the human heart their task is hopeless, for Christianity appeals to the noblest feelings of the human heart, and these are its noblest feelings.

' In the place of the vivid story of a struggle, old as humanity, real as life itself—a struggle between the Word of God and erring man—they have the insolence to set before us a sentiment of morality, borrowed from Heathen tombs, which had little if any existence in real life, or a ghastly parody of morality, stolen from the distant echoes of a lost Christianity itself. Of all the foul and slimy creatures that ever infested the world of thought, this is the slimiest and most contemptible—the fit and final offspring of that pseudo - intellect which would gain for humanity the knowledge of a Gas and lose it the presence of a God.

'I am not afraid that any of you will fall back upon the gastric juice. Let us try for a moment to realise the stupendous fact that this divine will is thwarted—this divine ideal frustrated every day. Righteousness and love and happiness set at naught, thwarted, every hour and every day! What mystery is this? Many of you work in arts in which natural laws are the forces in harmony with which you work. There is no uncertainty, no opposition here. These laws once known, you fear no disappointment—you cannot even conceive the fear that any failure in the regularity of their recurrence could befall. But of what avail is it that the obedience of inanimate matter is fixed and certain when man—made in the image of God—whose life is cursed, save in the light of God—prefers darkness, and misery, and cruelty, to light, and love, and peace? Nay, more than this—How can such things be? The will of God, being what it is —power and righteousness and blessing—how can anything else exist? To move in obedience to such a will, to live in such a light, is at once the characteristic and the boast of the highest intelligence,

" I am Gabriel, that stand in the presence of God."

And yet this will is frustrated every moment and hour of every earthly day!

'So impossible does this fact appear, when once its meaning is realised, that many thoughtful men have been driven into the denial of the existence of evil. There is no such thing, they say; there cannot be. It is inconceivable that there should be any opposition to the will of God. What seems evil does so only under a misapprehension and a mistake. In some sense something of this may be true; but the fact remains, it *seems* evil to us.   To the mother weeping over her fallen son—to the wife, despairing of even woman's love and tenderness to win a brutal husband—it *seems* evil: and the seeming for our purpose is enough.

'This is sin ; this is the mystery which was from the beginning, and which thwarts the will of God.

'Why ? Because the metals you deal with, the alkalies and gases in which the scientists believe, are senseless and stupid, but you are made in the image of God. You have the power of choice; you know good and evil; you can refuse the one and embrace the other. Would you give up this prerogative of the sonship of God for the monotony of material existence, for the safety of an irresponsible being, limited in existence by an invariable law ?

'This mistaken choice is sin. The choice

that refuses God. The creature refusing its Creator; the being formed for love refusing love; born to breathe a pure atmosphere, choosing an atmosphere tainted and impure; born for life and strength and energy, choosing sloth and impotence and suicide : and if there is one fact of history more certain than another it is this fact, that two thousand years ago human nature was reduced to such a state of fetid decay by this rejection of God that a few more years would have seen the world one gigantic dunghill of corruption and death. Then the great sacrifice took place : God, manifest in the flesh, died upon the cross, an eternal sacrifice to take away sin. A fresh, invigorating breeze swept through the putrifying mass of human life. Men faced for the first time the realities of existence with an unflinching faith—by pureness, by knowledge—in a divine life. The idea of sacrifice, which every nation under heaven had conceived, and blindly striven to work out, was fulfilled in the great sacrifice; and sin, no longer the ruler, became for ever the bruised and battered serpent only, loathed and despised even by those who submit to its slimy trail.

'For the will of God is an energising power in every heart that submits to the guidance of its gentle influence. "Existence," it has been well said, "begins with response to the divine voice." Before this is no existence. The ear hath not heard, nor hath the heart conceived, the things that are provided for him who is haply persuaded to follow the leading of this voice. He has a divine Friend ever by his side in the devious pathways of life. Amid the troubles and sorrows, the struggles and falls, that beset the wayfarer, constant in his ear is the divine consoling voice. And not only in consolation, but in suggestion of pure and holy thoughts, is life raised to an inconceivable clearness and purity. In the streets and in the turmoil of life this Friend is still at his side, and in the strength of this divine fellowship he is enabled to face the vexations of his daily life, to turn aside its scoffs and insults with a serenity that startles and surprises even the unconscious world. The gloomiest life is struck through with a sudden light, the dullest sky is brightened by the under-shining of a heavenly dawn.

'This persuasive voice is speaking now to every one of you. Will you resist the pleading of His gentle words? Will you not say to this heavenly Friend, " Abide with me ; Thou hast the words of eternal life " ?

'It is towards evening, and the day, with many of us at least, is far spent ; to-night heaven opens to you ; before it is too late let the choice be made.

'But most happy is he who, in his *youth*, gives himself up to this guidance, for he alone, in this life, can realise the fulness of the divine scheme and plan. From the moment of his birth the love and will of God has surrounded such an one. He begins with γένεσις, the birth of all things by the breath of God ; he ends with the τέλος κυρίου, the finished purpose of the will of the Lord.'

'That was a great preacher,' Percival said, as we drove away from the chapel, and he was very silent all the way home.

CHAPTER X

'WELL, Constance,' said the Duke, as we came into the drawing-room after the little supper we had had together, 'did you have a good sermon? I hope you are not too tired to play us a few airs. We cannot do without them, you know, on Sunday night.'

What I sang I do not remember now, but I know that as I played, all through the heart-melting rhythm of the melodious notes, and long afterward far on into the night in the intervals of a fitful slumber, there was present with me, as an echo of the preacher's voice, in inexpressible fulness, the sense of the presence of God. I had played as the last air the 'Pastoral Symphony,' and through the night there seemed to follow me, in the thin clear notes, the sense of a lofty refinement of thought—of an instinct of perfect clearness of spirit, whose dwelling-place is a purer sky—a shining, starlit world of purity and peace ineffable—high above the troubles, the tumults, the struggles of earth.

The morning broke clear and calm. I used, especially when I had not slept well, to go out before breakfast, in the summer mornings, on the terrace beyond the south garden, and I did so on this day. I had not been there long before Percival came on to the lawn through the door of the walled garden.

In the valley among the oaks, which lay beyond the gardens, where I had taken Percival on that first spring morning of our acquaintance, was a sacred well. In the old monkish days it was believed to have medicinal virtues, and had been formed into a stone bath, sheltered by a groined roof of some architectural beauty. The Duke, many years ago, had caused this bath to be cleaned out, and the stone-work of the roof repaired. The water was singularly clear, and some of the gentlemen used to go down there to bathe. Percival especially affected it. The plunge into the icy, shaded water, he used to say, was delicious. He came up from thence to-day. He looked handsomer than ever—more like the statue of a young Achilles, full of strength and life. He walked with me some steps along the terrace, then he said abruptly :

'Constance, I wish you would let me speak to you. I want to ask you to be my wife.'

I did not speak.

'I know very well,' he went on, 'that I am not worthy of you. I was not worthy of Virginia—how much less, then, of you! but I will do the best I can. I never knew any one I thought so much of as I do of you. You are a wonderful girl, Constance; you have made Lady Elizabeth Guion believe in you. Will you have me?'

He spoke without embarrassment, and with little, if any, shyness. We reached the eastern end of the terrace as he finished speaking, and we turned round. Before us lay the stretch of lawn, the tulip-trees, the groups of cedars and of elms, and beyond the long irregular front of the house, with its projecting mullions, and deep bays, and ivied, massy towers. This, then, was the moment to which what might have been was come at last!

Every word he spoke was honest, and, as far as he knew, true; but did he know what truth was? Did he know his own mind for a week together? 'I was not worthy of Virginia,' he had said. He belonged to her. She did not believe in a God. Should I, who professed to believe in a God of righteousness and truth, should I take him, who belonged to her, him whom she had claimed by her dying look and words—take him, who belonged to her, and the Guion money, that was hers by right? Surely no!

'Percival,' I said at last, 'be true! only be true! What does it matter what becomes of me? The only thing I long for—that I pray to God for day and night—is that you should become a good and a great man. You know you loved her. You love her memory now.'

'But she is dead, Constance,' he said; 'she is dead.'

'No, Percival,' I said, 'she is not dead. She is gone to that God whom she, poor lovely child, would not own. She is gone to that God whom she died serving, though she fancied that she did not know Him. Percival, she is not dead.'

He seemed to understand that he was dismissed, and he took it so lightly, without any sign of distress, that I knew more than ever that I was right. He had the air of a man who had done his duty and was content.

'It is curious, Constance,' he said, 'that you should use these words to me, "Only be true." That is just what Virginia said to me when I first told her that I loved her'—(he had asked *me* to be his wife). 'It was just here—no, not here—on the walk next the windows, where you first showed me the house. "Percival," she said, "I wonder— I wonder whether you are true?" and I stared at her, and I said, "Why?" and she said, "Are you quite sure—quite sure—that there is nothing between you and Constance Lisle?" and I laughed and said, "No—Constance! no. Only fancy Constance marrying me!" and she laughed a little and said, "What a boy you are, to say that to me!"'

Percival paused.

'And did she say no more?' I said.

'No,' he said; 'nothing more that I remember.'

'Nothing more about me?' I said. 'Do not be afraid to tell me if she did. I want to know.'

'No,' he said; 'no, I think not. I remember now,—I remember it all so well,' he went on, with a short laugh that was more than half a sob,—'I remember now. I thought she was going to say something else, and then she flushed all over and bit her lip, as she used to do. I remember I wondered what she had been going to say.'

I knew very well what it had been.

She had caught herself on the point of saying, 'She loves you with a love as deep as woman ever felt,' and her proud, girl's nature had struck her with a stinging shame that she had been so near betraying the secret of another girl.

'Percival,' I said, after we had walked a little farther on, and he did not seem to have anything more to say, 'be true to her. The "Morte d'Arthur" is not the only black-letter book the Duke has. I remember seeing the story of a girl in another, and these lines I shall never forget—

> " The God of her hath made an end,
>   And fro' this worldes fairie,
>   Hath taken her into companie."

Think of that when you think of her.'

'You are a strange girl, Constance,' he said, 'but I was warned. Lady Elizabeth told me how it would be. I went to say good-bye to her, and she said, "Good-bye, child; I wish you luck, but you won't succeed. There is only one girl in England who would refuse Sir Percival Massareen and the Guion money, but, unfortunately for our purpose, Constance Lisle is that girl." She said that.'

'I do not refuse Sir Percival Massareen,' I said smiling. All emotion seemed to die away before his contented smile. 'I hope always to keep him as a brother and as a friend;' and I held out my hand.

Percival stayed with us some days after this scene; indeed, though he had not seemed particularly pleased to come, I was surprised to see that he was loath to go away. He became wonderfully gentle and affectionate, and pleased with everything that he did with me. I blessed God a thousand times that I had been led to act as I had done. 'Now that he is relieved from the dread of marrying me,' I thought, 'he will love me as a sister, and all that is good and noble in him will be developed, not by me, but by the quiet and holy influence of the place.' Surely I had cause to rejoice.

We rode almost every day through the chase and to the dark tower over the channel, and he spoke to me a great deal about Virginia; and I saw, and rejoiced to see, that his love for her had indeed been real and deep—hitherto the one master-passion of his life. Her death had transferred it, as I hoped, from the change-ful and uncertain to the sure footing of the enduring and the ideal.   It is difficult even now to say whether I was right or not.

But one evening, a day or two before Percival was to leave us, all this received a shock, and I had another trial, the severest of all.

He had been so nice for many days, so loving and gentle in his manly strength, so thoughtful and affectionate and pure in heart, that I all but lost other sense save that of pleasure in being with him and of love of him. It seems to me, as I look back on those hours, wonderful—shall I say hardly fair?—that such a strain, such a task, should have been thrown upon a visionary, frail, unformed girl—but weakness is made strong in a strength which is not of this earth.

We had been riding one afternoon through the loneliest parts of the chase, 'overthwart and endlong in the wild forest,' as the 'Morte d'Arthur' says, 'and held no way but as wild adventure led' us, over the grassy ranges of the forest and underneath the branching ashes and oaks, and, coming back to Kingswood from towards the east, we found a stable-boy, as Percival said, 'up to some mischief,' and prevented its further development by giving him our horses to take home, while we ourselves entered the gardens by the mystic doorway in the wall. The western sun had cast a deep shade from the lofty wall and from the clumps of elms outside it in the chase, but as we opened the door a blaze of light and golden heat over the level lawns struck me with a sense of life and hope.

Percival turned to me suddenly as we stepped upon the lawn. The sense of light and brightness seemed to inspire him with a sudden thought. We were close to the tulip-tree, beneath which Virginia had lain that Sunday morning.

'Constance,' he said, 'I love you. Can

you give me no hope ? To-morrow I shall be gone.'

It was as though some one had struck me an unexpected blow. Stunned in heart and mind, I sent up a despairing cry for guidance, and for the space of a second I saw, as in a vision, a terrible future. I saw him wearied, his passing illusion outgrown, his life blighted by the consequence of a great mistake, his nature debased by the weakness of undecided action. I looked down, as it were, into a horrible pit, and saw what I dared not look at any more ; in a second or two I spoke.

'It were better not, Percival,' I said ; 'believe me, it were better not.'

'It is too late, then ?' he said sadly. 'I was blind and stupid, but I know better now.'

Should I tell him that he had made no mistake ? hardly that. Indeed for a moment or two I could not speak again ; then he went on :

'I know that you think that I am uncertain

and changeable, not to be depended on, but you might give me some hope. If a man has something to look forward to it steadies him, however poor a fellow he may be.'

'But suppose he changes soon,' I said almost in a whisper, 'and a girl has given him hope, what is to become of her?'

'You have a poor opinion of me, Constance,' he said sadly; 'perhaps it is not strange.'

'Only be true, Percival,' I said,—and I saw his face through the mist of tears,—'only be true. Hereafter in the years to come, when you are a great and noble man, and are married to some good and beautiful girl whom you love, we shall meet somewhere, and you will say, "My sister Constance told me this," and that she said "He is called Percival, a knight of the Holy Fellowship of the Table, not of Arthur, but of Christ."'

'It is too late,' he said somewhat bitterly; 'one mistake, and the door is closed for ever.'

'Why should you talk of a mistake?' I

said. 'You never thought of me before Virginia came. You loved her truly and honestly. Had she lived, she would have been your wife. Why do you call it a mistake?'

Every word of this was true. Perhaps it was not all the truth.

He shook his head.

'It was a mistake,' he said again; 'I see it now.'

The next morning he left. I went with him to the gate of the quadrangle, where he got into a dogcart and drove off, accompanied by his servant and a groom. At the corner of the nearest wood he turned and waved his hand. I never saw him again.

CHAPTER XI

About a week after Percival had left us I had a long letter from him which delighted me very much. He called me his dear sister Constance, and made no allusions to our conversations or to his suit; but he said that if he never saw Kingswood again he should remember it with love and gratitude for my sake. He said he should never forget what he had learnt there. He spoke of his future life, and he said that he was going in for another examination, and would devote himself to his profession, and that his earnest purpose and prayer was that he might become a good officer and a good man. He said that if it pleased God that it were so, he should owe it, under God, to his sister at Kingswood.

It was given to me then, in mercy, to see that I had been right. That had I accepted him,—had all things been made easy to him— what he thought at the moment to be earthly love, what certainly was earthly wealth, placed at his disposal, his beck and call,—he would have been tired and satiated in a few hours; but that, irritated and disappointed, disgusted for a moment with the world and its allurements, the serious side of his nature had been strengthened and encouraged afresh—a germ which might develop, by the grace of God, into a higher life.

As I read this letter in the summer morning, a sense of joy and peace filled my heart. The earthly sunshine seemed transfigured into the pureness of a crystal light—a light as of first Communion in the distant childhood, when the sunlight lay warm upon village church and spire, and upon the grassy hillocks of the dead.

He wrote to me every week, and although he never wrote so warmly again, yet his letters were all in the same strain. He was evidently becoming very much interested in his profession, and I could find no falling off from the earnest steadfastness with which he looked forward to his future career. I could not give thanks enough to God.

The year drew to a close with its wealth of autumn tints, its quiet hours, and its monotonous days and silent nights, 'in reverie, in faith and prayer,' as in the poem I had read at Merrivale. I used to wonder at the peace, nay, the happiness, that I enjoyed.

Towards the end of October the Marquis came down for a couple of days. The Duke was ageing very perceptibly, though he still kept up his rides, and his son came down oftener than before. I had not had a letter from Percival for a fortnight, and had begun to wonder whether he had forgotten to write.

'Oh, by the bye,' Lord Clare said to me at dinner, 'have you heard from Percival within the last few days? He is going with Sir Charles Sinclair to the West Coast.'

We all expressed our astonishment at the news.

'Yes,' the Marquis said, 'I was at the Guards' Club the other night at a dinner to Sir Charles, and he was very full of it. He had been dining somewhere a few nights before, he told us, and had been saying after dinner that he wished very much to find a young fellow whom he could depend upon to go out with him on the staff, but that it was very difficult to get the right man, it was such a beastly climate, you know; and he told us that, in the drawing-room, Massareen came up to him and said:

'"I think that I heard you say at dinner that you wanted a man to go out with you.

What should you say to me? I have passed all my exams., two or three extras indeed, and if I were of any use—I should be glad to go."

' "My dear fellow," said Sir Charles, "you are just the man ; but what on earth are you thinking of, with your prospects? It's the deuce of a climate."

' "I suppose there is plenty to do ?" he said.

' "Oh, lots !" said Sir Charles ; "lots of trouble with the slaves, and the missionaries, and blacks without end."

' "How can you explain it ?" we asked Sinclair.

' "It's inexplicable to me," he said, "the Guion money and all. I should guess that it is some love affair. But, at any rate," he finished up, "I am in luck, he is a—something—good fellow." I thought you would have heard all about it.'

' My dear,' my aunt said to me when we

got into the drawing-room, 'will you let him go? Cannot you forgive him? He was so young.'

'Aunt,' I said, 'I should have forgiven him long ago had there been anything to forgive. He never loved me. He does not love me now. Were I to marry him, with all the Guion money and all the life and luxury that it would bring, he would never be true to an ideal again. That girl's face would haunt him in his sleep. He would soon grow tired of me. The end would be too horrible even for a dream. I cannot marry him.'

Percival wrote a short letter a few days afterwards. He was full of his preparations. Lady Elizabeth was furious. Sir Charles was to leave at once. He did not propose to come down. I think that I was glad that it should be so.

We heard from him once or twice again, always full of courage and of hope. Then we saw in the papers that Sir Charles Sinclair had left England for Africa, accompanied by his staff.

Faint white mists from the channel floated over the chase, and became transmuted into wreaths of golden gossamer by the bright November sun. Against the pale but clear blue of the sky the tracery of the great oaks and elms, with here and there great yellow leaves trembling to their fall, rose in majestic silence, studded with myriad drops, like sparkling jewels. An intense peace and stillness seemed to have taken possession of the place and its inhabitants, and lulled them and it alike into an enchanted sleep. Day followed day in deeper and ever deeper repose. The Duke and Duchess were quieter than ever. The household moved more silently even than was their wont. We saw no one except Mr. de Foi, and once or twice Mrs. Merrivale from Merrivale. The Marquis also came down once or twice. For myself I began to realise what Mr. de Foi had often told me—that happiness is not the result of pleasure, commencing with enjoyment and turning naturally into the satiety of fruition, but of pain, dedicated to God by consecration, and transfigured by resignation into the peace that attends the practice of His presence.

Each morning as I awoke I was conscious always of an aching unrest, of a yearning after a lost hope and desire, but always, as the day advanced, the restless heart, which had recovered its liberty during the unconscious security of sleep, became gradually chastened and trained again by the sweet compulsion which led it through the peaceful paths of prayer and the quiet thoughts of holy men,

> ' When like somo long-forgotten strain,
>   Comes stealing o'er the heart forlorn,
>   What sunshine hours had taught in vain.'

I used at such times to wonder that any creature could be so happy as I was.

I read all that I could find about the West

Coast and its scenery, the dangers of its climate to Europeans, and its fatal fevers. The shuddering terror and shrinking with which I thought of Percival in the midst of such dangers was lost in a kind of joy at the thought that he too was worthy to suffer, and perchance to die, at the divine call of duty and sacrifice. Delicate girls had rejoiced when they saw their lovers taken to the cross—as poor Virginia had said, why should I be less brave than they were?

The old year died out; and, on the intense silence of the New-Year's morn, I once more heard that transcendental music of the bells, perceptible to the mental sense though lost to the physical. What gracious foretelling was wafted on the supernaturally clear and thrilling notes?

In the course of the spring there appeared in the papers telegrams from the West Coast stating that difficulties had arisen with the tribes and kings in the interior relating to the colonisation of European nations other than the English, and that the work of the missionaries was being much impeded, and some of them were even in danger of their lives. We had more than one long, lively letter from Percival, giving an account of his manner of life, and mentioning some of these facts; but we did not think much about them until one day we read a telegram from the governor to the Colonial Office relating alarming rumours as to the fate of an English bishop, who was on an expedition into the interior amongst fierce and warlike tribes. The governor stated that he had decided to send an envoy, accompanied only by trusty natives, by a direct but very difficult route to endeavour to intercept the bishop at the capital of the most savage of these native kings, where it was thought that the greatest danger existed, in the hope that the presence of an English officer might overawe the natives and their king. Sir Percival Massareen, of the staff, had volunteered for this dangerous and difficult duty, and, although other officers were willing to attempt it, the governor had decided to accept Sir Percival's offer, as he was peculiarly suited to encounter fatigue, and had been remarkably free from any attacks of fever since his arrival in the colony.   The expedition was to start at once.

After this we heard no more for many weeks.   Every now and then there were telegrams from the coast stating that native runners had arrived from the interior bringing intelligence that the bishop had been murdered ; then a day or two afterwards other telegrams appeared stating that he was perfectly safe, and much respected by the natives.   Nothing seemed to have been heard of the expedition to succour him.   The Marquis telegraphed to Sir Charles, and received an answer that many of the natives who accompanied the expedition had returned furtively, apparently discouraged or frightened by the difficulties or dangers of the task. He would telegraph the moment anything further was known. It was a time of considerable political excitement both on the Continent and at home. I suppose no one cared about these telegrams, except the friends of the Bishop— and the friends of Sir Percival Massareen.

The summer drew to a close, with weary waiting, and the gorgeous autumn tints once more decked the chase and woods. The monotony of our life knew no change. I had almost begun to think that there would be no change—that I should never hear anything more of Percival again.

Suddenly, one morning after breakfast, as I was sitting with the Duchess in her room, Mr. Giles, the butler, entered with a more than usually important air: a gentleman from the Colonial Office, he said, who had travelled all night, wished to see Miss Lisle.

He was told to bring the gentleman up, and a distinguished-looking young man entered the room.

I rose and met him as he came in, with a thrill of supreme excitement, almost of delight—the message, whatever it was, was to *me*.

'I am Miss Lisle,' I said; 'this is the Duchess. I fear that you bring us bad news.'

He held a small parcel, tied up very carefully, in his hand.

'I have the honour, madam,' he said, 'of being commissioned by Lord Cranbury to place this packet in your hands. It was received at the Colonial Office yesterday morning by special messenger from Sir Charles Sinclair. From the few lines of the despatch that accompanied the packet, I fear that there is no doubt that both the bishop and Sir Percival Massareen are dead.'

I took the packet in both hands, but I was not able to speak.

'My niece, sir,' said the Duchess, with that sweetness of dignity which never failed her at need, 'was sincerely attached to Sir Percival Massareen. It is a trying moment to her.'

The young man bowed very low, and retreated a few steps towards the door.

'I will take this to my room, I think, aunt,' I said.

'I hope, sir,' said my aunt, rising, 'that you will lunch here. As you have had a long journey you will probably wish to be shown a room. Afterwards I am sure that the Duke would be glad to make your acquaintance. I beg your pardon,' and she rang the bell, 'I think the servants did not give your name.'

'My name is Dayrolles, your Grace,' said the young man.

My aunt sent for Mr. Priest, and gave Mr. Dayrolles into his charge, requesting him to inform the Duke of his arrival.   I went to my room, but I did not open the packet there.

As I had stood, half-unconscious, holding the packet in my hands, there had flashed across my troubled memory the words I had read with Percival—ah, how long ago!

'And I saw a damoysel, all in white, with a vessel in both her hands.'

And I felt that in some way, at present unknown to me, I held in my hands a sacred trust—a letter to be read nowhere but before the altar of the Lord.

Mr. de Foi had a service in the little church at noon.   I had intended to be present, and, leaving word where I had gone, I left the house and walked along the pathway to the church.

I felt no impatience to open the packet. As I passed once more through the carved doorway in the wall, through scenes so constant to every thought and aspect of my life from a child that the material forms and shapes that met my eye were as nothing in comparison with the memories and sensations of the spirit that thronged the scene, it seemed to me that nothing is common or material, that no moment, no inanimate companion of my life hitherto, had been other than a messenger and angel of God. Surely it would not be otherwise now. I carried in my hands a sacred thing. In His time, and in His holy church, God would make known to me what it contained.

It was the Eve of All Saints. The church was very sweet with the flowers that decked the altar for the festival.

I went straight to the seat I usually occupied, facing the altar, and knelt down. It wanted nearly an hour to twelve o'clock.

Then I looked up suddenly, and broke the seals of the packet in my hand. Through my tears I saw the Victoria Cross—that priceless possession that, with all his affected indifference, I knew that Percival valued more than life, lying before me in its velvet case; and, beneath it, two sheets of foreign letter-paper, carefully written, as it seemed to me. Hardly knowing what I did, I spread the sheets of thin paper before me on the ledge, and laid the cross, which I had taken from its case, upon them.

This is then what I read:

'Sister Constance,' so the writing began, 'I am awake and in the hut alone. I feel another man to what I did last night, and I am irresistibly impelled to write to you, why? God knows; for how can I suppose that you will ever see what I write? The Bishop's paper and ink are here upon the table.

'But I must begin from the beginning. You will have heard from Sir Charles of the expedition from Cape Coast Castle to try to save the Bishop, and how Sir Charles chose me, though there were lots of fellows ready to go. I was immensely happy when we set out. I had a picked native team to go with me, with an awfully good fellow at the head, a Christian who was christened "Ned." It was rather a bad time of the year and very hot, but we did not think much of that. Sir Charles was very good. If I hadn't been so set upon it, I do not think that he would have let me go.

'At first we went on all right, through the cactus hedges and the palm-trees and the plantations; then we came upon the river, and had to strike out our route for ourselves. You could not fancy such a country, clever though Virginia used to say that you were; I never thought to see such a country. A sluggish, widespread river, with mud and mire on every side—an impassable, interminable thicket of immense forest trees, mangrove and other trees of which I know no names—with wild spreading branches and hanging roots and shoots reaching down to the water; along many of these branches we had to walk in single file. Then trees and leaves of every shape, long lance-like leaves, sharp as swords and knives, cut us, and stopped our way; and flowers and birds and wild beasts—monkeys and apes and tigers or leopards, I don't know which they were —all around us, crying out and flying off as we approached, and an awful stifling heat and perfume, so that one could hardly breathe.

'However, we kept on, and now and then we left the river and struck across the open plain, not altogether open, but less densely wooded, with rows of palms of all shapes and forms. I don't know which was worst. It was a choice between the moist, fetid heat of the river mud, and the blazing heat of the open—a fiery furnace, seven times heated in wrath. Then, every now and then, we came to villages and people — such villages and people as you never saw in a dream. Some of the houses quite large and fine, and covered with carvings and images of devils and Satans with grinning mouths; and fetish trees that stand in the midst of the houses, in the centre of the villages, where they stick up dolls of rags, and wretched guys and shapes of all sorts, and say that it is "fetish" or God! and the gold dust and the diamonds are buried beneath these trees, and no one, however depraved and wicked, dares to touch it because of the "fetish" in the thatched boughs: and women, or horrible shapes that bore a ghastly resemblance to women, came about us and brought us water, black and poisonous, to drink. But worst of all was the sickening heat and smell, and I never could sleep—only sometimes I was so worn out that I went off for a short time — for everywhere there was the cry of the wild beasts, and the chatter of the monkeys and the birds: and whenever we came to a village there was noise and beating of gongs, and hideous sounds all night long. I got to think that the heathen does not know what silence is. But, however, we kept on: but at every village we stopped at, or when we started again in the morning, I saw that some of our men were missing, and stayed behind; and at last there were so few that I had to speak to "Ned" about it, and I asked him what it meant, and he told me at last, after some trouble, that the great kings were leagued against the white men, and sworn to kill all white men that came to trouble them. He said that he was afraid that we should not get through; and when I saw the ghastly, grinning faces on the houses where we were, and the dances of devils—for they were nothing else—beneath the fetish trees on the village greens, and the leaping men, with long horns upon their heads, and the horrible girls, decked with feathers, and dancing in wild circles, I confess that I began to fear that he was right.

'However, we kept on. We left the river at last, and held on across the plain. It was hot, but it was dry, and we lay down under the great, roof-like palms, and sometimes it was quiet. But every morning, and sometimes in the day-time, one or other of the men slunk away, frightened at the rumours that were spread abroad on every side; and one morning when I awoke after a short sleep I was alone with " Ned."

'We were beneath a long grove or line of palm-trees, looking out over a wide plain, beyond which were rows of huts and lofty, strangely-shaped temples, indicating a considerable town.

'"We are through, Sir Percival," Ned said to me—he was a very clever man, and caught all the English phrases with great ease—" we are through, but we are alone. That is Yaoumie. I know that the Bishop is there. But what can we do? the kings are sworn to kill him and every white man. I see them coming out even now. Come back with me. It is easier going back than coming up. I will see you safe at the Castle again. I will die else, but it is easy; I will not die. Come back with me. Why is it that we should both die?"

'"That is all right," I said; "you are quite right; you have done all you promised to do, and done it well too. Go back. Tell them at the Coast that we got through. I will wait here till these fellows come, and they will take me to the Bishop. That is all I want."

'He looked at me for a moment or two, as I thought.

'"Do you know, Sir Percival," he said— "do you know what you say?"

'"Oh yes, my good fellow," I said, "I know: don't bother, it is so hot."

'As I spoke a long line of dark figures drew out from among the huts and came creeping towards us with swift and gliding pace. Ned turned and bolted into the bush.

'I don't very well know what happened after this, for I was dazed and blinded with the heat, and I thought that I was ill with fever, and I really didn't know what I did. I felt wearied out and ready to fall asleep. I suppose the blacks came about me and seized me, but I don't know that I told them any-thing or asked for the Bishop. All that I remember is that, after an interminable march, as it seemed, over the burning plain, there was a lot of noise, and a crowd of black figures, and a street of huts and strange temples, and I was pushed about a good deal; and then all at once I was in a cool, shaded hut, very lofty, out of the sun, and there were no blacks, but in front of me, by a table where he had been writing, there was a tall English gentleman that looked to me like a god. He was haggard-looking, and his dress was dishevelled and torn; but I never could have dreamt that I could be so delighted to see any man as I was when I saw him.

'He rose suddenly when he saw me, and a wonderful smile lighted his face.

'"The Lord hath heard me," he said; "blessed be the name of the Lord."

'"No," I said; "do not deceive yourself; let me speak, for I have only a few moments to do it in. I am Percival Massareen on the staff. We heard about you, and we thought on the Coast—Sir Charles thought—that if an English officer could get through, he might be of some use in overawing the king. I am through, but I am alone; all my people have deserted me, frightened by the rumours they heard. More than that, I am ill. I have the fever, and have only a few moments before me to keep my senses. Do not deceive yourself."

'He looked at me, still with the serene and happy smile.

'"I was not mistaken," he said; "the Lord *hath* heard me. Let us give thanks unto Him in His Holy Church."

'He came up to me and took my hand.

'"I think that you are wrong," he said; "I do not think that you have the fever.

You are worn out and blinded by the heat. What you must have gone through would have killed most men. You must lie down and sleep. But before that you will do me the greatest favour possible for man. I do not know how long I have to live. You will take the sacrament with me."

' I do not know how I remember all that he said, but I do recall every word.

' " We have no wine," he said, " and I have eaten all my bread for the day. It was a tradition of the Middle Ages, of which perhaps you may have heard, that if a man was dying on the field of battle, and if he eat three blades of grass with intention, he received the sacrament though other priest were none. You are not actually dying in battle, but you are dying on a nobler field —I see it in your eyes—a field where the Lord Jesus keeps the wager of battle against the world, the flesh, and hell."

' We knelt down, and he gathered some

blades of grass that grew up in the floor of the hut and forced their way under its wooden walls. He recited the Communion Service. I knew little of what passed; but I know that I eat the three blades of grass he gave me. Then I was lying down upon his rush-matted bed, and almost in a moment I was asleep.

'I must have slept a long time, for when I awoke it was morning, and the Bishop was gone. Standing by my bed was a native, who seemed to regard me with somewhat friendly eyes. When I had remembered where I was, I said to him :

'"Where is the Bishop?"

'"The Bishop is dead," he said. "When they came to fetch him he stood a moment by your side as you slept. 'He is dreaming of England,' he said; 'why should I wake nim?' and so he went out."

'"Who are you?" I said.

'"I am a Christian," said the black; "but——"

'A sudden thought struck me; I felt so fresh and strong after my sleep, and as I looked across the hut I saw the Bishop's paper and pens and ink on the table.

'"Look here!" I said; "here is gold. If I make up a parcel to-day will you promise me, —you say you are a Christian,—will you promise me to get it sent down to the Coast? The governor will pay the messenger who brings it well."

'"I promise," said the man. "I am a Christian. Give me the gold."

'"You can take all there is," I said.

'Then I got up and began to write. I am glad that I began so soon, for I could not have written it now. I think the Bishop must have been mistaken, and that I must have taken the fatal fever, for I have a strange uncertainty, and I cannot keep my thoughts.

'I have been asleep again; but whether I am awake or asleep it hardly seems to make

any difference, for I see the same things.   I
see the sweep of English forest, the oaks and
ashes, and the green expanse of leaves, and
the squirrels and the birds — and then, in
a moment, I see the strange palm-leaves, and
the cactus flowers, and the monkeys, and I
hear the wild discordant music, and I see the
dances of the blacks.   The Christian native is
come in again.

'"The Bishop is dead," he says; "your
turn is to-morrow.   When you hear the gongs
in the morning you will know that the idol
sacrifice is begun.   I am a Christian.   I will
come in in the morning, and see to the parcel
—and the gold."

'I have been asleep again.   I must have
slept well, for it is morning; but I hardly
know what I write.   I hardly know what I
see, for still the English forest is before me,
mixed with the groves of cactus and of palm.

'The gongs have begun to sound.   What is this?   Surely this cannot be death!

'I see the chase and the dark tower, and the flashing waters of the channel gleaming in light, and before me on her horse, beneath the oak-trees, an English girl.   Who is this, seated in her saddle beneath the rustling branches of the oak?   She turns her head towards me— Virginia?   No, it is Constance—Constance with the pleading eyes.   And the moment that she turns her look on me it all vanishes —the English oaks and ashes, and the groves of cactus and of palm—and the walls of the hut burst asunder to let in the dazzling light —and down the bright, clear spaces of the light files a long procession of noble forms— Constance! Constance!   Who is this?
And the armies that are in heaven follow Him upon white horses, clothed in fine linen white   and clean.'

This was what was written. It was not signed. The first portion was clearly and fairly written, but the last sentences were uneven and difficult to read. They wandered down the page in a broken fashion, with wide gaps, and the last two or three words were almost illegible. The packet had been carefully tied up, and was directed in his own hand with tolerable distinctness. More than this is known only to the savage heathen— and to God.

How long I lay with this writing before me and the bronze cross upon the words I do not know. I only know that when I looked up the sunshine was gilding the oaken benches and the escutcheons and tablets on the chancel walls, and in the fragments of stained glass in the eastern window, through which the green shimmer of the young oak leaves could be seen, I knew that the word 'Percival' was written.

'Lord, we have heard with our ears, and our fathers have declared unto us, the noble works that thou didst in their days and in the old time before them.'

THE END

Printed by R. & R. CLARK, *Edinburgh.*

MACMILLAN'S THREE-AND-SIXPENNY SERIES

OF

WORKS BY POPULAR AUTHORS.

In Crown 8vo.   Cloth extra.   Price 3s. 6d. each.

By Sir SAMUEL BAKER.
TRUE TALES FOR MY GRANDSONS.

Reprinted from the "TIMES."
BIOGRAPHIES OF EMINENT PERSONS. In 4 volumes.

By ROLF BOLDREWOOD
SATURDAY REVIEW—"Mr. Boldrewood can tell what he knows with great point and vigour, and there is no better reading than the adventurous parts of his books."
PALL MALL GAZETTE—"The volumes are brimful of adventure, in which gold, gold-diggers, prospectors, claim-holders, take an active part."

ROBBERY UNDER ARMS.	THE SQUATTER'S DREAM.
THE MINER'S RIGHT.	A SYDNEY-SIDE SAXON.
A COLONIAL REFORMER.	NEVERMORE.

By FRANCES HODGSON BURNETT.
LOUISIANA; AND THAT LASS O' LOWRIE'S.

By HUGH CONWAY.
MORNING POST—"Life-like and full of individuality."
DAILY NEWS—"Throughout written with spirit, good feeling, and ability, and a certain dash of humour."
LIVING OR DEAD? . | A FAMILY AFFAIR.

By Mrs. CRAIK.
(The Author of "JOHN HALIFAX, GENTLEMAN.")

OLIVE. With Illustrations by G. BOWERS.	TWO MARRIAGES.
THE OGILVIES. With Illustrations.	THE LAUREL BUSH.
AGATHA'S HUSBAND. With Illustrations.	MY MOTHER AND I. With Illustrations.
HEAD OF THE FAMILY. With Illustrations.	MISS TOMMY: A Mediæval Romance. Illustrated.
	KING ARTHUR: Not a Love Story.

SERMONS OUT OF CHURCH.

By F. MARION CRAWFORD.
SPECTATOR—"With the solitary exception of Mrs. Oliphant we have no living novelist more distinguished for variety of theme and range of imaginative outlook than Mr. Marion Crawford."

MR. ISAACS: A Tale of Modern India. Portrait of Author.	A TALE OF A LONELY PARISH.
DR. CLAUDIUS: A True Story.	PAUL PATOFF.
A ROMAN SINGER.	WITH THE IMMORTALS.
ZOROASTER.	GREIFENSTEIN.
MARZIO'S CRUCIFIX	SANT' ILARIO.
	A CIGARETTE-MAKER'S ROMANCE

KHALED.

By Sir HENRY CUNNINGHAM, K.C.I.E.
ST. JAMES'S GAZETTE—"Interesting as specimens of romance, the style of writing is so excellent—scholarly and at the same time easy and natural—that the volumes are worth reading on that account alone. But there is also masterly description of persons, places, and things; skilful analysis of character; a constant play of wit and humour; and a happy gift of instantaneous portraiture."
THE CŒRULEANS. | THE HERIOTS.
WHEAT AND TARES.

A CLASSIFIED
CATALOGUE OF BOOKS
IN GENERAL LITERATURE
PUBLISHED BY
MACMILLAN AND CO.
BEDFORD STREET, STRAND, LONDON, W.C.

For purely Educational Works see MACMILLAN AND CO.'s *Educational Catalogue*

AGRICULTURE.

(*See also* BOTANY; GARDENING.)

FRANKLAND (Prof. P. F.).—A HANDBOOK OF AGRICULTURAL CHEMICAL ANALYSIS. Cr. 8vo. 7s. 6d.

LAURIE (A. P.).—THE FOOD OF PLANTS. 18mo. 1s.

NICHOLLS (H. A. A.)—TEXT BOOK OF TROPICAL AGRICULTURE. Cr. 8vo. 6s.

TANNER (Henry).—ELEMENTARY LESSONS IN THE SCIENCE OF AGRICULTURAL PRACTICE. Fcp. 8vo. 3s. 6d.

—— FIRST PRINCIPLES OF AGRICULTURE. 18mo. 1s.

—— THE PRINCIPLES OF AGRICULTURE. For Use in Elementary Schools. Ext. fcp. 8vo.—THE ALPHABET OF THE PRINCIPLES OF AGRICULTURE. 6d.—FURTHER STEPS IN THE PRINCIPLES OF AGRICULTURE. 1s.—ELEMENTARY SCHOOL READINGS ON THE PRINCIPLES OF AGRICULTURE FOR THE THIRD STAGE. 1s.

—— THE ABBOT'S FARM; or, Practice with Science. Cr. 8vo. 3s. 6d.

ANATOMY, Human. (*See* PHYSIOLOGY.)

ANTHROPOLOGY.

BROWN (J. Allen).—PALÆOLITHIC MAN IN NORTH-WEST MIDDLESEX. 8vo. 7s. 6d.

DAWKINS (Prof. W. Boyd).—EARLY MAN IN BRITAIN AND HIS PLACE IN THE TERTIARY PERIOD. Med. 8vo. 25s.

DAWSON (James). — AUSTRALIAN ABORIGINES. Small 4to. 14s.

FINCK (Henry T.).—ROMANTIC LOVE AND PERSONAL BEAUTY. 2 vols. Cr. 8vo. 18s.

FISON (L.) and HOWITT (A. W.).—KAMILAROI AND KURNAI GROUP. Group-Marriage and Relationship, and Marriage by Elopement. 8vo. 15s.

FRAZER (J. G.).—THE GOLDEN BOUGH: A Study in Comparative Religion. 2 vols. 8vo. 28s.

GALTON (Francis).—ENGLISH MEN OF SCIENCE: THEIR NATURE AND NURTURE. 8vo. 8s. 6d.

—— INQUIRIES INTO HUMAN FACULTY AND ITS DEVELOPMENT. 8vo. 16s.

—— LIFE-HISTORY ALBUM: Being a Personal Note-book, combining Diary, Photograph Album, a Register of Height, Weight, and other Anthropometrical Observations, and a Record of Illnesses. 4to. 3s. 6d.—Or with Cards of Wool for Testing Colour Vision. 4s. 6d.

GALTON (Francis).—NATURAL INHERITANCE. 8vo. 9s.

—— RECORD OF FAMILY FACULTIES. Consisting of Tabular Forms and Directions for Entering Data. 4to. 2s. 6d.

—— HEREDITARY GENIUS: An Enquiry into its Laws and Consequences. Ext. cr. 8vo. 7s. net.

—— FINGER PRINTS. 8vo. 6s. net.

M'LENNAN (J. F.).—THE PATRIARCHAL THEORY. Edited and completed by DONALD M'LENNAN, M.A. 8vo. 14s.

—— STUDIES IN ANCIENT HISTORY. Comprising "Primitive Marriage." 8vo. 16s.

MONTELIUS—WOODS. — THE CIVILISATION OF SWEDEN IN HEATHEN TIMES. By Prof. OSCAR MONTELIUS. Translated by Rev. F. H. WOODS. Illustr. 8vo. 14s.

TURNER (Rev. Geo.).—SAMOA, A HUNDRED YEARS AGO AND LONG BEFORE. Cr. 8vo. 9s.

TYLOR (E. B.). — ANTHROPOLOGY. With Illustrations. Cr. 8vo. 7s. 6d.

WESTERMARCK (Dr. Edward).—THE HISTORY OF HUMAN MARRIAGE. With Preface by Dr. A. R. WALLACE. 8vo. 14s. net.

WILSON (Sir Daniel).—PREHISTORIC ANNALS OF SCOTLAND. Illustrated. 2 vols. 8vo. 36s.

—— PREHISTORIC MAN: Researches into the Origin of Civilisation in the Old and New World. Illustrated. 2 vols. 8vo. 36s.

—— THE RIGHT HAND: LEFT-HANDEDNESS. Cr. 8vo. 4s. 6d.

ANTIQUITIES.

(*See also* ANTHROPOLOGY.)

ATKINSON (Rev. J. C.).—FORTY YEARS IN A MOORLAND PARISH. Ext. cr. 8vo. 8s. 6d. net.—*Illustrated Edition.* 12s. net.

BURN (Robert).—ROMAN LITERATURE IN RELATION TO ROMAN ART. With Illustrations. Ext. cr. 8vo. 14s.

DILETTANTI SOCIETY'S PUBLICATIONS.

ANTIQUITIES OF IONIA. Vols. I.—III. 3l. 2s. each, or 5l. 5s. the set, net.—Vol. IV. Folio, half morocco, 3l. 13s. 6d. net.

AN INVESTIGATION OF THE PRINCIPLES OF ATHENIAN ARCHITECTURE. By F. C. PENROSE. Illustrated. Folio. 7l. 7s. net.

SPECIMENS OF ANCIENT SCULPTURE: EGYPTIAN, ETRUSCAN, GREEK, AND ROMAN. Vol. II. Folio. 5l. 5s. net.

ANTIQUITIES—*continued.*

DYER (Louis).—STUDIES OF THE GODS IN GREECE AT CERTAIN SANCTUARIES RECENTLY EXCAVATED. Ext. cr. 8vo. 8s. 6d. net.

FOWLER (W. W.).—THE CITY-STATE OF THE GREEKS AND ROMANS. Cr. 8vo. 5s.

GARDNER (Percy).—SAMOS AND SAMIAN COINS: An Essay. 8vo. 7s. 6d.

GOW (J., Litt.D.).—A COMPANION TO SCHOOL CLASSICS. Illustrated. 3rd Ed. Cr. 8vo. 6s.

HARRISON (Miss Jane) and VERRALL (Mrs.).—MYTHOLOGY AND MONUMENTS OF ANCIENT ATHENS. Illustrated. Cr. 8vo. 16s.

LANCIANI (Prof. R.).—ANCIENT ROME IN THE LIGHT OF RECENT DISCOVERIES. 4to. 24s.
—— PAGAN AND CHRISTIAN ROME. 4to. 24s.

MAHAFFY (Prof. J. P.).—A PRIMER OF GREEK ANTIQUITIES. 18mo. 1s.
—— SOCIAL LIFE IN GREECE FROM HOMER TO MENANDER. 6th Edit. Cr. 8vo. 9s.
—— RAMBLES AND STUDIES IN GREECE. Illustrated. 3rd Edit. Cr. 8vo. 10s. 6d. (*See also* HISTORY, p. 11.)

NEWTON (Sir C. T.).—ESSAYS ON ART AND ARCHÆOLOGY. 8vo. 12s. 6d.

SCHUCHHARDT (C.).—DR. SCHLIEMANN'S EXCAVATIONS AT TROY, TIRYNS, MYCENAE, ORCHOMENOS, ITHACA, IN THE LIGHT OF RECENT KNOWLEDGE. Trans. by EUGENIE SELLERS. Preface by WALTER LEAF, Litt.D. Illustrated. 8vo. 18s. net.

STRANGFORD. (*See* VOYAGES & TRAVELS.)

WALDSTEIN (C.).—CATALOGUE OF CASTS IN THE MUSEUM OF CLASSICAL ARCHÆOLOGY, CAMBRIDGE. Crown 8vo. 1s. 6d.—Large Paper Edition. Small 4to. 5s.

WHITE (Gilbert). (*See* NATURAL HISTORY.)

WILKINS (Prof. A. S.).—A PRIMER OF ROMAN ANTIQUITIES. 18mo. 1s.

ARCHÆOLOGY. (*See* ANTIQUITIES.)

ARCHITECTURE.

FREEMAN (Prof. E. A.).—HISTORY OF THE CATHEDRAL CHURCH OF WELLS. Cr. 8vo. 3s. 6d.

HULL (E.).—A TREATISE ON ORNAMENTAL AND BUILDING STONES OF GREAT BRITAIN AND FOREIGN COUNTRIES. 8vo. 12s.

MOORE (Prof. C. H.).—THE DEVELOPMENT AND CHARACTER OF GOTHIC ARCHITECTURE. Illustrated. Med. 8vo. 18s.

PENROSE (F. C.). (*See* ANTIQUITIES.)

STEVENSON (J. J.).—HOUSE ARCHITECTURE. With Illustrations. 2 vols. Roy. 8vo. 18s. each.—Vol. I. ARCHITECTURE; Vol. II. HOUSE PLANNING.

ART.

(*See also* MUSIC.)

ART AT HOME SERIES. Edited by W. J. LOFTIE, B.A. Cr. 8vo.
THE BEDROOM AND BOUDOIR. By Lady BARKER. 2s. 6d.
NEEDLEWORK. By ELIZABETH GLAISTER. Illustrated. 2s. 6d.
MUSIC IN THE HOUSE. By JOHN HULLAH. 4th edit. 2s. 6d.

ART AT HOME SERIES—*continued.*
THE DINING-ROOM. By Mrs. LOFTIE. With Illustrations. 2nd Edit. 2s. 6d.
AMATEUR THEATRICALS. By WALTER H. POLLOCK and LADY POLLOCK. Illustrated by KATE GREENAWAY. 2s. 6d.

ATKINSON (J. B.).—AN ART TOUR TO NORTHERN CAPITALS OF EUROPE. 8vo. 12s.

BURN (Robert). (*See* ANTIQUITIES.)

CARR (J. Comyns).—PAPERS ON ART. Cr. 8vo. 8s. 6d.

COLLIER (Hon. John).—A PRIMER OF ART. 18mo. 1s.

COOK (E. T.).—A POPULAR HANDBOOK TO THE NATIONAL GALLERY. Including Notes collected from the Works of Mr. RUSKIN. 3rd Edit. Cr. 8vo, half morocco. 14s.—Large paper Edition, 250 copies. 2 vols. 8vo.

DELAMOTTE (Prof. P. H.).—A BEGINNER'S DRAWING-BOOK. Cr. 8vo. 3s. 6d.

ELLIS (Tristram).—SKETCHING FROM NATURE. Illustr. by H. STACY MARKS, R.A., and the Author. 2nd Edit. Cr. 8vo. 3s. 6d.

HAMERTON (P. G.).—THOUGHTS ABOUT ART. New Edit. Cr. 8vo. 8s. 6d.

HERKOMER (H.).—ETCHING AND MEZZOTINT ENGRAVING. 4to. 42s. net.

HOOPER (W. H.) and PHILLIPS (W. C.).—A MANUAL OF MARKS ON POTTERY AND PORCELAIN. 16mo. 4s. 6d.

HUNT (W.).—TALKS ABOUT ART. With a Letter from Sir J. E. MILLAIS, Bart., R.A. Cr. 8vo. 3s. 6d.

HUTCHINSON (G. W. C.).—SOME HINTS ON LEARNING TO DRAW. Roy. 8vo. 8s. 6d.

LECTURES ON ART. By REGD. STUART POOLE, Professor W. B. RICHMOND, E. J. POYNTER, R.A., J. T. MICKLETHWAITE, and WILLIAM MORRIS. Cr. 8vo. 4s. 6d

NEWTON (Sir C. T.).—(*See* ANTIQUITIES.)

PALGRAVE (Prof. F. T.).—ESSAYS ON ART. Ext. fcp. 8vo. 6s.

PATER (W.).—THE RENAISSANCE: Studies in Art and Poetry. 4th Edit. Cr. 8vo. 10s. 6d.

PENNELL (Joseph).—PEN DRAWING AND PEN DRAUGHTSMEN. With 158 Illustrations. 4to. 3l. 13s. 6d. net.

PROPERT (J. Lumsden).—A HISTORY OF MINIATURE ART. Illustrated. Super roy. 4to. 3l. 13s. 6d.—Bound in vellum. 4l. 14s. 6d.

TURNER'S LIBER STUDIORUM: A DESCRIPTION AND A CATALOGUE. By W. G. RAWLINSON. Med. 8vo. 12s. 6d.

TYRWHITT (Rev. R. St. John).—OUR SKETCHING CLUB. 5th Edit. Cr. 8vo. 7s. 6d.

WYATT (Sir M. Digby).—FINE ART: A Sketch of its History, Theory, Practice, and Application to Industry. 8vo. 5s.

ASTRONOMY.

AIRY (Sir G. B.).—POPULAR ASTRONOMY. Illustrated. 7th Edit. Fcp. 8vo. 4s. 6d.
—— GRAVITATION. An Elementary Explanation of the Principal Perturbations in the Solar System. 2nd Edit. Cr. 8vo. 7s. 6d.

BLAKE (J. F.).—ASTRONOMICAL MYTHS. With Illustrations. Cr. 8vo. 9s.

CHEYNE (C. H. H.).—AN ELEMENTARY TREATISE ON THE PLANETARY THEORY. Cr. 8vo. 7s. 6d.

CLARK (L.) and SADLER (H.).—THE STAR GUIDE. Roy. 8vo. 5s.

CROSSLEY (E.), GLEDHILL (J.), and WILSON (J. M.).—A HANDBOOK OF DOUBLE STARS. 8vo. 21s.

—— CORRECTIONS TO THE HANDBOOK OF DOUBLE STARS. 8vo. 1s.

FORBES (Prof. George).—THE TRANSIT OF VENUS. Illustrated. Cr. 8vo. 3s. 6d.

GODFRAY (Hugh).—AN ELEMENTARY TREATISE ON THE LUNAR THEORY. 2nd Edit. Cr. 8vo. 5s. 6d.

—— A TREATISE ON ASTRONOMY, FOR THE USE OF COLLEGES AND SCHOOLS. 8vo. 12s. 6d.

LOCKYER (J. Norman, F.R.S.).—A PRIMER OF ASTRONOMY. Illustrated. 18mo. 1s.

—— ELEMENTARY LESSONS IN ASTRONOMY. Illustr. New Edition. Fcp. 8vo. 5s. 6d.

—— QUESTIONS ON THE SAME. By J. FORBES ROBERTSON. Fcp. 8vo. 1s. 6d.

—— THE CHEMISTRY OF THE SUN. Illustrated. 8vo. 14s.

—— THE METEORITIC HYPOTHESIS OF THE ORIGIN OF COSMICAL SYSTEMS. Illustrated. 8vo. 17s. net.

—— THE EVOLUTION OF THE HEAVENS AND THE EARTH. Illustrated. Cr. 8vo.

—— STAR-GAZING PAST AND PRESENT. Expanded from Notes with the assistance of G. M. SEABROKE. Roy. 8vo. 21s.

LODGE (O. J.).—PIONEERS OF SCIENCE. Ex. cr. 8vo. 7s. 6d.

MILLER (R. Kalley).—THE ROMANCE OF ASTRONOMY. 2nd Edit. Cr. 8vo. 4s. 6d.

NEWCOMB (Prof. Simon).—POPULAR ASTRONOMY. Engravings and Maps. 8vo. 18s.

RADCLIFFE (Charles B.).—BEHIND THE TIDES. 8vo. 4s. 6d.

ROSCOE—SCHUSTER. (See CHEMISTRY.)

ATLASES.

(See also GEOGRAPHY).

BARTHOLOMEW (J. G.).—ELEMENTARY SCHOOL ATLAS. 4to. 1s.

—— PHYSICAL AND POLITICAL SCHOOL ATLAS. 80 maps. 4to. 8s. 6d.; half mor. 10s. 6d.

—— LIBRARY REFERENCE ATLAS OF THE WORLD. With Index to 100,000 places. Folio. 52s. 6d. net.—Also in 7 parts. 5s. net; Geographical Index. 7s. 6d. net.

LABBERTON (R. H.).—NEW HISTORICAL ATLAS AND GENERAL HISTORY. 4to. 15s.

BIBLE. (See under THEOLOGY, p. 32.)

BIBLIOGRAPHY.

A BIBLIOGRAPHICAL CATALOGUE OF MACMILLAN AND CO.'S PUBLICATIONS, 1843—89. Med. 8vo. 10s. net.

BIBLIOGRAPHY—continued.

MAYOR (Prof. John E. B.).—A BIBLIOGRAPHICAL CLUE TO LATIN LITERATURE. Cr. 8vo. 10s. 6d.

RYLAND (F.).—CHRONOLOGICAL OUTLINES OF ENGLISH LITERATURE. Cr. 8vo. 6s.

BIOGRAPHY.

(See also HISTORY.)

For other subjects of BIOGRAPHY, *see* ENGLISH MEN OF LETTERS, ENGLISH MEN OF ACTION, TWELVE ENGLISH STATESMEN.

ABBOTT (E. A.).—THE ANGLICAN CAREER OF CARDINAL NEWMAN. 2 vols. 8vo. 25s. net.

AGASSIZ (Louis): HIS LIFE AND CORRESPONDENCE. Edited by ELIZABETH CARY AGASSIZ. 2 vols. Cr. 8vo. 18s.

ALBEMARLE (Earl of).—FIFTY YEARS OF MY LIFE. 3rd Edit., revised. Cr. 8vo. 7s. 6d.

ALFRED THE GREAT. By THOMAS HUGHES. Cr. 8vo. 6s.

AMIEL (H. F.)-THE JOURNAL INTIME. Trans. Mrs. HUMPHRY WARD. 2nd Ed. Cr. 8vo. 6s.

ANDREWS (Dr. Thomas). (See PHYSICS.)

ARNAULD, ANGELIQUE. By FRANCES MARTIN. Cr. 8vo. 4s. 6d.

ARTEVELDE. JAMES AND PHILIP VAN ARTEVELDE. By W. J. ASHLEY. Cr. 8vo. 6s.

BACON (Francis): AN ACCOUNT OF HIS LIFE AND WORKS. By E. A. ABBOTT. 8vo. 14s.

BARNES. LIFE OF WILLIAM BARNES, POET AND PHILOLOGIST. By his Daughter, LUCY BAXTER ("Leader Scott"). Cr. 8vo. 7s. 6d.

BERLIOZ (Hector): AUTOBIOGRAPHY OF. Trns. by R. & E. HOLMES. 2 vols. Cr. 8vo. 21s.

BERNARD (St.). THE LIFE AND TIMES OF ST. BERNARD, ABBOT OF CLAIRVAUX. By J. C. MORISON, M.A. Cr. 8vo. 6s.

BLACKBURNE. LIFE OF THE RIGHT HON. FRANCIS BLACKBURNE, late Lord Chancellor of Ireland, by his Son, EDWARD BLACKBURNE. With Portrait. 8vo. 12s.

BLAKE. LIFE OF WILLIAM BLAKE. With Selections from his Poems, etc. Illustr. from Blake's own Works. By ALEXANDER GILCHRIST. 2 vols. Med. 8vo. 42s.

BOLEYN (Anne): A CHAPTER OF ENGLISH HISTORY, 1527—36. By PAUL FRIEDMANN. 2 vols. 8vo. 28s.

BROOKE (Sir Jas.), THE RAJA OF SARAWAK (Life of). By GERTRUDE L. JACOB. 2 vols. 8vo. 25s.

BURKE. By JOHN MORLEY. Globe 8vo. 5s.

CALVIN. (See SELECT BIOGRAPHY, p. 6.)

CAMPBELL (Sir G.).—MEMOIRS OF MY INDIAN CAREER. Edited by Sir C. E. BERNARD. 2 vols. 8vo. 21s. net.

CARLYLE (Thomas). Edited by CHARLES E. NORTON. Cr. 8vo.
—— REMINISCENCES. 2 vols. 12s.
—— EARLY LETTERS, 1814—26. 2 vols. 18s.
—— LETTERS, 1826—36. 2 vols. 18s.
—— CORRESPONDENCE BETWEEN GOETHE AND CARLYLE. 9s.

BIOGRAPHY—*continued.*

CARSTARES (Wm.): A Character and Career of the Revolutionary Epoch (1649—1715). By R. H. Story. 8vo. 12s.

CAVOUR. (*See* Select Biography, p. 6.)

CHATTERTON: A Story of the Year 1770. By Prof. David Masson. Cr. 8vo. 5s.

—— A Biographical Study. By Sir Daniel Wilson. Cr. 8vo. 6s. 6d.

CLARK. Memorials from Journals and Letters of Samuel Clark, M.A. Edited by His Wife. Cr. 8vo. 7s. 6d.

CLOUGH (A. H.). (*See* Literature, p. 20.)

COMBE. Life of George Combe. By Charles Gibbon. 2 vols. 8vo. 32s.

CROMWELL. (*See* Select Biography, p. 6.)

DAMIEN (Father): A Journey from Cashmere to his Home in Hawaii. By Edward Clifford. Portrait. Cr. 8vo. 2s. 6d.

DANTE: and other Essays. By Dean Church. Globe 8vo. 5s.

DARWIN (Charles): Memorial Notices, By T. H. Huxley, G. J. Romanes, Sir Arch. Geikie, and W. Thiselton Dyer. With Portrait. Cr. 8vo. 2s. 6d.

DEÁK (Francis): Hungarian Statesman. A Memoir. 8vo. 12s. 6d.

DRUMMOND OF HAWTHORNDEN. By Prof. D. Masson. Cr. 8vo. 10s. 6d.

EADIE. Life of John Eadie, D.D. By James Brown, D.D. Cr. 8vo. 7s. 6d.

ELLIOTT. Life of H. V. Elliott, of Brighton. By J. Bateman. Cr. 8vo. 6s.

EMERSON. Life of Ralph Waldo Emerson. By J. L. Cabot. 2 vols. Cr. 8vo. 18s.

ENGLISH MEN OF ACTION. Cr. 8vo. With Portraits. 2s. 6d. each.

Clive. By Colonel Sir Charles Wilson.
Cook (Captain). By Walter Besant.
Dampier. By W. Clark Russell.
Drake. By Julian Corbett.
Gordon (General). By Col. Sir W. Butler.
Hastings (Warren). By Sir A. Lyall.
Havelock (Sir Henry). By A. Forbes.
Henry V. By the Rev. A. J. Church.
Lawrence (Lord). By Sir Rich. Temple.
Livingstone. By Thomas Hughes.
Monk. By Julian Corbett.
Montrose. By Mowbray Morris.
Moore (Sir John). By Col. Maurice. [*In prep.*
Napier (Sir Charles). By Colonel Sir Wm. Butler.
Peterborough. By W. Stebbing.
Rodney. By David Hannay.
Simon de Montfort. By G. W. Prothero. [*In prep.*
Strafford. By H. D. Traill.
Warwick, the King-Maker. By C. W. Oman.
Wellington. By George Hooper.

ENGLISH MEN OF LETTERS. Edited by John Morley. Cr. 8vo. 2s. 6d. each. Cheap Edition, 1s 6d. ; sewed, 1s.
Addison. By W. J. Courthope.
Bacon. By Dean Church.
Bentley. By Prof. Jebb.

ENGLISH MEN OF LETTERS—*contd.*
Bunyan. By J. A. Froude.
Burke. By John Morley.
Burns. By Principal Shairp.
Byron. By John Nichol.
Carlyle. By John Nichol.
Chaucer. By Prof. A. W. Ward.
Coleridge. By H. D. Traill.
Cowper. By Goldwin Smith.
Defoe. By W. Minto.
De Quincey. By Prof. Masson.
Dickens. By A. W. Ward.
Dryden. By G. Saintsbury.
Fielding. By Austin Dobson.
Gibbon. By J. Cotter Morison.
Goldsmith. By William Black.
Gray. By Edmund Gosse.
Hawthorne. By Henry James.
Hume. By T. H. Huxley.
Johnson. By Leslie Stephen.
Keats. By Sidney Colvin.
Lamb. By Rev. Alfred Ainger.
Landor. By Sidney Colvin.
Locke. By Prof. Fowler.
Macaulay. By J. Cotter Morison.
Milton. By Mark Pattison.
Pope. By Leslie Stephen.
Scott. By R. H. Hutton.
Shelley. By J. A. Symonds.
Sheridan. By Mrs. Oliphant.
Sidney. By J. A. Symonds.
Southey. By Prof. Dowden.
Spenser. By Dean Church.
Sterne. By H. D. Traill.
Swift. By Leslie Stephen.
Thackeray. By Anthony Trollope.
Wordsworth. By F. W. H. Myers.

ENGLISH STATESMEN, TWELVE Cr. 8vo. 2s. 6d. each.

William the Conqueror. By Edward A. Freeman, D.C.L., LL.D.
Henry II. By Mrs. J. R. Green.
Edward I. By T. F. Tout, M.A. [*In prep.*
Henry VII. By James Gairdner.
Cardinal Wolsey. By Bp. Creighton.
Elizabeth. By E. S. Beesly.
Oliver Cromwell. By F. Harrison.
William III. By H. D. Traill.
Walpole. By John Morley.
Chatham. By John Morley. [*In the Press.*
Pitt. By Lord Rosebery.
Peel. By J. R. Thursfield.

EPICTETUS. (*See* Select Biography, p 6)

FAIRFAX. Life of Robert Fairfax of Steeton, Vice-Admiral, Alderman, and Member for York, A.D. 1666-1725. By Clements R. Markham, C.B. 8vo. 12s. 6d

FITZGERALD (Edward). (*See* Literature, p. 21.)

FORBES (Edward): Memoir of. By George Wilson, M.P., and Sir Archibald Geikie, F.R.S., etc. Demy 8vo. 14s.

FRANCIS OF ASSISI. By Mrs. Oliphant. Cr. 8vo. 6s.

FRASER. James Fraser, Second Bishop of Manchester: A Memoir. By T. Hughes. Cr. 8vo. 6s.

GARIBALDI. (*See* Select Biography, p. 6.)

GOETHE: Life of. By Prof. Heinrich Düntzer. Translated by T. W. Lyster. 2 vols. Cr. 8vo. 21s.

GOETHE AND CARLYLE. (*See* CARLYLE.)

GORDON (General): A SKETCH. By REGINALD H. BARNES. Cr. 8vo. 1s.

—— LETTERS OF GENERAL C. G. GORDON TO HIS SISTER, M. A. GORDON. 4th Edit. Cr. 8vo. 3s. 6d.

HANDEL: LIFE OF. By W. S. ROCKSTRO. Cr. 8vo. 10s. 6d.

HAUSER (K.): TRUE STORY OF. By the DUCHESS OF CLEVELAND. Cr. 8vo. 4s. 6d.

HOBART. (*See* COLLECTED WORKS, p. 22.)

HODGSON. MEMOIR OF REV. FRANCIS HODGSON, B.D. By his Son, Rev. JAMES T. HODGSON, M.A. 2 vols. Cr. 8vo. 18s.

JEVONS (W. Stanley).—LETTERS AND JOURNAL. Edited by HIS WIFE. 8vo. 14s.

KAVANAGH (Rt. Hon. A. McMurrough): A BIOGRAPHY. From papers chiefly unpublished, compiled by his Cousin, SARAH L. STEELE. With Portrait. 8vo. 14s. net.

KINGSLEY: HIS LETTERS, AND MEMORIES OF HIS LIFE. Edited by HIS WIFE. 2 vols. Cr. 8vo. 12s.—Cheap Edition. 1 vol. 6s.

LAMB. THE LIFE OF CHARLES LAMB. By Rev. ALFRED AINGER, M.A. Globe 8vo. 5s.

LETHBRIDGE (Sir R.).—GOLDEN BOOK OF INDIA. Royal 8vo. 40s.

LOUIS (St.). (*See* SELECT BIOGRAPHY, p. 6.)

MACMILLAN (D.). MEMOIR OF DANIEL MACMILLAN. By THOMAS HUGHES, Q.C. With Portrait. Cr. 8vo. 4s. 6d.—Cheap Edition. Cr. 8vo, sewed. 1s.

MALTHUS AND HIS WORK. By JAMES BONAR. 8vo. 12s. 6d.

MARCUS AURELIUS. (*See* SELECT BIOGRAPHY, p. 6.)

MATHEWS. THE LIFE OF CHARLES J. MATHEWS. Edited by CHARLES DICKENS. With Portraits. 2 vols. 8vo. 25s.

MAURICE. LIFE OF FREDERICK DENISON MAURICE. By his Son, FREDERICK MAURICE, Two Portraits. 2 vols. 8vo. 36s.—Popular Edit. (4th Thousand). 2 vols. Cr. 8vo. 16s.

MAXWELL. PROFESSOR CLERK MAXWELL, A LIFE OF. By Prof. L. CAMPBELL, M.A., and W. GARNETT, M.A. Cr. 8vo. 7s. 6d.

MAZZINI (*See* SELECT BIOGRAPHY, p. 6.)

MELBOURNE. MEMOIRS OF VISCOUNT MELBOURNE. By W. M. TORRENS. With Portrait. 2nd Edit. 2 vols. 8vo. 32s.

MILTON. THE LIFE OF JOHN MILTON. By Prof. DAVID MASSON. Vol. I., 21s.; Vol. III., 18s.; Vols. IV. and V., 32s.; Vol. VI., with Portrait, 21s. (*See also* p. 16.)

MILTON, JOHNSON'S LIFE OF. With Introduction and Notes by K. DEIGHTON. Globe 8vo. 1s. 9d.

NAPOLEON I., HISTORY OF. By P. LANFREY. 4 vols. Cr. 8vo. 30s.

NELSON. SOUTHEY'S LIFE OF NELSON. With Introduction and Notes by MICHAEL MACMILLAN, B.A. Globe 8vo. 3s. 6d.

NORTH (M.).—RECOLLECTIONS OF A HAPPY LIFE. Being the Autobiography of MARIANNE NORTH. Ed. by Mrs. J. A. SYMONDS. 2nd Edit. 2 vols. Ex. cr. 8vo. 17s. net.

—— SOME FURTHER RECOLLECTIONS OF A HAPPY LIFE. Cr. 8vo. 8s. 6d. net.

OXFORD MOVEMENT, THE, 1833—45. By Dean CHURCH. Gl. 8vo. 5s.

PARKER (W. K.)—A BIOGRAPHICAL SKETCH. By His Son. Cr. 8vo. 4s. net.

PATTESON. LIFE AND LETTERS OF JOHN COLERIDGE PATTESON, D.D., MISSIONARY BISHOP. By C. M. YONGE. 2 vols. Cr. 8vo. 12s. (*See also* BOOKS FOR THE YOUNG, p. 41.)

PATTISON (M.).—MEMOIRS. Cr. 8vo. 8s. 6d.

PITT. (*See* SELECT BIOGRAPHY, p. 6.)

POLLOCK (Sir Frdk., 2nd Bart.).—PERSONAL REMEMBRANCES. 2 vols. Cr. 8vo. 16s.

POOLE, THOS., AND HIS FRIENDS. By Mrs. SANDFORD. 2nd edit. Cr. 8vo. 6s.

RENAN (Ernest).—IN MEMORIAM. By Sir M. E. GRANT DUFF. Cr. 8vo. 6s.

RITCHIE (Mrs.).—RECORDS OF TENNYSON, RUSKIN, AND BROWNING. Globe 8vo. 5s.

ROBINSON (Matthew): AUTOBIOGRAPHY OF. Edited by J. E. B. MAYOR. Fcp. 8vo. 5s.

ROSSETTI (Dante Gabriel): A RECORD AND A STUDY. By W. SHARP. Cr. 8vo. 10s. 6d.

RUMFORD. (*See* COLLECTED WORKS, p. 23.)

SCHILLER, LIFE OF. By Prof. H. DÜNTZER. Trans. by P. E. PINKERTON. Cr. 8vo. 10s. 6d.

SHELBURNE. LIFE OF WILLIAM, EARL OF SHELBURNE. By Lord EDMOND FITZMAURICE. In 3 vols.—Vol. I. 8vo. 12s.—Vol. II. 8vo. 12s.—Vol. III. 8vo. 16s.

SIBSON. (*See* MEDICINE.)

SMETHAM (Jas.).: LETTERS OF. Ed. by SARAH SMETHAM and W. DAVIES. Portrait. Globe 8vo. 5s.

TAIT. THE LIFE OF ARCHIBALD CAMPBELL TAIT, ARCHBISHOP OF CANTERBURY. By the BISHOP OF ROCHESTER and Rev. W. BENHAM, B.D. 2 vols. Cr. 8vo. 10s. net.

—— CATHARINE AND CRAWFURD TAIT, WIFE AND SON OF ARCHIBALD CAMPBELL, ARCHBISHOP OF CANTERBURY: A Memoir. Ed. by Rev. W. BENHAM, B.D. Cr. 8vo. 6s. —Popular Edit., abridged. Cr. 8vo. 2s. 6d.

THRING (Edward): A MEMORY OF. By J. H. SKRINE. Cr. 8vo. 6s.

VICTOR EMMANUEL II., FIRST KING OF ITALY. By G. S. GODKIN. Cr. 8vo. 6s.

WARD. WILLIAM GEORGE WARD AND THE OXFORD MOVEMENT. By his Son, WILFRID WARD. With Portrait. 8vo. 14s.

—— WILLIAM GEORGE WARD AND THE CATHOLIC REVIVAL. 8vo. 14s.

WATSON. A RECORD OF ELLEN WATSON. By ANNA BUCKLAND. Cr. 8vo. 6s.

WHEWELL. DR. WILLIAM WHEWELL, late Master of Trinity College, Cambridge. An Account of his Writings, with Selections from his Literary and Scientific Correspondence. By I. TODHUNTER, M.A. 2 vols. 8vo. 25s.

WILLIAMS (Montagu).—LEAVES OF A LIFE. Cr. 8vo. 3s. 6d.

—— LATER LEAVES. Being further Reminiscences. With Portrait. Cr. 8vo. 3s. 6d.

—— ROUND LONDON, DOWN EAST AND UP WEST. 8vo. 15s.

WILSON. MEMOIR OF PROF. GEORGE WILSON, M.D. By HIS SISTER. With Portrait. 2nd Edit. Cr. 8vo. 6s.

WORDSWORTH. DOVE COTTAGE, WORDSWORTH'S HOME 1800—8. Gl. 8vo, swd. 1s.

Select Biography.

BIOGRAPHIES OF EMINENT PERSONS. Reprinted from the *Times*. 4 vols. Cr. 8vo 3s. 6d. each.

FARRAR (Archdeacon).—SEEKERS AFTER GOD. Cr. 8vo. 3s. 6d.

FAWCETT (Mrs. H.). — SOME EMINENT WOMEN OF OUR TIMES. Cr. 8vo 2s. 6d.

GUIZOT.—GREAT CHRISTIANS OF FRANCE: ST. LOUIS AND CALVIN. Cr. 8vo. 6s.

HARRISON (Frederic).—THE NEW CALENDAR OF GREAT MEN. Ex. cr. 8vo. 7s. 6d. net.

MARRIOTT (J. A. R.).—THE MAKERS OF MODERN ITALY: MAZZINI, CAVOUR, GARIBALDI. Cr. 8vo. 1s. 6d.

MARTINEAU (Harriet). — BIOGRAPHICAL SKETCHES, 1852—75. Cr. 8vo. 6s.

NEW HOUSE OF COMMONS, JULY, 1892. Reprinted from the *Times*. 16mo 1s.

SMITH (Goldwin).—THREE ENGLISH STATESMEN: CROMWELL, PYM, PITT. Cr. 8vo. 5s.

STEVENSON (F. S.).—HISTORIC PERSONALITY. Cr. 8vo. 4s. 6d.

WINKWORTH (Catharine). — CHRISTIAN SINGERS OF GERMANY. Cr. 8vo. 4s. 6d.

YONGE (Charlotte M.).—THE PUPILS OF ST. JOHN. Illustrated. Cr. 8vo. 6s.
—— PIONEERS AND FOUNDERS; or, Recent Workers in the Mission Field. Cr. 8vo. 6s.
—— A BOOK OF WORTHIES. 18mo. 2s. 6d. net.
—— A BOOK OF GOLDEN DEEDS. 18mo. 2s. 6d. net.--*Glob. Readings Edition.* Gl. 8vo. 2s. *Abridged Edition.* Pott 8vo. 1s.

BIOLOGY.

(*See also* BOTANY; NATURAL HISTORY; PHYSIOLOGY; ZOOLOGY.)

BALFOUR (F. M.).—COMPARATIVE EMBRYOLOGY. Illustrated. 2 vols. 8vo. Vol. I. 18s. Vol. II. 21s.

BALL (W. P.).—ARE THE EFFECTS OF USE AND DISUSE INHERITED? Cr. 8vo. 3s. 6d.

BASTIAN (H. Charlton).—THE BEGINNINGS OF LIFE. 2 vols. Crown 8vo. 28s.
—— EVOLUTION AND THE ORIGIN OF LIFE. Cr. 8vo. 6s. 6d.

BATESON (W.).—MATERIALS FOR THE STUDY OF VARIATION IN ANIMALS. Part I. DISCONTINUOUS VARIATION. Illustr. 8vo.

BERNARD (H. M.).—THE APODIDAE. Cr. 8vo. 7s. 6d.

BIRKS (T. R.).— MODERN PHYSICAL FATALISM, AND THE DOCTRINE OF EVOLUTION. Including an Examination of Mr. Herbert Spencer's "First Principles." Cr. 8vo. 6s.

CALDERWOOD (H.).— EVOLUTION AND MAN'S PLACE IN NATURE. Cr. 8vo. 7s. 6d.

DE VARIGNY (H.).—EXPERIMENTAL EVOLUTION. Cr. 8vo. 5s.

EIMER (G. H. T.).—ORGANIC EVOLUTION AS THE RESULT OF THE INHERITANCE OF ACQUIRED CHARACTERS ACCORDING TO THE LAWS OF ORGANIC GROWTH. Translated by J. T. CUNNINGHAM, M.A. 8vo. 12s. 6d.

FISKE (John).—OUTLINES OF COSMIC PHILOSOPHY, BASED ON THE DOCTRINE OF EVOLUTION. 2 vols. 8vo. 25s.
—— MAN'S DESTINY VIEWED IN THE LIGHT OF HIS ORIGIN. Cr. 8vo. 3s. 6d.

FOSTER (Prof. M.) and BALFOUR (F. M.).—THE ELEMENTS OF EMBRYOLOGY. Ed. A. SEDGWICK, and WALTER HEAPE. Illus. 3rd Edit., revised and enlarged. Cr. 8vo. 10s. 6d.

HUXLEY (T. H.) and MARTIN (H. N.).—(*See under* ZOOLOGY, p. 43.)

KLEIN (Dr. E.).—MICRO-ORGANISMS AND DISEASE. With 121 Engravings. 3rd Edit. Cr. 8vo. 6s.

LANKESTER (Prof. E. Ray).—COMPARATIVE LONGEVITY IN MAN AND THE LOWER ANIMALS. Cr. 8vo. 4s. 6d.

LUBBOCK (Sir John, Bart.).—SCIENTIFIC LECTURES. Illustrated. 2nd Edit. 8vo. 8s. 6d.

MURPHY (J. J.).—NATURAL SELECTION. Gl. 8vo. 5s.

PARKER (T. Jeffery).—LESSONS IN ELEMENTARY BIOLOGY. Illustr. Cr. 8vo. 10s. 6d.

ROMANES (G. J.).—SCIENTIFIC EVIDENCES OF ORGANIC EVOLUTION. Cr. 8vo. 2s. 6d.

WALLACE (Alfred R.).—DARWINISM: An Exposition of the Theory of Natural Selection. Illustrated. 3rd Edit. Cr. 8vo. 9s.
—— CONTRIBUTIONS TO THE THEORY OF NATURAL SELECTION, AND TROPICAL NATURE: and other Essays. New Ed. Cr. 8vo. 6s.
—— THE GEOGRAPHICAL DISTRIBUTION OF ANIMALS. Illustrated. 2 vols. 8vo. 42s.
—— ISLAND LIFE. Illustr. Ext. Cr. 8vo. 6s.

BIRDS. (*See* ZOOLOGY; ORNITHOLOGY.)

BOOK-KEEPING.

THORNTON (J.).—FIRST LESSONS IN BOOK-KEEPING. New Edition. Cr. 8vo. 2s. 6d.
—— KEY. Oblong 4to. 10s. 6d.
—— PRIMER OF BOOK-KEEPING. 18mo. 1s.
—— KEY. Demy 8vo. 2s. 6d.
—— EXERCISES IN BOOK-KEEPING. 18mo. 1s.

BOTANY.

(*See also* AGRICULTURE; GARDENING.)

ALLEN (Grant). — ON THE COLOURS OF FLOWERS. Illustrated. Cr. 8vo. 3s. 6d.

BALFOUR (Prof. J. B.) and WARD (Prof. H. M.). — A GENERAL TEXT-BOOK OF BOTANY. 8vo. [*In preparation.*

BETTANY (G. T.).—FIRST LESSONS IN PRACTICAL BOTANY. 18mo. 1s.

BOWER (Prof. F. O.).—A COURSE OF PRACTICAL INSTRUCTION IN BOTANY. Cr. 8vo. 10s. 6d.—Abridged Edition. [*In preparation.*

CHURCH (Prof. A. H.) and VINES (S. H.).—MANUAL OF VEGETABLE PHYSIOLOGY. Illustrated. Crown 8vo. [*In preparation.*

GOODALE (Prof. G. L.).—PHYSIOLOGICAL BOTANY.—1. OUTLINES OF THE HISTOLOGY OF PHÆNOGAMOUS PLANTS; 2. VEGETABLE PHYSIOLOGY. 8vo. 10s. 6d.

GRAY (Prof. Asa).—STRUCTURAL BOTANY; or, Organography on the Basis of Morphology. 8vo. 10s. 6d.
—— THE SCIENTIFIC PAPERS OF ASA GRAY. Selected by C. S. SARGENT. 2 vols. 8vo. 21s.

HANBURY (Daniel).—SCIENCE PAPERS, CHIEFLY PHARMACOLOGICAL AND BOTANICAL. Med. 8vo. 14*s.*

HARTIG (Dr. Robert).—TEXT-BOOK OF THE DISEASES OF TREES. Transl. by Prof. WM. SOMERVILLE, B.Sc. With Introduction by Prof. H. MARSHALL WARD. 8vo.

HOOKER (Sir Joseph D.).—THE STUDENT'S FLORA OF THE BRITISH ISLANDS. 3rd Edit. Globe 8vo. 10*s.* 6*d.*
—— A PRIMER OF BOTANY. 18mo. 1*s.*

LASLETT (Thomas).—TIMBER AND TIMBER TREES, NATIVE AND FOREIGN. Cr. 8vo. 8*s.* 6*d.*

LUBBOCK (Sir John, Bart.).—ON BRITISH WILD FLOWERS CONSIDERED IN RELATION TO INSECTS. Illustrated. Cr. 8vo. 4*s.* 6*d.*
—— FLOWERS, FRUITS, AND LEAVES. With Illustrations. Cr. 8vo. 4*s.* 6*d.*

MÜLLER—THOMPSON.—THE FERTILISATION OF FLOWERS. By Prof. H. MÜLLER. Transl. by D'ARCY W. THOMPSON. Preface by CHARLES DARWIN, F.R.S. 8vo. 21*s.*

NISBET (J.).—BRITISH FOREST TREES AND THEIR AGRICULTURAL CHARACTERISTICS AND TREATMENT. Cr. 8vo. 6*s.*

OLIVER (Prof. Daniel).—LESSONS IN ELEMENTARY BOTANY. Illustr. Fcp. 8vo. 4*s.* 6*d.*
—— FIRST BOOK OF INDIAN BOTANY. Illustrated. Ext. fcp. 8vo. 6*s.* 6*d.*

PETTIGREW (J. Bell).—THE PHYSIOLOGY OF THE CIRCULATION IN PLANTS, IN THE LOWER ANIMALS, AND IN MAN. 8vo. 12*s.*

SMITH (J.).—ECONOMIC PLANTS, DICTIONARY OF POPULAR NAMES OF; THEIR HISTORY, PRODUCTS, AND USES. 8vo. 14*s.*

SMITH (W. G.).—DISEASES OF FIELD AND GARDEN CROPS, CHIEFLY SUCH AS ARE CAUSED BY FUNGI. Illust. Fcp. 8vo. 4*s.* 6*d.*

STEWART (S. A.) and CORRY (T. H.).—A FLORA OF THE NORTH-EAST OF IRELAND. Cr. 8vo. 5*s.* 6*d.*

WARD (Prof. H. M.).—TIMBER AND SOME OF ITS DISEASES. Illustrated. Cr. 8vo. 6*s.*

YONGE (C. M.).—THE HERB OF THE FIELD. New Edition, revised. Cr. 8vo. 5*s.*

BREWING AND WINE.

PASTEUR—FAULKNER.—STUDIES ON FERMENTATION: THE DISEASES OF BEER, THEIR CAUSES, AND THE MEANS OF PREVENTING THEM. By L. PASTEUR. Translated by FRANK FAULKNER. 8vo. 21*s.*

CHEMISTRY.

(*See also* METALLURGY.)

BRODIE (Sir Benjamin).—IDEAL CHEMISTRY. Cr. 8vo. 2*s.*

COHEN (J. B.).—THE OWENS COLLEGE COURSE OF PRACTICAL ORGANIC CHEMISTRY. Fcp. 8vo. 2*s.* 6*d.*

COOKE (Prof. J. P., jun.).—PRINCIPLES OF CHEMICAL PHILOSOPHY. New Ed. 8vo. 19*s.*

DOBBIN (L.) and WALKER (Jas.)—CHEMICAL THEORY FOR BEGINNERS. 18mo. 2*s.* 6*d.*

FLEISCHER (Emil).—A SYSTEM OF VOLUMETRIC ANALYSIS. Transl. with Additions, by M. M. P. MUIR, F.R.S.E. Cr. 8vo. 7*s.* 6*d.*

FRANKLAND (Prof. P. F.). (*See* AGRICULTURE.)

GLADSTONE (J. H.) and TRIBE (A.).—THE CHEMISTRY OF THE SECONDARY BATTERIES OF PLANTÉ AND FAURE. Cr. 8vo. 2*s.* 6*d.*

HARTLEY (Prof. W. N.).—A COURSE OF QUANTITATIVE ANALYSIS FOR STUDENTS. Globe 8vo. 5*s.*

HEMPEL (Dr. W.).—METHODS OF GAS ANALYSIS. Translated by L. M. DENNIS. Cr. 8vo. 7*s.* 6*d.*

HOFMANN (Prof. A. W.).—THE LIFE WORK OF LIEBIG IN EXPERIMENTAL AND PHILOSOPHIC CHEMISTRY. 8vo. 5*s.*

JONES (Francis).—THE OWENS COLLEGE JUNIOR COURSE OF PRACTICAL CHEMISTRY. Illustrated. Fcp. 8vo. 2*s.* 6*d.*
—— QUESTIONS ON CHEMISTRY. Fcp. 8vo. 3*s.*

LANDAUER (J.).—BLOWPIPE ANALYSIS. Translated by J. TAYLOR. Gl. 8vo. 4*s.* 6*d.*

LOCKYER (J. Norman, F.R.S.).—THE CHEMISTRY OF THE SUN. Illustr. 8vo. 14*s.*

LUPTON (S.).—CHEMICAL ARITHMETIC. With 1200 Problems. Fcp. 8vo. 4*s.* 6*d.*

MANSFIELD (C. B.).—A THEORY OF SALTS. Cr. 8vo. 14*s.*

MELDOLA (Prof. R.).—THE CHEMISTRY OF PHOTOGRAPHY. Illustrated. Cr. 8vo. 6*s.*

MEYER (E. von).—HISTORY OF CHEMISTRY FROM EARLIEST TIMES TO THE PRESENT DAY. Trans. G. McGOWAN. 8vo. 14*s.* net.

MIXTER (Prof. W. G.).—AN ELEMENTARY TEXT-BOOK OF CHEMISTRY. Cr. 8vo. 7*s.* 6*d.*

MUIR (M. M. P.).—PRACTICAL CHEMISTRY FOR MEDICAL STUDENTS (First M.B. Course). Fcp. 8vo. 1*s.* 6*d.*

MUIR (M. M. P.) and WILSON (D. M.).—ELEMENTS OF THERMAL CHEMISTRY. 12*s.* 6*d.*

OSTWALD (Prof.).—OUTLINES OF GENERAL CHEMISTRY. Trans. Dr. J. WALKER. 10*s.* net.

RAMSAY (Prof. William).—EXPERIMENTAL PROOFS OF CHEMICAL THEORY FOR BEGINNERS. 18mo. 2*s.* 6*d.*

REMSEN (Prof. Ira).—THE ELEMENTS OF CHEMISTRY. Fcp. 8vo. 2*s.* 6*d.*
—— AN INTRODUCTION TO THE STUDY OF CHEMISTRY (INORGANIC CHEMISTRY). Cr. 8vo. 6*s.* 6*d.*
—— A TEXT-BOOK OF INORGANIC CHEMISTRY. 8vo. 16*s.*
—— COMPOUNDS OF CARBON; or, An Introduction to the Study of Organic Chemistry. Cr. 8vo. 6*s.* 6*d.*

ROSCOE (Sir Henry E., F.R.S.).—A PRIMER OF CHEMISTRY. Illustrated. 18mo. 1*s.*
—— LESSONS IN ELEMENTARY CHEMISTRY, INORGANIC AND ORGANIC. Fcp. 8vo. 4*s.* 6*d.*

ROSCOE (Sir H. E.) and SCHORLEMMER (Prof. C.).—A COMPLETE TREATISE ON INORGANIC AND ORGANIC CHEMISTRY. Illustr. 8vo.—Vols. I. and II. INORGANIC CHEMISTRY: Vol. I. THE NON-METALLIC ELEMENTS, 2nd Edit., 21*s.* Vol. II. Parts I. and II. METALS, 18*s.* each.—Vol. III. ORGANIC CHEMISTRY: THE CHEMISTRY OF THE HYDRO-CARBONS AND THEIR DERIVATIVES. Parts I. II. IV. and VI. 21*s.*; Parts III. and V. 18*s.* each.

ROSCOE (Sir H. E.) and SCHUSTER (A.).—Spectrum Analysis. By Sir Henry E. Roscoe. 4th Edit., revised by the Author and A. Schuster, F.R.S. With Coloured Plates. 8vo. 21s.

THORPE (Prof. T. E.) and TATE (W.).—A Series of Chemical Problems. With Key. Fcp. 8vo. 2s.

THORPE (Prof. T. E.) and RÜCKER (Prof. A. W.).—A Treatise on Chemical Physics. Illustrated. 8vo. [In preparation.

WURTZ (Ad.).—A History of Chemical Theory. Transl. by H. Watts. Cr. 8vo. 6s.

CHRISTIAN CHURCH, History of the.
(See under Theology, p. 34.)

CHURCH OF ENGLAND, The.
(See under Theology, p. 34.)

COLLECTED WORKS.
(See under Literature, p. 20.)

COMPARATIVE ANATOMY.
(See under Zoology, p. 42.)

COOKERY.
(See under Domestic Economy, below.)

DEVOTIONAL BOOKS.
(See under Theology, p. 35.)

DICTIONARIES AND GLOSSARIES.
AUTENRIETH (Dr. G.).—An Homeric Dictionary. Translated from the German, by R. P. Keep, Ph.D. Cr. 8vo. 6s.

BARTLETT (J.).—Familiar Quotations. Cr. 8vo. 12s. 6d.

GROVE (Sir George).—A Dictionary of Music and Musicians. (See Music.)

HOLE (Rev. C.).—A Brief Biographical Dictionary. 2nd Edit. 18mo. 4s. 6d.

MASSON (Gustave).—A Compendious Dictionary of the French Language. Cr. 8vo. 3s. 6d.

PALGRAVE (R. H. I.).—A Dictionary of Political Economy. (See Political Economy.)

WHITNEY (Prof. W. D.).—A Compendious German and English Dictionary. Cr. 8vo. 5s.—German-English Part separately. 3s. 6d.

WRIGHT (W. Aldis).—The Bible Word-Book. 2nd Edit. Cr. 8vo. 7s. 6d.

YONGE (Charlotte M.).—History of Christian Names. Cr. 8vo. 7s. 6d.

DOMESTIC ECONOMY.
Cookery—Nursing—Needlework.
Cookery.
BARKER (Lady).—First Lessons in the Principles of Cooking. 3rd Ed. 18mo. 1s.

BARNETT (E. A.) and O'NEILL (H. C.).—Primer of Domestic Economy. 18mo. 1s.

MIDDLE-CLASS COOKERY BOOK, The. Compiled for the Manchester School of Cookery. Fcp. 8vo. 1s. 6d.

TEGETMEIER (W. B.).—Household Management and Cookery. 18mo. 1s.

WRIGHT (Miss Guthrie).—The School Cookery-Book. 18mo. 1s.

Nursing.
CRAVEN (Mrs. Dacre).—A Guide to District Nurses. Cr. 8vo. 2s. 6d.

FOTHERGILL (Dr. J. M.).—Food for the Invalid, the Convalescent, the Dyspeptic, and the Gouty. Cr. 8vo. 3s. 6d.

JEX-BLAKE (Dr. Sophia).—The Care of Infants. 18mo. 1s.

RATHBONE (Wm.).—The History and Progress of District Nursing, from 1859 to the Present Date. Cr. 8vo. 2s. 6d.

RECOLLECTIONS OF A NURSE. By E. D. Cr. 8vo. 2s.

STEPHEN (Caroline E.).—The Service of the Poor. Cr. 8vo. 6s. 6d.

Needlework.
GLAISTER (Elizabeth).—Needlework. Cr. 8vo. 2s. 6d.

GRAND'HOMME.—Cutting Out and Dressmaking. From the French of Mdlle. E. Grand'homme. 18mo. 1s.

GRENFELL (Mrs.)-Dressmaking. 18mo. 1s.

ROSEVEAR (E.).—Needlework, Knitting, and Cutting Out. Cr. 8vo. 6s.

DRAMA, The.
(See under Literature, p. 14.)

ELECTRICITY.
(See under Physics, p. 28.)

EDUCATION.
ARNOLD (Matthew).—Higher Schools and Universities in Germany. Cr. 8vo. 6s.

—— Reports on Elementary Schools, 1852-82. Ed. by Lord Sandford. 8vo. 3s. 6d.

—— A French Eton: or Middle Class Education and the State. Cr. 8vo. 6s.

BLAKISTON (J. R.).—The Teacher: Hints on School Management. Cr. 8vo. 2s. 6d.

CALDERWOOD (Prof. H.).—On Teaching. 4th Edit. Ext. fcp. 8vo. 2s. 6d.

COMBE (George).—Education: Its Principles and Practice as Developed by George Combe. Ed. by W. Jolly. 8vo. 15s.

CRAIK (Henry).—The State in its Relation to Education. Cr. 8vo. 3s. 6d.

FEARON (D. R.).—School Inspection. 6th Edit. Cr. 8vo. 2s. 6d.

FITCH (J. G.).—Notes on American Schools and Training Colleges. Reprinted by permission. Globe 8vo. 2s. 6d.

GLADSTONE (J. H.).—Spelling Reform from an Educational Point of View. 3rd Edit. Cr. 8vo. 1s. 6d.

HERTEL (Dr.).—OVERPRESSURE IN HIGH SCHOOLS IN DENMARK. With Introduction by Sir J. CRICHTON-BROWNE. Cr. 8vo. 3s. 6d.

KINGSLEY (Charles).—HEALTH AND EDUCATION. Cr. 8vo. 6s.

LUBBOCK (Sir John, Bart.).—POLITICAL AND EDUCATIONAL ADDRESSES. 8vo. 8s. 6d.

MAURICE (F. D.).—LEARNING AND WORKING. Cr. 8vo. 4s. 6d.

RECORD OF TECHNICAL AND SECONDARY EDUCATION. Crown 8vo. Sewed, 2s. net. No. I. Nov. 1891.

THRING (Rev. Edward).—EDUCATION AND SCHOOL. 2nd Edit. Cr. 8vo. 6s.

ENGINEERING.

ALEXANDER (T.) and THOMSON (A.W.)—ELEMENTARY APPLIED MECHANICS. Part II. TRANSVERSE STRESS. Cr. 8vo. 10s. 6d.

CHALMERS (J. B.).—GRAPHICAL DETERMINATION OF FORCES IN ENGINEERING STRUCTURES. Illustrated. 8vo. 24s.

COTTERILL (Prof. J. H.).—APPLIED MECHANICS: An Elementary General Introduction to the Theory of Structures and Machines. 3rd Edit. 8vo. 18s.

COTTERILL (Prof. J. H.) and SLADE (J. H.).—LESSONS IN APPLIED MECHANICS. Fcp. 8vo. 5s. 6d.

KENNEDY (Prof. A. B. W.).—THE MECHANICS OF MACHINERY. Cr. 8vo. 8s. 6d.

PEABODY (Prof. C. H.).—THERMODYNAMICS OF THE STEAM ENGINE AND OTHER HEAT-ENGINES. 8vo. 21s.

SHANN (G.).—AN ELEMENTARY TREATISE ON HEAT IN RELATION TO STEAM AND THE STEAM-ENGINE. Illustrated. Cr. 8vo. 4s. 6d.

WOODWARD (C. M.).—A HISTORY OF THE ST. LOUIS BRIDGE. 4to. 2l. 2s. net.

YOUNG (E. W.).—SIMPLE PRACTICAL METHODS OF CALCULATING STRAINS ON GIRDERS, ARCHES, AND TRUSSES. 8vo. 7s. 6d.

ENGLISH CITIZEN SERIES.
(See POLITICS.)

ENGLISH MEN OF ACTION.
(See BIOGRAPHY.)

ENGLISH MEN OF LETTERS.
(See BIOGRAPHY.)

ENGLISH STATESMEN, Twelve.
(See BIOGRAPHY.)

ENGRAVING. (See ART.)
ESSAYS. (See under LITERATURE, p. 20.)

ETCHING. (See ART.)
ETHICS. (See under PHILOSOPHY, p. 27.)

FATHERS, The.
(See under THEOLOGY, p. 35.)

FICTION, Prose.
(See under LITERATURE, p. 18.)

GARDENING.
(See also AGRICULTURE; BOTANY.)

BLOMFIELD (R.) and THOMAS (F. I.).—THE FORMAL GARDEN IN ENGLAND. Illustrated. Ex. cr. 8vo. 7s. 6d. net.

BRIGHT (H. A.).—THE ENGLISH FLOWER GARDEN. Cr. 8vo. 3s. 6d.
—— A YEAR IN A LANCASHIRE GARDEN. Cr. 8vo. 3s. 6d.

HOBDAY (E.).—VILLA GARDENING. A Handbook for Amateur and Practical Gardeners. Ext. cr. 8vo. 6s.

HOPE (Frances J.).—NOTES AND THOUGHTS ON GARDENS AND WOODLANDS. Cr. 8vo. 6s.

WRIGHT (J.).—A PRIMER OF PRACTICAL HORTICULTURE. 18mo. 1s.

GEOGRAPHY.
(See also ATLASES.)

BLANFORD (H. F.).—ELEMENTARY GEOGRAPHY OF INDIA, BURMA, AND CEYLON. Globe 8vo. 2s. 6d.

CLARKE (C. B.).—A GEOGRAPHICAL READER AND COMPANION TO THE ATLAS. Cr. 8vo. 2s.
—— A CLASS-BOOK OF GEOGRAPHY. With 18 Coloured Maps. Fcp. 8vo. 3s.; swd., 2s. 6d.

DAWSON (G. M.) and SUTHERLAND (A.).—ELEMENTARY GEOGRAPHY OF THE BRITISH COLONIES. Globe 8vo. 3s.

ELDERTON (W. A.).—MAPS AND MAP-DRAWING. Pott 8vo. 1s.

GEIKIE (Sir Archibald).—THE TEACHING OF GEOGRAPHY. A Practical Handbook for the use of Teachers. Globe 8vo. 2s.
—— GEOGRAPHY OF THE BRITISH ISLES. 18mo. 1s.

GREEN (J. R. and A. S.).—A SHORT GEOGRAPHY OF THE BRITISH ISLANDS. Fcp. 8vo. 3s. 6d.

GROVE (Sir George).—A PRIMER OF GEOGRAPHY. Maps. 18mo. 1s.

KIEPERT (H.).—MANUAL OF ANCIENT GEOGRAPHY. Cr. 8vo. 5s.

MILL (H. R.).—ELEMENTARY CLASS-BOOK OF GENERAL GEOGRAPHY. Cr. 8vo. 3s. 6d.

SIME (James).—GEOGRAPHY OF EUROPE. With Illustrations. Globe 8vo. 3s.

STRACHEY (Lieut.-Gen. R.).—LECTURES ON GEOGRAPHY. Cr. 8vo. 4s. 6d.

TOZER (H. F.).—A PRIMER OF CLASSICAL GEOGRAPHY. 18mo. 1s.

GEOLOGY AND MINERALOGY.

BLANFORD (W. T.).—GEOLOGY AND ZOOLOGY OF ABYSSINIA. 8vo. 21s.

COAL: ITS HISTORY AND ITS USES. By Profs. GREEN, MIALL, THORPE, RÜCKER, and MARSHALL. 8vo. 12s. 6d.

DAWSON (Sir J. W.).—THE GEOLOGY OF NOVA SCOTIA, NEW BRUNSWICK, AND PRINCE EDWARD ISLAND; or, Acadian Geology. 4th Edit. 8vo. 21s.

GEIKIE (Sir Archibald).—A PRIMER OF GEOLOGY. Illustrated. 18mo. 1s.
—— CLASS-BOOK OF GEOLOGY. Illustrated. Cr. 8vo. 4s. 6d.

GEOLOGY AND MINERALOGY—*contd.*

GEIKIE (Sir A.).—GEOLOGICAL SKETCHES AT HOME AND ABROAD. Illus. 8vo. 10s.6d.
—— OUTLINES OF FIELD GEOLOGY. With numerous Illustrations. Gl. 8vo. 3s. 6d.
—— TEXT-BOOK OF GEOLOGY. Illustrated. 2nd Edit. 7th Thousand. Med. 8vo. 28s.
—— THE SCENERY OF SCOTLAND. Viewed in connection with its Physical Geology. 2nd Edit. Cr. 8vo. 12s. 6d.

HULL (E.).—A TREATISE ON ORNAMENTAL AND BUILDING STONES OF GREAT BRITAIN AND FOREIGN COUNTRIES. 8vo. 12s.

PENNINGTON (Rooke).—NOTES ON THE BARROWS AND BONE CAVES OF DERBYSHIRE. 8vo. 6s.

RENDU—WILLS.—THE THEORY OF THE GLACIERS OF SAVOY. By M. LE CHANOINE RENDU. Trans. by A. WILLS, Q.C. 8vo. 7s.6d.

WILLIAMS (G. H.).—ELEMENTS OF CRY-STALLOGRAPHY. Cr. 8vo. 6s.

GLOBE LIBRARY. (*See* LITERATURE, p. 21.)

GLOSSARIES. (*See* DICTIONARIES.)

GOLDEN TREASURY SERIES. (*See* LITERATURE, p. 21.)

GRAMMAR. (*See* PHILOLOGY.)

HEALTH. (*See* HYGIENE.)

HEAT. (*See under* PHYSICS, p. 29.)

HISTOLOGY. (*See* PHYSIOLOGY.)

HISTORY.

(*See also* BIOGRAPHY.)

ANDREWS (C. M.).—THE OLD ENGLISH MANOR: A STUDY IN ECONOMIC HISTORY. Royal 8vo. 6s. net.

ANNALS OF OUR TIME. A Diurnal of Events, Social and Political, Home and Foreign. By JOSEPH IRVING. 8vo.—Vol. I June 20th, 1837, to Feb. 28th, 1871, 18s.; Vol. II. Feb. 24th, 1871, to June 24th, 1887, 18s. Also Vol. II. in 3 parts: Part I. Feb. 24th, 1871, to March 19th, 1874, 4s. 6d.; Part II. March 20th, 1874, to July 22nd, 1878, 4s. 6d.; Part III. July 23rd, 1878, to June 24th, 1887, 9s. Vol. III. By H. H. FYFE. Part I. June 25th, 1887, to Dec. 30th, 1890. 4s. 6d.; sewed, 3s. 6d. Part II. 1891, 1s. 6d.; sewed, 1s.

ANNUAL SUMMARIES. Reprinted from the *Times.* Vol. I. Cr. 8vo. 3s. 6d.

ARNOLD (T.).—THE SECOND PUNIC WAR. By THOMAS ARNOLD, D.D. Ed. by W. T. ARNOLD, M.A. With 8 Maps. Cr. 8vo. 5s.

ARNOLD (W. T.).—A HISTORY OF THE EARLY ROMAN EMPIRE. Cr. 8vo. [*In prep.*

BEESLY (Mrs.).—STORIES FROM THE HISTORY OF ROME. Fcp. 8vo. 2s. 6d.

BLACKIE (Prof. John Stuart).—WHAT DOES HISTORY TEACH? Globe 8vo. 2s. 6d.

BRETT (R. B.).—FOOTPRINTS OF STATESMEN DURING THE EIGHTEENTH CENTURY IN ENGLAND. Cr. 8vo. 6s.

BRYCE (James, M.P.).—THE HOLY ROMAN EMPIRE. 8th Edit. Cr. 8vo. 7s. 6d.—*Library Edition.* 8vo. 14s.

BUCKLEY (Arabella).—HISTORY OF ENGLAND FOR BEGINNERS. Globe 8vo. 3s.
—— PRIMER OF ENGLISH HISTORY. 18mo. 1s.

BURKE (Edmund). (*See* POLITICS.)

BURY (J. B.).—A HISTORY OF THE LATER ROMAN EMPIRE FROM ARCADIUS TO IRENE, A.D. 390—800. 2 vols. 8vo. 32s.

CASSEL (Dr. D.).—MANUAL OF JEWISH HISTORY AND LITERATURE. Translated by Mrs. HENRY LUCAS. Fcp. 8vo. 2s. 6d.

COX (G. V.).—RECOLLECTIONS OF OXFORD. 2nd Edit. Cr. 8vo. 6s.

ENGLISH STATESMEN, TWELVE. (*See* BIOGRAPHY, p. 4.)

FISKE (John).—THE CRITICAL PERIOD IN AMERICAN HISTORY, 1783—89. Ext. cr 8vo. 10s. 6d.
—— THE BEGINNINGS OF NEW ENGLAND; or, The Puritan Theocracy in its Relations to Civil and Religious Liberty. Cr. 8vo. 7s. 6d.
—— THE AMERICAN REVOLUTION. 2 vols. Cr. 8vo. 18s.
—— THE DISCOVERY OF AMERICA. 2 vols. Cr. 8vo. 18s.

FRAMJI (Dosabhai).—HISTORY OF THE PARSIS, INCLUDING THEIR MANNERS, CUSTOMS, RELIGION, AND PRESENT POSITION. With Illustrations. 2 vols. Med. 8vo. 36s.

FREEMAN (Prof. E. A.).—HISTORY OF THE CATHEDRAL CHURCH OF WELLS. Cr. 8vo. 3s. 6d.
—— OLD ENGLISH HISTORY. With 5 Coloured Maps. 9th Edit., revised. Ext. fcp. 8vo. 6s.
—— HISTORICAL ESSAYS. First Series. 4th Edit. 8vo. 10s. 6d.
—— —— Second Series. 3rd Edit., with Additional Essays. 8vo. 10s. 6d.
—— —— Third Series. 8vo. 12s.
—— —— Fourth Series. 8vo. 12s. 6d.
—— THE GROWTH OF THE ENGLISH CONSTITUTION FROM THE EARLIEST TIMES. 5th Edit. Cr. 8vo. 5s.
—— COMPARATIVE POLITICS. Lectures at the Royal Institution. To which is added "The Unity of History." 8vo. 14s.
—— SUBJECT AND NEIGHBOUR LANDS OF VENICE. Illustrated. Cr. 8vo. 10s. 6d.
—— ENGLISH TOWNS AND DISTRICTS. A Series of Addresses and Essays. 8vo. 14s.
—— THE OFFICE OF THE HISTORICAL PROFESSOR. Cr. 8vo. 2s.
—— DISESTABLISHMENT AND DISENDOWMENT; WHAT ARE THEY? Cr. 8vo. 2s.
—— GREATER GREECE AND GREATER BRITAIN: GEORGE WASHINGTON THE EXPANDER OF ENGLAND. With an Appendix on IMPERIAL FEDERATION. Cr. 8vo. 3s. 6d.
—— THE METHODS OF HISTORICAL STUDY. Eight Lectures at Oxford. 8vo. 10s. 6d.
—— THE CHIEF PERIODS OF EUROPEAN HISTORY. With Essay on "Greek Cities under Roman Rule." 8vo. 10s. 6d.
—— FOUR OXFORD LECTURES, 1887; FIFTY YEARS OF EUROPEAN HISTORY; TEUTONIC CONQUEST IN GAUL AND BRITAIN. 8vo. 5s.

FRIEDMANN (Paul). (*See* BIOGRAPHY.)

GIBBINS (H. de B.).—HISTORY OF COMMERCE IN EUROPE. Globe 8vo. 3s. 6d.

GREEN (John Richard).—A Short History of the English People. New Edit., revised. 159th Thousand. Cr. 8vo. 8s. 6d.—Also in Parts, with Analysis. 3s. each.—Part I. 607—1265; II. 1204—1553; III. 1540—1689; IV. 1660—1873.—Illustrated Edition, in Parts. Super roy. 8vo. 1s. each net.—Part I. Oct. 1891. Vols. I. and II. 12s. each net.
—— History of the English People. In 4 vols. 8vo. 16s. each.
—— The Making of England. 8vo. 16s.
—— The Conquest of England. With Maps and Portrait. 8vo. 18s.
—— Readings in English History. In 3 Parts. Fcp. 8vo. 1s. 6d. each.

GREEN (Alice S.).—The English Town in the 15th Century. 2 vols. 8vo.

GUEST (Dr. E.).—Origines Celticæ. Maps. 2 vols. 8vo. 32s.

GUEST (M. J.).—Lectures on the History of England. Cr. 8vo. 6s.

HISTORY PRIMERS. Edited by John Richard Green. 18mo. 1s. each.
Europe. By E. A. Freeman, M.A.
Greece. By C. A. Fyffe, M.A.
Rome. By Bishop Creighton.
France. By Charlotte M. Yonge.
English History. By A. B. Buckley.

HISTORICAL COURSE FOR SCHOOLS. Ed. by Edw. A. Freeman, D.C.L. 18mo.
General Sketch of European History. By E. A. Freeman. Maps. 3s. 6d.
History of England. By Edith Thompson. Coloured Maps. 2s. 6d.
History of Scotland. By Margaret Macarthur. 2s.
History of Italy. By the Rev. W. Hunt, M.A. With Coloured Maps. 3s. 6d.
History of Germany. By James Sime, M.A. 3s.
History of America. By J. A. Doyle. With Maps. 4s. 6d.
History of European Colonies. By E. J. Payne, M.A. Maps. 4s. 6d.
History of France. By Charlotte M. Yonge. Maps. 3s. 6d.

HOLE (Rev. C.).—Genealogical Stemma of the Kings of England and France. On a Sheet. 1s.

INGRAM (T. Dunbar).—A History of the Legislative Union of Great Britain and Ireland. 8vo. 10s. 6d.
—— Two Chapters of Irish History: 1. The Irish Parliament of James II.; 2. The Alleged Violation of the Treaty of Limerick. 8vo. 6s.

JEBB (Prof. R. C.).—Modern Greece. Two Lectures. Crown 8vo. 5s.

JENNINGS (A. C.).—Chronological Tables of Ancient History. 8vo. 5s.

KEARY (Annie).—The Nations Around Israel. Cr. 8vo. 3s. 6d.

KINGSLEY (Charles).—The Roman and the Teuton. Cr. 8vo. 3s. 6d.
—— Historical Lectures and Essays. Cr. 8vo. 3s. 6d.

LABBERTON (R. H.). (See Atlases.)

LEGGE (Alfred O.).—The Growth of the Temporal Power of the Papacy. Cr. 8vo. 8s. 6d.

LETHBRIDGE (Sir Roper).—A Short Manual of the History of India. Cr. 8vo. 5s.
—— The World's History. Cr. 8vo, swd. 1s.
—— Easy Introduction to the History of India. Cr. 8vo, sewed. 1s. 6d.
—— History of England. Cr. 8vo, swd. 1s. 6d.
—— Easy Introduction to the History and Geography of Bengal. Cr. 8vo. 1s. 6d.

LYTE (H. C. Maxwell).—A History of Eton College, 1440—1884. Illustrated. 8vo. 21s.
—— A History of the University of Oxford, from the Earliest Times to the Year 1530. 8vo. 16s.

MAHAFFY (Prof. J. P.).—Greek Life and Thought, from the Age of Alexander to the Roman Conquest. Cr. 8vo. 12s. 6d.
—— Social Life in Greece, from Homer to Menander. 6th Edit. Cr. 8vo. 9s.
—— The Greek World under Roman Sway, from Polybius to Plutarch. Cr. 8vo. 10s. 6d.
—— Problems in Greek History. Crown 8vo. 7s. 6d.

MARRIOTT (J. A. R.). (See Select Biography, p. 6.)

MICHELET (M.).—A Summary of Modern History. Translated by M. C. M. Simpson. Globe 8vo. 4s. 6d.

MULLINGER (J. B.).—Cambridge Characteristics in the Seventeenth Century. Cr. 8vo. 4s. 6d.

NORGATE (Kate).—England under the Angevin Kings. In 2 vols. 8vo. 32s.

OLIPHANT (Mrs. M. O. W.).—The Makers of Florence: Dante, Giotto, Savonarola, and their City. Illustr. Cr. 8vo. 10s. 6d.—Edition de Luxe. 8vo. 21s. net.
—— The Makers of Venice: Doges, Conquerors, Painters, and Men of Letters. Illustrated. Cr. 8vo. 10s. 6d.
—— Royal Edinburgh: Her Saints, Kings, Prophets, and Poets. Illustrated by G. Reid, R.S.A. Cr. 8vo. 10s. 6d.
—— Jerusalem, its History and Hope. Illust. 8vo. 21s.—Large Paper Edit. 50s. net.

OTTÉ (E. C.).—Scandinavian History. With Maps. Globe 8vo. 6s.

PALGRAVE (Sir F.).—History of Normandy and of England. 4 vols. 8vo. 4l. 4s.

PARKMAN (Francis). — Montcalm and Wolfe. Library Edition. Illustrated with Portraits and Maps. 2 vols. 8vo. 12s. 6d. each.
—— The Collected Works of Francis Parkman. Popular Edition. In 10 vols. Cr. 8vo. 7s. 6d. each; or complete, 3l. 13s. 6d.—Pioneers of France in the New World, 1 vol.; The Jesuits in North America, 1 vol.; La Salle and the Discovery of the Great West, 1 vol.; The Oregon Trail, 1 vol.; The Old Régime in Canada under Louis XIV., 1 vol.; Count Frontenac and New France under Louis XIV., 1 vol.; Montcalm and Wolfe, 2 vols.; The Conspiracy of Pontiac, 2 vols.
—— A Half Century of Conflict. 2 vols. 8vo. 25s.
—— The Oregon Trail. Illustrated. Med. 8vo. 21s.

PERKINS (J. B.).—France under the Regency. Cr. 8vo. 8s. 6d.

HISTORY—*continued*.

POOLE (R. L.).—A HISTORY OF THE HUGUE-NOTS OF THE DISPERSION AT THE RECALL OF THE EDICT OF NANTES. Cr. 8vo. 6s.

RHODES (J. F.).—HISTORY OF THE UNITED STATES FROM THE COMPROMISE OF 1850 TO 1880. 2 vols. 8vo. 24s.

ROGERS (Prof. J. E. Thorold).—HISTORICAL GLEANINGS. Cr. 8vo.—1st Series. 4s. 6d.—2nd Series. 6s.

SAYCE (Prof. A. H.).—THE ANCIENT EM-PIRES OF THE EAST. Cr. 8vo. 6s.

SEELEY (Prof. J. R.). — LECTURES AND ESSAYS. 8vo. 10s. 6d.

—— THE EXPANSION OF ENGLAND. Two Courses of Lectures. Cr. 8vo. 4s. 6d.

—— OUR COLONIAL EXPANSION. Extracts from the above. Cr. 8vo. 1s.

SEWELL (E. M.) and YONGE (C. M.).—EUROPEAN HISTORY, NARRATED IN A SERIES OF HISTORICAL SELECTIONS FROM THE BEST AUTHORITIES. 2 vols. 3rd Edit. Cr. 8vo. 6s. each.

SHUCKBURGH (E. S.).—A SCHOOL HIS-TORY OF ROME. Cr. 8vo. [*In preparation.*

STEPHEN (Sir J. Fitzjames, Bart.).—THE STORY OF NUNCOMAR AND THE IMPEACH-MENT OF SIR ELIJAH IMPEY. 2 vols. Cr. 8vo. 15s.

TAIT (C. W. A.).—ANALYSIS OF ENGLISH HISTORY, BASED ON GREEN'S "SHORT HIS-TORY OF THE ENGLISH PEOPLE." Cr. 8vo. 4s. 6d.

TOUT (T. F.).—ANALYSIS OF ENGLISH HIS-TORY. 18mo. 1s.

TREVELYAN (Sir Geo. Otto).—CAWNPORE. Cr. 8vo. 6s.

WHEELER (J. Talboys).—PRIMER OF IN-DIAN HISTORY, ASIATIC AND EUROPEAN. 18mo. 1s.

—— COLLEGE HISTORY OF INDIA, ASIATIC AND EUROPEAN. Cr. 8vo. 3s.; swd. 2s. 6d.

—— A SHORT HISTORY OF INDIA. With Maps. Cr. 8vo. 12s.

—— INDIA UNDER BRITISH RULE. 8vo. 12s. 6d.

WOOD (Rev. E. G.).—THE REGAL POWER OF THE CHURCH. 8vo. 4s. 6d.

YONGE (Charlotte).—CAMEOS FROM ENGLISH HISTORY. Ext. fcp. 8vo. 5s. each.—Vol. 1. FROM ROLLO TO EDWARD II.; Vol. 2. THE WARS IN FRANCE; Vol. 3. THE WARS OF THE ROSES; Vol. 4. REFORMATION TIMES; Vol. 5. ENGLAND AND SPAIN; Vol. 6. FORTY YEARS OF STEWART RULE (1603—43); Vol. 7. THE REBELLION AND RESTORATION (1642—1678).

—— THE VICTORIAN HALF-CENTURY. Cr. 8vo. 1s. 6d.; sewed, 1s.

—— THE STORY OF THE CHRISTIANS AND MOORS IN SPAIN. 18mo. 4s. 6d.

HORTICULTURE. (*See* GARDENING.)

HYGIENE.

BERNERS (J.)—FIRST LESSONS ON HEALTH. 18mo. 1s.

BLYTH (A. Wynter).—A MANUAL OF PUBLIC HEALTH. 8vo. 17s. net.

BROWNE (J. H. Balfour).—WATER SUPPLY. Cr. 8vo. 2s. 6d.

CORFIELD (Dr. W. H.).—THE TREATMENT AND UTILISATION OF SEWAGE. 3rd Edit. Revised by the Author, and by LOUIS C. PARKES, M.D. 8vo. 16s.

GOODFELLOW (J.).—THE DIETETIC VALUE OF BREAD. Cr. 8vo. 6s.

KINGSLEY (Charles).—SANITARY AND SO-CIAL LECTURES. Cr. 8vo. 3s. 6d.

—— HEALTH AND EDUCATION. Cr. 8vo. 6s.

MIERS (H. A.) and CROSSKEY (R.).—THE SOIL IN RELATION TO HEALTH. Cr. 8vo. 3s. 6d.

REYNOLDS (Prof. Osborne).—SEWER GAS, AND HOW TO KEEP IT OUT OF HOUSES. 3rd Edit. Cr. 8vo. 1s. 6d.

RICHARDSON (Dr. B. W.).—HYGEIA: A CITY OF HEALTH. Cr. 8vo. 1s.

—— THE FUTURE OF SANITARY SCIENCE. Cr. 8vo. 1s.

—— ON ALCOHOL. Cr. 8vo. 1s.

HYMNOLOGY.
(*See under* THEOLOGY, p. 35.)

ILLUSTRATED BOOKS.

BALCH (Elizabeth). — GLIMPSES OF OLD ENGLISH HOMES. Gl. 4to. 14s.

BLAKE. (*See* BIOGRAPHY, p. 3.)

BOUGHTON (G. H.) and ABBEY (E. A.). (*See* VOYAGES AND TRAVELS.)

CHRISTMAS CAROL (A). Printed in Colours, with Illuminated Borders. 4to. 21s.

DAYS WITH SIR ROGER DE COVER-LEY. From the *Spectator*. Illustrated by HUGH THOMSON. Cr. 8vo. 6s.—Also with uncut edges, paper label. 6s.

DELL (E. C.).—PICTURES FROM SHELLEY. Engraved by J. D. COOPER. Folio. 21s. net.

GASKELL (Mrs.).—CRANFORD. Illustrated by HUGH THOMSON. Cr. 8vo. 6s.—Also with uncut edges paper label. 6s.

GOLDSMITH (Oliver). — THE VICAR OF WAKEFIELD. New Edition, with 182 Illus-trations by HUGH THOMSON. Preface by AUSTIN DOBSON. Cr. 8vo. 6s.—Also with Uncut Edges, paper label. 6s.

GREEN (John Richard). — ILLUSTRATED EDITION OF THE SHORT HISTORY OF THE ENGLISH PEOPLE. In Parts. Sup. roy. 8vo. 1s. each net. Part I. Oct. 1891. Vols. I. and II. 12s. each net.

GRIMM. (*See* BOOKS FOR THE YOUNG.)

HALLWARD (R. F.).—FLOWERS OF PARA-DISE. Music, Verse, Design, Illustration. 6s.

HAMERTON (P. G.).—MAN IN ART. With Etchings and Photogravures. 3l. 13s. 6d. net.—Large Paper Edition. 10l. 10s. net.

HARRISON (F.).—ANNALS OF AN OLD MA-NOR HOUSE. SUTTON PLACE, GUILDFORD. 4to. 42s. net.

IRVING (Washington).—OLD CHRISTMAS. From the Sketch Book. Illustr. by RANDOLPH CALDECOTT. Gilt edges. Cr. 8vo. 6s.—Also with uncut edges, paper label. 6s.—Large Paper Edition. 30s. net.

—— BRACEBRIDGE HALL. Illustr. by RAN-DOLPH CALDECOTT. Gilt edges. Cr. 8vo. 6s.—Also with uncut edges, paper label. 6s.

—— OLD CHRISTMAS AND BRACEBRIDGE HALL. *Edition de Luxe.* Roy. 8vo. 21s.

KINGSLEY (Charles).—THE WATER BABIES. (*See* BOOKS FOR THE YOUNG.)
—— THE HEROES. (*See* BOOKS for the YOUNG.)
—— GLAUCUS. (*See* NATURAL HISTORY.)

LANG (Andrew).—THE LIBRARY. With a Chapter on Modern English Illustrated Books, by AUSTIN DOBSON. Cr. 8vo. 4*s*. 6*d*.
— Large Paper Edition. 21*s*. net.

LYTE (H. C. Maxwell). (*See* HISTORY.)

MAHAFFY (Rev. Prof. J. P.) and ROGERS (J. E.). (*See* VOYAGES AND TRAVELS.)

MEREDITH (L. A.).—BUSH FRIENDS IN TASMANIA. Native Flowers, Fruits, and Insects, with Prose and Verse Descriptions. Folio. 52*s*. 6*d*. net.

OLD SONGS. With Drawings by E. A. ABBEY and A. PARSONS. 4to, mor. gilt. 31*s*. 6*d*.

PROPERT (J. L.). (*See* ART.)

STUART, RELICS OF THE ROYAL HOUSE OF. Illustrated by 40 Plates in Colours drawn from Relics of the Stuarts by WILLIAM GIBB. With an Introduction by JOHN SKELTON, C.B., LL.D., and Descriptive Notes by W. ST. JOHN HOPE. Folio, half morocco, gilt edges. 10*l*. 10*s*. net.

TENNYSON (Lord H.).—JACK AND THE BEAN-STALK. English Hexameters. Illustrated by R. CALDECOTT. Fcp. 4to. 3*s*. 6*d*.

TRISTRAM (W. O.).—COACHING DAYS AND COACHING WAYS. Illust. H. RAILTON and HUGH THOMSON. Cr. 8vo. 6*s*.—Also with uncut edges, paper label, 6*s*.—Large Paper Edition, 30*s*. net.

TURNER'S LIBER STUDIORUM: A DESCRIPTION AND A CATALOGUE. By W. G. RAWLINSON. Med. 8vo. 12*s*. 6*d*.

WALTON and COTTON—LOWELL.—THE COMPLETE ANGLER. With Introduction by JAS. RUSSELL LOWELL. 2 vols. Ext. cr. 8vo. 52*s*. 6*d*. net.

LANGUAGE. (*See* PHILOLOGY.)

LAW.

BERNARD (M.).—FOUR LECTURES ON SUBJECTS CONNECTED WITH DIPLOMACY. 8vo. 9*s*.

BIGELOW (M. M.).—HISTORY OF PROCEDURE IN ENGLAND FROM THE NORMAN CONQUEST, 1066-1204. 8vo. 16*s*.

BOUTMY (E.). — STUDIES IN CONSTITUTIONAL LAW. Transl. by Mrs. DICEY. Preface by Prof. A. V. DICEY. Cr. 8vo. 6*s*.
—— THE ENGLISH CONSTITUTION. Transl. by Mrs. EADEN. Introduction by Sir F. POLLOCK, Bart. Cr. 8vo. 6*s*.

CHERRY (R. R.). — LECTURES ON THE GROWTH OF CRIMINAL LAW IN ANCIENT COMMUNITIES. 8vo. 5*s*. net.

DICEY (Prof. A. V.).—INTRODUCTION TO THE STUDY OF THE LAW OF THE CONSTITUTION. 4th Edit. 8vo. 12*s*. 6*d*.

ENGLISH CITIZEN SERIES, THE. (*See* POLITICS.)

HOLLAND (Prof. T. E.).—THE TREATY RELATIONS OF RUSSIA AND TURKEY, FROM 1774 TO 1853. Cr. 8vo. 2*s*.

HOLMES (O. W., jun.).—THE COMMON LAW. 8vo. 12*s*.

LIGHTWOOD (J. M.).—THE NATURE OF POSITIVE LAW. 8vo. 12*s*. 6*d*.

MAITLAND (F. W.).—PLEAS OF THE CROWN FOR THE COUNTY OF GLOUCESTER, A.D. 1221. 8vo. 7*s*. 6*d*.
—— JUSTICE AND POLICE. Cr. 8vo. 3*s*. 6*d*.

MONAHAN (James H.).—THE METHOD OF LAW. Cr. 8vo. 6*s*.

PATERSON (James).—COMMENTARIES ON THE LIBERTY OF THE SUBJECT, AND THE LAWS OF ENGLAND RELATING TO THE SECURITY OF THE PERSON. 2 vols. Cr. 8vo. 21*s*.
—— THE LIBERTY OF THE PRESS, SPEECH, AND PUBLIC WORSHIP. Cr. 8vo. 12*s*.

PHILLIMORE (John G.).—PRIVATE LAW AMONG THE ROMANS. 8vo. 6*s*.

POLLOCK (Sir F., Bart.).—ESSAYS IN JURISPRUDENCE AND ETHICS. 8vo. 10*s*. 6*d*.
—— THE LAND LAWS. Cr. 8vo. 3*s*. 6*d*.
—— LEADING CASES DONE INTO ENGLISH. Cr. 8vo. 3*s*. 6*d*.

RICHEY (Alex. G.).—THE IRISH LAND LAWS. Cr. 8vo. 3*s*. 6*d*.

SELBORNE (Earl of).—JUDICIAL PROCEDURE IN THE PRIVY COUNCIL. 8vo. 1*s*. net

STEPHEN (Sir J. F., Bart.).—A DIGEST OF THE LAW OF EVIDENCE. 6th Ed. Cr. 8vo. 6*s*.
—— A DIGEST OF THE CRIMINAL LAW: CRIMES AND PUNISHMENTS. 4th Ed. 8vo. 16*s*.
—— A DIGEST OF THE LAW OF CRIMINAL PROCEDURE IN INDICTABLE OFFENCES. By Sir J. F., Bart., and HERBERT STEPHEN, LL.M. 8vo. 12*s*. 6*d*.
—— A HISTORY OF THE CRIMINAL LAW OF ENGLAND. 3 vols. 8vo. 48*s*.
—— A GENERAL VIEW OF THE CRIMINAL LAW OF ENGLAND. 2nd Edit. 8vo. 14*s*.

STEPHEN (J. K.).—INTERNATIONAL LAW AND INTERNATIONAL RELATIONS. Cr. 8vo. 6*s*.

WILLIAMS (S. E.).—FORENSIC FACTS AND FALLACIES. Globe 8vo. 4*s*. 6*d*.

LETTERS. (*See under* LITERATURE, p. 20.)

LIFE-BOAT.

GILMORE (Rev. John).—STORM WARRIORS; or, Life-Boat Work on the Goodwin Sands. Cr. 8vo. 3*s*. 6*d*.

LEWIS (Richard).—HISTORY OF THE LIFE-BOAT AND ITS WORK. Cr. 8vo. 5*s*.

LIGHT. (*See under* PHYSICS, p. 29.)

LITERATURE.

History and Criticism of—Commentaries, etc.—Poetry and the Drama—Poetical Collections and Selections—Prose Fiction—Collected Works, Essays, Lectures, Letters, Miscellaneous Works.

History and Criticism of.

(*See also* ESSAYS, p. 20.)

ARNOLD (M.). (*See* ESSAYS. p. 20.)

BROOKE (Stopford A.).—A PRIMER OF ENGLISH LITERATURE. 18mo. 1*s*. — Large Paper Edition. 8vo. 7*s*. 6*d*.
—— A HISTORY OF EARLY ENGLISH LITERATURE. 2 vols. 8vo. 20*s*. net.

LITERATURE.

History and Criticism of—*continued.*

CLASSICAL WRITERS. Edited by JOHN RICHARD GREEN. Fcp. 8vo. 1s. 6d. each.
DEMOSTHENES. By Prof. BUTCHER, M.A.
EURIPIDES. By Prof. MAHAFFY.
LIVY. By the Rev. W. W. CAPES, M.A.
MILTON. By STOPFORD A. BROOKE.
SOPHOCLES. By Prof. L. CAMPBELL, M.A.
TACITUS. By Messrs. CHURCH and BRODRIBB.
VERGIL. By Prof. NETTLESHIP, M.A.

ENGLISH MEN OF LETTERS. (*See* BIOGRAPHY, p. 4.)

HISTORY OF ENGLISH LITERATURE. In 4 vols. Cr. 8vo.
EARLY ENGLISH LITERATURE. By STOPFORD BROOKE, M.A. [*In preparation.*
ELIZABETHAN LITERATURE (1560—1665). By GEORGE SAINTSBURY. 7s. 6d.
EIGHTEENTH CENTURY LITERATURE (1660—1780). By EDMUND GOSSE, M.A. 7s. 6d.
THE MODERN PERIOD. By Prof. DOWDEN. [*In preparation.*

JEBB (Prof. R. C.).—A PRIMER OF GREEK LITERATURE. 18mo. 1s.
—— THE ATTIC ORATORS, FROM ANTIPHON TO ISAEOS. 2 vols 8vo. 25s.

JOHNSON'S LIVES OF THE POETS. MILTON, DRYDEN, POPE, ADDISON, SWIFT, AND GRAY. With Macaulay's "Life of Johnson" Ed. by M. ARNOLD. Cr. 8vo. 4s. 6d.

KINGSLEY (Charles). — LITERARY AND GENERAL LECTURES. Cr. 8vo. 3s. 6d.

MAHAFFY (Prof. J. P.).—A HISTORY OF CLASSICAL GREEK LITERATURE. 2 vols. Cr. 8vo.—Vol. 1. THE POETS. With an Appendix on Homer by Prof. SAYCE. In 2 Parts.—Vol. 2. THE PROSE WRITERS. In 2 Parts. 4s. 6d. each.

MORLEY (John). (*See* COLLECTED WORKS, p. 23.)

NICHOL (Prof. J.) and McCORMICK (Prof (W. S.).—A SHORT HISTORY OF ENGLISH LITERATURE. Globe 8vo. [*In preparation.*

OLIPHANT (Mrs. M. O. W.).—THE LITERARY HISTORY OF ENGLAND IN THE END OF THE 18TH AND BEGINNING OF THE 19TH CENTURY. 3 vols. 8vo. 21s.

RYLAND (F.).—CHRONOLOGICAL OUTLINES OF ENGLISH LITERATURE. Cr. 8vo. 6s.

WARD (Prof. A. W.).—A HISTORY OF ENGLISH DRAMATIC LITERATURE, TO THE DEATH OF QUEEN ANNE. 2 vols. 8vo. 32s.

WILKINS (Prof. A. S.).—A PRIMER OF ROMAN LITERATURE. 18mo. 1s.

Commentaries, etc.

BROWNING.
A PRIMER ON BROWNING. By MARY WILSON. Cr. 8vo. 2s. 6d.

CHAUCER.
A PRIMER OF CHAUCER. By A. W. POLLARD. 18mo. 1s.

DANTE.
READINGS ON THE PURGATORIO OF DANTE. Chiefly based on the Commentary of Benvenuto da Imola. By the Hon. W. W. VERNON, M.A. With an Introduction by Dean CHURCH. 2 vols. Cr. 8vo. 24s.

HOMER.
HOMERIC DICTIONARY. (*See* DICTIONARIES.)
THE PROBLEM OF THE HOMERIC POEMS. By Prof. W. D. GEDDES. 8vo. 14s.
HOMERIC SYNCHRONISM. An Inquiry into the Time and Place of Homer. By the Rt. Hon. W. E. GLADSTONE. Cr. 8vo. 6s.
PRIMER OF HOMER. By the same. 18mo. 1s.
LANDMARKS OF HOMERIC STUDY, TOGETHER WITH AN ESSAY ON THE POINTS OF CONTACT BETWEEN THE ASSYRIAN TABLETS AND THE HOMERIC TEXT. By the same. Cr. 8vo. 2s. 6d.
COMPANION TO THE ILIAD FOR ENGLISH READERS. By W. LEAF, Litt.D. Crown 8vo. 7s. 6d.

HORACE.
STUDIES, LITERARY AND HISTORICAL, IN THE ODES OF HORACE. By A. W. VERRALL, Litt.D. 8vo. 8s. 6d.

SHAKESPEARE.
A PRIMER OF SHAKSPERE. By Prof. DOWDEN. 18mo. 1s.
A SHAKESPEARIAN GRAMMAR. By Rev. E. A. ABBOTT. Ext. fcp. 8vo. 6s.
SHAKESPEAREANA GENEALOGICA. By G. R. FRENCH. 8vo. 15s.
A SELECTION FROM THE LIVES IN NORTH'S PLUTARCH WHICH ILLUSTRATE SHAKESPEARE'S PLAYS. Edited by Rev. W. W. SKEAT, M.A. Cr. 8vo. 6s.
SHORT STUDIES OF SHAKESPEARE'S PLOTS. By Prof. CYRIL RANSOME. Cr. 8vo. 3s. 6d. —Also separately: HAMLET, 9d.; MACBETH, 9d.; TEMPEST, 9d.
CALIBAN: A Critique on "The Tempest" and "A Midsummer Night's Dream." By Sir DANIEL WILSON. 8vo. 10s. 6d.

TENNYSON.
A COMPANION TO "IN MEMORIAM." By ELIZABETH R. CHAPMAN. Globe 8vo. 2s.
LECTURES ON THE IDYLLS OF THE KING. By H. LITTLEDALE, M.A. Cr. 8vo. 4s. 6d.

WORDSWORTH.
WORDSWORTHIANA: A Selection of Papers read to the Wordsworth Society. Edited by W. KNIGHT. Cr. 8vo. 7s. 6d.

Poetry and the Drama.

ALDRICH (T. Bailey).—THE SISTERS' TRAGEDY: with other Poems, Lyrical and Dramatic. Fcp. 8vo. 3s. 6d. net.

AN ANCIENT CITY: AND OTHER POEMS. Ext. fcp. 8vo. 6s.

ANDERSON (A.).—BALLADS AND SONNETS. Cr. 8vo. 5s.

ARNOLD (Matthew). — THE COMPLETE POETICAL WORKS. New Edition. 3 vols. Cr. 8vo. 7s. 6d. each.
Vol. 1. EARLY POEMS, NARRATIVE POEMS AND SONNETS.
Vol. 2. LYRIC AND ELEGIAC POEMS.
Vol. 3. DRAMATIC AND LATER POEMS.
—— COMPLETE POETICAL WORKS. 1 vol. Cr. 8vo. 7s. 6d.
—— SELECTED POEMS. 18mo. 4s. 6d.

AUSTIN (Alfred).—POETICAL WORKS. New Collected Edition. 6 vols. Cr. 8vo. 5s. each.
    Vol. 1. THE TOWER OF BABEL.
    Vol. 2. SAVONAROLA, etc.
    Vol. 3. PRINCE LUCIFER.
    Vol. 4. THE HUMAN TRAGEDY.
    Vol. 5. LYRICAL POEMS.
    Vol. 6. NARRATIVE POEMS.
—— SOLILOQUIES IN SONG. Cr. 8vo. 6s.
—— AT THE GATE OF THE CONVENT: and other Poems. Cr. 8vo. 6s.
—— MADONNA'S CHILD. Cr. 4to. 3s. 6d.
—— ROME OR DEATH. Cr. 4to. 9s.
—— THE GOLDEN AGE. Cr. 8vo. 5s.
—— THE SEASON. Cr. 8vo. 5s.
—— LOVE'S WIDOWHOOD. Cr. 8vo. 6s.
—— ENGLISH LYRICS. Cr. 8vo. 3s. 6d.
—— FORTUNATUS THE PESSIMIST. Cr. 8vo. 6s.

BETSY LEE: A FO'C'S'LE YARN. Ext. fcp. 8vo. 3s. 6d.

BLACKIE (John Stuart).—MESSIS VITAE: Gleanings of Song from a Happy Life. Cr. 8vo. 4s. 6d.
—— THE WISE MEN OF GREECE. In a Series of Dramatic Dialogues. Cr. 8vo. 9s.
—— GOETHE'S FAUST. Translated into English Verse. 2nd Edit. Cr. 8vo. 9s.

BLAKE. (See BIOGRAPHY, p. 3.)

BROOKE (Stopford A.).—RIQUET OF THE TUFT: A Love Drama. Ext. cr. 8vo. 6s.
—— POEMS. Globe 8vo. 6s.

BROWN (T. E.).—THE MANX WITCH: and other Poems. Cr. 8vo. 6s.
—— OLD JOHN, AND OTHER POEMS. Crown 8vo. 6s.

BURGON (Dean).—POEMS. Ex. fcp. 8vo. 4s. 6d.

BURNS. THE POETICAL WORKS. With a Biographical Memoir by ALEXANDER SMITH. In 2 vols. Fcp. 8vo. 10s. (See also GLOBE LIBRARY, p. 21.)

BUTLER (Samuel).—HUDIBRAS. Edit. by ALFRED MILNES. Fcp. 8vo.—Part I. 3s. 6d.; Parts II. and III. 4s. 6d.

BYRON. (See GOLDEN TREASURY SERIES, p. 21.)

CALDERON.—SELECT PLAYS. Edited by NORMAN MACCOLL. Cr. 8vo. 14s.

CAUTLEY (G. S.).—A CENTURY OF EMBLEMS. With Illustrations by Lady MARION ALFORD. Small 4to. 10s. 6d.

CLOUGH (A. H.).—POEMS. Cr. 8vo. 7s. 6d.

COLERIDGE: POETICAL AND DRAMATIC WORKS. 4 vols. Fcp. 8vo. 31s. 6d.—Also an Edition on Large Paper, 2l. 12s. 6d.
—— COMPLETE POETICAL WORKS. With Introduction by J. D. CAMPBELL, and Portrait. Cr. 8vo. 7s. 6d.

COLQUHOUN.—RHYMES AND CHIMES. By F. S. COLQUHOUN (née F. S. FULLER MAITLAND). Ext. fcp. 8vo. 2s. 6d.

COWPER. (See GLOBE LIBRARY, p. 21; GOLDEN TREASURY SERIES, p. 21.)

CRAIK (Mrs.).—POEMS. Ext. fcp. 8vo. 6s.

DE VERE (A.).—POETICAL WORKS. 6 vols. Cr. 8vo. 5s. each.

DOYLE (Sir F. H.).—THE RETURN OF THE GUARDS: and other Poems. Cr. 8vo. 7s. 6d.

DRYDEN. (See GLOBE LIBRARY, p. 21.)

EMERSON. (See COLLECTED WORKS, p. 21.)

EVANS (Sebastian). — BROTHER FABIAN'S MANUSCRIPT: and other Poems. Fcp. 8vo. 6s.
—— IN THE STUDIO: A Decade of Poems. Ext. fcp. 8vo. 5s.

FITZ GERALD (Caroline).—VENETIA VICTRIX: and other Poems. Ext. fcp. 8vo. 3s. 6d.

FITZGERALD (Edward).—THE RUBÁIYÁT OF OMAR KHÁYYÁM. Ext. cr. 8vo. 10s. 6d.

FO'C'SLE YARNS, including "Betsy Lee," and other Poems. Cr. 8vo. 6s.

FRASER-TYTLER. — SONGS IN MINOR KEYS. By C. C. FRASER-TYTLER (Mrs. EDWARD LIDDELL). 2nd Edit. 18mo. 6s.

FURNIVALL (F. J.).—LE MORTE ARTHUR. Edited from the Harleian MSS. 2252, in the British Museum. Fcp. 8vo. 7s. 6d.

GARNETT (R.).—IDYLLS AND EPIGRAMS. Chiefly from the Greek Anthology. Fcp. 8vo. 2s. 6d.

GOETHE.—FAUST. (See BLACKIE.)
—— REYNARD THE FOX. Transl. into English Verse by A. D. AINSLIE. Cr. 8vo. 7s. 6d.

GOLDSMITH.—THE TRAVELLER AND THE DESERTED VILLAGE. With Introduction and Notes, by ARTHUR BARRETT, B.A. 1s. 9d.; sewed, 1s. 6d.—THE TRAVELLER (separately), sewed, 1s.—By J. W. HALES. Cr. 8vo. 6d. (See also GLOBE LIBRARY, p. 21.)

GRAHAM (David).—KING JAMES I. An Historical Tragedy. Globe 8vo. 7s.

GRAY.—POEMS. With Introduction and Notes, by J. BRADSHAW, LL.D. Gl. 8vo. 1s. 9d.; sewed, 1s. 6d. (See also COLLECTED WORKS, p. 22.)

HALLWARD. (See ILLUSTRATED BOOKS.)

HAYES (A.).—THE MARCH OF MAN: and other Poems. Fcp. 8vo. 3s. 6d. net.

HERRICK. (See GOLDEN TREASURY SERIES, p. 21.)

HOPKINS (Ellice).—AUTUMN SWALLOWS: A Book of Lyrics. Ext. fcp. 8vo. 6s.

HOSKEN (J. D.).—PHAON AND SAPPHO, AND NIMROD. Fcp. 8vo. 5s.

JONES (H. A.).—SAINTS AND SINNERS. Ext. fcp. 8vo. 3s. 6d.
—— THE CRUSADERS. Fcp. 8vo. 2s. 6d.

KEATS. (See GOLDEN TREASURY SERIES, p. 21.)

KINGSLEY (Charles).—POEMS. Cr. 8vo. 3s. 6d.—Pocket Edition. 18mo. 1s. 6d.—Eversley Edition. 2 vols. Cr. 8vo. 10s.

LAMB. (See COLLECTED WORKS, p. 22.)

LANDOR. (See GOLDEN TREASURY SERIES, p. 22.)

LONGFELLOW. (See GOLDEN TREASURY SERIES, p. 22.)

LOWELL (Jas. Russell).—COMPLETE POETICAL WORKS. 18mo. 4s. 6d.
—— With Introduction by THOMAS HUGHES, and Portrait. Cr. 8vo. 7s. 6d.
—— HEARTSEASE AND RUE. Cr. 8vo. 5s.
—— OLD ENGLISH DRAMATISTS. Cr. 8vo. 5s. (See also COLLECTED WORKS, p. 23.)

LUCAS (F.).—SKETCHES OF RURAL LIFE. Poems. Globe 8vo. 5s.

LITERATURE.

Poetry and the Drama—*continued*.

MEREDITH (George). — A READING OF EARTH. Ext. fcp. 8vo. 5s.

—— POEMS AND LYRICS OF THE JOY OF EARTH. Ext. fcp. 8vo. 6s.

—— BALLADS AND POEMS OF TRAGIC LIFE. Cr. 8vo. 6s.

—— MODERN LOVE. Ex. fcap. 8vo. 5s.

—— THE EMPTY PURSE. Fcp. 8vo. 5s.

MILTON.—POETICAL WORKS. Edited, with Introductions and Notes, by Prof. DAVID MASSON, M.A. 3 vols. 8vo. 2l. 2s.—[Uniform with the Cambridge Shakespeare.]

—— —— Edited by Prof. MASSON. 3 vols. Globe 8vo. 15s.

—— —— *Globe Edition.* Edited by Prof. MASSON. Globe 8vo. 3s. 6d.

—— PARADISE LOST, BOOKS 1 and 2. Edited by MICHAEL MACMILLAN, B.A. 1s. 9d.; sewed, 1s. 6d.—BOOKS 1 and 2 (separately), 1s. 3d. each; sewed, 1s. each.

—— L'ALLEGRO, IL PENSEROSO, LVCIDAS, ARCADES, SONNETS, ETC. Edited by WM. BELL, M.A. 1s. 9d.; sewed, 1s. 6d.

—— COMUS. By the same. 1s. 3d.; swd. 1s.

—— SAMSON AGONISTES. Edited by H. M. PERCIVAL, M.A. 2s.; sewed, 1s. 9d.

MOULTON (Louise Chandler). — IN THE GARDEN OF DREAMS: Lyrics and Sonnets. Cr. 8vo. 6s.

—— SWALLOW FLIGHTS. Cr. 8vo. 6s.

MUDIE (C. E.).—STRAY LEAVES: Poems. 4th Edit. Ext. fcp. 8vo. 3s. 6d.

MYERS (E.).—THE PURITANS: A Poem. Ext. fcp. 8vo. 2s. 6d.

—— POEMS. Ext. fcp. 8vo. 4s. 6d.

—— THE DEFENCE OF ROME: and other Poems. Ext. fcp. 8vo. 5s.

—— THE JUDGMENT OF PROMETHEUS: and other Poems. Ext. fcp. 8vo. 3s. 6d.

MYERS (F. W. H.).—THE RENEWAL OF YOUTH: and other Poems. Cr. 8vo. 7s. 6d.

—— ST. PAUL: A Poem. Ext. fcp. 8vo. 2s. 6d.

NORTON (Hon. Mrs.).—THE LADY OF LA GARAYE. 9th Edit. Fcp. 8vo. 4s. 6d.

PALGRAVE (Prof. F. T.).—ORIGINAL HYMNS. 3rd Edit. 18mo. 1s. 6d.

—— LYRICAL POEMS. Ext. fcp. 8vo. 6s.

—— VISIONS OF ENGLAND. Cr. 8vo. 7s. 6d.

—— AMENOPHIS. 18mo. 4s. 6d.

PALGRAVE (W. G.).—A VISION OF LIFE: SEMBLANCE AND REALITY. Cr. 8vo. 7s. net.

PEEL (Edmund).—ECHOES FROM HOREB: and other Poems. Cr. 8vo. 3s. 6d

POPE. (*See* GLOBE LIBRARY, p. 21.)

RAWNSLEY (H. D.).—POEMS, BALLADS, AND BUCOLICS. Fcp. 8vo. 5s.

ROSCOE (W. C.).—POEMS. Edit. by E. M. ROSCOE. Cr. 8vo. 7s. net.

ROSSETTI (Christina).—POEMS. New Collected Edition. Globe 8vo. 7s. 6d.

SCOTT.—THE LAY OF THE LAST MINSTREL, and THE LADY OF THE LAKE. Edited by Prof. F. T. PALGRAVE. 1s.

—— THE LAY OF THE LAST MINSTREL. By G. H. STUART, M.A., and E. H. ELLIOT, B.A. Globe 8vo. 2s.; sewed, 1s. 9d.—Canto I. 9d.—Cantos I.—III. and IV.—VI. 1s. 3d. each; sewed, 1s. each.

—— MARMION. Edited by MICHAEL MACMILLAN, B.A. 3s.; sewed, 2s. 6d.

—— MARMION, and THE LORD OF THE ISLES. By Prof. F. T. PALGRAVE. 1s.

—— THE LADY OF THE LAKE. By G. H. STUART, M.A. Gl. 8vo. 2s. 6d.; swd. 2s.

—— ROKEBY. By MICHAEL MACMILLAN, B.A. 3s.; sewed, 2s. 6d.

(*See also* GLOBE LIBRARY, p. 21.)

SHAIRP (John Campbell).—GLEN DESSERAY: and other Poems, Lyrical and Elegiac. Ed. by F. T. PALGRAVE. Cr. 8vo. 6s.

SHAKESPEARE.—THE WORKS OF WILLIAM SHAKESPEARE. *Cambridge Edition.* New and Revised Edition, by W. ALDIS WRIGHT, M.A. 9 vols. 8vo. 10s. 6d. each.

—— *Victoria Edition.* In 3 vols.—COMEDIES; HISTORIES; TRAGEDIES. Cr. 8vo. 6s. each.

—— THE TEMPEST. With Introduction and Notes, by K. DEIGHTON.. Gl. 8vo. 1s. 9d.; sewed, 1s. 6d.

—— MUCH ADO ABOUT NOTHING. 2s.; sewed, 1s. 9d.

—— A MIDSUMMER NIGHT'S DREAM. 1s. 9d.; sewed, 1s. 6d.

—— THE MERCHANT OF VENICE. 1s. 9d.; sewed, 1s. 6d.

—— AS YOU LIKE IT. 1s. 9d.; sewed, 1s. 6d.

—— TWELFTH NIGHT. 1s. 9d.; sewed, 1s. 6d.

—— THE WINTER'S TALE. 2s.; sewed, 1s. 9d.

—— KING JOHN. 1s. 9d.; sewed, 1s. 6d.

—— RICHARD II. 1s. 9d.; sewed, 1s. 6d.

—— HENRY V. 1s. 9d.; sewed, 1s. 6d.

—— RICHARD III. By C. H. TAWNEY, M.A. 2s. 6d.; sewed, 2s.

—— CORIOLANUS. By K. DEIGHTON. 2s. 6d.; sewed, 2s.

—— JULIUS CÆSAR. 1s. 9d.; sewed, 1s. 6d.

—— MACBETH. 1s. 9d.; sewed, 1s. 6d.

—— HAMLET. 2s. 6d.; sewed, 2s.

—— KING LEAR. 1s. 9d.; sewed, 1s. 6d.

—— OTHELLO. 2s.; sewed, 1s. 9d.

—— ANTONY AND CLEOPATRA. 2s. 6d.; swd. 2s.

—— CYMBELINE. 2s. 6d.; sewed, 2s.

(*See also* GLOBE LIBRARY, p. 21; GOLDEN TREASURY SERIES, p. 21.)

SHELLEY.—COMPLETE POETICAL WORKS. Edited by Prof. DOWDEN. Portrait. Cr. 8vo. 7s. 6d. (*See* GOLDEN TREASURY SERIES, p. 21.)

SMITH (C. Barnard).—POEMS. Fcp. 8vo. 5s.

SMITH (Horace).—POEMS. Globe 8vo. 5s.

—— INTERLUDES. Cr. 8vo. 5s.

SPENSER.—FAIRIE QUEENE. Book I. By H. M. PERCIVAL, M.A. Gl. 8vo. 3s.; swd., 2s. 6d. (*See also* GLOBE LIBRARY, p. 21.)

STEPHENS (J. B.).—CONVICT ONCE: and other Poems. Cr. 8vo. 7s. 6d.

STRETTELL (Alma).—SPANISH AND ITALIAN FOLK SONGS. Illustr. Roy. 16mo. 12s. 6d.

SYMONS (Arthur). — DAYS AND NIGHTS. Globe 8vo. 6s.

TENNYSON (Lord).—COMPLETE WORKS. New and Enlarged Edition, with Portrait. Cr. 8vo. 7s. 6d.—*School Edition.* In Four Parts. Cr. 8vo. 2s. 6d. each.

—— POETICAL WORKS. *Pocket Edition.* 18mo, morocco, gilt edges. 7s. 6d. net.

—— WORKS. *Library Edition.* In 8 vols. Globe 8vo. 5s. each. [Each volume may be had separately.]—POEMS, 2 vols.—IDYLLS OF THE KING.—THE PRINCESS, and MAUD.—ENOCH ARDEN, and IN MEMORIAM.—BALLADS, and other Poems.—QUEEN MARY, and HAROLD.—BECKET, and other Plays.

—— WORKS. *Ext. fcp. 8vo. Edition,* on Hand-made Paper. In 10 vols. (supplied in sets only). 5l. 5s. 0d.—EARLY POEMS.—LUCRETIUS, and other Poems.—IDYLLS OF THE KING.—THE PRINCESS, and MAUD.—ENOCH ARDEN, and IN MEMORIAM.—QUEEN MARY, and HAROLD.—BALLADS, and other Poems. —BECKET, THE CUP.—THE FORESTERS, THE FALCON, THE PROMISE OF MAY.— TIRESIAS, and other Poems.

—— WORKS. *Miniature Edition,* in 16 vols., viz. THE POETICAL WORKS. 12 vols. in a box. 25s.—THE DRAMATIC WORKS. 4 vols. in a box. 10s. 6d.

—— WORKS. *Miniature Edition on India Paper.* POETICAL AND DRAMATIC WORKS. 8 vols. in a box. 40s. net.

—— *The Original Editions.* Fcp. 8vo. POEMS. 6s.
MAUD: and other Poems. 3s. 6d.
THE PRINCESS. 3s. 6d.
THE HOLY GRAIL: and other Poems. 4s. 6d.
BALLADS: and other Poems. 5s.
HAROLD: A Drama. 6s.
QUEEN MARY: A Drama. 6s.
THE CUP, and THE FALCON. 5s.
BECKET. 6s.
TIRESIAS: and other Poems. 6s.
LOCKSLEY HALL SIXTY YEARS AFTER, etc. 6s.
DEMETER: and other Poems. 6s.
THE FORESTERS: ROBIN HOOD AND MAID MARIAN. 6s.
THE DEATH OF OENONE, AKBAR'S DREAM, AND OTHER POEMS. 6s.
POEMS BY TWO BROTHERS. 6s.

—— *The Royal Edition.* 1 vol. 8vo. 16s.

—— THE TENNYSON BIRTHDAY BOOK. Edit. by EMILY SHAKESPEAR. 18mo. 2s. 6d.

—— THE BROOK. With 20 Illustrations by A. WOODRUFF. 32mo. 2s. 6d.

—— SONGS FROM TENNYSON'S WRITINGS. Square 8vo. 2s. 6d.

—— SELECTIONS FROM TENNYSON. With Introduction and Notes, by F. J. ROWE, M.A., and W. T. WEBB, M.A. Globe 8vo. 3s. 6d.

—— ENOCH ARDEN. By W. T. WEBB, M.A. Globe 8vo. 2s. 6d.

—— AYLMER'S FIELD. By W. T. WEBB, M.A. Globe 8vo. 2s. 6d.

—— THE COMING OF ARTHUR, and THE PASSING OF ARTHUR. By F. J. ROWE. Gl. 8vo. 2s. 6d.

—— THE PRINCESS. By P. M. WALLACE, M.A. Globe 8vo. 3s. 6d.

—— GARETH AND LYNETTE. By G. C. MACAULAY, M.A. 2s. 6d.

—— GERAINT AND ENID. By G. C. MACAULAY, M.A. 2s. 6d.

—— THE HOLY GRAIL. By G. C. MACAULAY, M.A. 2s. 6d.

—— TENNYSON FOR THE YOUNG. By Canon AINGER. 18mo. 1s. net.—Large Paper, uncut, 3s. 6d.; gilt edges, 4s. 6d.

TENNYSON (Lord).—BECKET. As arranged for the Stage by H. IRVING. 8vo. swd. 2s. net.

TENNYSON (Frederick).—THE ISLES OF GREECE: SAPPHO AND ALCAEUS. Cr. 8vo. 7s. 6d.

—— DAPHNE: and other Poems. Cr. 8vo. 7s. 6d.

TENNYSON (Lord H.). (*See* ILLUSTRATED BOOKS.)

TRUMAN (Jos.).—AFTER-THOUGHTS: Poems. Cr. 8vo. 3s. 6d.

TURNER (Charles Tennyson).—COLLECTED SONNETS, OLD AND NEW. Ext. fcp. 8vo. 7s. 6d.

TYRWHITT (R. St. John).—FREE FIELD. Lyrics, chiefly Descriptive. Gl. 8vo. 3s. 6d.

—— BATTLE AND AFTER, CONCERNING SERGEANT THOMAS ATKINS, GRENADIER GUARDS: and other Verses. Gl. 8vo. 3s. 6d.

WARD (Samuel).—LYRICAL RECREATIONS. Fcp. 8vo. 6s.

WATSON (W.).—POEMS. Fcap. 8vo. 5s.

—— LACHRYMAE MUSARUM. Fcp. 8vo. 4s. 6d. (*See also* GOLDEN TREASURY SERIES, p. 22.)

WHITTIER.—COMPLETE POETICAL WORKS OF JOHN GREENLEAF WHITTIER. With Portrait. 18mo. 4s. 6d. (*See also* COLLECTED WORKS, p. 23.)

WILLS (W. G.).—MELCHIOR. Cr. 8vo. 9s.

WOOD (Andrew Goldie).—THE ISLES OF THE BLEST: and other Poems. Globe 8vo. 5s.

WOOLNER (Thomas). — MY BEAUTIFUL LADY. 3rd Edit. Fcp. 8vo. 5s.

—— PYGMALION. Cr. 8vo. 7s. 6d.

—— SILENUS. Cr. 8vo. 6s.

WORDSWORTH. — COMPLETE POETICAL WORKS. Copyright Edition. With an Introduction by JOHN MORLEY, and Portrait. Cr. 8vo. 7s. 6d.

—— THE RECLUSE. Fcp. 8vo. 2s. 6d.—Large Paper Edition. 8vo. 10s. 6d.

(*See also* GOLDEN TREASURY SERIES, p. 21.)

Poetical Collections and Selections.

(*See also* GOLDEN TREASURY SERIES, p. 21; BOOKS FOR THE YOUNG, p. 41.)

HALES (Prof. J. W.).—LONGER ENGLISH POEMS. With Notes, Philological and Explanatory, and an Introduction on the Teaching of English. Ext. fcp. 8vo. 4s. 6d.

MACDONALD (George).—ENGLAND'S ANTIPHON. Cr. 8vo. 4s. 6d.

MARTIN (F.). (*See* BOOKS FOR THE YOUNG, p. 41.)

MASSON (R. O. and D.).—THREE CENTURIES OF ENGLISH POETRY. Being Selections from Chaucer to Herrick. Globe 8vo. 3s. 6d.

PALGRAVE (Prof. F. T.).—THE GOLDEN TREASURY OF THE BEST SONGS AND LYRICAL POEMS IN THE ENGLISH LANGUAGE. Large Type. Cr. 8vo. 10s. 6d. (*See also* GOLDEN TREASURY SERIES, p. 21; BOOKS FOR THE YOUNG, p. 41.)

WARD (T. H.).—ENGLISH POETS. Selections, with Critical Introductions by various Writers, and a General Introduction by MATTHEW ARNOLD. Edited by T. H. WARD, M.A. 4 vols. 2nd Edit. Cr. 8vo. 7s. 6d. each.— Vol. I. CHAUCER TO DONNE; II. BEN JONSON TO DRYDEN; III. ADDISON TO BLAKE; IV. WORDSWORTH TO ROSSETTI.

LITERATURE.

WOODS (M. A.).—A First Poetry Book. Fcp. 8vo. 2s. 6d.
—— A Second Poetry Book. 2 Parts. Fcp. 8vo. 2s. 6d. each.—Complete, 4s. 6d.
—— A Third Poetry Book. Fcp. 8vo. 4s. 6d.

WORDS FROM THE POETS. With a Vignette and Frontispiece. 12th Edit. 18mo. 1s.

Prose Fiction.

BIKELAS (D.).—Loukis Laras; or, The Reminiscences of a Chiote Merchant during the Greek War of Independence. Translated by J. Gennadius. Cr. 8vo. 7s. 6d.

BJÖRNSON (B.).—Synnövë Solbakken. Translated by Julie Sutter. Cr. 8vo. 6s.

BOLDREWOOD (Rolf).—*Uniform Edition.* Cr. 8vo. 3s. 6d. each.
Robbery Under Arms.
The Miner's Right.
The Squatter's Dream.
A Sydney-Side Saxon.
A Colonial Reformer.
Nevermore.

BURNETT (F. H.).—Haworth's. Gl. 8vo. 2s.
—— Louisiana, and That Lass o' Lowrie's. Illustrated. Cr. 8vo. 3s. 6d.

CALMIRE. 2 vols. Cr. 8vo. 21s.

CARMARTHEN (Marchioness of).—A Lover of the Beautiful. Cr. 8vo. 6s.

CONWAY (Hugh).—A Family Affair. Cr. 8vo. 3s. 6d.
—— Living or Dead. Cr. 8vo. 3s. 6d.

CORBETT (Julian).—The Fall of Asgard: A Tale of St. Olaf's Day. 2 vols. Gl. 8vo. 12s.
—— For God and Gold. Cr. 8vo. 6s.
—— Kophetua the Thirteenth. 2 vols. Globe 8vo. 12s.

CRAIK (Mrs.).—*Uniform Edition.* Cr. 8vo. 3s. 6d. each.
Olive.
The Ogilvies. Also Globe 8vo, 2s.
Agatha's Husband. Also Globe 8vo, 2s.
The Head of the Family.
Two Marriages. Also Globe 8vo, 2s.
The Laurel Bush.
My Mother and I.
Miss Tommy: A Mediæval Romance.
King Arthur: Not a Love Story.

CRAWFORD (F. Marion).—*Uniform Edition.* Cr. 8vo. 3s. 6d. each.
Mr. Isaacs: A Tale of Modern India.
Dr. Claudius.
A Roman Singer.
Zoroaster.
A Tale of a Lonely Parish.
Marzio's Crucifix.
Paul Patoff.
With the Immortals.
Greifenstein.
Sant' Ilario.
A Cigarette Maker's Romance.
Khaled: A Tale of Arabia.
The Witch of Prague.
The Three Fates.
—— Don Orsino. 3 vols. Cr. 8vo. 31s. 6d.
—— Children of the King. 2 vols. 12s.
—— Pietro Ghisleri. 3 vols. Cr. 8vo. 31s. 6d.

CUNNINGHAM (Sir H. S.).—The Cœruleans: A Vacation Idyll. Cr. 8vo. 3s. 6d.
—— The Heriots. Cr. 8vo. 3s. 6d.
—— Wheat and Tares. Cr. 8vo. 3s. 6d.

DAGONET THE JESTER. Cr. 8vo. 4s. 6d.

DAHN (Felix).—Felicitas. Translated by M. A. C. E. Cr. 8vo. 4s. 6d.

DAY (Rev. Lal Behari).—Bengal Peasant Life. Cr. 8vo. 6s.
—— Folk Tales of Bengal. Cr. 8vo. 4s. 6d.

DEFOE (D.). (*See* Globe Library, p. 21: Golden Treasury Series, p. 22.)

DEMOCRACY: An American Novel. Cr. 8vo. 4s. 6d.

DICKENS (Charles). — *Uniform Edition.* Cr. 8vo. 3s. 6d. each.
The Pickwick Papers.
Oliver Twist.
Nicholas Nickleby.
Martin Chuzzlewit.
The Old Curiosity Shop.
Barnaby Rudge.
Dombey and Son.
Christmas Books.
Sketches by Boz.
David Copperfield.
American Notes, and Pictures from Italy.
—— The Posthumous Papers of the Pickwick Club. Illust. Edit. by C. Dickens, Jun. 2 vols. Ext. cr. 8vo. 21s.

DICKENS (M. A.).—A Mere Cypher. 3 vols. Cr. 8vo. 31s. 6d.

DILLWYN (E. A.).—Jill. Cr. 8vo. 6s.
—— Jill and Jack. 2 vols. Globe 8vo. 12s.

DUNSMUIR (Amy).—Vida: Study of a Girl. 3rd Edit. Cr. 8vo. 6s.

EBERS (Dr. George).—The Burgomaster's Wife. Transl. by C. Bell. Cr. 8vo. 4s. 6d.
—— Only a Word. Translated by Clara Bell. Cr. 8vo. 4s. 6d.

"ESTELLE RUSSELL" (The Author of).—Harmonia. 3 vols. Cr. 8vo. 31s. 6d.

FALCONER (Lanoe).—Cecilia de Noel. Cr. 8vo. 3s. 6d.

FLEMING (G.).—A Nile Novel. Gl. 8vo. 2s.
—— Mirage: A Novel. Globe 8vo. 2s.
—— The Head of Medusa. Globe 8vo. 2s.
—— Vestigia. Globe 8vo. 2s.

FRATERNITY: A Romance. 2 vols. Cr. 8vo. 21s.

"FRIENDS IN COUNCIL" (The Author of).—Realmah. Cr. 8vo. 6s.

GRAHAM (John W.).—Neæra: A Tale of Ancient Rome. Cr. 8vo. 6s.

HARBOUR BAR, THE. Cr. 8vo. 6s.

HARDY (Arthur Sherburne).—But Yet a Woman: A Novel. Cr. 8vo. 4s. 6d.
—— The Wind of Destiny. 2 vols. Gl. 8vo. 12s.

HARDY (Thomas). — The Woodlanders. Cr. 8vo. 3s. 6d.
—— Wessex Tales. Cr. 8vo. 3s. 6d.

HARTE (Bret).—Cressy. Cr. 8vo. 3s. 6d.
—— The Heritage of Dedlow Marsh: and other Tales. Cr. 8vo. 3s. 6d.
—— A First Family of Tasajara. Cr. 8vo. 3s. 6d.

"HOGAN, M.P." (The Author of).—HOGAN, M.P. Cr. 8vo. 3s. 6d.
—— THE HON. MISS FERRARD. Gl. 8vo. 2s.
—— FLITTERS, TATTERS, AND THE COUNSELLOR, ETC. Globe 8vo. 2s.
—— CHRISTY CAREW. Globe 8vo. 2s.
—— ISMAY'S CHILDREN. Globe 8vo. 2s.

HOPPUS (Mary).—A GREAT TREASON: A Story of the War of Independence. 2 vols. Cr. 8vo. 9s.

HUGHES (Thomas).—TOM BROWN'S SCHOOL DAYS. By AN OLD BOY.—Golden Treasury Edition. 2s. 6d. net.—Uniform Edit. 3s. 6d. —People's Edition. 2s.—People's Sixpenny Edition. Illustr. Med. 4to. 6d.—Uniform with Sixpenny Kingsley. Med. 8vo. 6d.
—— TOM BROWN AT OXFORD. Cr. 8vo. 3s. 6d.
—— THE SCOURING OF THE WHITE HORSE, and THE ASHEN FAGGOT. Cr. 8vo. 3s. 6d.

IRVING (Washington). (See ILLUSTRATED BOOKS, p. 12.)

JACKSON (Helen).—RAMONA. Gl. 8vo. 2s.

JAMES (Henry).—THE EUROPEANS: A Novel. Cr. 8vo. 6s.; 18mo, 2s.
—— DAISY MILLER: and other Stories. Cr. 8vo. 6s.; Globe 8vo, 2s.
—— THE AMERICAN. Cr. 8vo. 6s.—18mo. 2 vols. 4s.
—— RODERICK HUDSON. Cr. 8vo. 6s.; Gl. 8vo, 2s.; 18mo, 2 vols. 4s.
—— THE MADONNA OF THE FUTURE: and other Tales. Cr. 8vo. 6s.; Globe 8vo, 2s.
—— WASHINGTON SQUARE, THE PENSION BEAUREPAS. Globe 8vo. 2s.
—— THE PORTRAIT OF A LADY. Cr. 8vo. 6s. 18mo, 3 vols. 6s.
—— STORIES REVIVED. In Two Series. Cr. 8vo. 6s. each.
—— THE BOSTONIANS. Cr. 8vo. 6s.
—— NOVELS AND TALES. Pocket Edition. 18mo. 2s. each volume.
CONFIDENCE. 1 vol.
THE SIEGE OF LONDON; MADAME DE MAUVES. 1 vol.
AN INTERNATIONAL EPISODE; THE PENSION BEAUREPAS; THE POINT OF VIEW. 1 vol.
DAISY MILLER, a Study; FOUR MEETINGS; LONGSTAFF'S MARRIAGE; BENVOLIO. 1 vol.
THE MADONNA OF THE FUTURE; A BUNDLE OF LETTERS; THE DIARY OF A MAN OF FIFTY; EUGENE PICKERING. 1 vol.
—— TALES OF THREE CITIES. Cr. 8vo. 4s. 6d.
—— THE PRINCESS CASAMASSIMA. Cr. 8vo. 6s.; Globe 8vo, 2s.
—— THE REVERBERATOR. Cr. 8vo. 6s.
—— THE ASPERN PAPERS; LOUISA PALLANT; THE MODERN WARNING. Cr. 8vo. 3s. 6d.
—— A LONDON LIFE. Cr. 8vo. 3s. 6d.
—— THE TRAGIC MUSE. Cr. 8vo. 3s. 6d.
—— THE LESSON OF THE MASTER, AND OTHER STORIES. Cr. 8vo. 6s.
—— THE REAL THING, AND OTHER TALES. Cr. 8vo. 6s.

KEARY (Annie).—JANET'S HOME. Cr. 8vo. 3s. 6d.
—— CLEMENCY FRANKLYN. Globe 8vo. 2s.
—— OLDBURY. Cr. 8vo. 3s. 6d.
—— A YORK AND A LANCASTER ROSE. Cr. 8vo. 3s. 6d.
—— CASTLE DALY. Cr. 8vo. 3s. 6d.
—— A DOUBTING HEART. Cr. 8vo. 3s. 6d.

KENNEDY (P.).—LEGENDARY FICTIONS OF THE IRISH CELTS. Cr. 8vo. 3s. 6d.

KINGSLEY (Charles).—Eversley Edition. 13 vols. Globe 8vo. 5s. each.—WESTWARD HO! 2 vols.—TWO YEARS AGO. 2 vols.—HYPATIA. 2 vols.—YEAST. 1 vol.—ALTON LOCKE. 2 vols.—HEREWARD THE WAKE. 2 vols.
—— Complete Edition. Cr. 8vo. 3s. 6d. each. —WESTWARD HO! With a Portrait.—HYPATIA.—YEAST.—ALTON LOCKE.—TWO YEARS AGO.—HEREWARD THE WAKE.
—— Sixpenny Edition. Med. 8vo. 6d. each. — WESTWARD HO! — HYPATIA. — YEAST.—ALTON LOCKE.—TWO YEARS AGO. —HEREWARD THE WAKE.

KIPLING (Rudyard).—PLAIN TALES FROM THE HILLS. Cr. 8vo. 6s.
—— THE LIGHT THAT FAILED. Cr. 8vo. 6s.
—— LIFE'S HANDICAP: Being Stories of mine own People. Cr. 8vo. 6s.
—— MANY INVENTIONS. Cr. 8vo. 6s.

LAFARGUE (Philip).—THE NEW JUDGMENT OF PARIS. 2 vols. Globe 8vo. 12s.

LEE (Margaret).—FAITHFUL AND UNFAITHFUL. Cr. 8vo. 3s. 6d.

LEVY (A.).—REUBEN SACHS. Cr. 8vo. 3s. 6d.

LITTLE PILGRIM IN THE UNSEEN, A. 24th Thousand. Cr. 8vo. 2s. 6d.

"LITTLE PILGRIM IN THE UNSEEN, A" (Author of).—THE LAND OF DARKNESS. Cr. 8vo. 5s.

LYSAGHT (S. R.).—THE MARPLOT. 3 vols. Cr. 8vo. 31s. 6d.

LYTTON (Earl of).—THE RING OF AMASIS: A Romance. Cr. 8vo. 3s. 6d.

McLENNAN (Malcolm).—MUCKLE JOCK; and other Stories of Peasant Life in the North. Cr. 8vo. 3s. 6d.

MACQUOID (K. S.).—PATTY. Gl. 8vo. 2s.

MADOC (Fayr).—THE STORY OF MELICENT. Cr. 8vo. 4s. 6d.

MALET (Lucas).—MRS. LORIMER: A Sketch in Black and White. Cr. 8vo. 3s. 6d.

MALORY (Sir Thos.). (See GLOBE LIBRARY, p. 21.)

MINTO (W.).—THE MEDIATION OF RALPH HARDELOT. 3 vols. Cr. 8vo. 31s. 6d.

MITFORD (A. B.).—TALES OF OLD JAPAN. With Illustrations. Cr. 8vo. 3s. 6d.

MIZ MAZE (THE); OR, THE WINKWORTH PUZZLE. A Story in Letters by Nine Authors. Cr. 8vo. 4s. 6d.

MURRAY (D. Christie). — AUNT RACHEL. Cr. 8vo. 3s. 6d.
—— SCHWARTZ. Cr. 8vo. 3s. 6d.
—— THE WEAKER VESSEL. Cr. 8vo. 3s. 6d.
—— JOHN VALE'S GUARDIAN. Cr. 8vo. 3s. 6d.

LITERATURE.
Prose Fiction—*continued.*

MURRAY (D. Christie) and HERMAN (H.). —HE FELL AMONG THIEVES. Cr. 8vo. 3s. 6d.

NEW ANTIGONE, THE: A ROMANCE. Cr. 8vo. 3s. 6d.

NOEL (Lady Augusta).—HITHERSEA MERE. 3 vols. Cr. 8vo. 31s. 6d.

NORRIS (W. E.).—MY FRIEND JIM. Globe 8vo. 2s.
—— CHRIS. Globe 8vo. 2s.

NORTON (Hon. Mrs.).—OLD SIR DOUGLAS. Cr. 8vo. 6s.

OLIPHANT (Mrs. M. O. W.).—A SON OF THE SOIL. Globe 8vo. 2s.
—— THE CURATE IN CHARGE. Globe 8vo. 2s.
—— YOUNG MUSGRAVE. Globe 8vo. 2s.
—— HE THAT WILL NOT WHEN HE MAY. Cr. 8vo. 3s. 6d.—Globe 8vo. 2s.
—— SIR TOM. Cr. 8vo. 3s. 6d.—Gl. 8vo. 2s.
—— HESTER. Cr. 8vo. 3s. 6d.
—— THE WIZARD'S SON. Globe 8vo. 2s.
—— THE COUNTRY GENTLEMAN AND HIS FAMILY. Globe 8vo. 2s.
—— THE SECOND SON. Globe 8vo. 2s.
—— NEIGHBOURS ON THE GREEN. Cr. 8vo. 3s. 6d.
—— JOYCE. Cr. 8vo. 3s. 6d.
—— A BELEAGUERED CITY. Cr. 8vo. 3s. 6d.
—— KIRSTEEN. Cr. 8vo. 3s. 6d.
—— THE RAILWAY MAN AND HIS CHILDREN. Cr. 8vo. 3s. 6d.
—— THE MARRIAGE OF ELINOR Cr. 8vo. 3s. 6d.
—— THE HEIR-PRESUMPTIVE AND THE HEIR-APPARENT. 3 vols. Cr. 8vo. 31s. 6d

PALMER (Lady Sophia).—MRS. PENICOTT'S LODGER: and other Stories. Cr. 8vo. 2s. 6d.

PARRY (Gambier). —THE STORY OF DICK. Cr. 8vo. 3s. 6d.

PATER (Walter).—MARIUS THE EPICUREAN: HIS SENSATIONS AND IDEAS. 3rd Edit. 2 vols. 8vo. 12s.

RHOADES (J.).—THE STORY OF JOHN TREVENNICK. 3 vols. Cr. 8vo. 31s. 6d.

ROSS (Percy).—A MISGUIDIT LASSIE. Cr. 8vo. 4s. 6d.

ROY (J.).—HELEN TREVERYAN: OR, THE RULING RACE. 3 vols. Cr. 8vo. 31s. 6d.

RUSSELL (W. Clark).—MAROONED. Cr. 8vo. 3s. 6d.
—— A STRANGE ELOPEMENT. Cr. 8vo. 3s. 6d.

ST. JOHNSTON (A.). — A SOUTH SEA LOVER: A Romance. Cr. 8vo. 6s.

SHORTHOUSE (J. Henry).—*Uniform Edition.* Cr. 8vo. 3s. 6d. each.
JOHN INGLESANT: A Romance.
SIR PERCIVAL: A Story of the Past and of the Present.
THE LITTLE SCHOOLMASTER MARK: A Spiritual Romance.
THE COUNTESS EVE.
A TEACHER OF THE VIOLIN: and other Tales.
—— BLANCHE, LADY FALAISE. Cr. 8vo. 6s.

SLIP IN THE FENS, A. Globe 8vo. 2s.

THEODOLI (Marchesa)—UNDER PRESSURE. 2 vols. Globe 8vo. 12s.

TIM. Cr. 8vo. 6s.

TOURGÉNIEF.—VIRGIN SOIL. Translated by ASHTON W. DILKE. Cr. 8vo. 6s.

VELEY (Margaret).—A GARDEN OF MEMORIES; MRS. AUSTIN; LIZZIE'S BARGAIN. Three Stories. 2 vols. Globe 8vo. 12s.

VICTOR (H.).—MARIAM: OR TWENTY ONE DAYS. Cr. 8vo. 6s.

VOICES CRYING IN THE WILDERNESS: A NOVEL. Cr. 8vo. 7s. 6d.

WARD (Mrs. T. Humphry).—MISS BRETHERTON. Cr. 8vo. 3s. 6d.

WEST (M.).—A BORN PLAYER. Cr. 8vo. 6s.

WORTHEY (Mrs.).—THE NEW CONTINENT: A Novel. 2 vols. Globe 8vo. 12s.

YONGE (C. M.).—GRISLY GRISELL. 2 vols. Cr. 8vo. 12s. (*See also* p. 23.)

YONGE (C. M.) and COLERIDGE (C. R.) —STROLLING PLAYERS. Cr. 8vo. 6s.

Collected Works; Essays; Lectures; Letters; Miscellaneous Works.

ADDISON.—SELECTIONS FROM THE "SPECTATOR." With Introduction and Notes by K. DEIGHTON. Globe 8vo. 2s. 6d.

AN AUTHOR'S LOVE. Being the Unpublished Letters of PROSPER MÉRIMÉE'S "Inconnue." 2 vols. Ext. cr. 8vo. 12s.

ARNOLD (Matthew).—ESSAYS IN CRITICISM. 6th Edit. Cr. 8vo. 9s.
—— ESSAYS IN CRITICISM. Second Series. Cr. 8vo. 7s. 6d.
—— DISCOURSES IN AMERICA. Cr. 8vo. 4s. 6d.

BACON.—ESSAYS. With Introduction and Notes, by F. G. SELBY, M.A. Gl. 8vo. 3s.; swd., 2s. 6d.
—— ADVANCEMENT OF LEARNING. Book I. By the same. Globe 8vo. 2s.
(*See also* GOLDEN TREASURY SERIES, p. 21.)

BLACKIE (J. S.).—LAY SERMONS. Cr. 8vo. 6s.

BRIDGES (John A.).—IDYLLS OF A LOST VILLAGE. Cr. 8vo. 7s. 6d.

BRIMLEY (George).—ESSAYS. Globe 8vo. 5s.

BUNYAN (John).—THE PILGRIM'S PROGRESS FROM THIS WORLD TO THAT WHICH IS TO COME. 18mo. 2s. 6d. net.

BUTCHER (Prof. S. H.)—SOME ASPECTS OF THE GREEK GENIUS. Cr. 8vo. 7s. 6d. net.

CARLYLE (Thomas). (*See* BIOGRAPHY.)

CHURCH (Dean).—MISCELLANEOUS WRITINGS. Collected Edition. 6 vols. Globe 8vo. 5s. each.—Vol. I. MISCELLANEOUS ESSAYS.—II. DANTE: AND OTHER ESSAYS.—III. ST. ANSELM.—IV. SPENSER.—V. BACON.—VI. THE OXFORD MOVEMENT, 1833—45.

CLIFFORD (Prof. W. K.). LECTURES AND ESSAYS. Edited by LESLIE STEPHEN and Sir F. POLLOCK. Cr. 8vo. 8s. 6d.

CLOUGH (A. H.).—PROSE REMAINS. With a Selection from his Letters, and a Memoir by HIS WIFE. Cr. 8vo. 7s. 6d.

COLLINS (J. Churton).—THE STUDY OF ENGLISH LITERATURE. Cr. 8vo. 4s. 6d.

CRAIK (H.).—ENGLISH PROSE SELECTIONS. With Critical Introductions by various writers, and General Introductions to each Period. Edited by H. CRAIK, C.B. Vol. I. Crown 8vo. 7s. 6d.

CRAIK (Mrs.).—CONCERNING MEN: and other Papers. Cr. 8vo. 4s. 6d.

CRAIK (Mrs.).—ABOUT MONEY: and other Things. Cr. 8vo. 6s.
—— SERMONS OUT OF CHURCH. Cr. 8vo. 3s. 6d.

CRAWFORD (F. M.).—THE NOVEL: WHAT IT IS. 18mo. 3s.

CUNLIFFE (J. W.).—THE INFLUENCE OF SENECA ON ELIZABETHAN TRAGEDY. 4to. 4s. net.

DE VERE (Aubrey).—ESSAYS CHIEFLY ON POETRY. 2 vols. Globe 8vo. 12s.
—— ESSAYS, CHIEFLY LITERARY AND ETHICAL. Globe 8vo. 6s.

DICKENS.—LETTERS OF CHARLES DICKENS. Edited by his Sister-in-Law and MARY DICKENS. Cr. 8vo. 3s. 6d.

DRYDEN, ESSAYS OF. Edited by Prof. C. D. YONGE. Fcp. 8vo. 2s. 6d. (See also GLOBE LIBRARY, below.)

DUFF (Rt. Hon. Sir M. E. Grant).—MISCELLANIES, Political and Literary. 8vo. 10s. 6d.

EMERSON (Ralph Waldo).—THE COLLECTED WORKS. 6 vols. Globe 8vo. 5s. each.— I. MISCELLANIES. With an Introductory Essay by JOHN MORLEY.—II. ESSAYS.— III. POEMS.—IV. ENGLISH TRAITS; REPRESENTATIVE MEN.—V. CONDUCT OF LIFE; SOCIETY AND SOLITUDE.—VI. LETTERS; SOCIAL AIMS, ETC.

FITZGERALD (Edward): LETTERS AND LITERARY REMAINS OF. Ed. by W. ALDIS WRIGHT, M.A. 3 vols. Cr. 8vo. 31s. 6d.

GLOBE LIBRARY. Gl. 8vo. 3s. 6d. each:
BOSWELL'S LIFE OF JOHNSON. Introduction by MOWBRAY MORRIS.
BURNS.—COMPLETE POETICAL WORKS AND LETTERS. Edited, with Life and Glossarial Index, by ALEXANDER SMITH.
COWPER.—POETICAL WORKS. Edited by the Rev. W. BENHAM, B.D.
DEFOE.—THE ADVENTURES OF ROBINSON CRUSOE. Introduction by H. KINGSLEY.
DRYDEN.—POETICAL WORKS. A Revised Text and Notes. By W. D. CHRISTIE, M.A.
GOLDSMITH. — MISCELLANEOUS WORKS. Edited by Prof. MASSON.
HORACE.—WORKS. Rendered into English Prose by JAMES LONSDALE and S. LEE.
MALORY.—LE MORTE D'ARTHUR. Sir Thos. Malory's Book of King Arthur and of his Noble Knights of the Round Table. The Edition of Caxton, revised for modern use. By Sir E. STRACHEY, Bart.
MILTON.—POETICAL WORKS. Edited, with Introductions, by Prof. MASSON.
POPE.—POETICAL WORKS. Edited, with Memoir and Notes, by Prof. WARD.
SCOTT.—POETICAL WORKS. With Essay by Prof. PALGRAVE.
SHAKESPEARE.—COMPLETE WORKS. Edit. by W. G. CLARK and W. ALDIS WRIGHT. India Paper Edition. Cr. 8vo, cloth extra, gilt edges. 10s. 6d. net.
SPENSER.—COMPLETE WORKS Edited by R. MORRIS. Memoir by J. W. HALES, M.A.
VIRGIL.—WORKS. Rendered into English Prose by JAMES LONSDALE and S. LEE.

GOLDEN TREASURY SERIES.—Uniformly printed in 18mo, with Vignette Titles by Sir J. E. MILLAIS, Sir NOEL PATON, T. WOOLNER, W. HOLMAN HUNT, ARTHUR HUGHES, etc. 2s. 6d. net each.

GOLDEN TREASURY SERIES—contd.
THE GOLDEN TREASURY OF THE BEST SONGS AND LYRICAL POEMS IN THE ENGLISH LANGUAGE. Selected and arranged, with Notes, by Prof. F. T. PALGRAVE.—Large Paper Edition. 8vo. 10s. 6d. net.
THE CHILDREN'S GARLAND FROM THE BEST POETS. Selected by COVENTRY PATMORE.
BUNYAN.—THE PILGRIM'S PROGRESS FROM THIS WORLD TO THAT WHICH IS TO COME. —Large Paper Edition. 8vo. 10s. 6d. net.
BACON.—ESSAYS, and COLOURS OF GOOD AND EVIL. With Notes and Glossarial Index by W. ALDIS WRIGHT, M.A.—Large Paper Edition. 8vo. 10s. 6d net.
THE BOOK OF PRAISE. From the Best English Hymn Writers. Selected by ROUNDELL, EARL OF SELBORNE.
SHELLEY.—POEMS. Edited by STOPFORD A. BROOKE.—Large Paper Edit. 12s. 6d.
THE FAIRY BOOK: THE BEST POPULAR FAIRY STORIES. Selected by Mrs. CRAIK, Author of "John Halifax, Gentleman."
WORDSWORTH.—POEMS. Chosen and Edited by M. ARNOLD.—Large Paper Edition. 10s. 6d net.
PLATO.—THE TRIAL AND DEATH OF SOCRATES. Being the Euthyphron, Apology, Crito and Phaedo of Plato. Trans. by F. J. CHURCH.
THE JEST BOOK. The Choicest Anecdotes and Sayings. Arranged by MARK LEMON.
HERRICK.—CHRYSOMELA. Edited by Prof. F. T. PALGRAVE.
THE BALLAD BOOK. A Selection of the Choicest British Ballads. Edited by WILLIAM ALLINGHAM.
THE SUNDAY BOOK OF POETRY FOR THE YOUNG. Selected by C. F. ALEXANDER.
A BOOK OF GOLDEN DEEDS. By C. M. YONGE.
A BOOK OF WORTHIES. By C. M. YONGE.
KEATS.—THE POETICAL WORKS. Edited by Prof. F. T. PALGRAVE.
PLATO.—THE REPUBLIC. Translated by J. LL. DAVIES, M.A., and D. J. VAUGHAN. —Large Paper Edition. 8vo. 10s. 6d. net.
ADDISON.—ESSAYS. Chosen and Edited by JOHN RICHARD GREEN.
DEUTSCHE LYRIK. The Golden Treasury of the best German Lyrical Poems. Selected by Dr. BUCHHEIM.
SIR THOMAS BROWNE.—RELIGIO MEDICI, LETTER TO A FRIEND, &C., AND CHRISTIAN MORALS. Ed. W. A. GREENHILL.
LAMB.—TALES FROM SHAKSPEARE. Edited by Rev. ALFRED AINGER, M.A.
THE SONG BOOK. Words and Tunes selected and arranged by JOHN HULLAH.
SCOTTISH SONG. Compiled by MARY CARLYLE AITKEN.
LA LYRE FRANÇAISE. Selected and arranged, with Notes, by G. MASSON.
BALLADEN UND ROMANZEN. Being a Selection of the best German Ballads and Romances. Edited, with Introduction and Notes, by Dr. BUCHHEIM.
A BOOK OF GOLDEN THOUGHTS. By Sir HENRY ATTWELL.
MATTHEW ARNOLD.—SELECTED POEMS.
BYRON.—POETRY. Chosen and arranged by M. ARNOLD.—Large Paper Edit. 9s.
COWPER.—SELECTIONS FROM POEMS. With an Introduction by Mrs. OLIPHANT.

LITERATURE.

Collected Works; Essays; Lectures; Letters; Miscellaneous Works—*contd.*

GOLDEN TREASURY SERIES—*contd.*

COWPER.—LETTERS. Edited, with Introduction. by Rev. W. BENHAM.

DEFOE.—THE ADVENTURES OF ROBINSON CRUSOE. Edited by J. W. CLARK, M.A.

GOLDEN TREASURY PSALTER. By Four Friends.

BALTHASAR GRACIAN'S ART OF WORLDLY WISDOM. Translated by J. JACOBS.

HUGHES.—TOM BROWN'S SCHOOL DAYS.

LANDOR.—SELECTIONS. Ed. by S. COLVIN.

LONGFELLOW. — BALLADS, LYRICS, AND SONNETS.

MOHAMMAD.—SPEECHES AND TABLE-TALK. Translated by STANLEY LANE-POOLE.

NEWCASTLE.—THE CAVALIER AND HIS LADY. Selections from the Works of the First Duke and Duchess of Newcastle. With an Introductory Essay by E. JENKINS.

PALGRAVE.—CHILDREN'S TREASURY OF LYRICAL POETRY.

PLATO. —THE PHAEDRUS, LYSIS, AND PROTAGORAS. Translated by J. WRIGHT.

SHAKESPEARE.—SONGS AND SONNETS. Ed. with Notes, by Prof. F. T. PALGRAVE.

THEOCRITUS.—BION, AND MOSCHUS. Rendered into English Prose by ANDREW LANG.—Large Paper Edition. 9s.

WATSON.—LYRIC LOVE: An Anthology.

WINKWORTH.—THEOLOGIA GERMANICA.

CHARLOTTE M. YONGE.—THE STORY OF THE CHRISTIANS AND MOORS IN SPAIN.

HARE.—GUESSES AT TRUTH. By Two Brothers. 4s. 6d.

LONGFELLOW.—POEMS OF PLACES: ENGLAND AND WALES. Edited by H. W. LONGFELLOW. 2 vols. 9s.

TENNYSON.—LYRICAL POEMS. Selected and Annotated by Prof. F. T. PALGRAVE. 4s. 6d. —Large Paper Edition. 9s.

— IN MEMORIAM. 4s. 6d.—Large Paper Edition. 9s.

GOLDSMITH, ESSAYS OF. Edited by C. D. YONGE, M.A. Fcp. 8vo. 2s. 6d. (*See also* GLOBE LIBRARY, p. 21; ILLUSTRATED BOOKS, p. 12.)

GRAY (Thomas).—WORKS. Edited by EDMUND GOSSE. In 4 vols. Globe 8vo. 20s.—Vol. I. POEMS, JOURNALS, AND ESSAYS.—II. LETTERS.—III. LETTERS.—IV. NOTES ON ARISTOPHANES AND PLATO.

GREEN (J. R.).—STRAY STUDIES FROM ENGLAND AND ITALY. Globe 8vo. 5s.

HAMERTON (P. G.).—THE INTELLECTUAL LIFE. Cr. 8vo. 10s. 6d.

—— HUMAN INTERCOURSE. Cr. 8vo. 8s. 6d.

—— FRENCH AND ENGLISH: A Comparison. Cr. 8vo. 10s. 6d.

HARRISON (Frederic).—THE CHOICE OF BOOKS. Gl. 8vo. 6s.—Large Paper Ed. 15s.

HARWOOD (George).—FROM WITHIN. Cr. 8vo. 6s.

HELPS (Sir Arthur).—ESSAYS WRITTEN IN THE INTERVALS OF BUSINESS. With Introduction and Notes, by F. J. ROWE, M.A., and W. T. WEBB, M.A. 1s. 9d.; swd. 1s. 6d.

HOBART (Lord).—ESSAYS AND MISCELLANEOUS WRITINGS. With Biographical Sketch. Ed. Lady HOBART. 2 vols. 8vo. 25s.

HUTTON (R. H.).—ESSAYS ON SOME OF THE MODERN GUIDES OF ENGLISH THOUGHT IN MATTERS OF FAITH. Globe 8vo. 6s.

—— ESSAYS. 2 vols. Gl. 8vo. 6s. each. – Vol. I. Literary; II. Theological.

HUXLEY (Prof. T. H.).—LAY SERMONS, ADDRESSES, AND REVIEWS. 8vo. 7s. 6d.

—— CRITIQUES AND ADDRESSES. 8vo. 10s. 6d.

—— AMERICAN ADDRESSES, WITH A LECTURE ON THE STUDY OF BIOLOGY. 8vo. 6s. 6d.

—— SCIENCE AND CULTURE, AND OTHER ESSAYS. 8vo. 10s. 6d.

—— INTRODUCTORY SCIENCE PRIMER. 18mo. 1s.

—— ESSAYS UPON SOME CONTROVERTED QUESTIONS. 8vo. 14s.

JAMES (Henry).—FRENCH POETS AND NOVELISTS. New Edition. Gl. 8vo. 5s.

—— PORTRAITS OF PLACES. Cr. 8vo. 7s. 6d.

—— PARTIAL PORTRAITS. Cr. 8vo. 6s.

KEATS.—LETTERS. Edited by SIDNEY COLVIN. Globe 8vo. 6s.

KINGSLEY (Charles).—COMPLETE EDITION OF THE WORKS OF CHARLES KINGSLEY. Cr. 8vo. 3s. 6d. each.

WESTWARD HO! With a Portrait.

HYPATIA.

YEAST.

ALTON LOCKE.

TWO YEARS AGO.

HEREWARD THE WAKE.

POEMS.

THE HEROES; or, Greek Fairy Tales for my Children.

THE WATER BABIES: A Fairy Tale for a Land Baby.

MADAM HOW AND LADY WHY; or, First Lesson in Earth-Lore for Children.

AT LAST: A Christmas in the West Indies.

PROSE IDYLLS.

PLAYS AND PURITANS.

THE ROMAN AND THE TEUTON. With Preface by Professor MAX MÜLLER.

SANITARY AND SOCIAL LECTURES.

HISTORICAL LECTURES AND ESSAYS.

SCIENTIFIC LECTURES AND ESSAYS.

LITERARY AND GENERAL LECTURES.

THE HERMITS.

GLAUCUS; or, The Wonders of the Sea-Shore. With Coloured Illustrations.

VILLAGE AND TOWN AND COUNTRY SERMONS.

THE WATER OF LIFE, AND OTHER SERMONS.

SERMONS ON NATIONAL SUBJECTS: AND THE KING OF THE EARTH.

SERMONS FOR THE TIMES.

GOOD NEWS OF GOD.

THE GOSPEL OF THE PENTATEUCH: AND DAVID.

DISCIPLINE, AND OTHER SERMONS.

WESTMINSTER SERMONS.

ALL SAINTS' DAY, AND OTHER SERMONS.

LAMB (Charles).—COLLECTED WORKS. Ed., with Introduction and Notes, by the Rev. ALFRED AINGER, M.A. Globe 8vo. 5s. each volume.—I. ESSAYS OF ELIA.—II. PLAYS, POEMS, AND MISCELLANEOUS ESSAYS.—III. MRS. LEICESTER'S SCHOOL; THE ADVENTURES OF ULYSSES; AND OTHER ESSAYS.—IV. TALES FROM SHAKESPEARE.—V. and VI. LETTERS. Newly arranged, with additions.

—— TALES FROM SHAKESPEARE. 18mo. 4s. 6d.

LANKESTER (Prof. E. Ray).—THE ADVANCE-
MENT OF SCIENCE. Occasional Essays and
Addresses. 8vo. 10s. 6d.

LETTERS FROM SOUTH AFRICA. Reprinted from the *Times*. Cr. 8vo. 2s. 6d.

LETTERS FROM QUEENSLAND. Reprinted from the *Times*. Cr. 8vo. 2s. 6d.

LIGHTFOOT (Bishop).—ESSAYS. 2 vols. 8vo.
I. DISSERTATIONS ON THE APOSTOLIC AGE
14s.—II. MISCELLANEOUS.

LODGE (Prof. Oliver).—THE PIONEERS OF
SCIENCE. Illustrated. Ext. cr. 8vo. 7s. 6d.

LOWELL (Jas. Russell).—COMPLETE WORKS.
10 vols. Cr. 8vo. 6s. each.—Vols. I.—IV.
LITERARY ESSAYS.—V. POLITICAL ESSAYS.
—VI. LITERARY AND POLITICAL ADDRESSES.
VII.—X. POETICAL WORKS.
—— POLITICAL ESSAYS. Ext. cr. 8vo. 7s. 6d.
—— LATEST LITERARY ESSAYS. Cr. 8vo. 6s.

LUBBOCK (Rt. Hon. Sir John, Bart.).—SCI-
ENTIFIC LECTURES. Illustrated. 2nd Edit.
revised. 8vo. 8s. 6d.
—— POLITICAL AND EDUCATIONAL AD-
DRESSES. 8vo. 8s. 6d.
—— FIFTY YEARS OF SCIENCE: Address to
the British Association, 1881. 5th Edit.
Cr. 8vo. 2s. 6d.
—— THE PLEASURES OF LIFE. New Edit. 60th
Thousand. Gl. 8vo. Part I. 1s. 6d.; swd. 1s.—
Library Edition. 3s. 6d.—Part II. 1s. 6d.;
sewed, 1s.—*Library Edition.* 3s. 6d.—Com-
plete in 1 vol. 2s. 6d.
—— THE BEAUTIES OF NATURE. Cr. 8vo. 6s.

LYTTELTON (E.).—MOTHERS AND SONS.
Cr. 8vo. 3s. 6d.

MACMILLAN (Rev. Hugh).—ROMAN MO-
SAICS, or, Studies in Rome and its Neighbourhood. Globe 8vo. 6s.

MAHAFFY (Prof. J. P.).—THE PRINCIPLES
OF THE ART OF CONVERSATION. Cr. 8vo. 4s. 6d.

MAURICE (F. D.).—THE FRIENDSHIP OF
BOOKS: and other Lectures. Cr. 8vo. 3s. 6d.

MORLEY (John).—WORKS. Collected Edit.
In 11 vols. Globe 8vo. 5s. each.—VOLTAIRE.
1 vol.—ROUSSEAU. 2 vols.—DIDEROT AND
THE ENCYCLOPÆDISTS. 2 vols.—ON COM-
PROMISE. 1 vol.—MISCELLANIES. 3 vols.—
BURKE. 1 vol.—STUDIES IN LITERATURE.
1 vol.

MYERS (F. W. H.).—ESSAYS. 2 vols. Cr. 8vo.
4s. 6d. each.—I. CLASSICAL; II. MODERN.
—— SCIENCE AND A FUTURE LIFE. Gl. 8vo. 5s.

NADAL (E. S.).—ESSAYS AT HOME AND
ELSEWHERE. Cr. 8vo. 6s.

OLIPHANT (T. L. Kington).—THE DUKE AND
THE SCHOLAR: and other Essays. 8vo. 7s. 6d.

OWENS COLLEGE ESSAYS AND AD-
DRESSES. By Professors and Lecturers
of the College. 8vo. 14s.

PATER (W.).—THE RENAISSANCE; Studies
in Art and Poetry. 4th Ed. Cr. 8vo. 10s. 6d.
—— IMAGINARY PORTRAITS. Cr. 8vo. 6s.
—— APPRECIATIONS. With an Essay on
"Style." 2nd Edit. Cr. 8vo. 8s. 6d.
—— MARIUS THE EPICUREAN. 2 vols. Cr.
8vo. 12s.
—— PLATO AND PLATONISM. Ex. cr. 8vo. 8s. 6d.

PICTON (J. A.).—THE MYSTERY OF MATTER:
and other Essays. Cr. 8vo. 6s.

POLLOCK (Sir F., Bart.).—OXFORD LEC-
TURES: and other Discourses. 8vo. 9s.

POOLE (M. E.).—PICTURES OF COTTAGE
LIFE IN THE WEST OF ENGLAND. 2nd Ed.
Cr. 8vo. 3s. 6d.

POTTER (Louisa).—LANCASHIRE MEMORIES.
Cr. 8vo. 6s.

PRICKARD (A. O.).—ARISTOTLE ON THE
ART OF POETRY. Cr. 8vo. 3s. 6d.

RUMFORD.—COMPLETE WORKS OF COUNT
RUMFORD. Memoir by G. ELLIS. Portrait. 5 vols. 8vo. 4l. 14s. 6d.

SCIENCE LECTURES AT SOUTH KEN-
SINGTON. Illustr. 2 vols. Cr. 8vo. 6s. each.

SMALLEY (George W.).—LONDON LETTERS
AND SOME OTHERS. 2 vols. 8vo. 32s.

STEPHEN (Sir James F., Bart.).—HORÆ
SABBATICÆ. Three Series. Gl. 8vo. 5s.
each.

THRING (Edward).—THOUGHTS ON LIFE
SCIENCE. 2nd Edit. Cr. 8vo. 7s. 6d.

WESTCOTT (Bishop). (*See* THEOLOGY, p. 39.)

WILSON (Dr. George).—RELIGIO CHEMICI.
Cr. 8vo. 8s. 6d.
—— THE FIVE GATEWAYS OF KNOWLEDGE.
9th Edit. Ext. fcp. 8vo. 2s. 6d.

WHITTIER (John Greenleaf). THE COM-
PLETE WORKS. 7 vols. Cr. 8vo. 6s. each.—
Vol. I. NARRATIVE AND LEGENDARY POEMS.
—II. POEMS OF NATURE; POEMS SUBJEC-
TIVE AND REMINISCENT; RELIGIOUS POEMS.
—III. ANTI-SLAVERY POEMS; SONGS OF
LABOUR AND REFORM.—IV. PERSONAL
POEMS; OCCASIONAL POEMS; THE TENT ON
THE BEACH; with the Poems of ELIZABETH
H. WHITTIER, and an Appendix containing
Early and Uncollected Verses.—V. MAR-
GARET SMITH'S JOURNAL; TALES AND
SKETCHES.—VI. OLD PORTRAITS AND MO-
DERN SKETCHES; PERSONAL SKETCHES AND
TRIBUTES; HISTORICAL PAPERS.—VII. THE
CONFLICT WITH SLAVERY, POLITICS, AND
REFORM; THE INNER LIFE, CRITICISM.

YONGE (Charlotte M.).—*Uniform Edition.*
Cr. 8vo. 3s. 6d. each.

THE HEIR OF REDCLYFFE.
HEARTSEASE.
HOPES AND FEARS.
DYNEVOR TERRACE.
THE DAISY CHAIN.
THE TRIAL: More Links of the Daisy Chain.
PILLARS OF THE HOUSE. Vol. I.
PILLARS OF THE HOUSE. Vol. II.
THE YOUNG STEPMOTHER.
CLEVER WOMAN OF THE FAMILY.
THE THREE BRIDES.
MY YOUNG ALCIDES.
THE CAGED LION.
THE DOVE IN THE EAGLE'S NEST.
THE CHAPLET OF PEARLS.
LADY HESTER, and THE DANVERS PAPERS.
MAGNUM BONUM.
LOVE AND LIFE.
UNKNOWN TO HISTORY.
STRAY PEARLS.
THE ARMOURER'S PRENTICES.
THE TWO SIDES OF THE SHIELD.
NUTTIE'S FATHER.

LITERATURE.

Collected Works; Essays: Lectures; Letters; Miscellaneous Works—*contd.*

YONGE (Charlotte M.).—*Uniform Edition.* Cr. 8vo. 3s. 6d. each.
  SCENES AND CHARACTERS.
  CHANTRY HOUSE.
  A MODERN TELEMACHUS.
  BYE WORDS.
  BEECHCROFT AT ROCKSTONE.
  MORE BYWORDS.
  A REPUTED CHANGELING.
  THE LITTLE DUKE, RICHARD THE FEARLESS.
  THE LANCES OF LYNWOOD.
  THE PRINCE AND THE PAGE.
  P's AND Q's: LITTLE LUCY'S WONDERFUL GLOBE.
  THE TWO PENNILESS PRINCESSES.
  THAT STICK.
  AN OLD WOMAN'S OUTLOOK.

LOGIC. (*See under* PHILOSOPHY, p. 27.)

MAGAZINES. (*See* PERIODICALS, p. 26).

MAGNETISM. (*See under* PHYSICS, p. 28.)

MATHEMATICS, History of.

BALL (W. W. R.).—A SHORT ACCOUNT OF THE HISTORY OF MATHEMATICS. 2nd Ed. Cr. 8vo. 10s. net.
—— MATHEMATICAL RECREATIONS AND PROBLEMS. Cr. 8vo. 7s. net.

MEDICINE.

(*See also* DOMESTIC ECONOMY; NURSING; HYGIENE; PHYSIOLOGY.)

ACLAND (Sir H. W.).—THE ARMY MEDICAL SCHOOL: Address at Netley Hospital. 1s.

ALLBUTT (Dr. T. Clifford).—ON THE USE OF THE OPHTHALMOSCOPE. 8vo. 15s.

ANDERSON (Dr. McCall).—LECTURES ON CLINICAL MEDICINE. Illustr. 8vo. 10s. 6d.

BALLANCE (C. A.) and EDMUNDS (Dr. W.). LIGATION IN CONTINUITY. Illustr. Roy. 8vo. 30s. net.

BARWELL (Richard, F.R.C.S.). — THE CAUSES AND TREATMENT OF LATERAL CURVATURE OF THE SPINE. Cr. 8vo. 5s.
—— ON ANEURISM, ESPECIALLY OF THE THORAX AND ROOT OF THE NECK. 3s. 6d.

BASTIAN (H. Charlton).—ON PARALYSIS FROM BRAIN DISEASE IN ITS COMMON FORMS. Cr. 8vo. 10s. 6d.

BICKERTON (T. H.).—ON COLOUR BLINDNESS. Cr. 8vo.

BRAIN: A JOURNAL OF NEUROLOGY. Edited for the Neurological Society of London, by A. DE WATTEVILLE, Quarterly. 8vo. 3s. 6d. (Part I. in Jan. 1878.) Vols. I. to XII. 8vo. 15s. each. [Cloth covers for binding, 1s. each.]

BRUNTON (Dr. T. Lauder). — A TEXT-BOOK OF PHARMACOLOGY, THERAPEUTICS, AND MATERIA MEDICA. 3rd Edit. Med. 8vo. 21s.—Or in 2 vols. 22s. 6d.—SUPPLEMENT, 1s.

BRUNTON (Dr. T. Lauder).—DISORDERS OF DIGESTION: THEIR CONSEQUENCES AND TREATMENT. 8vo. 10s. 6d.
—— PHARMACOLOGY AND THERAPEUTICS; or, Medicine Past and Present. Cr. 8vo. 6s.
—— TABLES OF MATERIA MEDICA: A Companion to the Materia Medica Museum. 8vo. 5s.
—— AN INTRODUCTION TO MODERN THERAPEUTICS. Croonian Lectures on the Relationship between Chemical Structure and Physiological Action. 8vo. 3s. 6d net.

BUCKNILL (Dr.).—THE CARE OF THE INSANE. Cr. 8vo. 3s. 6d.

CARTER (R. Brudenell, F.C.S.).—A PRACTICAL TREATISE ON DISEASES OF THE EYE. 8vo. 16s.
—— EYESIGHT, GOOD AND BAD. Cr. 8vo. 6s.
—— MODERN OPERATIONS FOR CATARACT. 8vo. 6s.

CHRISTIE (J.).—CHOLERA EPIDEMICS IN EAST AFRICA. 8vo. 15s.

COWELL (George).—LECTURES ON CATARACT: ITS CAUSES, VARIETIES, AND TREATMENT. Cr. 8vo. 4s. 6d.

FLÜCKIGER (F. A.) and HANBURY (D.). —PHARMACOGRAPHIA. A History of the Principal Drugs of Vegetable Origin met with in Great Britain and India. 8vo. 21s.

FOTHERGILL (Dr. J. Milner).—THE PRACTITIONER'S HANDBOOK OF TREATMENT; or, The Principles of Therapeutics. 8vo. 16s.
—— THE ANTAGONISM OF THERAPEUTIC AGENTS, AND WHAT IT TEACHES. Cr. 8vo. 6s.
—— FOOD FOR THE INVALID, THE CONVALESCENT, THE DYSPEPTIC, AND THE GOUTY. 2nd Edit. Cr. 8vo. 3s. 6d.

FOX (Dr. Wilson). — ON THE ARTIFICIAL PRODUCTION OF TUBERCLE IN THE LOWER ANIMALS. With Plates. 4to. 5s. 6d.
—— ON THE TREATMENT OF HYPERPYREXIA, AS ILLUSTRATED IN ACUTE ARTICULAR RHEUMATISM BY MEANS OF THE EXTERNAL APPLICATION OF COLD. 8vo. 2s. 6d.

GRIFFITHS (W. H.).—LESSONS ON PRESCRIPTIONS AND THE ART OF PRESCRIBING. New Edition. 18mo. 3s. 6d.

HAMILTON (Prof. D. J.).—ON THE PATHOLOGY OF BRONCHITIS, CATARRHAL PNEUMONIA, TUBERCLE, AND ALLIED LESIONS OF THE HUMAN LUNG. 8vo. 8s. 6d.
—— A TEXT-BOOK OF PATHOLOGY, SYSTEMATIC AND PRACTICAL. Illustrated. Vol. I. 8vo. 25s.

HANBURY (Daniel). — SCIENCE PAPERS, CHIEFLY PHARMACOLOGICAL AND BOTANICAL. Med. 8vo. 14s.

KLEIN (Dr. E.).—MICRO-ORGANISMS AND DISEASE. An Introduction into the Study of Specific Micro-Organisms. Cr. 8vo. 6s.
—— THE BACTERIA IN ASIATIC CHOLERA. Cr. 8vo. 5s.

LEPROSY INVESTIGATION COMMITTEE, JOURNAL OF THE. Edited by P. S. ABRAHAM, M.A. Nos. 2—4. 2s. 6d. each net.

LINDSAY (Dr. J. A.). — THE CLIMATIC TREATMENT OF CONSUMPTION. Cr. 8vo. 5s.

MACLAGAN (Dr. T.).—THE GERM THEORY. 8vo. 10s. 6d.

MACLEAN (Surgeon-General W. C.).—DISEASES OF TROPICAL CLIMATES. Cr. 8vo. 10s. 6d.

MACNAMARA (C.).—A HISTORY OF ASIATIC CHOLERA. Cr. 8vo. 10s. 6d.
—— ASIATIC CHOLERA, HISTORY UP TO JULY 15, 1892: CAUSES AND TREATMENT. 8vo. 2s. 6d.

MERCIER (Dr. C.).—THE NERVOUS SYSTEM AND THE MIND. 8vo. 12s. 6d.

PIFFARD (H. G.).—AN ELEMENTARY TREATISE ON DISEASES OF THE SKIN. 8vo. 16s.

PRACTITIONER, THE: A MONTHLY JOURNAL OF THERAPEUTICS AND PUBLIC HEALTH. Edited by T. LAUDER BRUNTON F.R.S., etc.; DONALD MACALISTER, M.A., M.D., and J. MITCHELL BRUCE, M.D. 1s. 6d. monthly. Vols. I.—XLIX. Half yearly vols. 10s. 6d. each. [Cloth covers for binding, 1s. each.]

REYNOLDS (J. R.).—A SYSTEM OF MEDICINE. Edited by J. RUSSELL REYNOLDS, M.D., In 5 vols. Vols. I.—III. and V. 8vo. 25s. each.—Vol. IV. 21s.

RICHARDSON (Dr. B. W.).—DISEASES OF MODERN LIFE. Cr. 8vo.
—— THE FIELD OF DISEASE. A Book of Preventive Medicine. 8vo. 25s.

SEATON (Dr Edward C.).—A HANDBOOK OF VACCINATION. Ext. fcp. 8vo. 8s. 6d.

SEILER (Dr. Carl). — MICRO-PHOTOGRAPHS IN HISTOLOGY, NORMAL AND PATHOLOGICAL. 4to. 31s. 6d.

SIBSON (Dr. Francis).—COLLECTED WORKS Edited by W. M. ORD, M.D. Illustrated. 4 vols. 8vo. 3l. 3s.

SPENDER (J. Kent).—THERAPEUTIC MEANS FOR THE RELIEF OF PAIN. 8vo. 8s. 6d.

SURGERY (THE INTERNATIONAL ENCYCLOPAEDIA OF). A Systematic Treatise on the Theory and Practice of Surgery by Authors of various Nations. Edited by JOHN ASHHURST, jun., M.D. 6 vols. Roy. 8vo. 31s. 6d. each.

THORNE (Dr. Thorne).—DIPHTHERIA. Cr. 8vo. 8s. 6d.

WHITE (Dr. W. Hale).—A TEXT-BOOK OF GENERAL THERAPEUTICS. Cr. 8vo. 8s. 6d.

ZIEGLER (Ernst).—A TEXT-BOOK OF PATHOLOGICAL ANATOMY AND PATHOGENESIS. Translated and Edited by DONALD MACALISTER, M.A., M.D. Illustrated. 8vo.—Part I. GENERAL PATHOLOGICAL ANATOMY 12s. 6d.—Part II. SPECIAL PATHOLOGICAL ANATOMY. Sections I.—VIII. and IX.—XII. 8vo. 12s. 6d. each.

METALLURGY.
(*See also* CHEMISTRY.)

HIORNS (Arthur H.).—A TEXT-BOOK OF ELEMENTARY METALLURGY. Gl. 8vo. 4s.
—— PRACTICAL METALLURGY AND ASSAYING. Illustrated. 2nd Edit. Globe 8vo. 6s.

HIORNS (Arthur H.).—IRON AND STEEL MANUFACTURE. Illustrated. Globe 8vo. 3s. 6d.
—— MIXED METALS OR METALLIC ALLOYS. Globe 8vo. 6s.
—— METAL COLOURING AND BRONZING. Globe 8vo. 5s.

PHILLIPS (J. A.).—A TREATISE ON ORE DEPOSITS. Illustrated. Med. 8vo. 25s.

METAPHYSICS.
(*See under* PHILOSOPHY, p. 27.)

MILITARY ART AND HISTORY.

ACLAND (Sir H. W.). (*See* MEDICINE.)

AITKEN (Sir W.).—THE GROWTH OF THE RECRUIT AND YOUNG SOLDIER. Cr. 8vo. 8s. 6d.

CUNYNGHAME (Gen. Sir A. T.). — MY COMMAND IN SOUTH AFRICA, 1874—78. 8vo. 12s. 6d.

DILKE (Sir C.) and WILKINSON (S.).—IMPERIAL DEFENCE. Cr. 8vo. 3s. 6d.

HOZIER (Lieut.-Col. H. M.).—THE SEVEN WEEKS' WAR. 3rd Edit. Cr. 8vo. 6s.
—— THE INVASIONS OF ENGLAND. 2 vols. 8vo. 28s.

MARTEL (Chas.).—MILITARY ITALY. With Map. 8vo. 12s. 6d.

MAURICE (Lt.-Col.).—WAR. 8vo. 5s. net.
—— THE NATIONAL DEFENCES. Cr. 8vo.

MERCUR (Prof. J.).—ELEMENTS OF THE ART OF WAR. 8vo. 17s.

SCRATCHLEY — KINLOCH COOKE. — AUSTRALIAN DEFENCES AND NEW GUINEA. Compiled from the Papers of the late Major-General Sir PETER SCRATCHLEY, R.E., by C. KINLOCH COOKE. 8vo. 14s.

THROUGH THE RANKS TO A COMMISSION. New Edition. Cr. 8vo. 2s. 6d.

WILKINSON (S.). — THE BRAIN OF AN ARMY. A Popular Account of the German General Staff. Cr. 8vo. 2s. 6d.

WINGATE (Major F. R.).—MAHDIISM AND THE EGYPTIAN SUDAN. An Account of the Rise and Progress of Mahdiism, and of Subsequent Events in the Sudan to the Present Time. With 17 Maps. 8vo. 30s. net.

WOLSELEY (General Viscount).—THE SOLDIER'S POCKET-BOOK FOR FIELD SERVICE. 5th Edit. 16mo, roan. 5s.
—— FIELD POCKET-BOOK FOR THE AUXILIARY FORCES. 16mo. 1s. 6d.

MINERALOGY. (*See* GEOLOGY.)

MISCELLANEOUS WORKS.
(*See under* LITERATURE, p. 20.)

MUSIC.

FAY (Amy).—MUSIC-STUDY IN GERMANY Preface by Sir GEO. GROVE. Cr. 8vo. 4s. 6d.

MUSIC—*continued*.

GROVE (Sir George).—A DICTIONARY OF MUSIC AND MUSICIANS, A.D. 1450—1889. Edited by Sir GEORGE GROVE, D.C.L. In 4 vols. 8vo. 21*s*. each. With Illustrations in Music Type and Woodcut.—Also published in Parts. Parts I.—XIV., XIX.—XXII. 3*s*. 6*d*. each; XV. XVI. 7*s*.; XVII. XVIII. 7*s*.; XXIII.—XXV., Appendix. Edited by J. A. FULLER MAITLAND, M.A. 9*s*. [Cloth cases for binding the volumes, 1*s*. each.]

—— A COMPLETE INDEX TO THE ABOVE. By Mrs. E. WODEHOUSE. 8vo. 7*s*. 6*d*.

HULLAH (John).—MUSIC IN THE HOUSE. 4th Edit. Cr. 8vo. 2*s*. 6*d*.

TAYLOR (Franklin).—A PRIMER OF PIANOFORTE PLAYING. 18mo. 1*s*.

TAYLOR (Sedley).—SOUND AND MUSIC. 2nd Edit. Ext. cr. 8vo. 8*s*. 6*d*.

—— A SYSTEM OF SIGHT-SINGING FROM THE ESTABLISHED MUSICAL NOTATION. 8vo. 5*s*. net.

—— RECORD OF THE CAMBRIDGE CENTENARY OF W. A. MOZART. Cr. 8vo. 2*s*. 6*d*. net.

NATURAL HISTORY.

ATKINSON (J. C.). (*See* ANTIQUITIES, p. 1.)

BAKER (Sir Samuel W.). (*See* SPORT, p. 32.)

BLANFORD (W. T.).—GEOLOGY AND ZOOLOGY OF ABYSSINIA. 8vo. 21*s*.

FOWLER (W. W.).—TALES OF THE BIRDS. Illustrated. Cr. 8vo. 3*s*. 6*d*.

—— A YEAR WITH THE BIRDS. trated. Cr. 8vo. 3*s*. 6*d*.

KINGSLEY (Charles).—MADAM HOW AND LADY WHY; or, First Lessons in Earth-Lore for Children. Cr. 8vo. 3*s*. 6*d*.

—— GLAUCUS; or, The Wonders of the Sea-Shore. With Coloured Illustrations. Cr. 8vo. 3*s*. 6*d*.—*Presentation Edition*. Cr. 8vo, extra cloth. 7*s*. 6*d*.

KLEIN (E.).—ETIOLOGY AND PATHOLOGY OF GROUSE DISEASE. 8vo. 7*s*. net.

WALLACE (Alfred Russel).—THE MALAY ARCHIPELAGO: The Land of the Orang Utang and the Bird of Paradise. Maps and Illustrations. Ext. cr. 8vo. 6*s*. (*See also* BIOLOGY.)

WATERTON (Charles).—WANDERINGS IN SOUTH AMERICA, THE NORTH-WEST OF THE UNITED STATES, AND THE ANTILLES. Edited by Rev. J. G. WOOD. Illustrated. Cr. 8vo. 6*s*.—People's Edition. 4to. 6*d*.

WHITE (Gilbert).—NATURAL HISTORY AND ANTIQUITIES OF SELBORNE. Ed. by FRANK BUCKLAND. With a Chapter on Antiquities by the EARL OF SELBORNE. Cr. 8vo. 6*s*.

NATURAL PHILOSOPHY. (*See* PHYSICS.)

NAVAL SCIENCE.

KELVIN (Lord).—POPULAR LECTURES AND ADDRESSES.—Vol. III. NAVIGATION. Cr. 8vo. 7*s*. 6*d*.

ROBINSON (Rev. J. L.).—MARINE SURVEYING, AN ELEMENTARY TREATISE ON. For Younger Naval Officers. Illustrated. Cr. 8vo. 7*s*. 6*d*.

SHORTLAND (Admiral).—NAUTICAL SURVEYING. 8vo. 21*s*.

NOVELS. (*See* PROSE FICTION, p. 18.)

NURSING.

(*See under* DOMESTIC ECONOMY, p. 8.)

OPTICS (or LIGHT). (*See* PHYSICS, p. 28.)

PAINTING. (*See* ART, p. 2.)

PATHOLOGY. (*See* MEDICINE, p. 24.)

PERIODICALS.

AMERICAN JOURNAL OF PHILOLOGY, THE. (*See* PHILOLOGY.)

BRAIN. (*See* MEDICINE.)

ECONOMIC JOURNAL, THE. (*See* POLITICAL ECONOMY.)

ECONOMICS, THE QUARTERLY JOURNAL OF. (*See* POLITICAL ECONOMY.)

NATURAL SCIENCE: A MONTHLY REVIEW OF SCIENTIFIC PROGRESS. 8vo. 1*s*. net. No. 1. March 1892.

NATURE: A WEEKLY ILLUSTRATED JOURNAL OF SCIENCE. Published every Thursday. Price 6*d*. Monthly Parts, 2*s*. and 2*s*. 6*d*.; Current Half-yearly vols., 15*s*. each. Vols. I.—XLVII. [Cases for binding vols. 1*s*. 6*d*. each.]

HELLENIC STUDIES, THE JOURNAL OF. Published Half-Yearly from 1880. 8vo. 30*s*.; or each Part, 15*s*. Vol. XIII. Part I. 15*s*. net.

The Journal will be sold at a reduced price to Libraries wishing to subscribe, but official application must in each case be made to the Council. Information on this point, and upon the conditions of Membership, may be obtained on application to the Hon. Sec., Mr. George Macmillan, 29, Bedford Street, Covent Garden.

LEPROSY INVESTIGATION COMMITTEE, JOURNAL OF. (*See* MEDICINE.)

MACMILLAN'S MAGAZINE. Published Monthly. 1*s*.—Vols. I.-LXVII. 7*s*. 6*d*. each. [Cloth covers for binding, 1*s*. each.]

PHILOLOGY, THE JOURNAL OF. (*See* PHILOLOGY.)

PRACTITIONER, THE. (*See* MEDICINE.)

RECORD OF TECHNICAL AND SECONDARY EDUCATION. (*See* EDUCATION, p. 8.)

PHILOLOGY.

AMERICAN JOURNAL OF PHILOLOGY, THE. Edited by Prof. BASIL L. GILDERSLEEVE. 4*s*. 6*d*. each No. (quarterly).

PHILOLOGY—*continued.*

CORNELL UNIVERSITY STUDIES IN CLASSICAL PHILOLOGY. Edited by I. FLAGG, W. G. HALE, and B. I. WHEELER. I. THE *C U M*-CONSTRUCTIONS: their History and Functions. Part I. Critical. 1s. 8d. net. Part II. Constructive. By W. G. HALE. 3s. 4d. net.—II. ANALOGY AND THE SCOPE OF ITS APPLICATION IN LANGUAGE. By B. I. WHEELER. 1s. 3d. net.

GILES (P.).—A SHORT MANUAL OF PHILOLOGY FOR CLASSICAL STUDENTS. Cr. 8vo.

JOURNAL OF SACRED AND CLASSICAL PHILOLOGY. 4 vols. 8vo. 12s. 6d. each.

JOURNAL OF PHILOLOGY. New Series. Edited by W. A. WRIGHT, M.A., I. BYWATER, M.A., and H. JACKSON, M.A. 4s. 6d. each No. (half-yearly).

KELLNER (Dr. L.).—HISTORICAL OUTLINES IN ENGLISH SYNTAX. Globe 8vo. 6s.

MORRIS (Rev. Richard, LL.D.).—PRIMER OF ENGLISH GRAMMAR. 18mo. 1s.

—— ELEMENTARY LESSONS IN HISTORICAL ENGLISH GRAMMAR. 18mo. 2s. 6d.

—— HISTORICAL OUTLINES OF ENGLISH ACCIDENCE. Extra fcp. 8vo. 6s.

MORRIS (R.) and BOWEN (H. C.).—ENGLISH GRAMMAR EXERCISES. 18mo. 1s.

OLIPHANT (T. L. Kington). — THE OLD AND MIDDLE ENGLISH. Globe 8vo. 9s.

—— THE NEW ENGLISH. 2 vols. Cr. 8vo. 21s.

PEILE (John).—A PRIMER OF PHILOLOGY. 18mo. 1s.

PELLISSIER (E.).—FRENCH ROOTS AND THEIR FAMILIES. Globe 8vo. 6s.

TAYLOR (Isaac).—WORDS AND PLACES. 9th Edit. Maps. Globe 8vo. 6s.

—— ETRUSCAN RESEARCHES. 8vo. 14s.

—— GREEKS AND GOTHS: A Study of the Runes. 8vo. 9s.

WETHERELL (J.).—EXERCISES ON MORRIS'S PRIMER OF ENGLISH GRAMMAR. 18mo. 1s.

YONGE (C. M.).—HISTORY OF CHRISTIAN NAMES. New Edit., revised. Cr. 8vo. 7s. 6d.

PHILOSOPHY.

Ethics and Metaphysics—Logic—Psychology.

Ethics and Metaphysics.

BIRKS (Thomas Rawson).—FIRST PRINCIPLES OF MORAL SCIENCE. Cr. 8vo. 8s. 6d.

—— MODERN UTILITARIANISM; or, The Systems of Paley, Bentham, and Mill Examined and Compared. Cr. 8vo. 6s. 6d.

—— MODERN PHYSICAL FATALISM, AND THE DOCTRINE OF EVOLUTION. Including an Examination of Mr. Herbert Spencer's "First Principles." Cr. 8vo. 6s.

CALDERWOOD (Prof. H.).—A HANDBOOK OF MORAL PHILOSOPHY. Cr. 8vo. 6s.

FISKE (John).—OUTLINES OF COSMIC PHILOSOPHY, BASED ON THE DOCTRINE OF EVOLUTION. 2 vols. 8vo. 25s.

FOWLER (Rev. Thomas). — PROGRESSIVE MORALITY: An Essay in Ethics. Cr. 8vo. 5s.

HARPER (Father Thomas).—THE METAPHYSICS OF THE SCHOOL. In 5 vols.—Vols. I. and II. 8vo. 18s. each.—Vol. III. Part I. 12s.

HUXLEY (Prof. T. H.).—EVOLUTION AND ETHICS. 8vo. 2s. net.

KANT.—KANT'S CRITICAL PHILOSOPHY FOR ENGLISH READERS. By J. P. MAHAFFY, D.D., and J. H. BERNARD, B.D. 2 vols. Cr. 8vo.—Vol. I. THE KRITIK OF PURE REASON EXPLAINED AND DEFENDED. 7s. 6d.—Vol. II. THE PROLEGOMENA. Translated, with Notes and Appendices. 6s.

—— KRITIK OF JUDGMENT. Translated by J. H. BERNARD, D.D. 8vo. 10s. net.

KANT—MAX MÜLLER. — CRITIQUE OF PURE REASON BY IMMANUEL KANT. Translated by F. MAX MÜLLER. With Introduction by LUDWIG NOIRÉ. 2 vols. 8vo. 16s. each (sold separately).—Vol. I. HISTORICAL INTRODUCTION, by LUDWIG NOIRÉ, etc.—Vol. II. CRITIQUE OF PURE REASON.

MAURICE (F. D.).—MORAL AND METAPHYSICAL PHILOSOPHY. 2 vols. 8vo. 16s.

McCOSH (Rev. Dr. James).—THE METHOD OF THE DIVINE GOVERNMENT, PHYSICAL AND MORAL. 8vo. 10s. 6d.

—— THE SUPERNATURAL IN RELATION TO THE NATURAL. Cr. 8vo. 7s. 6d.

—— INTUITIONS OF THE MIND. 8vo. 10s. 6d.

—— AN EXAMINATION OF MR. J. S. MILL'S PHILOSOPHY. 8vo. 10s. 6d.

—— CHRISTIANITY AND POSITIVISM. Lectures on Natural Theology and Apologetics. Cr. 8vo. 7s. 6d.

—— THE SCOTTISH PHILOSOPHY FROM HUTCHESON TO HAMILTON, BIOGRAPHICAL, EXPOSITORY, CRITICAL. Roy. 8vo. 16s.

—— REALISTIC PHILOSOPHY DEFENDED IN A PHILOSOPHIC SERIES. 2 vols.—Vol. I. EXPOSITORY. Vol. II. HISTORICAL AND CRITICAL. Cr. 8vo. 14s.

—— FIRST AND FUNDAMENTAL TRUTHS. Being a Treatise on Metaphysics. 8vo. 9s.

—— THE PREVAILING TYPES OF PHILOSOPHY: CAN THEY LOGICALLY REACH REALITY? 8vo. 3s. 6d.

—— OUR MORAL NATURE. Cr. 8vo. 2s. 6d.

MASSON (Prof. David).—RECENT BRITISH PHILOSOPHY. 3rd Edit. Cr. 8vo. 6s.

SIDGWICK (Prof. Henry).—THE METHODS OF ETHICS. 4th Edit., revised. 8vo. 14s.

—— A SUPPLEMENT TO THE SECOND EDITION. Containing all the important Additions and Alterations in the Fourth Edition. 8vo. 6s.

—— OUTLINES OF THE HISTORY OF ETHICS FOR ENGLISH READERS. Cr. 8vo. 3s. 6d.

THORNTON (W. T.). — OLD-FASHIONED ETHICS AND COMMON-SENSE METAPHYSICS. 8vo. 10s. 6d.

WILLIAMS (C. M.)—A REVIEW OF THE SYSTEMS OF ETHICS FOUNDED ON THE THEORY OF EVOLUTION. Cr. 8vo. 12s. net.

PHILOSOPHY.
Logic.

BOOLE (George). — THE MATHEMATICAL ANALYSIS OF LOGIC. 8vo. sewed. 5s.

CARROLL (Lewis).—THE GAME OF LOGIC. Cr. 8vo. 3s. net.

JEVONS (W. Stanley).—A PRIMER OF LOGIC. 18mo. 1s.

—— ELEMENTARY LESSONS IN LOGIC, DEDUCTIVE AND INDUCTIVE. 18mo. 3s. 6d.

—— STUDIES IN DEDUCTIVE LOGIC. 2nd Edit. Cr. 8vo. 6s.

—— THE PRINCIPLES OF SCIENCE: Treatise on Logic and Scientific Method. Cr. 8vo. 12s. 6d.

—— PURE LOGIC: and other Minor Works. Edited by R. ADAMSON, M.A., and HARRIET A. JEVONS. 8vo. 10s. 6d.

KEYNES (J. N.).—STUDIES AND EXERCISES IN FORMAL LOGIC. 2nd Edit. Cr. 8vo. 10s. 6d.

McCOSH (Rev. Dr.).—THE LAWS OF DISCURSIVE THOUGHT. A Text-Book of Formal Logic. Cr. 8vo. 5s.

RAY (Prof. P. K.).—A TEXT-BOOK OF DEDUCTIVE LOGIC. 4th Edit. Globe 8vo. 4s. 6d.

VENN (Rev. John).—THE LOGIC OF CHANCE. 2nd Edit. Cr. 8vo. 10s. 6d.

—— SYMBOLIC LOGIC. Cr. 8vo. 10s. 6d.

—— THE PRINCIPLES OF EMPIRICAL OR INDUCTIVE LOGIC. 8vo. 18s.

Psychology.

BALDWIN (Prof. J. M.).—HANDBOOK OF PSYCHOLOGY: Senses and Intellect. 8vo. 12s. 6d.

—— FEELING AND WILL. 8vo. 12s. 6d.

CALDERWOOD (Prof. H.). — THE RELATIONS OF MIND AND BRAIN. 3rd Ed. 8vo. 8s.

CLIFFORD (W. K.).—SEEING AND THINKING. Cr. 8vo. 3s. 6d.

HÖFFDING (Prof. H.).—OUTLINES OF PSYCHOLOGY. Translated by M. E. LOWNDES. Cr. 8vo. 6s.

JAMES (Prof. William).—THE PRINCIPLES OF PSYCHOLOGY. 2 vols. Demy 8vo. 25s. net.

—— TEXT-BOOK OF PSYCHOLOGY. Cr. 8vo. 7s. net.

JARDINE (Rev. Robert).—THE ELEMENTS OF THE PSYCHOLOGY OF COGNITION. 3rd Edit. Cr. 8vo. 6s. 6d.

McCOSH (Rev. Dr.).—PSYCHOLOGY. Cr. 8vo. I. THE COGNITIVE POWERS. 6s. 6d.—II. THE MOTIVE POWERS. 6s. 6d.

—— THE EMOTIONS. 8vo. 9s.

MAUDSLEY (Dr. Henry).—THE PHYSIOLOGY OF MIND. Cr. 8vo. 10s. 6d.

—— THE PATHOLOGY OF MIND. 8vo. 18s.

—— BODY AND MIND. Cr. 8vo. 6s. 6d.

MURPHY (J. J.).—HABIT AND INTELLIGENCE. 2nd Edit. Illustrated. 8vo. 16s.

PHOTOGRAPHY.

MELDOLA (Prof. R.).—THE CHEMISTRY OF PHOTOGRAPHY. Cr. 8vo. 6s.

PHYSICS OR NATURAL PHILOSOPHY.
General—Electricity and Magnetism—Heat, Light, and Sound.

General.

ANDREWS (Dr. Thomas): THE SCIENTIFIC PAPERS OF THE LATE. With a Memoir by Profs. TAIT and CRUM BROWN. 8vo. 18s.

BARKER (G. F.). — PHYSICS: ADVANCED COURSE. 8vo. 21s.

DANIELL (A.)—A TEXT-BOOK OF THE PRINCIPLES OF PHYSICS. Illustrated. 2nd Edit. Med. 8vo. 21s.

EVERETT (Prof. J. D.).—THE C. G. S. SYSTEM OF UNITS, WITH TABLES OF PHYSICAL CONSTANTS. New Edit. Globe 8vo. 5s.

FESSENDEN (C.).—ELEMENTS OF PHYSICS. Fcp. 8vo. 3s.

FISHER (Rev. Osmond).—PHYSICS OF THE EARTH'S CRUST. 2nd Edit. 8vo. 12s.

GUILLEMIN (Amédée).—THE FORCES OF NATURE. A Popular Introduction to the Study of Physical Phenomena. 455 Woodcuts. Roy. 8vo. 21s.

KELVIN (Lord).—POPULAR LECTURES AND ADDRESSES.—Vol. I. CONSTITUTION OF MATTER. Cr. 8vo. 7s. 6d.

KEMPE (A. B.).—HOW TO DRAW A STRAIGHT LINE. Cr. 8vo. 1s. 6d.

LOEWY (B.).—QUESTIONS AND EXAMPLES IN EXPERIMENTAL PHYSICS, SOUND, LIGHT, HEAT, ELECTRICITY, AND MAGNETISM. Fcp. 8vo. 2s.

—— A GRADUATED COURSE OF NATURAL SCIENCE. Part I. Gl. 8vo. 2s.—Part II. 2s. 6d.

MOLLOY (Rev. G.).—GLEANINGS IN SCIENCE: A Series of Popular Lectures on Scientific Subjects. 8vo. 7s. 6d.

STEWART (Prof. Balfour). — A PRIMER OF PHYSICS. Illustrated. 18mo. 1s.

—— LESSONS IN ELEMENTARY PHYSICS. Illustrated. Fcp. 8vo. 4s. 6d.

—— QUESTIONS. By T. H. CORE. 18mo. 2s.

STEWART (Prof. Balfour) and GEE (W. W. Haldane).—LESSONS IN ELEMENTARY PRACTICAL PHYSICS. Illustrated.—GENERAL PHYSICAL PROCESSES. Cr. 8vo. 6s.

TAIT (Prof. P. G.).—LECTURES ON SOME RECENT ADVANCES IN PHYSICAL SCIENCE. 3rd Edit. Cr. 8vo. 9s.

Electricity and Magnetism.

CUMMING (Linnæus).—AN INTRODUCTION TO ELECTRICITY. Cr. 8vo. 8s. 6d.

DAY (R. E.).—ELECTRIC LIGHT ARITHMETIC. 18mo. 2s.

GRAY (Prof. Andrew).—THE THEORY AND PRACTICE OF ABSOLUTE MEASUREMENTS IN ELECTRICITY AND MAGNETISM. 2 vols. Cr. 8vo. Vol. I. 12s. 6d.—Vol. II. 2 parts. 25s.

—— ABSOLUTE MEASUREMENTS IN ELECTRICITY AND MAGNETISM. Fcp. 8vo. 5s. 6d.

GUILLEMIN (A.).—ELECTRICITY AND MAGNETISM. A Popular Treatise. Translated and Edited by Prof. SILVANUS P. THOMPSON. Super Roy. 8vo. 31s. 6d.

HEAVISIDE (O.) — ELECTRICAL PAPERS. 2 vols. 8vo. 30s. net.

KELVIN (Lord). — PAPERS ON ELECTROSTATICS AND MAGNETISM. 8vo. 18s.

LODGE (Prof. Oliver). — MODERN VIEWS OF ELECTRICITY. Illust. Cr. 8vo. 6s. 6d.

MENDENHALL (T. C.). — A CENTURY OF ELECTRICITY. Cr. 8vo. 4s. 6d.

STEWART (Prof. Balfour) and GEE (W. W. Haldane). — LESSONS IN ELEMENTARY PRACTICAL PHYSICS. Cr. 8vo. Illustrated. — ELECTRICITY AND MAGNETISM. 7s. 6d.
—— PRACTICAL PHYSICS FOR SCHOOLS. Gl. 8vo. — ELECTRICITY AND MAGNETISM. 2s. 6d.

THOMPSON (Prof. Silvanus P.). — ELEMENTARY LESSONS IN ELECTRICITY AND MAGNETISM. Illustrated. Fcp. 8vo. 4s. 6d.

TURNER (H. H.). — EXAMPLES ON HEAT AND ELECTRICITY. Cr. 8vo. 2s. 6d.

Heat, Light, and Sound.

AIRY (Sir G. B.). — ON SOUND AND ATMOSPHERIC VIBRATIONS. Cr. 8vo. 9s.

CARNOT—THURSTON.—REFLECTIONS ON THE MOTIVE POWER OF HEAT, AND ON MACHINES FITTED TO DEVELOP THAT POWER. From the French of N. L. S. CARNOT. Edited by R. H. THURSTON, LL.D. Cr. 8vo. 7s. 6d.

JOHNSON (Amy). — SUNSHINE. Illustrated. Cr. 8vo. 6s.

JONES (Prof. D. E.). — HEAT, LIGHT, AND SOUND. Globe 8vo. 2s. 6d.
—— LESSONS IN HEAT AND LIGHT. Globe 8vo. 3s. 6d.

MAYER (Prof. A. M.). — SOUND. A Series of Simple Experiments. Illustr. Cr. 8vo. 3s. 6d.

MAYER (Prof. A. M.) and BARNARD (C.) — LIGHT. A Series of Simple Experiments. Illustrated. Cr. 8vo. 2s. 6d.

PARKINSON (S.). — A TREATISE ON OPTICS. 4th Edit., revised. Cr. 8vo. 10s. 6d.

PEABODY (Prof. C. H.). — THERMODYNAMICS OF THE STEAM ENGINE AND OTHER HEAT-ENGINES. 8vo. 21s.

PERRY (Prof. J.). — STEAM: An Elementary Treatise. 18mo. 4s. 6d.

PRESTON (T.). — THE THEORY OF LIGHT. Illustrated. 8vo. 15s. net.
—— THE THEORY OF HEAT. 8vo.

RAYLEIGH (Lord). — THEORY OF SOUND. 8vo. Vol. I. 12s. 6d. — Vol. II. 12s. 6d.

SHANN (G.). — AN ELEMENTARY TREATISE ON HEAT IN RELATION TO STEAM AND THE STEAM-ENGINE. Illustr. Cr. 8vo. 4s. 6d.

SPOTTISWOODE (W.). — POLARISATION OF LIGHT. Illustrated. Cr. 8vo. 3s. 6d.

STEWART (Prof. Balfour) and GEE (W. W. Haldane). — LESSONS IN ELEMENTARY PRACTICAL PHYSICS. Cr. 8vo. Illustrated. — OPTICS, HEAT, AND SOUND.
—— PRACTICAL PHYSICS FOR SCHOOLS. Gl. 8vo. — HEAT, LIGHT, AND SOUND.

STOKES (Sir George G.). — ON LIGHT. The Burnett Lectures. Cr. 8vo. 7s. 6d.

STONE (W. H.). — ELEMENTARY LESSONS ON SOUND. Illustrated. Fcp. 8vo. 3s. 6d.

TAIT (Prof. P. G.). — HEAT. With Illustrations. Cr. 8vo. 6s.

TAYLOR (Sedley). — SOUND AND MUSIC. 2nd Edit. Ext. cr. 8vo. 8s. 6d.

TURNER (H. H.). (See ELECTRICITY.)

WRIGHT (Lewis). — LIGHT. A Course of Experimental Optics. Illust. Cr. 8vo. 7s. 6d.

PHYSIOGRAPHY and METEOROLOGY.

ARATUS. — THE SKIES AND WEATHER FORECASTS OF ARATUS. Translated by E. POSTE, M.A. Cr. 8vo. 3s. 6d.

BLANFORD (H. F.). — THE RUDIMENTS OF PHYSICAL GEOGRAPHY FOR THE USE OF INDIAN SCHOOLS. Illustr. Cr. 8vo. 2s. 6d.
—— A PRACTICAL GUIDE TO THE CLIMATES AND WEATHER OF INDIA, CEYLON AND BURMAH, AND THE STORMS OF INDIAN SEAS. 8vo. 12s. 6d.

FERREL (Prof. W.). — A POPULAR TREATISE ON THE WINDS. 2nd Ed. 8vo. 17s. net.

FISHER (Rev. Osmond). — PHYSICS OF THE EARTH'S CRUST. 2nd Edit. 8vo. 12s.

GEIKIE (Sir Archibald). — A PRIMER OF PHYSICAL GEOGRAPHY. Illustrated. 18mo. 1s.
—— ELEMENTARY LESSONS IN PHYSICAL GEOGRAPHY. Illustrated. Fcp. 8vo. 4s. 6d.
—— QUESTIONS ON THE SAME. 1s. 6d.

HUXLEY (Prof. T. H.). — PHYSIOGRAPHY. Illustrated. Cr. 8vo. 6s.

LOCKYER (J. Norman). — OUTLINES OF PHYSIOGRAPHY: THE MOVEMENTS OF THE EARTH. Illustrated. Cr. 8vo, swd. 1s. 6d.

MELDOLA (Prof. R.) and WHITE (Wm.). — REPORT ON THE EAST ANGLIAN EARTHQUAKE OF APRIL 22ND, 1884. 8vo. 3s. 6d.

PHYSIOLOGY.

FEARNLEY (W.). — A MANUAL OF ELEMENTARY PRACTICAL HISTOLOGY. Cr. 8vo. 7s. 6d.

FOSTER (Prof. Michael). — A TEXT-BOOK OF PHYSIOLOGY. Illustrated. 5th Edit. 8vo. — Part I. Book I. BLOOD: THE TISSUES OF MOVEMENT, THE VASCULAR MECHANISM. 10s. 6d. — Part II. Book II. THE TISSUES OF CHEMICAL ACTION, WITH THEIR RESPECTIVE MECHANISMS: NUTRITION. 10s. 6d. — Part III. Book III. THE CENTRAL NERVOUS SYSTEM. 7s. 6d. — Part IV. Book III. THE SENSES, AND SOME SPECIAL MUSCULAR MECHANISMS. — BOOK IV. THE TISSUES AND MECHANISMS OF REPRODUCTION. 10s. 6d. — Appendix, by A. S. LEA. 7s. 6d.
—— A PRIMER OF PHYSIOLOGY. 18mo. 1s.

FOSTER (Prof. M.) and LANGLEY (J. N.). — A COURSE OF ELEMENTARY PRACTICAL PHYSIOLOGY AND HISTOLOGY. Cr. 8vo. 7s. 6d.

GAMGEE (Arthur). — A TEXT-BOOK OF THE PHYSIOLOGICAL CHEMISTRY OF THE ANIMAL BODY. Vol. I. 8vo. 18s. Vol. II.

PHYSIOLOGY—*continued.*

HUMPHRY (Prof. Sir G. M.).—THE HUMAN FOOT AND THE HUMAN HAND. Illustrated. Fcp. 8vo. 4s. 6d.

HUXLEY (Prof. Thos. H.).—LESSONS IN ELEMENTARY PHYSIOLOGY. Fcp. 8vo. 4s. 6d.
—— QUESTIONS. By T. ALCOCK. 18mo. 1s.6d.

MIVART (St. George).—LESSONS IN ELEMENTARY ANATOMY. Fcp. 8vo. 6s. 6d.

PETTIGREW (J. Bell).—THE PHYSIOLOGY OF THE CIRCULATION IN PLANTS IN THE LOWER ANIMALS AND IN MAN. 8vo. 12s.

SEILER (Dr. Carl).—MICRO-PHOTOGRAPHS IN HISTOLOGY, NORMAL AND PATHOLOGICAL. 4to. 31s. 6d.

POETRY. (*See under* LITERATURE, p. 14.)

POLITICAL ECONOMY.

BASTABLE (Prof. C. F.).—PUBLIC FINANCE. 12s. 6d. net.

BÖHM-BAWERK (Prof.).—CAPITAL AND INTEREST. Trans. by W. SMART. 8vo. 12s.net.
—— THE POSITIVE THEORY OF CAPITAL. By the same Translator. 12s. net.

BOISSEVAIN (G. M.).—THE MONETARY QUESTION. 8vo, sewed. 3s. net.

BONAR (James).—MALTHUS AND HIS WORK. 8vo. 12s. 6d.

CAIRNES (J. E.).—SOME LEADING PRINCIPLES OF POLITICAL ECONOMY NEWLY EXPOUNDED. 8vo. 14s.
—— THE CHARACTER AND LOGICAL METHOD OF POLITICAL ECONOMY. Cr. 8vo. 6s.

CANTILLON.—ESSAI SUR LE COMMERCE. 12mo. 7s. net.

CLARE (G).—A B C OF THE FOREIGN EXCHANGES. Cr. 8vo. 3s. net.

CLARKE (C. B.). — SPECULATIONS FROM POLITICAL ECONOMY. Cr. 8vo. 3s. 6d.

DICTIONARY OF POLITICAL ECONOMY, A. By various Writers. Ed. R. H. I. PALGRAVE. 3s.6d. net. (Part I. July, 1891.)

ECONOMIC JOURNAL, THE. — THE JOURNAL OF THE BRITISH ECONOMIC ASSOCIATION. Edit. by Prof. F. Y. EDGEWORTH. Published Quarterly. 8vo. 5s. (Part I. April, 1891.) Vol. I. 21s. [Cloth Covers for binding Volumes, 1s. 6d. each.]

ECONOMICS : THE QUARTERLY JOURNAL OF. Vol. II. Parts II. III. IV. 2s. 6d. each. —Vol. III. 4 parts. 2s. 6d. each.—Vol. IV. 4 parts. 2s.6d. each.—Vol. V. 4 parts. 2s.6d. each.—Vol. VI. 4 parts. 2s. 6d. each.

FAWCETT (Henry).—MANUAL OF POLITICAL ECONOMY. 7th Edit. Cr. 8vo. 12s.
—— AN EXPLANATORY DIGEST OF THE ABOVE. By C. A. WATERS. Cr. 8vo. 2s.6d.
—— FREE TRADE AND PROTECTION. 6th Edit. Cr. 8vo. 3s. 6d.

FAWCETT (Mrs. H.).—POLITICAL ECONOMY FOR BEGINNERS, WITH QUESTIONS. 7th Edit. 18mo. 2s. 6d.

FIRST LESSONS IN BUSINESS MATTERS. By A BANKER'S DAUGHTER. 2nd Edit. 18mo. 1s.

GILMAN (N. P.).—PROFIT-SHARING BETWEEN EMPLOYER AND EMPLOYEE. Cr. 8vo. 7s. 6d.

GOSCHEN (Rt. Hon. George J.).—REPORTS AND SPEECHES ON LOCAL TAXATION. 8vo. 5s.

GUIDE TO THE UNPROTECTED : IN EVERY-DAY MATTERS RELATING TO PROPERTY AND INCOME. Ext. fcp. 8vo. 3s. 6d.

GUNTON (George).—WEALTH AND PROGRESS. Cr. 8vo. 6s.

HORTON (Hon. S. Dana).—THE SILVER POUND AND ENGLAND'S MONETARY POLICY SINCE THE RESTORATION. 8vo. 14s.

HOWELL (George).—THE CONFLICTS OF CAPITAL AND LABOUR. Cr. 8vo. 7s. 6d.

JEVONS (W. Stanley).—A PRIMER OF POLITICAL ECONOMY. 18mo. 1s.
—— THE THEORY OF POLITICAL ECONOMY. 3rd Ed. 8vo. 10s. 6d.
—— INVESTIGATIONS IN CURRENCY AND FINANCE. Edit. by H. S. FOXWELL. 8vo. 21s.

KEYNES (J. N.).—THE SCOPE AND METHOD OF POLITICAL ECONOMY. Cr. 8vo. 7s. net.

MARSHALL (Prof. Alfred).—PRINCIPLES OF ECONOMICS. 2 vols. 8vo. Vol. I. 12s.6d. net.
—— ELEMENTS OF ECONOMICS OF INDUSTRY. Crown 8vo. 3s. 6d.

MARTIN (Frederick).—THE HISTORY OF LLOYD'S, AND OF MARINE INSURANCE IN GREAT BRITAIN. 8vo. 14s.

PRICE (L. L. F. R.).—INDUSTRIAL PEACE : ITS ADVANTAGES, METHODS, AND DIFFICULTIES. Med. 8vo. 6s.

SIDGWICK (Prof. Henry).—THE PRINCIPLES OF POLITICAL ECONOMY. 2nd Edit. 8vo. 16s.

SMART (W.).—AN INTRODUCTION TO THE THEORY OF VALUE. Cr. 8vo. 3s. net.

THOMPSON (H. M.).—THE THEORY OF WAGES AND ITS APPLICATION TO THE EIGHT HOURS QUESTION. Cr. 8vo. 3s. 6d.

WALKER (Francis A.).—FIRST LESSONS IN POLITICAL ECONOMY. Cr. 8vo. 5s.
—— A BRIEF TEXT-BOOK OF POLITICAL ECONOMY. Cr. 8vo. 6s. 6d.
—— POLITICAL ECONOMY. 8vo. 12s. 6d.
—— THE WAGES QUESTION. Ext. cr. 8vo. 8s. 6d. net.
—— MONEY. New Edit. Ext.cr.8vo. 8s.6d.net.
—— MONEY IN ITS RELATION TO TRADE AND INDUSTRY. Cr. 8vo. 7s. 6d.
—— LAND AND ITS RENT. Fcp. 8vo. 3s. 6d.

WALLACE (A. R.).—BAD TIMES : An Essay. Cr. 8vo. 2s. 6d.

WICKSTEED (Ph. H.).—THE ALPHABET OF ECONOMIC SCIENCE.—I. ELEMENTS OF THE THEORY OF VALUE OR WORTH. Gl.8vo. 2s.6d.

POLITICS.

(*See also* HISTORY, p. 10.)

ADAMS (Sir F. O.) and CUNNINGHAM (C.).—THE SWISS CONFEDERATION. 8vo. 14s.

BAKER (Sir Samuel W.).—THE EGYPTIAN QUESTION. 8vo, sewed. 2s.

BATH (Marquis of).—OBSERVATIONS ON BULGARIAN AFFAIRS. Cr. 8vo. 3s. 6d.

BRIGHT (John).—SPEECHES ON QUESTIONS OF PUBLIC POLICY. Edit. by J. E. THOROLD ROGERS. With Portrait. 2 vols. 8vo. 25s. —Popular Edition. Ext. fcp. 8vo. 3s. 6d.
—— PUBLIC ADDRESSES. Edited by J. E. T. ROGERS. 8vo. 14s.

BRYCE (Jas., M.P.).—THE AMERICAN COMMONWEALTH. 2 vols. Ext. cr. 8vo. 25s.

BUCKLAND (Anna).—OUR NATIONAL INSTITUTIONS. 18mo. 1s.

BURKE (Edmund).—LETTERS, TRACTS, AND SPEECHES ON IRISH AFFAIRS. Edited by MATTHEW ARNOLD, with Preface. Cr. 8vo. 6s.
—— REFLECTIONS ON THE FRENCH REVOLUTION. Ed. by F. G. SELBY. Globe 8vo. 5s.

CAIRNES (J. E.).—POLITICAL ESSAYS. 8vo. 10s. 6d.
—— THE SLAVE POWER. 8vo. 10s. 6d.

COBDEN (Richard).—SPEECHES ON QUESTIONS OF PUBLIC POLICY. Ed. by J. BRIGHT and J. E. THOROLD ROGERS. Gl. 8vo. 3s. 6d.

DICEY (Prof. A. V.).—LETTERS ON UNIONIST DELUSIONS. Cr. 8vo. 2s. 6d.

DILKE (Rt. Hon. Sir Charles W.).—GREATER BRITAIN. 9th Edit. Cr. 8vo. 6s.
—— PROBLEMS OF GREATER BRITAIN. Maps. 3rd Edit. Ext. cr. 8vo. 12s. 6d.

DONISTHORPE (Wordsworth). — INDIVIDUALISM: A System of Politics. 8vo. 14s.

DUFF (Rt. Hon. Sir M. E. Grant).—MISCELLANIES, POLITICAL AND LITERARY. 8vo. 10s. 6d.

ENGLISH CITIZEN, THE.—His Rights and Responsibilities. Ed. by HENRY CRAIK, C.B. New Edit. Monthly Volumes from Oct. 1892. Cr. 8vo. 2s. 6d. each.

CENTRAL GOVERNMENT. By H. D. TRAILL.

THE ELECTORATE AND THE LEGISLATURE. By SPENCER WALPOLE.

THE LAND LAWS. By Sir F. POLLOCK, Bart. 2nd Edit.

THE PUNISHMENT AND PREVENTION OF CRIME. By Col. Sir EDMUND DU CANE.

LOCAL GOVERNMENT. By M. D. CHALMERS.

COLONIES AND DEPENDENCIES: Part I. INDIA. By J. S. COTTON, M.A.—II. THE COLONIES. By E. J. PAYNE.

THE STATE IN ITS RELATION TO EDUCATION. By HENRY CRAIK, C.B.

THE STATE AND THE CHURCH. By Hon. ARTHUR ELLIOTT, M.P.

THE STATE IN ITS RELATION TO TRADE. By Sir T. H. FARRER, Bart.

THE POOR LAW. By the Rev. T. W. FOWLE.

THE STATE IN RELATION TO LABOUR. By W. STANLEY JEVONS.

JUSTICE AND POLICE. By F. W. MAITLAND.

THE NATIONAL DEFENCES. By Colonel MAURICE, R.A. [In the Press.

FOREIGN RELATIONS. By S. WALPOLE.

THE NATIONAL BUDGET; NATIONAL DEBT; TAXES AND RATES. By A. J. WILSON.

FAWCETT (Henry).—SPEECHES ON SOME CURRENT POLITICAL QUESTIONS. 8vo. 10s. 6d.
—— FREE TRADE AND PROTECTION. 6th Edit. Cr. 8vo. 3s. 6d.

FAWCETT (Henry and Mrs. H.).—ESSAYS AND LECTURES ON POLITICAL AND SOCIAL SUBJECTS. 8vo. 10s. 6d.

FISKE (John).—AMERICAN POLITICAL IDEAS VIEWED FROM THE STAND-POINT OF UNIVERSAL HISTORY. Cr. 8vo. 4s.
—— CIVIL GOVERNMENT IN THE UNITED STATES CONSIDERED WITH SOME REFERENCE TO ITS ORIGIN. Cr. 8vo. 6s. 6d.

FREEMAN (E. A.). — DISESTABLISHMENT AND DISENDOWMENT. WHAT ARE THEY? 4th Edit. Cr. 8vo. 1s.
—— THE GROWTH OF THE ENGLISH CONSTITUTION. 5th Edit. Cr. 8vo. 5s.

HARWOOD (George).—DISESTABLISHMENT: or, a Defence of the Principle of a National Church. 8vo. 12s.
—— THE COMING DEMOCRACY. Cr. 8vo. 6s.

HILL (Florence D.).—CHILDREN OF THE STATE. Edited by FANNY FOWKE. Crown 8vo. 6s.

HILL (Octavia).—OUR COMMON LAND, AND OTHER ESSAYS. Ext. fcp. 8vo. 3s. 6d.

HOLLAND (Prof. T. E.).—THE TREATY RELATIONS OF RUSSIA AND TURKEY, FROM 1774 TO 1853. Cr. 8vo. 2s.

JENKS (Prof. Edward).—THE GOVERNMENT OF VICTORIA (AUSTRALIA). 8vo. 14s.

JEPHSON (H.).—THE PLATFORM: ITS RISE AND PROGRESS. 2 vols. 8vo. 21s.

LOWELL (J. R.). (See COLLECTED WORKS.)

LUBBOCK (Sir J.). (See COLLECTED WORKS.)

PALGRAVE (W. Gifford). — ESSAYS ON EASTERN QUESTIONS. 8vo. 10s. 6d.

PARKIN (G. R.).—IMPERIAL FEDERATION. Cr. 8vo. 4s. 6d.

POLLOCK (Sir F., Bart.).—INTRODUCTION TO THE HISTORY OF THE SCIENCE OF POLITICS. Cr. 8vo. 2s. 6d.
—— LEADING CASES DONE INTO ENGLISH. Crown 8vo. 3s. 6d.

PRACTICAL POLITICS. 8vo. 6s.

ROGERS (Prof. J. E. T.).—COBDEN AND POLITICAL OPINION. 8vo. 10s. 6d.

ROUTLEDGE (Jas.).—POPULAR PROGRESS IN ENGLAND. 8vo. 16s.

RUSSELL (Sir Charles).—NEW VIEWS ON IRELAND. Cr. 8vo. 2s. 6d.
—— THE PARNELL COMMISSION: THE OPENING SPEECH FOR THE DEFENCE. 8vo. 10s. 6d. —Popular Edition. Sewed. 2s.

SIDGWICK (Prof. Henry).—THE ELEMENTS OF POLITICS. 8vo. 14s. net.

POLITICS.

SMITH (Goldwin).—CANADA AND THE CANADIAN QUESTION. 8vo. 8s. net.

STATESMAN'S YEAR-BOOK, THE. (*See below under* STATISTICS.)

STATHAM (R.).—BLACKS, BOERS, AND BRITISH. Cr. 8vo. 6s.

THORNTON (W. T.).—A PLEA FOR PEASANT PROPRIETORS. New Edit. Cr. 8vo. 7s. 6d.
—— INDIAN PUBLIC WORKS, AND COGNATE INDIAN TOPICS. Cr. 8vo. 8s. 6d.

TRENCH (Capt. F.).—THE RUSSO-INDIAN QUESTION. Cr. 8vo. 7s. 6d.

WALLACE (Sir Donald M.).—EGYPT AND THE EGYPTIAN QUESTION. 8vo. 14s.

PSYCHOLOGY.

(*See under* PHILOSOPHY, p. 28.)

SCULPTURE. (*See* ART.)

SOCIAL ECONOMY.

BOOTH (C.).—A PICTURE OF PAUPERISM. Cr. 8vo. 5s.—Cheap Edit. 8vo. Swd., 6d.
—— LIFE AND LABOUR OF THE PEOPLE OF LONDON. 4 vols. Cr. 8vo. 3s. 6d. each.—Maps to illustrate the above. 5s.

FAWCETT (H. and Mrs. H.). (*See* POLITICS.)

GILMAN (N. P.).—SOCIALISM AND THE AMERICAN SPIRIT. Cr. 8vo. 6s. 6d.

HILL (Octavia).—HOMES OF THE LONDON POOR. Cr. 8vo, sewed. 1s.

HUXLEY (Prof. T. H.).—SOCIAL DISEASES AND WORSE REMEDIES: Letters to the "Times." Cr. 8vo. sewed. 1s. net.

JEVONS (W. Stanley).—METHODS OF SOCIAL REFORM. 8vo. 10s. 6d.

PEARSON (C. H.).—NATIONAL LIFE AND CHARACTER: A FORECAST. 8vo. 10s. net.

STANLEY (Hon. Maude). — CLUBS FOR WORKING GIRLS. Cr. 8vo. 3s. 6d.

SOUND. (*See under* PHYSICS, p. 29.)

SPORT.

BAKER (Sir Samuel W.).—WILD BEASTS AND THEIR WAYS: REMINISCENCES OF EUROPE, ASIA, AFRICA, AMERICA, FROM 1845—88. Illustrated. Ext. cr. 8vo. 12s. 6d.

CHASSERESSE (D.).—SPORTING SKETCHES. Illustrated. Cr. 8vo. 3s. 6d.

EDWARDS-MOSS (Sir J. E., Bart.). — A SEASON IN SUTHERLAND. Cr. 8vo. 1s. 6d.

STATISTICS.

STATESMAN'S YEAR-BOOK, THE. Statistical and Historical Annual of the States of the World for the Year 1893. Revised after Official Returns. Ed. by J. SCOTT KELTIE. Cr. 8vo. 10s. 6d.

SURGERY. (*See* MEDICINE.)

SWIMMING.

LEAHY (Sergeant).—THE ART OF SWIMMING IN THE ETON STYLE. Cr. 8vo. 2s.

THEOLOGY.

The Bible—History of the Christian Church—The Church of England—Devotional Books—The Fathers—Hymnology—Sermons, Lectures, Addresses, and Theological Essays.

The Bible.

History of the Bible—
THE ENGLISH BIBLE; An External and Critical History of the various English Translations of Scripture. By Prof. JOHN EADIE. 2 vols. 8vo. 28s.
THE BIBLE IN THE CHURCH. By Right Rev. Bp. WESTCOTT. 10th edit. 18mo. 4s. 6d.

Biblical History—
BIBLE LESSONS. By Rev. E. A. ABBOTT. Cr. 8vo. 4s. 6d.
SIDE-LIGHTS UPON BIBLE HISTORY. By Mrs. SYDNEY BUXTON. Cr. 8vo. 5s.
STORIES FROM THE BIBLE. By Rev. A. J. CHURCH. Illust. Cr. 8vo. 2 parts. 3s. 6d. each.
BIBLE READINGS SELECTED FROM THE PENTATEUCH AND THE BOOK OF JOSHUA. By Rev. J. A. CROSS. Gl. 8vo. 2s. 6d.
THE CHILDREN'S TREASURY OF BIBLE STORIES. By Mrs. H. GASKOIN. 18mo. 1s. each.—Part I. Old Testament; II. New Testament; III. The Apostles.
THE NATIONS AROUND ISRAEL. By A. KEARY. Cr. 8vo. 3s. 6d.
A CLASS-BOOK OF OLD TESTAMENT HISTORY. By Rev. Dr. MACLEAR. 18mo. 4s. 6d.
A CLASS-BOOK OF NEW TESTAMENT HISTORY. By the same. 18mo. 5s. 6d.
A SHILLING BOOK OF OLD TESTAMENT HISTORY. By the same. 18mo. 1s.
A SHILLING BOOK OF NEW TESTAMENT HISTORY. By the same. 18mo. 1s.

The Old Testament—
SCRIPTURE READINGS FOR SCHOOLS AND FAMILIES. By C. M. YONGE. Globe 8vo. 1s. 6d. each: also with comments, 3s. 6d. each. — GENESIS TO DEUTERONOMY. — JOSHUA TO SOLOMON.—KINGS AND THE PROPHETS.—THE GOSPEL TIMES.—APOSTOLIC TIMES.
THE PATRIARCHS AND LAWGIVERS OF THE OLD TESTAMENT. By F. D. MAURICE. Cr. 8vo. 3s. 6d.
THE PROPHETS AND KINGS OF THE OLD TESTAMENT. By same. Cr. 8vo. 3s. 6d.
THE CANON OF THE OLD TESTAMENT. By Prof. H. E. RYLE. Cr. 8vo. 6s.

The Pentateuch—
AN HISTORICO-CRITICAL INQUIRY INTO THE ORIGIN AND COMPOSITION OF THE HEXATEUCH (PENTATEUCH AND BOOK OF JOSHUA). By Prof. A. KUENEN. Trans. by P. H. WICKSTEED, M.A. 8vo. 14s.

The Psalms—
THE PSALMS CHRONOLOGICALLY ARRANGED. By FOUR FRIENDS. Cr. 8vo. 5s. net.
GOLDEN TREASURY PSALTER. Student's Edition of the above. 18mo. 3s. 6d.
THE PSALMS. With Introduction and Notes. By A. C. JENNINGS, M.A., and W. H. LOWE, M.A. 2 vols. Cr. 8vo. 10s. 6d. each.
INTRODUCTION TO THE STUDY AND USE OF THE PSALMS. By Rev. J. F. THRUPP. 2nd Edit. 2 vols. 8vo. 21s.

Isaiah—
ISAIAH XL.—LXVI. With the Shorter Prophecies allied to it. Edited by MATTHEW ARNOLD. Cr. 8vo. 5s.

Isaiah—

ISAIAH OF JERUSALEM. In the Authorised English Version, with Introduction and Notes. By MATTHEW ARNOLD. Cr. 8vo. 4s. 6d.

A BIBLE-READING FOR SCHOOLS. The Great Prophecy of Israel's Restoration (Isaiah xl.—lxvi.). Arranged and Edited for Young Learners. By the same. 18mo. 1s.

COMMENTARY ON THE BOOK OF ISAIAH: Critical, Historical, and Prophetical; including a Revised English Translation. By T. R. BIRKS. 2nd Edit. 8vo. 12s. 6d.

THE BOOK OF ISAIAH CHRONOLOGICALLY ARRANGED. By T. K. CHEYNE. Cr. 8vo. 7s. 6d.

Zechariah—

THE HEBREW STUDENT'S COMMENTARY ON ZECHARIAH, Hebrew and LXX. By W. H. LOWE, M.A. 8vo. 10s. 6d.

The New Testament—

THE NEW TESTAMENT. Essay on the Right Estimation of MS. Evidence in the Text of the New Testament. By T. R. BIRKS. Cr. 8vo. 3s. 6d.

THE MESSAGES OF THE BOOKS. Discourses and Notes on the Books of the New Testament. By Archd. FARRAR. 8vo. 14s.

THE CLASSICAL ELEMENT IN THE NEW TESTAMENT. Considered as a Proof of its Genuineness, with an Appendix on the Oldest Authorities used in the Formation of the Canon. By C. H. HOOLE. 8vo. 10s. 6d.

ON A FRESH REVISION OF THE ENGLISH NEW TESTAMENT. With an Appendix on the last Petition of the Lord's Prayer. By Bishop LIGHTFOOT. Cr. 8vo. 7s. 6d.

THE UNITY OF THE NEW TESTAMENT. By F. D. MAURICE. 2 vols. Cr. 8vo. 12s.

THE SYNOPTIC PROBLEM FOR ENGLISH READERS. By A. J. JOLLEY. Cr. 8vo. 3s. net.

A GENERAL SURVEY OF THE HISTORY OF THE CANON OF THE NEW TESTAMENT DURING THE FIRST FOUR CENTURIES. By Bishop WESTCOTT. Cr. 8vo. 10s. 6d.

THE NEW TESTAMENT IN THE ORIGINAL GREEK. The Text revised by Bishop WESTCOTT, D.D., and Prof. F. J. A. HORT, D.D. 2 vols. Cr. 8vo. 10s. 6d. each.—Vol. I. Text.—Vol. II. Introduction and Appendix.

SCHOOL EDITION OF THE ABOVE. 18mo, 4s. 6d.; 18mo, roan, 5s. 6d.; morocco, gilt edges, 6s. 6d.

The Gospels—

THE COMMON TRADITION OF THE SYNOPTIC GOSPELS. In the Text of the Revised Version. By Rev. E. A. ABBOTT and W. G. RUSHBROOKE. Cr. 8vo. 3s. 6d.

SYNOPTICON: An Exposition of the Common Matter of the Synoptic Gospels. By W. G. RUSHBROOKE. Printed in Colours. In Six Parts, and Appendix. 4to.—Part I. 3s. 6d. —Parts II. and III. 7s.—Parts IV. V. and VI., with Indices, 10s. 6d.—Appendices, 10s. 6d.—Complete in 1 vol. 35s.

INTRODUCTION TO THE STUDY OF THE FOUR GOSPELS. By Bp. WESTCOTT. Cr. 8vo. 10s. 6d.

THE COMPOSITION OF THE FOUR GOSPELS. By Rev. ARTHUR WRIGHT. Cr. 8vo. 5s.

Gospel of St. Matthew—

THE GREEK TEXT, with Introduction and Notes by Rev. A. SLOMAN. Fcp. 8vo. 2s. 6d.

CHOICE NOTES ON ST. MATTHEW. Drawn from Old and New Sources. Cr. 8vo. 4s. 6d. (St. Matthew and St. Mark in 1 vol. 9s.)

Gospel of St. Mark—

SCHOOL READINGS IN THE GREEK TESTAMENT. Being the Outlines of the Life of our Lord as given by St. Mark, with additions from the Text of the other Evangelists. Edited, with Notes and Vocabulary, by Rev. A. CALVERT, M.A. Fcp. 8vo. 2s. 6d.

CHOICE NOTES ON ST. MARK. Drawn from Old and New SOURCES. Cr. 8vo. 4s. 6d. (St. Matthew and St. Mark in 1 vol. 9s.)

Gospel of St. Luke—

GREEK TEXT, with Introductions and Notes by Rev. J. BOND, M.A. Fcp. 8vo. 2s. 6d.

CHOICE NOTES ON ST. LUKE. Drawn from Old and New Sources. Cr. 8vo. 4s. 6d.

THE GOSPEL OF THE KINGDOM OF HEAVEN. A Course of Lectures on the Gospel of St. Luke. By F. D. MAURICE. Cr. 8vo. 3s. 6d.

Gospel of St. John—

THE GOSPEL OF ST. JOHN. By F. D. MAURICE. Cr. 8vo. 3s. 6d.

CHOICE NOTES ON ST. JOHN. Drawn from Old and New Sources. Cr. 8vo. 4s. 6d.

The Acts of the Apostles—

GREEK TEXT, with Notes by T. E. PAGE, M.A. Fcp. 8vo. 3s. 6d.

THE CHURCH OF THE FIRST DAYS: THE CHURCH OF JERUSALEM, THE CHURCH OF THE GENTILES, THE CHURCH OF THE WORLD. Lectures on the Acts of the Apostles. By Very Rev. C. J. VAUGHAN. Cr. 8vo. 10s. 6d.

The Epistles of St. Paul—

THE EPISTLE TO THE ROMANS. The Greek Text, with English Notes. By the Very Rev. C. J. VAUGHAN. 7th Edit. Cr. 8vo. 7s. 6d.

THE EPISTLES TO THE CORINTHIANS. Greek Text, with Commentary. By Rev. W. KAY. 8vo. 9s.

THE EPISTLE TO THE GALATIANS. A Revised Text, with Introduction, Notes, and Dissertations. By Bishop LIGHTFOOT. 10th Edit. 8vo. 12s.

THE EPISTLE TO THE PHILIPPIANS. A Revised Text, with Introduction, Notes, and Dissertations. By the same. 8vo. 12s.

THE EPISTLE TO THE PHILIPPIANS. With Translation, Paraphrase, and Notes for English Readers. By the Very Rev. C. J. VAUGHAN. Cr. 8vo. 5s.

THE EPISTLES TO THE COLOSSIANS AND TO PHILEMON. A Revised Text, with Introductions, etc. By Bishop LIGHTFOOT. 9th Edit. 8vo. 12s.

THE EPISTLES TO THE EPHESIANS, THE COLOSSIANS, AND PHILEMON. With Introduction and Notes. By Rev. J. LL. DAVIES. 2nd Edit. 8vo. 7s. 6d.

THE FIRST EPISTLE TO THE THESSALONIANS. By Very Rev. C. J. VAUGHAN. 8vo, sewed. 1s. 6d.

THE EPISTLES TO THE THESSALONIANS. Commentary on the Greek Text. By Prof. JOHN EADIE. 8vo. 12s.

THEOLOGY.
The Bible—*continued.*

The Epistle of St. James—
THE GREEK TEXT, with Introduction and Notes. By Rev. JOSEPH B. MAYOR. 8vo. 14*s.*

The Epistles of St. John—
THE EPISTLES OF ST. JOHN. By F. D. MAURICE. Cr. 8vo. 3*s.* 6*d.*
— The Greek Text, with Notes, by Bishop WESTCOTT. 3rd Edit. 8vo. 12*s.* 6*d.*

The Epistle to the Hebrews—
GREEK AND ENGLISH. Edited by Rev. FREDERIC RENDALL. Cr. 8vo. 6*s.*
ENGLISH TEXT, with Commentary. By the same. Cr. 8vo. 7*s.* 6*d.*
THE GREEK TEXT, with Notes, by Very Rev C. J. VAUGHAN. Cr. 8vo. 7*s.* 6*d.*
THE GREEK TEXT, with Notes and Essays, by Bishop WESTCOTT. 8vo. 14*s.*

Revelation—
LECTURES ON THE APOCALYPSE. By F. D. MAURICE. Cr. 8vo. 3*s.* 6*d.*
THE REVELATION OF ST. JOHN. By Rev. Prof. W. MILLIGAN. Cr. 8vo. 7*s.* 6*d.*
LECTURES ON THE APOCALYPSE. By the same. Crown 8vo. 5*s.*
DISCUSSIONS ON THE APOCALYPSE. By the same. Cr. 8vo. 5*s.*
LECTURES ON THE REVELATION OF ST. JOHN. By Very Rev. C. J. VAUGHAN. 5th Edit. Cr. 8vo. 10*s.* 6*d.*

THE BIBLE WORD-BOOK. By W. ALDIS WRIGHT. 2nd Edit. Cr. 8vo. 7*s.* 6*d.*

History of the Christian Church.

CHURCH (Dean).—THE OXFORD MOVEMENT, 1833—45. Gl. 8vo. 5*s.*

CUNNINGHAM (Rev. John).—THE GROWTH OF THE CHURCH IN ITS ORGANISATION AND INSTITUTIONS. 8vo. 9*s.*

CUNNINGHAM (Rev. William). — THE CHURCHES OF ASIA : A Methodical Sketch of the Second Century. Cr. 8vo. 6*s.*

DALE (A. W. W.).—THE SYNOD OF ELVIRA, AND CHRISTIAN LIFE IN THE FOURTH CENTURY. Cr. 8vo. 10*s.* 6*d.*

HARDWICK (Archdeacon).—A HISTORY OF THE CHRISTIAN CHURCH : MIDDLE AGE. Edited by Bp. STUBBS. Cr. 8vo. 10*s.* 6*d.*
—— A HISTORY OF THE CHRISTIAN CHURCH DURING THE REFORMATION. 9th Edit., revised by Bishop STUBBS. Cr. 8vo. 10*s.* 6*d.*

HORT (Dr. F. J. A.).—TWO DISSERTATIONS. I. ON ΜΟΝΟΓΕΝΗΣ ΘΕΟΣ IN SCRIPTURE AND TRADITION. II. ON THE "CONSTANTINOPOLITAN" CREED AND OTHER EASTERN CREEDS OF THE FOURTH CENTURY. 8vo. 7*s.* 6*d.*

KILLEN (W. D.).—ECCLESIASTICAL HISTORY OF IRELAND, FROM THE EARLIEST DATE TO THE PRESENT TIME. 2 vols. 8vo. 25*s.*

SIMPSON (Rev. W.).—AN EPITOME OF THE HISTORY OF THE CHRISTIAN CHURCH. 7th Edit. Fcp. 8vo 3*s.* 6*d.*

VAUGHAN (Very Rev. C. J.).—THE CHURCH OF THE FIRST DAYS : THE CHURCH OF JERUSALEM, THE CHURCH OF THE GENTILES, THE CHURCH OF THE WORLD. Cr. 8vo. 10*s.* 6*d.*

WARD (W.).—WILLIAM GEORGE WARD AND THE OXFORD MOVEMENT. 8vo. 14*s.*
—— W. G. WARD AND THE CATHOLIC REVIVAL. 8vo. 14*s.*

The Church of England.
Catechism of—
A CLASS-BOOK OF THE CATECHISM OF THE CHURCH OF ENGLAND. By Rev. Canon MACLEAR. 18mo. 1*s.* 6*d.*
A FIRST CLASS-BOOK OF THE CATECHISM OF THE CHURCH OF ENGLAND. By the same. 18mo. 6*d.*
THE ORDER OF CONFIRMATION. With Prayers and Devotions. By the same. 32mo. 6*d.*

Collects—
COLLECTS OF THE CHURCH OF ENGLAND. With a Coloured Floral Design to each Collect. Cr. 8vo. 12*s.*

Disestablishment—
DISESTABLISHMENT AND DISENDOWMENT. WHAT ARE THEY? By Prof. E. A. FREEMAN. 4th Edit. Cr. 8vo. 1*s.*
DISESTABLISHMENT ; or, A Defence of the Principle of a National Church. By GEO. HARWOOD. 8vo. 12*s.*
A DEFENCE OF THE CHURCH OF ENGLAND AGAINST DISESTABLISHMENT. By ROUNDELL, EARL OF SELBORNE. Cr. 8vo. 2*s.* 6*d.*
ANCIENT FACTS AND FICTIONS CONCERNING CHURCHES AND TITHES By the same. 2nd Edit. Cr. 8vo. 7*s.* 6*d.*

Dissent in its Relation to—
DISSENT IN ITS RELATION TO THE CHURCH OF ENGLAND. By Rev. G. H. CURTEIS. Bampton Lectures for 1871. Cr. 8vo. 7*s.* 6*d.*

Holy Communion—
THE COMMUNION SERVICE FROM THE BOOK OF COMMON PRAYER. With Select Readings from the Writings of the Rev. F. D. MAURICE. Edited by Bishop COLENSO. 6th Edit. 16mo. 2*s.* 6*d.*
BEFORE THE TABLE : An Inquiry, Historical and Theological, into the Meaning of the Consecration Rubric in the Communion Service of the Church of England. By Very Rev. J. S. HOWSON. 8vo. 7*s.* 6*d.*
FIRST COMMUNION. With Prayers and Devotions for the newly Confirmed. By Rev. Canon MACLEAR. 32mo. 6*d.*
A MANUAL OF INSTRUCTION FOR CONFIRMATION AND FIRST COMMUNION. With Prayers and Devotions. By the same. 32mo. 2*s.*

Liturgy—
AN INTRODUCTION TO THE CREEDS. By Rev. Canon MACLEAR. 18mo. 3*s.* 6*d.*
AN INTRODUCTION TO THE THIRTY-NINE ARTICLES. By same. 18mo. [*In the Press.*
A HISTORY OF THE BOOK OF COMMON PRAYER. By Rev F. PROCTER. 18th Edit. Cr. 8vo. 10*s.* 6*d.*

Liturgy—

AN ELEMENTAY INTRODUCTION TO THE BOOK OF COMMON PRAYER. By Rev. F. PROCTER and Rev. Canon MACLEAR. 18mo. 2s. 6d.

TWELVE DISCOURSES ON SUBJECTS CONNECTED WITH THE LITURGY AND WORSHIP OF THE CHURCH OF ENGLAND. By Very Rev. C. J. VAUGHAN. Fcp. 8vo. 6s.

A COMPANION TO THE LECTIONARY. By Rev. W. BENHAM, B.D. Cr. 8vo. 4s. 6d.

Devotional Books.

EASTLAKE (Lady).—FELLOWSHIP: LETTERS ADDRESSED TO MY SISTER-MOURNERS. Cr. 8vo. 2s. 6d.

IMITATIO CHRISTI. Libri IV. Printed in Borders after Holbein, Dürer, and other old Masters, containing Dances of Death, Acts of Mercy, Emblems, etc. Cr. 8vo. 7s. 6d.

KINGSLEY (Charles).—OUT OF THE DEEP: WORDS FOR THE SORROWFUL. From the Writings of CHARLES KINGSLEY. Ext. fcp. 8vo. 3s. 6d.

—— DAILY THOUGHTS. Selected from the Writings of CHARLES KINGSLEY. By His WIFE. Cr. 8vo. 6s.

—— FROM DEATH TO LIFE. Fragments of Teaching to a Village Congregation. Edit. by His WIFE. Fcp. 8vo. 2s. 6d.

MACLEAR (Rev. Canon).—A MANUAL OF INSTRUCTION FOR CONFIRMATION AND FIRST COMMUNION, WITH PRAYERS AND DEVOTIONS. 32mo. 2s.

—— THE HOUR OF SORROW; or, The Office for the Burial of the Dead. 32mo. 2s.

MAURICE (F. D.).—LESSONS OF HOPE Readings from the Works of F. D. MAURICE. Selected by Rev. J. LL. DAVIES, M.A. Cr. 8vo. 5s.

RAYS OF SUNLIGHT FOR DARK DAYS. With a Preface by Very Rev. C. J. VAUGHAN. D.D. New Edition. 18mo. 3s. 6d.

SERVICE (Rev. J.).—PRAYERS FOR PUBLIC WORSHIP. Cr. 8vo. 4s. 6d.

THE WORSHIP OF GOD, AND FELLOWSHIP AMONG MEN. By Prof. MAURICE and others. Fcp. 8vo. 3s. 6d.

WELBY-GREGORY (Hon. Lady).—LINKS AND CLUES. 2nd Edit. Cr. 8vo. 6s.

WESTCOTT (Rt. Rev. Bishop).—THOUGHTS ON REVELATION AND LIFE. Selections from the Writings of Bishop WESTCOTT. Edited by Rev. S. PHILLIPS. Cr. 8vo. 6s.

WILBRAHAM (Francis M.).—IN THE SERE AND YELLOW LEAF: THOUGHTS AND RECOLLECTIONS FOR OLD AND YOUNG. Globe 8vo. 3s. 6d.

The Fathers.

DONALDSON (Prof. James).—THE APOSTOLIC FATHERS. A Critical Account of their Genuine Writings, and of their Doctrines. 2nd Edit. Cr. 8vo. 7s. 6d.

Works of the Greek and Latin Fathers:

THE APOSTOLIC FATHERS. Revised Texts, with Introductions, Notes, Dissertations, and Translations. By Bishop LIGHTFOOT. —Part I. ST. CLEMENT OF ROME. 2 vols. 8vo. 32s.—Part II. ST. IGNATIUS TO ST. POLYCARP. 3 vols. 2nd Edit. 8vo. 48s. THE APOSTOLIC FATHERS. Abridged Edit. With Short Introductions, Greek Text, and English Translation. By same. 8vo. 16s. THE EPISTLE OF ST. BARNABAS. Its Date and Authorship. With Greek Text, Latin Version, Translation and Commentary. By Rev. W. CUNNINGHAM. Cr. 8vo. 7s. 6d.

Hymnology.

BROOKE (S. A.).—CHRISTIAN HYMNS. Gl. 8vo. 2s. 6d. net.—CHRISTIAN HYMNS AND SERVICE BOOK OF BEDFORD CHAPEL, BLOOMSBURY. Gl. 8vo. 3s. 6d. net.—SERVICE BOOK. Gl. 8vo. 1s. net.

PALGRAVE (Prof. F. T.).—ORIGINAL HYMNS. 3rd Edit. 18mo. 1s. 6d.

SELBORNE (Roundell, Earl of).—THE BOOK OF PRAISE. 18mo. 2s. 6d. net.

—— A HYMNAL. Chiefly from "The Book of Praise."—A. Royal 32mo, limp. 6d.—B. 18mo, larger type. 1s.—C. Fine paper. 1s. 6d. —With Music, Selected, Harmonised, and Composed by JOHN HULLAH. 18mo. 3s. 6d.

WOODS (Miss M. A.).—HYMNS FOR SCHOOL WORSHIP. 18mo. 1s. 6d.

Sermons, Lectures, Addresses, and Theological Essays.

ABBOT (F. E.).—SCIENTIFIC THEISM. Cr. 8vo. 7s. 6d.

—— THE WAY OUT OF AGNOSTICISM; or, The Philosophy of Free Religion. Cr. 8vo. 4s. 6d.

ABBOTT (Rev. E. A.).—CAMBRIDGE SERMONS. 8vo. 6s.

—— OXFORD SERMONS. 8vo. 7s. 6d.

—— PHILOMYTHUS. A discussion of Cardinal Newman's Essay on Ecclesiastical Miracles. Cr. 8vo. 3s. 6d.

—— NEWMANIANISM. Cr. 8vo. 1s. net.

AINGER (Canon).—SERMONS PREACHED IN THE TEMPLE CHURCH. Ext. fcp. 8vo. 6s.

ALEXANDER (W., Bishop of Derry and Raphoe).—THE LEADING IDEAS OF THE GOSPELS. New Edit. Cr. 8vo. 6s.

BAINES (Rev. Edward).—SERMONS. Preface and Memoir by Bishop BARRY. Cr. 8vo. 6s.

BATHER (Archdeacon).—ON SOME MINISTERIAL DUTIES, CATECHISING, PREACHING, Etc. Edited, with a Preface, by Very Rev. C. J. VAUGHAN, D.D. Fcp. 8vo. 4s. 6d.

BERNARD (Canon).—THE CENTRAL TEACHING OF CHRIST. Cr. 8vo. 7s. 6d.

BETHUNE-BAKER (J. F.).—THE INFLUENCE OF CHRISTIANITY ON WAR. 8vo. 5s.

—— THE STERNNESS OF CHRIST'S TEACHING, AND ITS RELATION TO THE LAW OF FORGIVENESS. Cr. 8vo. 2s. 6d.

BINNIE (Rev. W.).—SERMONS. Cr. 8vo. 6s.

THEOLOGY.

Sermons, Lectures, Addresses, and Theological Essays—*continued*.

BIRKS (Thomas Rawson).—THE DIFFICULTIES OF BELIEF IN CONNECTION WITH THE CREATION AND THE FALL, REDEMPTION, AND JUDGMENT. 2nd Edit. Cr. 8vo. 5*s.*
—— JUSTIFICATION AND IMPUTED RIGHTEOUSNESS. A Review. Cr. 8vo. 6*s.*
—— SUPERNATURAL REVELATION; or, First Principles of Moral Theology. 8vo. 8*s.*

BROOKE S. A.).—SHORT SERMONS. Crown 8vo. 6*s.*

BROOKS (Bishop Phillips).—THE CANDLE OF THE LORD: and other Sermons. Cr. 8vo. 6*s.*
—— SERMONS PREACHED IN ENGLISH CHURCHES. Cr. 8vo. 6*s.*
—— TWENTY SERMONS. Cr. 8vo. 6*s.*
—— TOLERANCE. Cr. 8vo. 2*s.* 6*d.*
—— THE LIGHT OF THE WORLD. Cr. 8vo. 3*s.* 6*d.*

BRUNTON (T. Lauder).—THE BIBLE AND SCIENCE. Illustrated. Cr. 8vo. 10*s.* 6*d.*

BUTLER (Archer).—SERMONS, DOCTRINAL AND PRACTICAL. 11th Edit. 8vo. 8*s.*
—— SECOND SERIES OF SERMONS. 8vo. 7*s.*
—— LETTERS ON ROMANISM. 8vo. 10*s.* 6*d.*

BUTLER (Rev. Geo.).—SERMONS PREACHED IN CHELTENHAM COLL. CHAPEL. 8vo. 7*s.* 6*d.*

CAMPBELL (Dr. John M'Leod).—THE NATURE OF THE ATONEMENT. Cr. 8vo. 6*s.*
—— REMINISCENCES AND REFLECTIONS. Edited by his Son, DONALD CAMPBELL, M.A. Cr. 8vo. 7*s.* 6*d.*
—— THOUGHTS ON REVELATION. Cr. 8vo. 5*s.*
—— RESPONSIBILITY FOR THE GIFT OF ETERNAL LIFE. Compiled from Sermons preached 1829—31. Cr. 8vo. 5*s.*

CANTERBURY (Edward White, Archbishop of).—BOY-LIFE: ITS TRIAL, ITS STRENGTH, ITS FULNESS. Sundays in Wellington College, 1859—73. Cr. 8vo. 6*s.*
—— THE SEVEN GIFTS. Primary Visitation Address. Cr. 8vo. 6*s.*
—— CHRIST AND HIS TIMES. Second Visitation Address. Cr. 8vo. 6*s.*
—— A PASTORAL LETTER TO THE DIOCESE OF CANTERBURY, 1890. 8vo, sewed. 1*d.*

CARPENTER (W. Boyd, Bishop of Ripon).—TRUTH IN TALE. Addresses, chiefly to Children. Cr. 8vo. 4*s.* 6*d.*
—— THE PERMANENT ELEMENTS OF RELIGION. 2nd Edit. Cr. 8vo. 6*s.*

CAZENOVE (J. Gibson).—CONCERNING THE BEING AND ATTRIBUTES OF GOD. 8vo. 5*s.*

CHURCH (Dean).—HUMAN LIFE AND ITS CONDITIONS. Cr. 8vo. 6*s.*
—— THE GIFTS OF CIVILISATION: and other Sermons and Letters. Cr. 8vo. 7*s.* 6*d.*
—— DISCIPLINE OF THE CHRISTIAN CHARACTER; and other Sermons. Cr. 8vo. 4*s.* 6*d.*
—— ADVENT SERMONS, 1885. Cr. 8vo. 4*s.* 6*d.*
—— VILLAGE SERMONS. Cr. 8vo. 6*s.*
—— CATHEDRAL AND UNIVERSITY SERMONS. Cr. 8vo. 6*s.*

CLERGYMAN'S SELF-EXAMINATION CONCERNING THE APOSTLES' CREED. Ext. fcp. 8vo. 1*s.* 6*d.*

CONGREVE (Rev. John).—HIGH HOPES AND PLEADINGS FOR A REASONABLE FAITH, NOBLER THOUGHTS, AND LARGER CHARITY. Cr. 8vo. 5*s.*

COOKE (Josiah P., jun.).—RELIGION AND CHEMISTRY. Cr. 8vo. 7*s.* 6*d.*

COTTON (Bishop).—SERMONS PREACHED TO ENGLISH CONGREGATIONS IN INDIA. Cr. 8vo. 7*s.* 6*d.*

CUNNINGHAM (Rev. W.).—CHRISTIAN CIVILISATION, WITH SPECIAL REFERENCE TO INDIA. Cr. 8vo. 5*s.*

CURTEIS (Rev. G. H.).—THE SCIENTIFIC OBSTACLES TO CHRISTIAN BELIEF. The Boyle Lectures, 1884. Cr. 8vo. 6*s.*

DAVIES (Rev. J. Llewelyn).—THE GOSPEL AND MODERN LIFE. Ext. fcp. 8vo. 6*s.*
—— SOCIAL QUESTIONS FROM THE POINT OF VIEW OF CHRISTIAN THEOLOGY. Cr. 8vo. 6*s.*
—— WARNINGS AGAINST SUPERSTITION. Ext. fcp. 8vo. 2*s.* 6*d.*
—— THE CHRISTIAN CALLING. Ext. fp. 8vo. 6*s.*
—— ORDER AND GROWTH AS INVOLVED IN THE SPIRITUAL CONSTITUTION OF HUMAN SOCIETY. Cr. 8vo. 3*s.* 6*d.*
—— BAPTISM, CONFIRMATION, AND THE LORD'S SUPPER. Addresses. 18mo. 1*s.*

DIGGLE (Rev. J. W.).—GODLINESS AND MANLINESS. Cr. 8vo. 6*s.*

DRUMMOND (Prof. Jas.).—INTRODUCTION TO THE STUDY OF THEOLOGY. Cr. 8vo. 5*s.*

DU BOSE (W. P.).—THE SOTERIOLOGY OF THE NEW TESTAMENT. By W. P. Du Bose. Cr. 8vo. 7*s.* 6*d.*

ECCE HOMO: A SURVEY OF THE LIFE AND WORK OF JESUS CHRIST. Globe 8vo. 6*s.*

ELLERTON (Rev. John).—THE HOLIEST MANHOOD, AND ITS LESSONS FOR BUSY LIVES. Cr. 8vo. 6*s.*

FAITH AND CONDUCT: AN ESSAY ON VERIFIABLE RELIGION. Cr. 8vo. 7*s.* 6*d.*

FARRAR (Ven. Archdeacon).—WORKS. *Uniform Edition*. Cr. 8vo. 3*s.* 6*d.* each. Monthly from December, 1891.
SEEKERS AFTER GOD.
ETERNAL HOPE. Westminster Abbey Sermons.
THE FALL OF MAN: and other Sermons.
THE WITNESS OF HISTORY TO CHRIST. Hulsean Lectures, 1870.
THE SILENCE AND VOICES OF GOD. Sermons.
IN THE DAYS OF THY YOUTH. Marlborough College Sermons.
SAINTLY WORKERS. Five Lenten Lectures.
EPHPHATHA; or, The Amelioration of the MERCY AND JUDGMENT. [World.
SERMONS AND ADDRESSES DELIVERED IN AMERICA.
—— THE HISTORY OF INTERPRETATION. Bampton Lectures, 1885. 8vo. 16*s.*

FISKE (John).—MAN'S DESTINY VIEWED IN THE LIGHT OF HIS ORIGIN. Cr. 8vo. 3*s.* 6*d.*

FORBES (Rev. Granville).—THE VOICE OF GOD IN THE PSALMS. Cr. 8vo. 6*s.* 6*d.*

FOWLE (Rev. T. W.).—A NEW ANALOGY BETWEEN REVEALED RELIGION AND THE COURSE AND CONSTITUTION OF NATURE. Cr. 8vo. 6*s.*

FRASER (Bishop).—SERMONS. Edited by JOHN W. DIGGLE. 2 vols. Cr. 8vo. 6s. each.

HAMILTON (John).—ON TRUTH AND ERROR. Cr. 8vo. 5s.
—— ARTHUR'S SEAT; or, The Church of the Banned. Cr. 8vo. 6s.
—— ABOVE AND AROUND: Thoughts on God and Man. 12mo. 2s. 6d.

HARDWICK (Archdeacon).—CHRIST AND OTHER MASTERS. 6th Edit. Cr. 8vo. 10s. 6d.

HARE (Julius Charles).—THE MISSION OF THE COMFORTER. New Edition. Edited by Dean PLUMPTRE. Cr. 8vo. 7s. 6d.

HARPER (Father Thomas).—THE META-PHYSICS OF THE SCHOOL. Vols. I. and II. 8vo. 18s. each.—Vol. III. Part I. 12s.

HARRIS (Rev. G. C.).—SERMONS. With a Memoir by C. M. YONGE. Ext. fcp. 8vo. 6s.

HUTTON (R. H.). (See p. 22.)

ILLINGWORTH (Rev. J. R.).—SERMONS PREACHED IN A COLLEGE CHAPEL. Cr. 8vo. 5s.
—— UNIVERSITY AND CATHEDRAL SERMONS. Crown 8vo. 5s.

JACOB (Rev. J. A.).—BUILDING IN SILENCE: and other Sermons. Ext. fcp. 8vo. 6s.

JAMES (Rev. Herbert).—THE COUNTRY CLERGYMAN AND HIS WORK. Cr. 8vo. 6s.

JEANS (Rev. G. E.).—HAILEYBURY CHAPEL: and other Sermons. Fcp. 8vo. 3s. 6d.

JELLETT (Rev. Dr.).—THE ELDER SON: and other Sermons. Cr. 8vo. 6s.
—— THE EFFICACY OF PRAYER. Cr. 8vo. 5s.

KELLOGG (Rev. S. H.).—THE LIGHT OF ASIA AND THE LIGHT OF THE WORLD. Cr. 8vo. 7s. 6d.
—— GENESIS AND GROWTH OF RELIGION. Cr. 8vo. 6s.

KINGSLEY (Charles). (See COLLECTED WORKS, p. 22.)

KIRKPATRICK (Prof.).—THE DIVINE LI-BRARY OF THE OLD TESTAMENT. Cr. 8vo. 3s. net.
—— DOCTRINE OF THE PROPHETS. Cr. 8vo. 6s.

KYNASTON (Rev. Herbert, D.D.).—CHEL-TENHAM COLLEGE SERMONS. Cr. 8vo. 6s.

LEGGE (A. O.).—THE GROWTH OF THE TEM-PORAL POWER OF THE PAPACY. Cr. 8vo. 8s. 6d.

LIGHTFOOT (Bishop).—LEADERS IN THE NORTHERN CHURCH: Sermons. Cr. 8vo. 6s.
—— ORDINATION ADDRESSES AND COUNSELS TO CLERGY. Cr. 8vo. 6s.
—— CAMBRIDGE SERMONS. Cr. 8vo. 6s.
—— SERMONS PREACHED IN ST. PAUL'S CATHEDRAL. Cr. 8vo. 6s.
—— SERMONS ON SPECIAL OCCASIONS. 8vo. 6s.
—— A CHARGE DELIVERED TO THE CLERGY OF THE DIOCESE OF DURHAM, 1886. 8vo. 2s.
—— ESSAYS ON THE WORK ENTITLED "SU-PERNATURAL RELIGION." 8vo. 10s. 6d.
—— ON A FRESH REVISION OF THE ENGLISH NEW TESTAMENT. Cr. 8vo. 7s. 6d.
—— DISSERTATIONS ON THE APOSTOLIC AGE. 8vo. 14s.

MACLAREN (Rev. A.).—SERMONS PREACHED AT MANCHESTER. 11th Ed. Fcp. 8vo. 4s. 6d.
—— SECOND SERIES. 7th Ed. Fcp. 8vo. 4s. 6d.
—— THIRD SERIES. 6th Ed. Fcp. 8vo. 4s. 6d.
—— WEEK-DAY EVENING ADDRESSES. 4th Edit. Fcp. 8vo. 2s. 6d.
—— THE SECRET OF POWER: and other Ser-mons. Fcp. 8vo. 4s. 6d.

MACMILLAN (Rev. Hugh).—BIBLE TEACH-INGS IN NATURE. 15th Edit. Globe 8vo. 6s.
—— THE TRUE VINE; or, The Analogies of our Lord's Allegory. 5th Edit. Gl. 8vo. 6s.
—— THE MINISTRY OF NATURE. 8th Edit. Globe 8vo. 6s.
—— THE SABBATH OF THE FIELDS. 6th Edit. Globe 8vo. 6s.
—— THE MARRIAGE IN CANA. Globe 8vo. 6s.
—— TWO WORLDS ARE OURS. Gl. 8vo. 6s.
—— THE OLIVE LEAF. Globe 8vo. 6s.
—— THE GATE BEAUTIFUL: and other Bible Teachings for the Young. Cr. 8vo. 3s. 6d.

MAHAFFY (Prof. J. P.).—THE DECAY OF MODERN PREACHING. Cr. 8vo. 3s. 6d.

MATURIN (Rev. W.).—THE BLESSEDNESS OF THE DEAD IN CHRIST. Cr. 8vo. 7s. 6d.

MAURICE (Frederick Denison).—THE KING-DOM OF CHRIST. 3rd Ed. 2 vols. Cr. 8vo. 12s.
—— EXPOSITORY SERMONS ON THE PRAYER-BOOK, AND THE LORD'S PRAYER. Cr. 8vo. 6s.
—— SERMONS PREACHED IN COUNTRY CHURCHES. 2nd Edit. Cr. 8vo. 6s.
—— THE CONSCIENCE: Lectures on Casuistry. 3rd Edit. Cr. 8vo. 4s. 6d.
—— DIALOGUES ON FAMILY WORSHIP. Cr. 8vo. 4s. 6d.
—— THE DOCTRINE OF SACRIFICE DEDUCED FROM THE SCRIPTURES. 2nd Edit. Cr. 8vo. 6s.
—— THE RELIGIONS OF THE WORLD. 6th Edit. Cr. 8vo. 4s. 6d.
—— ON THE SABBATH DAY; THE CHARACTER OF THE WARRIOR; AND ON THE INTERPRE-TATION OF HISTORY. Fcp. 8vo. 2s. 6d.
—— LEARNING AND WORKING. Cr. 8vo. 4s. 6d.
—— THE LORD'S PRAYER, THE CREED, AND THE COMMANDMENTS. 18mo. 1s.
—— SERMONS PREACHED IN LINCOLN'S INN CHAPEL. 6 vols. Cr. 8vo. 3s. 6d. each.
—— COLLECTED WORKS. Monthly Volumes from Oct. 1892. Cr. 8vo. 3s. 6d. each.
CHRISTMAS DAY AND OTHER SERMONS.
THEOLOGICAL ESSAYS.
PROPHETS AND KINGS.
PATRIARCHS AND LAWGIVERS.
THE GOSPEL OF THE KINGDOM OF HEAVEN.
GOSPEL OF ST. JOHN.
EPISTLE OF ST. JOHN
LECTURES ON THE APOCALYPSE.
FRIENDSHIP OF BOOKS.
SOCIAL MORALITY.
PRAYER BOOK AND LORD'S PRAYER.
THE DOCTRINE OF SACRIFICE.

MILLIGAN (Rev. Prof. W.).—THE RESUR-RECTION OF OUR LORD. 2nd Edit. Cr. 8vo. 5s.
—— THE ASCENSION AND HEAVENLY PRIEST-HOOD OF OUR LORD. Cr. 8vo. 7s. 6d.

MOORHOUSE (J., Bishop of Manchester).—JACOB: Three Sermons. Ext. fcp. 8vo. 3s. 6d.
—— THE TEACHING OF CHRIST: its Condi-tions, Secret, and Results. Cr. 8vo. 3s. net.

MYLNE (L. G., Bishop of Bombay).—SERMONS PREACHED IN ST. THOMAS'S CATHEDRAL, BOMBAY. Cr. 8vo. 6s.

THEOLOGY.

Sermons, Lectures, Addresses, and Theological Essays—*continued.*

NATURAL RELIGION. By the Author of "Ecce Homo." 3rd Edit. Globe 8vo. 6s.

PATTISON (Mark).—SERMONS. Cr. 8vo. 6s.

PAUL OF TARSUS. 8vo. 10s. 6d.

PHILOCHRISTUS: MEMOIRS OF A DISCIPLE OF THE LORD. 3rd. Edit. 8vo. 12s.

PLUMPTRE (Dean).—MOVEMENTS IN RELIGIOUS THOUGHT. Fcp. 8vo. 3s. 6d.

POTTER (R.).—THE RELATION OF ETHICS TO RELIGION. Cr. 8vo. 2s. 6d.

REASONABLE FAITH: A SHORT ESSAY By "Three Friends." Cr. 8vo. 1s.

REICHEL (C. P., Bishop of Meath).—THE LORD'S PRAYER. Cr. 8vo. 7s. 6d.
—— CATHEDRAL AND UNIVERSITY SERMONS. Cr. 8vo. 6s.

RENDALL (Rev. F.).—THE THEOLOGY OF THE HEBREW CHRISTIANS. Cr. 8vo. 5s.

REYNOLDS (H. R.).—NOTES OF THE CHRISTIAN LIFE. Cr. 8vo. 7s. 6d.

ROBINSON (Prebendary H. G.).—MAN IN THE IMAGE OF GOD: and other Sermons. Cr. 8vo. 7s. 6d.

RUSSELL (Dean).—THE LIGHT THAT LIGHTETH EVERY MAN: Sermons. With an Introduction by Dean PLUMPTRE, D.D. Cr. 8vo. 6s.

RYLE (Rev. Prof. H.).—THE EARLY NARRATIVES OF GENESIS. Cr. 8vo. 3s. net.

SALMON (Rev. George, D.D.).—NON-MIRACULOUS CHRISTIANITY: and other Sermons. 2nd Edit. Cr. 8vo. 6s.
—— GNOSTICISM AND AGNOSTICISM: and other Sermons. Cr. 8vo. 7s. 6d.

SANDFORD (Rt. Rev. C. W., Bishop of Gibraltar).—COUNSEL TO ENGLISH CHURCHMEN ABROAD. Cr. 8vo. 6s.

SCOTCH SERMONS, 1880. By Principal CAIRD and others. 3rd Edit. 8vo. 10s. 6d.

SERVICE (Rev. J.).—SERMONS. Cr. 8vo. 6s.

SHIRLEY (W. N.).—ELIJAH: Four University Sermons. Fcp. 8vo. 2s. 6d.

SMITH (Rev. Travers).—MAN'S KNOWLEDGE OF MAN AND OF GOD. Cr. 8vo. 6s.

SMITH (W. Saumarez).—THE BLOOD OF THE NEW COVENANT: An Essay. Cr. 8vo. 2s. 6d.

STANLEY (Dean).—THE NATIONAL THANKSGIVING. Sermons Preached in Westminster Abbey. 2nd Edit. Cr. 8vo. 2s. 6d.
—— ADDRESSES AND SERMONS delivered in America, 1878. Cr. 8vo. 6s.

STEWART (Prof. Balfour) and TAIT (Prof. P. G.).—THE UNSEEN UNIVERSE, OR PHYSICAL SPECULATIONS ON A FUTURE STATE. 15th Edit. Cr. 8vo. 6s.
—— PARADOXICAL PHILOSOPHY: A Sequel to the above. Cr. 8vo. 7s. 6d.

STUBBS (Rev. C. W.).—FOR CHRIST AND CITY. Sermons and Addresses. Cr. 8vo. 6s.

TAIT (Archbp.).—THE PRESENT CONDITION OF THE CHURCH OF ENGLAND. Primary Visitation Charge. 3rd Edit. 8vo. 3s. 6d.
—— DUTIES OF THE CHURCH OF ENGLAND. Second Visitation Addresses. 8vo. 4s. 6d.
—— THE CHURCH OF THE FUTURE. Quadrennial Visitation Charges. Cr. 8vo. 3s. 6d.

TAYLOR (Isaac).—THE RESTORATION OF BELIEF. Cr. 8vo. 8s. 6d.

TEMPLE (Frederick, Bishop of London).—SERMONS PREACHED IN THE CHAPEL OF RUGBY SCHOOL. Second Series. Ex. fcp. 8vo. 6s. Third Series 4th Edit. Ext. fcp. 8vo. 6s.
—— THE RELATIONS BETWEEN RELIGION AND SCIENCE. Bampton Lectures, 1884. 7th and Cheaper Edition. Cr. 8vo. 6s.

TRENCH (Archbishop). — THE HULSEAN LECTURES FOR 1845—6. 8vo. 7s. 6d.

TULLOCH (Principal).—THE CHRIST OF THE GOSPELS AND THE CHRIST OF MODERN CRITICISM. Ext. fcp. 8vo. 4s. 6d.

VAUGHAN (C. J., Dean of Landaff).—MEMORIALS OF HARROW SUNDAYS. 8vo. 10s. 6d.
—— EPIPHANY, LENT, AND EASTER. 8vo. 10s. 6d.
—— HEROES OF FAITH. 2nd Edit. Cr. 8vo. 6s.
—— LIFE'S WORK AND GOD'S DISCIPLINE. Ext. fcp. 8vo. 2s. 6d.
—— THE WHOLESOME WORDS OF JESUS CHRIST. 2nd Edit. Fcp. 8vo. 3s. 6d.
—— FOES OF FAITH. 2nd Edit. Fcp. 8vo. 3s. 6d.
—— CHRIST SATISFYING THE INSTINCTS OF HUMANITY. 2nd Edit. Ext. fcp. 8vo. 3s. 6d.
—— COUNSELS FOR YOUNG STUDENTS. Fcp. 8vo. 2s. 6d.
—— THE TWO GREAT TEMPTATIONS. 2nd Edit. Fcp. 8vo. 3s. 6d.
—— ADDRESSES FOR YOUNG CLERGYMEN. Ext. fcp. 8vo. 4s. 6d.
—— "MY SON, GIVE ME THINE HEART." Ext. fcp. 8vo. 5s.
—— REST AWHILE. Addresses to Toilers in the Ministry. Ext. fcp. 8vo. 5s.
—— TEMPLE SERMONS. Cr. 8vo. 10s. 6d.
—— AUTHORISED OR REVISED? Sermons. Cr. 8vo. 7s. 6d.
—— LESSONS OF THE CROSS AND PASSION; WORDS FROM THE CROSS; THE REIGN OF SIN; THE LORD'S PRAYER. Four Courses of Lent Lectures. Cr. 8vo. 10s. 6d.
—— UNIVERSITY SERMONS, NEW AND OLD. Cr. 8vo. 10s. 6d.
—— THE PRAYERS OF JESUS CHRIST. Globe 8vo. 3s. 6d.
—— DONCASTER SERMONS; LESSONS OF LIFE AND GODLINESS; WORDS FROM THE GOSPELS. Cr. 8vo. 10s. 6d.
—— NOTES FOR LECTURES ON CONFIRMATION. 14th Edit. Fcp. 8vo. 1s. 6d.
—— RESTFUL THOUGHTS IN RESTLESS TIMES. Crown 8vo. 5s.

VAUGHAN (Rev. D. J.).—THE PRESENT TRIAL OF FAITH. Cr. 8vo. 9s.

VAUGHAN (Rev. E. T.).—SOME REASONS OF OUR CHRISTIAN HOPE. Hulsean Lectures for 1875. Cr. 8vo. 6s. 6d.

VAUGHAN (Rev. Robert).—STONES FROM THE QUARRY. Sermons. Cr. 8vo. 5s.

VENN (Rev. John).—ON SOME CHARACTERISTICS OF BELIEF, SCIENTIFIC, AND RELIGIOUS. Hulsean Lectures, 1869. 8vo. 6s. 6d.

WELLDON (Rev. J. E. C.).—THE SPIRITUAL LIFE: and other Sermons. Cr. 8vo. 6s.

WESTCOTT (Rt. Rev. B. F., Bishop of Durham).—ON THE RELIGIOUS OFFICE OF THE UNIVERSITIES. Sermons. Cr. 8vo. 4s. 6d.
—— GIFTS FOR MINISTRY. Addresses to Candidates for Ordination. Cr. 8vo. 1s. 6d.
—— THE VICTORY OF THE CROSS. Sermons Preached in 1888. Cr. 8vo. 3s. 6d.
—— FROM STRENGTH TO STRENGTH. Three Sermons (In Memoriam J. B. D.). Cr. 8vo. 2s.
—— THE REVELATION OF THE RISEN LORD. 4th Edit. Cr. 8vo. 6s.
—— THE HISTORIC FAITH. Cr. 8vo. 6s.
—— THE GOSPEL OF THE RESURRECTION. 6th Edit. Cr. 8vo. 6s.
—— THE REVELATION OF THE FATHER. Cr. 8vo. 6s.
—— CHRISTUS CONSUMMATOR. Cr. 8vo. 6s.
—— SOME THOUGHTS FROM THE ORDINAL. Cr. 8vo. 1s. 6d.
—— SOCIAL ASPECTS OF CHRISTIANITY. Cr. 8vo. 6s.
—— THE GOSPEL OF LIFE. Cr. 8vo. 6s.
—— ESSAYS IN THE HISTORY OF RELIGIOUS THOUGHT IN THE WEST. Globe 8vo. 6s.

WICKHAM (Rev. E. C.).—WELLINGTON COLLEGE SERMONS. Cr. 8vo. 6s.

WILKINS (Prof. A. S.).—THE LIGHT OF THE WORLD: An Essay. 2nd Ed. Cr. 8vo. 3s. 6d.

WILLINK (A.).—THE WORLD OF THE UNSEEN. Cr. 8vo. 3s. 6d.

WILSON (J. M., Archdeacon of Manchester).—SERMONS PREACHED IN CLIFTON COLLEGE CHAPEL. 2nd Series, 1888–90. Cr. 8vo. 6s.
—— ESSAYS AND ADDRESSES. Cr. 8vo. 4s. 6d.
—— SOME CONTRIBUTIONS TO THE RELIGIOUS THOUGHT OF OUR TIME. Cr. 8vo. 6s.

WOOD (C. J.).—SURVIVALS IN CHRISTIANITY. Crown 8vo. 6s.

WOOD (Rev. E. G.).—THE REGAL POWER OF THE CHURCH. 8vo. 4s. 6d.

THERAPEUTICS. (See MEDICINE, p. 24.)

TRANSLATIONS.

From the Greek—From the Italian—From the Latin—Into Latin and Greek Verse.

From the Greek.

AESCHYLUS.—THE SUPPLICES. With Translation, by T. G. TUCKER, Litt. D. 8vo. 10s. 6d.
—— THE SEVEN AGAINST THEBES. With Translation, by A. W. VERRALL, Litt. D. 8vo. 7s. 6d.
—— THE CHOEPHORI. With Translation. By the same. 8vo. 12s.
—— EUMENIDES. With Verse Translation, by BERNARD DRAKE, M.A. 8vo. 5s.

ARATUS. (See PHYSIOGRAPHY, p. 29.)

ARISTOPHANES.—THE BIRDS. Trans. into English Verse, by B. H. KENNEDY. 8vo. 6s.

ARISTOTLE ON FALLACIES; OR, THE SOPHISTICI ELENCHI. With Translation, by E. POSTE M.A. 8vo. 8s. 6d.

ARISTOTLE.—THE FIRST BOOK OF THE METAPHYSICS OF ARISTOTLE. By a Cambridge Graduate. 8vo. 5s.
—— THE POLITICS. By J. E. C. WELLDON, M.A. 10s. 6d.
—— THE RHETORIC. By same. Cr. 8vo. 7s. 6d.
—— THE NICOMACHEAN ETHICS. By same. Cr. 8vo. 7s. 6d.

ARISTOTLE.—ON THE CONSTITUTION OF ATHENS. By E. POSTE. 2nd Edit. Cr. 8vo. 3s. 6d.

BION. (See THEOCRITUS.)

HERODOTUS.—THE HISTORY. By G. C. MACAULAY, M.A. 2 vols. Cr. 8vo. 18s.

HOMER.—THE ODYSSEY DONE INTO ENGLISH PROSE, by S. H. BUTCHER, M.A., and A. LANG, M.A. Cr. 8vo. 6s.
—— THE ODYSSEY. Books I.—XII. Transl. into English Verse by EARL OF CARNARVON. Cr. 8vo. 7s. 6d.
—— THE ILIAD DONE INTO ENGLISH PROSE, by ANDREW LANG, WALTER LEAF, and ERNEST MYERS. Cr. 8vo. 12s. 6d.

MELEAGER.—FIFTY POEMS. Translated into English Verse by WALTER HEADLAM. Fcp. 4to. 7s. 6d.

MOSCHUS. (See THEOCRITUS).

PINDAR.—THE EXTANT ODES. By ERNEST MYERS. Cr. 8vo. 5s.

PLATO.—TIMÆUS. With Translation, by R. D. ARCHER-HIND, M.A. 8vo. 16s. (See also GOLDEN TREASURY SERIES, p. 20.)

POLYBIUS.—THE HISTORIES. By E. S. SHUCKBURGH. Cr. 8vo. 24s.

SOPHOCLES.—ŒDIPUS THE KING. Translated into English Verse by E. D. A. MORSHEAD, M.A. Fcp. 8vo. 3s. 6d.

THEOCRITUS, BION, AND MOSCHUS. By A. LANG, M.A. 18mo. 2s. 6d. net.—Large Paper Edition. 8vo. 9s.

XENOPHON. —THE COMPLETE WORKS. By H. G. DAKYNS, M.A. Cr. 8vo.—Vols. I. and II. 10s. 6d. each.

From the Italian.

DANTE.—THE PURGATORY. With Transl. and Notes, by A. J. BUTLER. Cr. 8vo. 12s. 6d.
—— THE PARADISE. By the same. 2nd Edit. Cr. 8vo. 12s. 6d.
—— THE HELL. By the same. Cr. 8vo. 12s. 6d.
—— DE MONARCHIA. By F. J. CHURCH. 8vo. 4s. 6d.
—— THE DIVINE COMEDY. By C. E. NORTON. I. HELL. II. PURGATORY. III. PARADISE. Cr. 8vo. 6s. each.
—— NEW LIFE OF DANTE. Transl. by C. E. NORTON. 5s.
—— THE PURGATORY. Transl. by C. L. SHADWELL. Ext. cr. 8vo. 10s. net.

From the Latin.

CICERO.—THE LIFE AND LETTERS OF MARCUS TULLIUS CICERO. By the Rev. G. E. JEANS, M.A. 2nd Edit. Cr. 8vo. 10s. 6d.
—— THE ACADEMICS. By J. S. REID. 8vo. 5s. 6d.

HORACE: THE WORKS OF. By J. LONSDALE, M.A., and S. LEE, M.A. Gl. 8vo. 3s. 6d.
—— THE ODES IN A METRICAL PARAPHRASE. By R. M. HOVENDEN, B.A. Ext. fcp. 8vo. 4s. 6d.
—— LIFE AND CHARACTER: AN EPITOME OF HIS SATIRES AND EPISTLES. By R. M. HOVENDEN, B.A. Ext. fcp. 8vo. 4s. 6d.
—— WORD FOR WORD FROM HORACE: The Odes Literally Versified. By W. T. THORNTON, C.B. Cr. 8vo. 7s. 6d.

JUVENAL.—THIRTEEN SATIRES. By ALEX. LEEPER, LL.D. New Ed. Cr. 8vo. 3s. 6d.

TRANSLATIONS—*continued.*

LIVY.—BOOKS XXI.—XXV. THE SECOND PUNIC WAR. By A. J. CHURCH, M.A., and W. J. BRODRIBB, M.A. Cr. 8vo. 7s. 6d.

MARCUS AURELIUS ANTONINUS.— BOOK IV. OF THE MEDITATIONS. With Translation and Commentary, by H. CROSSLEY, M.A. 8vo. 6s.

SALLUST.—THE CONSPIRACY OF CATILINE AND THE JUGURTHINE WAR. By A. W. POLLARD. Cr. 8vo. 6s.—CATILINE. 3s.

TACITUS, THE WORKS OF. By A. J. CHURCH, M.A., and W. J. BRODRIBB, M.A. THE HISTORY. 4th Edit. Cr. 8vo. 6s. THE AGRICOLA AND GERMANIA. With the Dialogue on Oratory. Cr. 8vo. 4s. 6d. THE ANNALS. 5th Edit. Cr. 8vo. 7s. 6d.

VIRGIL: THE WORKS OF. By J. LONSDALE, M.A., and S. LEE, M.A. Globe 8vo. 3s. 6d.
—— THE ÆNEID. By J. W. MACKAIL, M.A. Cr. 8vo. 7s. 6d.

Into Latin and Greek Verse.

CHURCH (Rev. A. J.).—LATIN VERSION OF SELECTIONS FROM TENNYSON. By Prof. CONINGTON, Prof. SEELEY, Dr. HESSEY, T. E. KEBBEL, &c. Edited by A. J. CHURCH, M.A. Ext. fcp. 8vo. 6s.

GEDDES (Prof. W. D.).—FLOSCULI GRÆCI BOREALES. Cr. 8vo. 6s.

KYNASTON (Herbert D.D.).—EXEMPLARIA CHELTONIENSIA. Ext. fcp. 8vo. 5s.

VOYAGES AND TRAVELS.

(*See also* HISTORY, p. 10; SPORT, p. 32.)

APPLETON (T. G.).—A NILE JOURNAL. Illustrated by EUGENE BENSON. Cr. 8vo. 6s.

"BACCHANTE." THE CRUISE OF H.M.S. "BACCHANTE," 1879—1882. Compiled from the Private Journals, Letters and Note-books of PRINCE ALBERT VICTOR and PRINCE GEORGE OF WALES. By the Rev. Canon DALTON. 2 vols. Med. 8vo. 52s. 6d.

BAKER (Sir Samuel W.).—ISMAILIA. A Narrative of the Expedition to Central Africa for the Suppression of the Slave Trade, organised by ISMAIL, Khedive of Egypt. Cr. 8vo. 6s.
—— THE NILE TRIBUTARIES OF ABYSSINIA, AND THE SWORD HUNTERS OF THE HAMRAN ARABS. Cr. 8vo. 6s.
—— THE ALBERT N'YANZA GREAT BASIN OF THE NILE AND EXPLORATION OF THE NILE SOURCES. Cr. 8vo. 6s.
—— CYPRUS AS I SAW IT IN 1879. 8vo. 12s. 6d.

BARKER (Lady).—A YEAR'S HOUSEKEEPING IN SOUTH AFRICA. Illustr. Cr. 8vo. 3s. 6d.
—— STATION LIFE IN NEW ZEALAND. Cr. 8vo. 3s. 6d.
—— LETTERS TO GUY. Cr. 8vo. 5s.

BOUGHTON (G. H.) and ABBEY (E. A.).— SKETCHING RAMBLES IN HOLLAND. With Illustrations. Fcp. 4to. 21s.

BRYCE (James, M.P.). — TRANSCAUCASIA AND ARARAT. 3rd Edit. Cr. 8vo. 9s.

CAMERON (V. L.).—OUR FUTURE HIGHWAY TO INDIA. 2 vols. Cr. 8vo. 21s.

CAMPBELL (J. F.).—MY CIRCULAR NOTES. Cr. 8vo. 6s.

CARLES (W. R.).—LIFE IN COREA. 8vo. 12s. 6d.

CAUCASUS: NOTES ON THE. By "WANDERER." 8vo. 9s.

CRAIK (Mrs.).—AN UNKNOWN COUNTRY. Illustr. by F. NOEL PATON. Roy. 8vo. 7s. 6d.
—— AN UNSENTIMENTAL JOURNEY THROUGH CORNWALL. Illustrated. 4to. 12s. 6d.

DILKE (Sir Charles). (*See* pp. 25. 31.)

DUFF (Right Hon. Sir M. E. Grant).—NOTES OF AN INDIAN JOURNEY. 8vo. 10s. 6d.

FORBES (Archibald).—SOUVENIRS OF SOME CONTINENTS. Cr. 8vo. 6s.
—— BARRACKS, BIVOUACS, AND BATTLES. Cr. 8vo. 7s. 6d.

FULLERTON (W. M.).—IN CAIRO. Fcp. 8vo. 3s. 6d.

GONE TO TEXAS: LETTERS FROM OUR BOYS. Ed. by THOS. HUGHES. Cr. 8vo. 4s. 6d.

GORDON (Lady Duff). — LAST LETTERS FROM EGYPT, TO WHICH ARE ADDED LETTERS FROM THE CAPE. 2nd Edit. Cr. 8vo. 9s.

GREEN (W. S.).—AMONG THE SELKIRK GLACIERS. Cr. 8vo. 7s. 6d.

HOOKER (Sir Joseph D.) and BALL (J.).— JOURNAL OF A TOUR IN MAROCCO AND THE GREAT ATLAS. 8vo. 21s.

HÜBNER (Baron von).—A RAMBLE ROUND THE WORLD. Cr. 8vo. 6s.

HUGHES (Thos.).—RUGBY, TENNESSEE. Cr. 8vo. 4s. 6d.

KALM.—ACCOUNT OF HIS VISIT TO ENGLAND. Trans. by J. LUCAS. Illus. 8vo. 12s. net.

KINGSLEY (Charles).—AT LAST: A Christmas in the West Indies. Cr. 8vo. 3s. 6d.

KINGSLEY (Henry). — TALES OF OLD TRAVEL. Cr. 8vo. 3s. 6d.

KIPLING (J. L.).—BEAST AND MAN IN INDIA. Illustrated. Ext. cr. 8vo. 7s. 6d.

MAHAFFY (Prof. J. P.).—RAMBLES AND STUDIES IN GREECE. Illust. Cr. 8vo. 10s. 6d.

MAHAFFY (Prof. J. P.) and ROGERS (J. E.).—SKETCHES FROM A TOUR THROUGH HOLLAND AND GERMANY. Illustrated by J. E. ROGERS. Ext. cr. 8vo. 10s. 6d.

NORDENSKIÖLD. — VOYAGE OF THE "VEGA" ROUND ASIA AND EUROPE. By Baron A. E. VON NORDENSKIÖLD. Trans. by ALEX. LESLIE. 400 Illustrations, Maps, etc. 2 vols. 8vo. 45s.—*Popular Edit.* Cr. 8vo. 6s.

OLIPHANT (Mrs.). (*See* HISTORY, p. 11.)

OLIVER (Capt. S. P.).—MADAGASCAR: AN HISTORICAL AND DESCRIPTIVE ACCOUNT OF THE ISLAND. 2 vols. Med. 8vo. 52s. 6d.

PALGRAVE (W. Gifford).—A NARRATIVE OF A YEAR'S JOURNEY THROUGH CENTRAL AND EASTERN ARABIA, 1862-63. Cr. 8vo. 6s.
—— DUTCH GUIANA. 8vo. 9s.
—— ULYSSES; or, Scenes and Studies in many Lands. 8vo. 12s. 6d.

PERSIA, EASTERN. AN ACCOUNT OF THE JOURNEYS OF THE PERSIAN BOUNDARY COMMISSION, 1870-71-72. 2 vols. 8vo. 42*s.*

PIKE (W.)—THE BARREN GROUND OF NORTHERN CANADA. 8vo. 10*s.* 6*d.*

ST. JOHNSTON (A.)—CAMPING AMONG CANNIBALS. Cr. 8vo. 4*s.* 6*d.*

SANDYS (J. E.)—AN EASTER VACATION IN GREECE. Cr. 8vo. 3*s.* 6*d.*

SMITH (G.)—A TRIP TO ENGLAND. 18mo. 3*s.*

STRANGFORD (Viscountess). — EGYPTIAN SEPULCHRES AND SYRIAN SHRINES. New Edition. Cr. 8vo. 7*s.* 6*d.*

TAVERNIER (Baron): TRAVELS IN INDIA OF JEAN BAPTISTE TAVERNIER. Transl. by V. BALL, LL.D. 2 vols. 8vo. 42*s.*

TRISTRAM. (*See* ILLUSTRATED BOOKS.)

TURNER (Rev. G.). (*See* ANTHROPOLOGY.)

WALLACE (A. R.). (*See* NATURAL HISTORY.)

WATERTON (Charles).—WANDERINGS IN SOUTH AMERICA, THE NORTH-WEST OF THE UNITED STATES, AND THE ANTILLES. Edited by Rev. J. G. WOOD. Illustr. Cr. 8vo. 6*s.*—*People's Edition.* 4to. 6*d.*

WATSON (R. Spence).—A VISIT TO WAZAN, THE SACRED CITY OF MOROCCO. 8vo. 10*s.* 6*d.*

YOUNG, Books for the.

(*See also* BIBLICAL HISTORY, p. 32.)

ÆSOP—CALDECOTT.—SOME OF ÆSOP'S FABLES, with Modern Instances, shown in Designs by RANDOLPH CALDECOTT. 4to. 5*s.*

ARIOSTO.—PALADIN AND SARACEN. Stories from Ariosto. By H. C. HOLLWAY-CALTHROP. Illustrated. Cr. 8vo. 6*s.*

ATKINSON (Rev. J. C.).—THE LAST OF THE GIANT KILLERS. Globe 8vo. 3*s.* 6*d.*
—— WALKS, TALKS, TRAVELS, AND EXPLOITS OF TWO SCHOOLBOYS. Cr. 8vo. 3*s.* 6*d.*
—— PLAYHOURS AND HALF-HOLIDAYS, OR FURTHER EXPERIENCES OF TWO SCHOOLBOYS. Cr. 8vo. 3*s* 6*d*
—— SCENES IN FAIRYLAND. Cr. 8vo. 4*s.* 6*d.*

AWDRY (Frances).—THE STORY OF A FELLOW SOLDIER. (A Life of Bishop Patteson for the Young.) Globe 8vo. 2*s.* 6*d.*

BAKER (Sir S. W.).—TRUE TALES FOR MY GRANDSONS. Illustrated. Cr. 8vo. 3*s.* 6*d.*
—— CAST UP BY THE SEA: OR, THE ADVENTURES OF NED GRAY. Illus. Cr. 8vo. 6*s.*

BUMBLEBEE BOGO'S BUDGET. By a RETIRED JUDGE. Illust. Cr. 8vo. 2*s.* 6*d.*

CARROLL (Lewis).—ALICE'S ADVENTURES IN WONDERLAND. With 42 Illustrations by TENNIEL. Cr. 8vo. 6*s.* net.
People's Edition. With all the original Illustrations. Cr. 8vo. 2*s.* 6*d.* net.
A GERMAN TRANSLATION OF THE SAME. Cr. 8vo. 6*s.* net. —A FRENCH TRANSLATION OF THE SAME. Cr. 8vo. 6*s.* net. AN ITALIAN TRANSLATION OF THE SAME. Cr. 8vo. 6*s.* net.
—— ALICE'S ADVENTURES UNDER-GROUND. Being a Fascimile of the Original MS. Book, afterwards developed into "Alice's Adventures in Wonderland." With 27 Illustrations by the Author. Cr. 8vo. 4*s* net.

CARROLL (Lewis).—THROUGH THE LOOKING-GLASS AND WHAT ALICE FOUND THERE. With 50 Illustrations by TENNIEL. Cr. 8vo. 6*s.* net.
People's Edition. With all the original Illustrations. Cr. 8vo. 2*s.* 6*d.* net.
People's Edition of "Alice's Adventures in Wonderland," and "Through the Looking-Glass." 1 vol. Cr. 8vo. 4*s.* 6*d.* net.
—— RHYME? AND REASON? With 65 Illustrations by ARTHUR B. FROST, and 9 by HENRY HOLIDAY. Cr. 8vo. 6*s.* net.
—— A TANGLED TALE. With 6 Illustrations by ARTHUR B. FROST. Cr. 8vo. 4*s.* 6*d.* net.
—— SYLVIE AND BRUNO. With 46 Illustrations by HARRY FURNISS. Cr. 8vo. 7*s.* 6*d.* net.
—— THE NURSERY "ALICE." Twenty Coloured Enlargements from TENNIEL'S Illustrations to "Alice's Adventures in Wonderland," with Text adapted to Nursery Readers. 4to. 4*s.* net.—*People's Edition.* 4to. 2*s.* net.
—— THE HUNTING OF THE SNARK, AN AGONY IN EIGHT FITS. With 9 Illustrations by HENRY HOLIDAY. Cr. 8vo. 4*s.* 6*d.* net.

CLIFFORD (Mrs. W. K.).—ANYHOW STORIES. With Illustrations by DOROTHY TENNANT. Cr. 8vo. 1*s.* 6*d.*; paper covers, 1*s.*

CORBETT (Julian).—FOR GOD AND GOLD. Cr. 8vo. 6*s.*

CRAIK (Mrs.).—ALICE LEARMONT: A FAIRY TALE. Illustrated. Globe 8vo. 4*s.* 6*d.*
—— THE ADVENTURES OF A BROWNIE. Illustrated by Mrs. ALLINGHAM. Gl. 8vo. 4*s.* 6*d.*
—— THE LITTLE LAME PRINCE AND HIS TRAVELLING CLOAK. Illustrated by J. McL. RALSTON. Cr. 8vo. 4*s.* 6*d.*
—— OUR YEAR: A CHILD'S BOOK IN PROSE AND VERSE. Illustrated. Gl. 8vo. 2*s.* 6*d.*
—— LITTLE SUNSHINE'S HOLIDAY. Globe 8vo. 2*s.* 6*d.*
—— THE FAIRY BOOK: THE BEST POPULAR FAIRY STORIES. 18mo. 2*s.* 6*d.* net.
—— CHILDREN'S POETRY. Ex. fcp. 8vo. 4*s.* 6*d.*
—— SONGS OF OUR YOUTH. Small 4to. 6*s.*

DE MORGAN (Mary).—THE NECKLACE OF PRINCESS FIORIMONDE, AND OTHER STORIES. Illustrated by WALTER CRANE. Ext. fcp. 8vo. 3*s.* 6*d.*—Large Paper Ed., with Illustrations on India Paper. 100 copies printed.

FOWLER (W. W.). (*See* NATURAL HISTORY.)

GREENWOOD (Jessy E.). — THE MOON MAIDEN: AND OTHER STORIES. Cr. 8vo. 2*s.* 6*d.*

GRIMM'S FAIRY TALES. Translated by LUCY CRANE, and Illustrated by WALTER CRANE. Cr. 8vo. 6*s.*

KEARY (A. and E.). — THE HEROES OF ASGARD. Tales from Scandinavian Mythology. Globe 8vo. 2*s.* 6*d*

KEARY (E.)—THE MAGIC VALLEY. Illustr. by "E. V. B." Globe 8vo. 4*s.* 6*d.*

KINGSLEY (Charles).—THE HEROES; or, Greek Fairy Tales for my Children. Cr. 8vo. 3*s.* 6*d.*—*Presentation Ed.*, gilt edges. 7*s.* 6*d.* MADAM HOW AND LADY WHY; or, First Lessons in Earth-Lore. Cr. 8vo. 3*s.* 6*d.*
THE WATER-BABIES: A Fairy Tale for a Land Baby. Cr. 8vo. 3*s.* 6*d.*—New Edit. Illus. by L. SAMBOURNE. Fcp. 4to. 12*s.* 6*d.*

BOOKS FOR THE YOUNG—*continued.*

MACLAREN (Arch.).—THE FAIRY FAMILY. A Series of Ballads and Metrical Tales. Cr. 8vo. 5s.

MACMILLAN (Hugh). (*See* p. 37.)

MADAME TABBY'S ESTABLISHMENT. By KARI. Illust. by L. WAIN. Cr. 8vo. 4s. 6d.

MAGUIRE (J. F.).—YOUNG PRINCE MARIGOLD. Illustrated. Globe 8vo. 4s. 6d.

MARTIN (Frances).—THE POET'S HOUR. Poetry selected for Children. 18mo. 2s. 6d.

—— SPRING-TIME WITH THE POETS. 18mo. 2s. 6d.

MAZINI (Linda).—IN THE GOLDEN SHELL. With Illustrations. Globe 8vo. 4s. 6d.

MOLESWORTH (Mrs.).—WORKS. Illust. by WALTER CRANE. Globe 8vo. 2s. 6d. each.
"CARROTS," JUST A LITTLE BOY.
A CHRISTMAS CHILD.
CHRISTMAS-TREE LAND.
THE CUCKOO CLOCK.
FOUR WINDS FARM.
GRANDMOTHER DEAR.
HERR BABY.
LITTLE MISS PEGGY.
THE RECTORY CHILDREN.
ROSY.
THE TAPESTRY ROOM.
TELL ME A STORY.
TWO LITTLE WAIFS.
"US": An Old-Fashioned Story.
CHILDREN OF THE CASTLE.

—— A CHRISTMAS POSY. Illustrated by WALTER CRANE. Cr. 8vo. 4s. 6d.

—— FOUR GHOST STORIES. Cr. 8vo. 6s.

—— NURSE HEATHERDALE'S STORY. Illust. by LESLIE BROOKE. Cr. 8vo. 4s. 6d.

—— THE GIRLS AND I. Illust. by L. BROOKE. Cr. 8vo. 4s. 6d.

OLIPHANT (Mrs.). —AGNES HOPETOUN'S SCHOOLS AND HOLIDAYS. Illust. Gl. 8vo. 2s. 6d.

PALGRAVE (Francis Turner).—THE FIVE DAYS' ENTERTAINMENTS AT WENTWORTH GRANGE. Small 4to. 6s.

—— THE CHILDREN'S TREASURY OF LYRICAL POETRY. 18mo. 2s. 6d.—Or in 2 parts, 1s. each.

PATMORE (C.).—THE CHILDREN'S GARLAND FROM THE BEST POETS. 18mo. 2s. 6d. net.

ROSSETTI (Christina). —SPEAKING LIKENESSES. Illust. by A. HUGHES. Cr. 8vo. 4s. 6d.

RUTH AND HER FRIENDS: A STORY FOR GIRLS. Illustrated. Globe 8vo. 2s. 6d.

ST. JOHNSTON (A.).—CAMPING AMONG CANNIBALS. Cr. 8vo. 4s. 6d.

—— CHARLIE ASGARDE: THE STORY OF A FRIENDSHIP. Illustrated by HUGH THOMSON. Cr. 8vo. 5s.

"ST. OLAVE'S" (Author of). Illustrated. Globe 8vo.
WHEN I WAS A LITTLE GIRL. 2s. 6d.
NINE YEARS OLD. 2s. 6d.
WHEN PAPA COMES HOME. 4s. 6d.
PANSIE'S FLOUR BIN. 4s. 6d.

STEWART (Aubrey).—THE TALE OF TROY. Done into English. Globe 8vo. 2s. 6d.

TENNYSON (Hon. Hallam).—JACK AND THE BEAN-STALK. English Hexameters. Illust. by R. CALDECOTT. Fcp. 4to. 3s. 6d.

"WANDERING WILLIE" (Author of).—CONRAD THE SQUIRREL. Globe 8vo. 2s. 6d.

WARD (Mrs. T. Humphry).—MILLY AND OLLY. With Illustrations by Mrs. ALMA TADEMA. Globe 8vo. 2s. 6d.

WEBSTER (Augusta).—DAFFODIL AND THE CROÄXAXICANS. Cr. 8vo. 6s.

WILLOUGHBY (F.).—FAIRY GUARDIANS. Illustr. by TOWNLEY GREEN. Cr. 8vo. 5s.

WOODS (M. A.). (*See* COLLECTIONS, p. 17.)

YONGE (Charlotte M.).—THE PRINCE AND THE PAGE. Cr. 8vo. 2s. 6d.

—— A BOOK OF GOLDEN DEEDS. 18mo. 2s. 6d. net. Globe 8vo. 2s.—*Abridged Edition.* 1s.

—— LANCES OF LYNWOOD. Cr. 8vo. 3s. 6d.

—— P's AND Q's; and LITTLE LUCY'S WONDERFUL GLOBE. Illustrated. Cr. 8vo. 3s. 6d.

—— A STOREHOUSE OF STORIES. 2 vols. Globe 8vo. 2s. 6d. each.

—— THE POPULATION OF AN OLD PEAR-TREE; or, Stories of Insect Life. From E. VAN BRUYSSEL. Illustr. Gl. 8vo. 2s. 6d.

ZOOLOGY.

Comparative Anatomy—Practical Zoology—Entomology—Ornithology.

(*See also* BIOLOGY; NATURAL HISTORY; PHYSIOLOGY.)

Comparative Anatomy.

FLOWER (Sir W. H.).—AN INTRODUCTION TO THE OSTEOLOGY OF THE MAMMALIA. Illustrated. 3rd Edit., revised with the assistance of HANS GADOW, Ph.D. Cr. 8vo. 10s. 6d.

HUMPHRY (Prof. Sir G. M.).—OBSERVATIONS IN MYOLOGY. 8vo. 6s.

LANG (Prof. Arnold).—TEXT-BOOK OF COMPARATIVE ANATOMY. Transl. by H. M. and M. BERNARD. Preface by Prof. E. HAECKEL. Illustr. 2 vols. 8vo. Part I. 17s. net.

PARKER (T. Jeffery).—A COURSE OF INSTRUCTION IN ZOOTOMY (VERTEBRATA). Illustrated. Cr. 8vo. 8s. 6d.

PETTIGREW (J. Bell).—THE PHYSIOLOGY OF THE CIRCULATION IN PLANTS, IN THE LOWER ANIMALS, AND IN MAN. 8vo. 12s.

SHUFELDT (R. W.).—THE MYOLOGY OF THE RAVEN (*Corvus corax Sinuatus*). A Guide to the Study of the Muscular System in Birds. Illustrated. 8vo. 13s. net.

WIEDERSHEIM (Prof. R.).—ELEMENTS OF THE COMPARATIVE ANATOMY OF VERTEBRATES. Adapted by W. NEWTON PARKER. With Additions. Illustrated. 8vo. 12s. 6d.

Practical Zoology.

HOWES (Prof. G. B.).—AN ATLAS OF PRACTICAL ELEMENTARY BIOLOGY. With a Preface by Prof. HUXLEY. 4to. 14s.

HUXLEY (T. H.) and MARTIN (H. N.).—A COURSE OF PRACTICAL INSTRUCTION IN ELEMENTARY BIOLOGY. Revised and extended by Prof. G. B. HOWES and D. H. SCOTT, Ph.D. Cr. 8vo. 10s. 6d

THOMSON (Sir C. Wyville).—THE VOYAGE OF THE "CHALLENGER": THE ATLANTIC. With Illustrations, Coloured Maps, Charts, etc 2 vols. 8vo. 45s.

THOMSON (Sir C. Wyville).—THE DEPTHS OF THE SEA. An Account of the Results of the Dredging Cruises of H.M.SS. "Lightning" and "Porcupine," 1868-69-70. With Illustrations, Maps, and Plans. 8vo. 31s.6d.

Entomology.

BUCKTON (G. B.).—MONOGRAPH OF THE BRITISH CICADÆ, OR TETTIGIDÆ. 2 vols. 33s. 6d. each net; or in 8 Parts. 8s. each net.

LUBBOCK (Sir John).—THE ORIGIN AND METAMORPHOSES OF INSECTS. Illustrated. Cr. 8vo. 3s. 6d.

SCUDDER (S. H.).—FOSSIL INSECTS OF NORTH AMERICA. Map and Plates. 2 vols. 4to. 90s. net.

Ornithology.

COUES (Elliott).—KEY TO NORTH AMERICAN BIRDS. Illustrated. 8vo. 2l. 2s.

—— HANDBOOK OF FIELD AND GENERAL ORNITHOLOGY. Illustrated. 8vo. 10s. net.

FOWLER (W. W.). (See NATURAL HISTORY.

WHITE (Gilbert). (See NATURAL HISTORY.

INDEX.

INDEX.

MACMILLAN AND CO., LONDON.

J. PALMER, PRINTER, ALEXANDRA STREET, CAMBRIDGE.

9/50/6/93